YOUNG GERBER

FRIEDRICH TORBERG

YOUNG GERBER

Translated from the German by
Anthea Bell

PUSHKIN PRESS
LONDON

Original text © Paul Zsolnay Verlag, Vienna 1958
English language translation © Anthea Bell 2012

Young Gerber first published in German as
Der Schüler Gerber in 1930 by Paul Zsolnay Verlag, Vienna

This edition first published in 2012 by
Pushkin Press
71-75 Shelton Street,
London WC2H 9JQ

ISBN 978 1 906548 89 6

Cover Illustration: *Self-portrait with a Striped Shirt*, Egon Schiele
© Leopold Museum, Vienna

Frontispiece: *Friedrich Torberg*
© Paul Zsolnay Verlag, Vienna

Set in 10 on 12 Monotype Baskerville
by Tetragon, London

Proudly printed and bound in Great Britain by TJ International,
Padstow, Cornwall, on Munken Premium White 90gsm

www.pushkinpress.com

CONTENTS

YOUNG GERBER

Translator's Foreword

Exam pressure on young people is nothing new, as readers will discover from this novel, first published in 1930. Its author, Friedrich Torberg (a pseudonym; his real surname was Kantor), is regarded as an Austrian writer, although as a young man he held Czech citizenship. His family was from the same German-speaking Jewish middle class of Prague as Kafka's, although Friedrich was born in 1908 in Vienna, where his father's work had taken them. In his teenage years the family moved back to Prague; his last school years were spent in that city at the German *Realgymnasium* (grammar school or high school), which still used antiquated educational methods dating from the old Austro-Hungarian monarchy. Some reforms were already being introduced in Vienna at this time, but *Young Gerber* contains autobiographical elements.

After leaving school (he passed his final exams at the second attempt), and abandoning his university studies, Torberg worked as a journalist in both Prague and Vienna. *Young Gerber* was his first novel, and he was encouraged to send it to a publisher by Max Brod, Kafka's confidant and the man who famously ignored instructions to destroy all his friend's unpublished work after his death. Torberg's novel was a great success, but only three years after its publication it was banned in Nazi Germany at the time of the first book-burnings, along with the works of many other German-language writers of Jewish origin. When the Nazis annexed Austria in 1938, Torberg happened to be in Prague, and armed with his Czech citizenship he emigrated first to Switzerland, then to France, before becoming one of a party of "Ten Outstanding German Writers" invited to the United States by the PEN Club in New York. During the war he worked in the States as a translator, freelance journalist and theatrical critic, and took American citizenship, which he retained even after his return to Austria in 1951. He lived there for the rest of his life, and died in Vienna in 1979.

Young Gerber's instant success suggests that it aroused painful memories in the minds of those of its original readers who had been through the German and Austrian educational system of those days. Kurt Gerber, the 18-year-old protagonist, is persecuted during his final year at school by a man who, it is to be hoped, would be recognized today as a sadistic psychopath: Professor Kupfer, teacher of mathematics and descriptive geometry. "Professor" was evidently a kind of courtesy title for all the teachers in such secondary schools, and denoted no particular academic rank; we learn that Kupfer did not even have a doctoral degree.

The school-leaving examination itself, known as the *Abitur* in Germany, the *Matura* or *Reifeprüfung* in Austria, had a firmly established structure at the time described by Torberg. It was in two parts, first the written papers, then an oral examination. The compulsory subjects were mathematics and descriptive geometry (involving the representation of three-dimensional objects, useful if you intended to be an engineer or architect); a foreign language, either classical or modern; as well as German, history and geography. While physics, chemistry and natural history were studied, they did not feature as examination subjects. Only students who had passed the written papers were admitted to the oral part of the exam, which, as Torberg presents it, was vitally important. This fact explains the constant anxiety felt throughout their last year by the students in this novel when they are to be tested in class. Only if they pass the oral examination will they really have gained their *Matura*.

The long final chapter describes the course of this oral exam. Best of all was to pass with a distinction (*Vorzug*); second best was to be passed unanimously by all the examiners (*Stimmeneinheit*); students who did not quite achieve that could still claim the *Matura* with a majority of pass marks (*Mehrheit*). Interestingly, one of the girls in the class, Anny Kohl, is distressed by the prospect of getting only a unanimous pass; she wanted to emulate the other girls who had passed with distinction that day. Evidently girls with academic ambitions had to be competitive; Lisa, whom Kurt loves, has opted out as the book begins, leaving school to work in an arts and crafts studio and be a good-time girl. In Kurt's class of final-year students there are few girls, only six of them among many more boys (and they sit segregated at the front of the class, where the teachers, all of them men, can have a good look at their legs). Exam pressure may still be felt today, but mercifully such details of the old Austro-Hungarian system are a thing of the past.

ANTHEA BELL

The whole world rests upon three things:
on truth, on justice, and on love.

Rabbi Shimon ben Gamliel

The author began writing this book in the winter of early 1929, a year after his first draft of it. Within a single week of that winter, from 27th January to 3rd February 1929, his attention was drawn to newspaper announcements of ten suicides by school students.

I

God Almighty Kupfer

IT WAS A MILD, late-summer morning, and the classroom door was open. Amidst all the noise, no one noticed when young Gerber came in. He went to his desk in the back row, sat down and looked at the scene before him at his leisure. It was just the same as on any other day at school. And Kurt Gerber, in line with the habit he had acquired from much reading of seeing everything that went on around him as if he remembered it, as if it were an account of something already in the past, registered it as almost a recapitulation of previous events.

The students in their last year at High School XVI had assembled in their classroom. They were sitting or standing around in groups, their conversations were loud, excited and incessant, even headlong; they had so much to tell each other after two summer months, their final long school holidays. For the last time they knew, with familiar certainty, that the end of those months meant the beginning of a new school year, but they also knew for the first time, and with an intriguing sense of novelty, that it would be their last.

Their last school year! Those four words had always had a magical aura—they were about to enter the world of reality, and the face and behaviour of every one of the thirty-two eighth-year students reflected that fact. Between 28th June and 1st September they had visibly been adjusting to adulthood, and now, in high spirits, they acted as if they already had this last year behind them. As if there were not another ten months still ahead of them, ten more months of being the school students they had been for the last seven years. Except that everything would carry the extra significance of being for the last time: preparing for exams, taking them, making mistakes, skipping lessons, homework, entries in the register, work marked from Very Good to Unsatisfactory. All that, thought Kurt, looking at the eighth-year students as they cheerfully talked, would be as it had always been since their first year. And not so very much had changed about themselves either, although Körner sported a moustache, and Sittig was kissing the hands of the Reinhard sisters who had just come in (they hadn't grown any prettier in all that time). They would all behave badly, and less frequently well, just as they did before, and they would quake with fear of the exams and laugh at their teachers' jokes. However, if Rimmel hooted with shrill merriment as he was doing now when Schleich recited the latest double entendres in a song about a randy landlady, and if it wasn't a teacher's joke he was laughing at, then first he would get his face slapped, and second he would have a black mark entered against him in the register—which in the eighth class, just before the final examination, was a far more serious matter than before. I'd happily give you a black mark myself, you toady, thought Kurt Gerber. Well, there we are. And now let the school year begin…

Kurt Gerber looked around. None of the chattering groups particularly attracted him.

Where was Lisa Berwald?

When he got home, he had found a picture postcard from Italy sending him her warm good wishes. "I'm afraid I don't know where you are spending the summer," she wrote, "or I might have looked in there myself. Well, see you when we're back home again." He wanted to know whether she would really have visited him on holiday, or if those were only empty words, like just about everything she said to him and did. But Lisa Berwald wasn't here yet.

So who to talk to? It was simplest to join the group on his left by the window. Kaulich was there, with Gerald, Schleich and Blank.

After loud greetings the conversation was soon in full flow. Soon Hobbelmann, who had obviously just arrived, joined them.

"Hello, Scheri! I have news for you!" (Scheri was Kurt's nickname. It had started out "Geri" with a hard "g" sound, short for Gerber, and then, Heaven knows why, had become Scheri, with a soft initial sound.) "Who do you think is going to be our class teacher?"

"No idea."

Hobbelmann looked around. "None of the rest of you, either? Go on, then, have a guess!"

"Seelig?" asked Kurt.

"Wrong."

"Mattusch?"

"Wrong again."

"Unless you're going to say you don't know either—who is it?"

"God Almighty Kupfer."

Kurt jumped. His head shot forward. He felt the blood rising to his face. Next moment he had seized the startled Hobbelmann and was shaking him. "What did you say? *Who?*"

Everyone knew that although Professor Kupfer had never taught Kurt Gerber, he did not like him– but the effect of this sudden explosion was so funny that everyone burst out laughing. That brought Kurt to his senses. He let go of the gasping Hobbelmann, struck the top of the desk in front of him and cried, with comically exaggerated emotion, "Then all my wishes are finally granted!"

And his account of a meeting with Kupfer during the summer holidays came pouring out. The Professor stalked past him three times, ignoring him, and even when he came upon Kurt in the forest, and they were on their own, he did not return his civil greeting but said only, in a sharp tone of voice, "It appears that you have recovered very well from the seventh-year examinations," and walked on before Kurt could say anything—"I could have hit the conceited fool". And later, when by chance Kupfer was introduced to Kurt Gerber's father, and his first words were: "Oh… Gerber? The father of that lad going up into the eighth year? Well, your son would have nothing to laugh about in *my* form. I know how to bring slackers like that into line!" there had been an argument. His father wanted him to change to a different school, but Kurt had persuaded him that, after all, it was far from certain that Kupfer was really going to be his class teacher—and now there he was, God Almighty Kupfer…

Silence reigned for a while. Then there was a buzz of voices.

"I heard there was going to be a new teacher.—How does Hobbelmann know, anyway?—It's not set in stone.—Why not Mattusch as our class teacher again?—God Almighty's not so bad, you just have to keep on the right side of him.—That's true.—I'm staying out of this.—God Almighty Kupfer is all right.—Don't expect me to swallow that. He's failed me once already.—Let's go on strike.—Down with Kupfer.—Don't be ridiculous.—I'm telling you, Rothbart will stay where he is and Niesset will be our form master…"

Then the bell rang, only faintly audible at first in all the hubbub, but it soon died down. Eight o'clock. School was beginning. Someone closed the classroom door from the outside, and now all was quiet.

But then the noise swelled again. It was a familiar phenomenon, and its nonsensical nature hadn't changed since the students' first day at school: as soon as the bell rang they went to their places—without any pushing and shoving—where they continued the conversation they had broken off. Real silence fell only when the class teacher, often several minutes later, opened the door. And today of all days, when there were no lessons, only the class teacher's official opening of the year of studies, which—as if to lead them gently from leisure to hard work—always began a little late, so that you didn't really know whether to count it as a school day or still the holidays—well, today of all days, then, there was no real reason to preserve an anxious silence. Soon there was general conversation again.

Only Kurt Gerber sat there in silence. His thoughts were in confusion, he tried in vain to gather them all together and begin sorting them out, he could grasp nothing clearly but that name, the idea of it, the quintessence of that idea:

Professor Kupfer, God Almighty. What to do? How was he to behave to him? Submissively? Knuckling under from the start, without waiting for the first blow, ducking so that it would fall on empty air? That would mean he didn't even find out whether Kupfer really meant "to deal with" a "slacker" like him! Or, on the contrary, should he fight back? Brace himself to resist at the first occasion for it: I am not going to duck! But, for Heaven's sake—this was the last year at school, the crucial year when you had to, *had to* pass the final examination, known in Austrian schools as the *Matura*. What should he do? Wait and see, that's best, he thought. Maybe he won't really be as bad as all that, and I'll be able to get along with him without losing face. Some people speak well of him. Yes, and anyway—who says for certain that he's going to be our class teacher? Why shouldn't Mattusch stay with us, or maybe it will be the descriptive geometry master Rothbart, or Hussak who teaches maths and physics? Why is it to be Kupfer all of a sudden teaching us maths *and* descriptive geometry *and* being our class teacher? Why? Just because Hobbelmann wanted to show off by imparting a sensational piece of news? Nonsense. God Almighty Kupfer won't be coming here…

"Here comes God Almighty Kupfer!"

Mertens, who had been keeping watch outside the door, rushed in and sat down in his place as good as gold. The noise broke off abruptly.

So it was true. Or maybe he was on his way to another class?

He ought to be here by now.

Was Mertens trying to fool us?

There—now… nothing.

The sound of the door handle being pushed suddenly down was like a shot breaking the deep silence. Kurt started with alarm, and his knees felt weak as he got to his feet.

The others had risen as well and stood motionless as Professor Artur Kupfer, known among the students as God Almighty Kupfer on account of the infallibility to which he often and emphatically laid claim, strode past the right-hand row of students to the teacher's desk.

Professor Kupfer was about forty years old, and rather too corpulent for a man of medium height. Areas of his short fair hair bore witness to unsuccessful efforts with the brush to arrange it neatly at the back of his head. His moderately high forehead, like the whole of his rather bloated face, was an undistinguished red in colour, despite the attention he obviously devoted to it, and on his thin, prominent, aquiline nose that effect was enhanced by the little red veins running over it. Steely blue eyes behind oval, rimless glasses looked persistently for something that wasn't present. Today he wore a casual pale-grey suit with a matching tie. He had draped a raincoat over the arm in which he was clutching the large green class register; his free hand, as usual, was plucking at his carefully trimmed blond moustache.

Professor Kupfer had reached the lectern that was the teacher's desk. He mounted the step up to it, still with his back turned to the students, and threw the raincoat carelessly over the back of his chair. Then he swung swiftly round, looked expressionlessly at all of them now standing to attention, and said very quietly, with a slight nod of his head, "Sit down!" For the first time that remark, heard five times every day for hundreds of weeks, had a special effect on the students. It was almost a relief, coming from the mouth of the man whose appearance had imposed such unusual and almost paralytic rigidity on the eighth-year class. He actually speaks, they thought, God Almighty Kupfer speaks like any human being. Doesn't make his stern will known in brief gestures. Says just, "Sit down", like the other teachers, and now there he stands saying nothing, as any human being might say nothing.

"I will wait until we have total peace and quiet," says Professor Kupfer in a sharp voice, without moving, without looking at anyone. And only when the class is sitting as motionless as it was standing before, only then does *he* move, apparently in order to illustrate the contrast between the students, who must sit still at his bidding, and him, whom no one here can command, and who now moves all the more freely.

Kurt Gerber had not looked away from him yet; he was staring at him spellbound, as if looking for some vulnerable spot in the enemy with whom he was about to enter the ring for a ten-month wrestling match.

Now Professor Kupfer made a movement like a man waking from profound and distant thought, leant against the tall lectern, hands in his jacket pockets, and suddenly began to smile. Instantly, he had so transformed both himself and the mood of the class that all he had previously said and done became an artificial prelude, one he had performed almost without thinking. Now, however, now that God Almighty Kupfer was really here, now the real game began.

His voice had an entirely different sound—and once again Kurt jumped, just as he had when the door handle was pressed down, although both times he had known what was coming next.

"Well, so here we all are." Kupfer fell silent, as if thinking hard. He wanted to give what he said the appearance of improvisation, as if he were voluntarily exposing his own little human weaknesses. (Hoping to appear "jovial", he often adopted a stilted manner.)

"Let's see who's here." His glance swept around the room. Kurt sat there in fevered expectation. What would happen when God Almighty Kupfer noticed him?

"Lewy," said Kupfer, with his mouth hardly open, "we've already had the pleasure—Lengsfeld, yes, all old acquaintances—and I see Gerber is also here—you liked the summer holidays better than this, eh?" he asked as Kurt, who had risen to his feet, red in the face and unsure of himself, silently bowed.

"Yes." Kurt said this barely audibly, and quickly sat down again.

"Good. We'll start with a roll-call of the register."

He opened it and began reading out the names; each time a student said, "Here," he made a note in the book without looking up.

"Altschul!"

"Here!"

"Benda!"

"Here!"

Kurt, listening carefully as he waited for his own name to be called, expected to hear "Berwald" at this point, and he looked at Lisa's place. It was still empty. In his surprise, he didn't hear Kupfer murmuring, "Berwald has left the school," nor did he hear him reading on, calling the names of Blank, Brodetzky and Duffek, he didn't hear Gerald's name or his own. His thoughts had abruptly taken another direction, and in the same way as they had previously been circling around "Kupfer", they were now circling in mindless haste around "Lisa"… Lisa, Lisa, he thought, where's Lisa? And now, when Hobbelmann turns and urgently whispers "Scheri", he jumps, and his carefully prepared "Here" comes out in such a strange tone that no one can help laughing, and even Kupfer, who has called "Gerber!" three times with increasing impatience, only shakes his head and, without castigating him for inattention, reads on through the register. Halpern, Hergeth, Hobbelmann. Once again, Kurt hears nothing, but stares at the green-painted wood of the desk in front of him and thinks: Lisa… He was planning to invite her out to a cake shop for the last free morning when she might not be surrounded by twenty others; he'd meant to work out a plan with her for the school term ahead, one last moment of free time, entirely free—you're back from Italy, Lisa, where no one knew you were still at school, and you and I and everyone know that I'm almost past my schooldays, we're much older than we used to be, and we'll behave accordingly, no one must notice anything, we won't talk on our own in break, those childish idiots mustn't have anything to see and gossip about, Lisa—but Lisa wasn't here…

Professor Kupfer had closed the register and stepped forward to deliver his opening address to the class, with the same smile on his lips as he had assumed earlier. It really did suggest a touch of goodwill, even a kind of modesty. He was trying to come down, as far as possible, to an earthly level. But the obvious care he took to do so made his intentions clear: they were to notice how far he had to descend from those heights where he usually sat enthroned in order to appear to the students a member of the human race like themselves. Look, his tone of voice and the tenor of his address implied, I am taking a great deal of trouble to make myself understood. But thank heavens, I can only regret that it doesn't work. I am steeped too far in knowledge that is denied to you, in experience that you could not understand—yet something of it *must* come through to you in my words, and for your sake I did intend to keep them as easy as I possibly could. However, no one can stay far below his own level for long. So, as I proceed further in my address, I must give more meaning and richness to my words, seemingly at the expense of the subject. You will not be able to follow me, but I can't help myself. I trust you will not take offence at my considering you stupid. But should anyone dare not to hide his inferiority under a cloak of humble shame, and instead try to express it in any way whatsoever, thus making me aware that I am, after all, among hopeless idiots, it will be the worse for him! And I shall be careful that not the slightest expression of your stupidity escapes me!

What he said, out loud, was: "Captain Kupfer—for I held the rank of captain in the Great War—sees everything, takes note of everything, knows everything." Kupfer uttered these words perfectly seriously, and Kurt's astonishment (for the time being he was still incapable of any other feeling) increased immeasurably. He had listened intently to what Kupfer said as, after beginning in the traditional way, he moved more and more into the first person, punctuating his remarks with instances of self-glorification, at first in parenthesis but then coming thicker and thicker, climbing higher and higher up artificial hills of pomposity, and now the inflated address had reached the peak of the vanity of the man delivering it, to no one's pleasure but his own. Kurt had listened to all this. Now he was waiting for whatever outrageous comment would follow what the speaker had been at such pains to express.

"You see, you must know that it is impossible to deceive me, and it will be in your own interests not even to try. Do not think you might succeed after all, and don't listen to anyone else's whispered suggestions. It is inadvisable to lend an ear to such advice. I have never done so. Nor do I ever follow the crowd. The crowd always does something stupid and regrets it later. That is life. The stupid shed tears afterwards, it is the clever who laugh. I am in the habit of laughing."

"Ha, ha," said someone in the artificial pause that followed this.

Kurt had not actually laughed; he said, "Ha, ha," aloud and slowly, as he contemplated this shallow admirer of his own reflection, thinking himself undisturbed in the cloudy fields of his divinity, and was possessed by an uncontrollable wish to take him down a peg or two and return him to his rightful place at the teacher's desk.

Undisturbed, Kupfer looked at the desk where Kurt was sitting, and raised his eyebrows. Everyone turned to him. Kurt sat leaning forward, smiling right into the Professor's face, as if he shared his opinion that the clever are in the habit of laughing. He was glad, he found, that the moment of showdown between him and Kupfer had come so soon.

"Gerber!" said Kupfer slowly. "You may be one of those who shed tears afterwards."

With that, so far as Kupfer was concerned and much to the regret of Kurt and the class, the subject was closed. Soon he concluded his address with the words: "I don't need you to show mathematical genius, and I won't demand the impossible of you. What I do want, you can all easily achieve by dint of hard work and goodwill. Anyone who cannot or will not achieve that is immature, and only the genuinely mature will pass the final examination, the *Matura*. I give you my assurance today that in this crucial year there will be no acts of mercy. Anyone who happens to have reached the eighth year as the result of an act of mercy will have a very hard time with me. I would prefer weak students to leave the school at once. I will not have the *Matura* degraded to a mere formality, not I. In particular, I advise those who hope to make up for their laziness by impudence to be on their guard. You will do best not to take me on. Now you know more or less how you must behave in my class. Regular lessons begin at eight a.m. tomorrow."

Professor Kupfer turned round and picked up his coat. Suddenly he remembered something.

"And as to the seating plan—is that how you were sitting last year?"

A few students were bold enough to answer with a loud "Yes".

"Very well. It can stay the same for now. Only someone will have to move into Berwald's place now that it's vacant… let's see… Lengsfeld, all right? Oh, and who is missing there, in the same row as Gerber. That's right, Weinberg. He can stay. I want a seating plan of the whole class tomorrow. Who has good handwriting?"

"Reinhard… Kaulich… Not me… Severin."

"Oh, agree among yourselves who does it!" said Kupfer in sudden annoyance, turning to leave. The class immediately rose to their feet and stood without a sound, but once Kupfer had closed the door behind him, hubbub broke out.

The eighth-year students milled around in agitation, unable to make up their minds about Kupfer. For neither the "He's not so bad" group nor the larger "He's an absolute bastard" group could cite any evidence for their opinions except that they had just expressed them. Volubility had to make do for the absence of logic.

Kurt Gerber took no part in this debate. He sat there thinking of Lisa and only Lisa. He was indignant that Kupfer had even spoken her name. And the fact that he would have no further occasion to do so made him very anxious. Lisa Berwald had left the school. Why? And why hadn't she told him?

Someone clapped him on the shoulder with a heavy hand; it was the bearlike Kaulich, with a satisfied grin on his broad face.

"Well done, Scheri, you let him have it!"

Meanwhile some of the others had joined them. Nowak said, "That wasn't a great idea of yours. Why do you have to get across everyone right away? What do you get out of it?" A number of students agreed with him, others didn't. "It's a good thing for God Almighty Kupfer to find he can't go too far."

Kurt, thinking things over, asked as casually as possible, "Does anyone know what all this about Lisa Berwald is?"

Several answers came in. "Left school.—I heard she's going to get married soon.—Not a bit of it, she's simply sick and tired of this place.—Can't say I blame her."

"If you ask me, young Lisa's no fool—she's fed to the teeth with swanning round school," versified Pollak, bowing to his laughing audience. Most of the students were in good humour now, and they decided to go to the morning concert at the bandstand in the municipal park. Kurt was in no mood for it. He unobtrusively slipped away and went home.

Full of dissatisfaction in general, he turned his back on the day's events, dragging his feet.

At home, he flung himself on the sofa. Might as well sleep off a foul day like this. If you didn't have to go to school. And today he didn't.

Professor Artur Kupfer, on the other hand, was extremely satisfied with the day, as indeed he was with almost all days in the school year. After two empty summer months—empty because he had gone around like one human being among others and not a god among school students, because there was no one he could cause to tremble before his omnipotence, because the many people he saw could not be forced into what his need for domination required—after this period of exile he flung himself body and soul into the empire now restored to him. He had felt warm enjoyment of that first "Sit down", he had caressed it in advance with his palate and tongue and lips, like a man sucking the last fibres of fruit off a peach stone before spitting it out. But Kupfer hadn't spat anything out. It had passed his lips lovingly (and therefore gently), not a peach stone to be thrown away, more like a little diamond of incalculable value, successfully brought over the border by a jewel-smuggler who now lets it slip out of his mouth with care and trembling delight. Kupfer felt a similar tremor of delight. During the annual summer exile he was always tormented by the same sombre fear: that while he was away everything could have changed, that after his return to the throne, suddenly, for some unfathomable

33

reason, "Sit down" would no longer mean "Sit down", and when he commanded his subjects to sit down they might stay on their feet, or walk around the room. It was an agonizing fear, and he couldn't understand it; he felt it was pointless, and yet it brought him terrible visions on many a sleepless night. When, on holiday in mountainous country, he came to a peak whose height failed to meet his imperious expectations after one such night, he had wanted to tell it, "Unsatisfactory, sit down!" but next moment had felt ridiculous in the fact of that great, silent entity standing there in icy immobility, letting it be known that it was not about to move, and even before the command was given announcing that it was not minded to carry it out—rather like a defiant school student. And he, Kupfer, had therefore been obliged to refrain from giving the order at the last moment, so he hated that mountain and hated the entire landscape and hated all the people he encountered. Most of all he hated Kurt Gerber, whom he happened to meet there and who could not yet be told to "Sit down!" But soon, soon—oh, soon he would be telling students to sit down, sit down, sit down…

And now his hour came. He said, "Sit down" and many human beings, a whole room full of them, sat down. He spoke the names of those human beings, and each of them stood up and announced, "Here". As a whole and as individuals they were at his disposal again. Nothing had gone wrong while he was away, it all worked. He gave orders, and his orders were obeyed. He called, and he was answered. He said, "I want peace and quiet!" and there was peace and quiet. He spoke—and was surrounded by the bright light of authority and radiant perfection. God Almighty Kupfer.

He knew that was the students' nickname for him. He also knew that nothing can be done about nicknames. So he was determined to live up to his, and since he succeeded in that, he had no objection to hearing it. Yes, he was God Almighty Kupfer, and he was a jealous god, avenging the sins of the students even unto the third and the fourth semester that he forced them to spend in the same class… He was also a slave to his vanity, and would not tolerate the slightest offence to it. And he was anxiously intent on issuing commandments to avert anything that might impair his omnipotence. He was well disposed only to students who looked up at him in obsequious humility, who pitifully begged him for mercy when all was not well with them, and thanked him, bowing low, when it was. Moreover, his splendour hung only from a thread, depending on a single, tiny decision: were they going to believe in him or were they not?

Since the students did believe in him, he was God Almighty to them. He was considered a great authority on mathematics, particularly descriptive geometry. His textbook of descriptive geometry with exercises, in four parts (to him, "in four parts" meant as good as twice the usual number of fists to hit with) was set for study in almost all high schools, so that his name as an expert was accepted without question by the students. He consolidated his position in every lesson. There was no way anyone could contend with him. Kupfer was Kismet. He had built up a reputation for invincibility, and now it went before him into every new classroom, opened the door to him, sat at the teacher's desk and spread universal fear. When Kupfer entered the room he had only to take over from his reputation by replacing it with himself. He was, in a way, a body cast by his own shadow instead of vice versa, he was the justification of what was expected of him, and he had no difficulty in proving his point. He did it convincingly. Anyone who dared to make a fuss was inexorably struck by one of his thunderbolts, and there was no lightning conductor. Kupfer himself seldom uttered threats. Usually a glance, a gesture, a tone of voice, the course of a test gave warning of what lay ahead, and it was like a doctor's final diagnosis of an incurable sickness. You were doomed. Any flicker of the flame of life—a good word put in for you, a test passed—was only a flash in the pan, a delusion. The adder never relaxed its bite, never let you go. And slowly the deadly venom spread through its victim, who felt that his legs were getting weaker and weaker, and that he was sure to sink to the ground at exactly the appointed time.

Some made desperate attempts to save themselves at the last minute, lowering themselves to grovel mindlessly, doglike, licking up the saliva dripping from the victor's slavering jaws, or tried to resist the inevitable with hands raised in plead-ing, writhing and whimpering beneath the knee weighing down on their chests, immersing themselves in their books, crazily hammering facts into their hot heads with fevered haste—only to find out, standing before the examiner with cheeks that did not owe their pallor to fear, and eyes red but not from weeping, that unfortunately it had all been too late. Yes, there were some like that. Others gave up the race and fell by the wayside. Resigned, they let themselves drift towards the end with a weary smile and received the verdict with a nod of the head. "I knew that ages ago." But as for a student who in answer to Kupfer's nasal, "Well, let's see who's going to draw the short straw here!" would reply, "I only want to try it out, I'm ready to have a go!", a student who would fight to the end and emerge from the battle the same as he had been at the start of it—no such student existed.

So far Kupfer had always won just as he wanted. He had come to take that for granted, and coolly took note of his success. When he had carefully crushed his victim between the millstones of his intentions he felt no triumph, either noisily vaunted or relished with hidden malice. He did not rejoice. Quietly, with gentle regret, he established the fact that it must necessarily turn out like this. That meant that in a way he was apologizing to the victim, to the spectators watching the victim's sacrifice, and also, if very seldom, to himself.

The manner of his victory also determined the style of his attack. Kupfer did not come up from behind. He did not need to lull the chosen victim into a sense of security and then strike unexpectedly—after all, his victory was certain from the start. He was also careful not to use flagrantly obvious methods, not to do anything that could be shown to be more incorrect than was tacitly admitted to be his due as the more powerful party in the contest. What he needed came his way as if by chance, and he made use of it to the utmost extent that the rules allowed. Nothing was too slight to arouse his ire and bring it into action. Seizing the most inconspicuous opportunities and using them for his own ends sometimes allowed him to dispense with the more conspicuous kind, thus suddenly giving himself the appearance of generous objectivity.

He did not mind exactly where he struck; there were other ways open to him.

He paid great attention to his point of departure. He chose his victim like a gourmet selecting the tastiest of game; he sought out the choicest parts of the roast, and carved it up with a relish that was satisfying in itself. He consumed those who were wholly incapable of achievement, entirely stupid, as side dishes, swallowing them just as they came to hand. They offered no stimulation, and he was not particularly concerned with them. Their written tests were easily marked "Unsatisfactory", and to make doubly sure he followed that up with his dreaded venom-tipped arrow: the questions he asked in class as they sat at their desks which, if they went unanswered (and only then), counted towards their exam results. Otherwise he wanted nothing to do with such students, the scrapings of the barrel, and ignored them. He fixed his eye all the more keenly on the main objects marked out for destruction. Weaklings who might have collapsed at the first hurdle never to recover, hysterical students who might have done something unexpected in a sudden fit of fury, the naturally indifferent with the hide of an elephant—he steered clear of those with a sure instinct. He wanted students who were firmly based. There was a special piquancy when one of them also came of a wealthy family or had a reputation for special intelligence. In that case, those who were not equipped with either money or brains gleefully kept track of Kupfer's progress. And there was something else that, to his advantage, set him apart from all other teachers—or rather could have set him apart if he had not taken it too far: it was a matter of total indifference to him whether his victim was male or female. He was so indifferent that even the greatest misogynists in the eighth year felt uncomfortable when he snapped at a girl student and, further stimulated by her tears, bombarded her with patronizing remarks through the entire lesson. Ultimately, however, even that helped to surround him with an armour of incorruptibility that kept off all his adversaries, including the shrewdest. God Almighty Kupfer had no weak spots; students were all alike to him...

And he would have liked to see them all dressed alike as well. He wanted to be the only person present who was elegantly clad. Even wearing a new tie in one of his lessons was enough to earn you an "Unsatisfactory", because that was tantamount to claiming an unseemly advantage over him. Kupfer would tolerate no such thing, and was furious with anyone who ventured to claim it. This attitude sometimes brought some idiot son of a patrician into his clutches, or an oaf wearing a deliberate grin because he enjoyed protection in high places. Kupfer, with unwavering tenacity, would wrest him from the hands that protected him and bring him to grief. Because that looked legal, it earned him the respect or even the admiration of those students who, from the first, had got themselves into a reasonably secure position by consistent diligence. But Kupfer himself preferred students who, because he seemed to like them, did not know why: the reason was that with his goodwill towards them and the latitude he allowed them, he only wanted to spur on the enslaved to new hatred, a hatred that became darker and darker and more and more helpless. So he dallied with his students, sowing envy and resentment among them, ensuring that they did not form a united front against him, playing off one against another and calculating the points he had won with cold pleasure. They served his purposes far beyond the hours of lessons. And in his lessons, their inferiority left the despicable creatures known as students with no option but to be the tools he used to bring his absolute power into action, dominating them by such means. In fact it was never clear to him for what work exactly they were to be his tools. It was at this point that the equation was reduced to zero. Infinity—not of the kind where parallels intersect—intervened in Kupfer's calculations and made one factor stand out. The word for that factor was sense.

Kupfer was satisfied with this solution. He thought no more about it, and did not want to put infinity to the test (sometimes it felt quite close, like a black chasm promising an unpleasant outcome if you fell into it). Nor was it necessary to do so. He carried weight all the same, or perhaps for that very reason. Class after class, young people with the blood pulsing through them, who became a rigid bulwark against all doubt at his behest, came again and again to confirm that to him with subservient nods. And he needed that confirmation, and even the smallest of the evidence of it they gave, he held the thought of them lustfully close, as excited as if he were possessing a naked, pleading woman…

Because he had been given that confirmation again today, after a long period of abstinence, with immediacy and at full force, seasoned by a promising little episode, Professor Artur Kupfer was extremely pleased with his day. He had managed the prelude to the Gerber case excellently. "You may be one of those who shed tears afterwards," he had told him. It had been a hint and at the same time a clever retort, and on top of that it followed on from what he had said. He could indeed have dismissed him with an even wittier play on words, since the German noun *Gerber* means a tanner ("Gerber, we'll tan your hide for you," he could have said, or something like that; tee-hee), but he kept that for another time. It did not escape him, just as Gerber would not escape him. That young

Gerber! Kupfer looked forward to dealing with him like a child looking forward to a new toy; he was going to ruin him. It was not least for that reason that Kupfer had campaigned to have himself appointed class teacher for the eighth-year students. Over the years, when the teachers complained of some new misdeed of Gerber's, declaring themselves power-less in the face of his unruly behaviour, so different from that of the other students—over the years Kupfer had always said, with insulting surprise, "It amazes me, my dear colleague, that you can't cope with such a stupid, brazen boy as that!" And when it was pointed out to him that Gerber was by no means stupid, but by far the most intelligent of his class, if not in the entire school, nor was he brazen, he just had a way of expressing his opinion that did not belong at a school desk, and above all he was not exactly a boy but, on the contrary, so mature that it was impossible to decide to fail him, Kupfer would say dismissively, "I don't believe it." (He was referring to the information that a student was intelligent; the utter implausibility of this circumstance made all else an illusion.) "If I were ever to get young Gerber in my class, I'd soon bring him into line. Not that I'd wish that on him." But he did, and now his wish had been fulfilled. Mattusch had firmly turned down the idea of carrying on as class teacher to "that unruly gang"; Rothbart, the next to be considered, had too heavy a workload; Hussak was too young, Prochaska too old—and so Kupfer became class teacher for the eighth-year students. Now they'd see what he was capable of! So, too, thought several other professors; the leniency so far shown to young Gerber went against the grain with them. They were curious to see the outcome of the duel that had been announced, and their thoughts followed Professor Artur Kupfer, who

was to be judge of the case, to the eighth-year classroom…
where on the very first day, young Gerber revealed his own
weaknesses first by failing to pay attention, and then with an
impudent interruption. So much for his famous intelligence!
You fool, Kupfer would have liked to tell him, you don't seem
to have any inkling of what lies ahead of you. But he did
not say it out loud. The retort he had in fact given was more
elegant. And feeling rather sorry that the Gerber case might
not be nearly as complicated as he had expected, Kupfer had
left the classroom.

On the stairs, he met Professor Seelig. "My dear colleague," he said, "tell me what you really think of Gerber."

"Gerber? An unusually talented young man. There's not
really much left for him to do at school—"

"Are you so sure of that?"

"Well, I know that he doesn't exactly shine in your subjects.
But he's probably not going to practise a profession in which
he'll need them. In other respects, however, he is—"

"He also strikes me as impudent. I've heard this and that
about him. You yourself said, Seelig—"

"Oh well… that's nothing to speak of. Yes, he's a little
wild. However—and here I speak from experience, my dear
Kupfer—that's probably nothing but his natural youthful
temperament. The opportunities open to him here at this
school simply aren't enough for him. Fundamentally, so far
as I can judge, my dear Kupfer, it's easy enough to get on
with him, you have only to—"

"Well, time will show!" rasped Kupfer, and he said a quick
goodbye to his colleague.

Kupfer took short steps, thinking that his slightly rocking
gait was still a satisfactory test of the elasticity of his muscles.

As he walked along the streets he looked straight ahead, so that he could intentionally fail to see anyone who might be expected to address him. Kupfer never returned a greeting. He was the first to greet those whose company he wanted to cultivate, and took no notice of the others—most of them were school students anyway. He ignored them, however, in such a way that they did not know whether he didn't want to see the greeting or really hadn't seen it. Consequently his anxious students would greet him a second and a third time and still get no reaction. However, if one of them did not try to greet him at all, Captain Kupfer immediately took him to task, and disciplinary procedures followed.

Kupfer had reached his home. The building was in a narrow alley off the city centre, and his first-floor apartment belonged to a widowed baroness. Her husband, a holder of high military rank, had fallen in the Great War, and ever since then she had worn black and cut herself off increasingly from the outside world. When word got around that for financial reasons she was thinking of letting three of her six rooms to a tenant, she was bombarded with enticing applications, for her exquisite taste in the pre-war years was famous. Kupfer won the day in the face of all rivals. Perhaps his former rank of captain, which he brought into play to good effect in applying, helped him. Perhaps the baroness hoped that in this former officer she might find a friend who would satisfy her need for reminiscence. Kupfer moved into the rooms, and maintaining them put him to considerable expense. As he had inherited money and was a bachelor, however, he could afford the rooms, could even afford more when, after a while, the baroness wanted to sell him their furnishings. The old lady misinterpreted the trouble he was taking with her, and made gentle overtures of friendship. But soon she was repelled by his boastful, hollow nature, and now she lived entirely retired from the world. The one thing she asked him for was permission to pass through his rooms while he was out, and Kupfer agreed.

Now the three rooms were his alone. He had plain wallpaper hung on the walls of the smallest and made it his study. In case his own taste spoilt anything, he emphasized simplicity. He might almost have succeeded if the bay window had not been adorned by a little rococo table on which lay the manuscript of his descriptive-geometry textbook plus exercises, in four parts, carefully kept in heavy, red plush folders, and the first edition of the books themselves, bound in silk. Another folder contained letters of appreciation and other papers showing the author in a good light. The crowning touch was a framed photograph of Kupfer in a thoughtful pose. In the middle of the room there was an oval table with an oilcloth cover, surrounded by brown wooden chairs, against one wall a sofa and against another a cupboard containing all Kupfer's mathematical instruments. He also kept his library in this room; he had had shelves built in along one wall and provided with a curtain. The curtain was never more than half drawn, and revealed his books: all the classics and their contemporaries, many titles in French, a de luxe edition of Schopenhauer in which the passages dealing with vanity were marked in red, several works on social policy, here and there choice editions of very modern writers, but otherwise little by living authors (because the extent of their importance could not be known for certain), apart from the works to be found on station bookstalls that did not oblige the reader to form an opinion of them. The pages of all the books had been cut, many bought in antiquarian bookshops had thus already been read—for the rest, the volumes stood side by side at random and unclassified. The idea was to make it look as if the library was much used, and above all to convey an impression of artistic confusion. For, one day, Artur Kupfer had decided to be bohemian. He resolved to remind himself daily how good it felt, after the rigid, boring rules and regulations of school, to bathe in the waters of informality, which he considered suited his real nature much better! Kupfer took meticulous care to let disorder reign in his study. The desk was heavily laden with colourful heaps of books, newspapers, letters, exercise books and loose sheets of paper. He snapped at the cleaner if she tidied the piles of material while she was dusting, or if she placed the ruler neatly beside his writing case instead of letting it peep out of the pages of an illustrated magazine, from which he was in the habit of taking it, or if she failed to leave the ashtray, the calendar, the blotting pad and all other items in the places where it was their daily purpose not to belong. (Places and objects were changed around at certain intervals of time.) The drawers of his desk were also very untidy. And when a visitor asked to see his study, Kupfer would say, "Oh, I'm quite ashamed to take you in there, it's in terrible disorder. I really think I shall have to fire the cleaning lady."

Kupfer had changed nothing in the appearance of the other two rooms, except that in the salon, under the curved Saracen sabre that hung on the wall flanked by two Turkish slippers, there were now three photographs of Kupfer. They showed Kupfer in uniform, Kupfer in riding dress on horseback, and Kupfer attired for a game of tennis. Otherwise the rooms had retained all their old atmosphere

of aristocratic gloom, all the distinguished calm with which
Kupfer's notions did not seem to be at home. When Kupfer
had drawn the heavy curtains in the evening, and walked
about the rooms in the muted light of a lamp in a niche, he
thought, with a chilly shudder, that he felt the cold breath
of their nobility. Then he took off his glasses, put a monocle
in his eye, stood in front of the heavily framed wall mirror
with a cigarette casually held in the corner of his mouth,
and realized that he suited this place very well, and should
really have come into the world as Artur Maria Baron von
Kupfer somewhere in Pomerania, instead of being the son
of an respectable if narrow-minded provincial in Mährisch
Trübau, and the old baroness now sleeping in the other half
of the apartment ought to have been his mother. Then there
would have been a different kind of attraction in the fact
that she could not hear prostitutes moaning in transports of
lust (as specified in their tariff) in the broad, soft bed in his
bedroom. They were seldom street-walkers—usually they
were barmaids, dancers, cocottes who did not offer their
bodies immediately (they liked to have their hands kissed
first), but allowed a kind of wooing to enter the game of their
work. As far as Kupfer was concerned, there was an end to
all that the moment they set foot in his apartment. A girl
who let herself sink into one of his comfortable armchairs
cheerfully or with sultry sensuality, prepared to continue
the game to its predestined end, was summarily ordered by
Kupfer to undress in order to reach that end by the means
that desires verging on the sick suggested: she must kneel
before him, for instance, begging him to take her body as a
penance that she deserved. If she objected, or demanded a
higher price for the extra play-acting, he would chase her

out of the house with pretended composure. Generally, however, the girls shrugged their shoulders and complied with Kupfer's wishes...

Such nights (and they were followed by a sense of shame next morning, but very muted and as if coming from far away) were the only means he had of confirming his godlike omnipotence. Beyond that it failed dismally. He had never had a real lover. After brief attempts, he had realized that ultimately there was no prospect of such a thing, and withdrew. Indeed, he realized with a precision that was nearly always correct just where his limits lay. He knew that as soon as he was outside his sphere of influence, the school, he could not impress anyone in any way. A layman has little respect for knowledge that does not interest him. The fact that he could construct the regular section of a prism by discovering its trace points and by using affinity was not going to fill many people with awe-stricken respect. He knew that. And because he could offer nothing else, he had to develop his personality as a teacher, making it so feared that it overshadowed and determined his personality as a private individual. Not the other way around. He was not the man Artur Kupfer who assumed the profession of a professor of mathematics, he was the professor of mathematics—*the* Professor of Mathematics—who assumed the character of Artur Kupfer. He did not practise his profession but was practised by it. Its radiance surrounded him at the café table where, with familiarity and heavy humour that he had learnt by heart, he sought the approval and admiration of average citizens, some of them the parents of students whom he favoured. It glittered around him in a club or association where he could debate without presumption and with undemanding if nondescript ingenuity. A glint of the same radiance still danced around him when he was lying on the beach at the seaside, and the waves, seeing it, whispered to one another: there lies Professor Artur Kupfer, private individual…

He was no god to other people, but still, they knew that he was treated as a god somewhere. And now it was a question of whether that at least impressed them. Where it did, Kupfer became, if not exactly more popular, at least more welcome and in a way, on occasion, more interesting company. Where it did not, people turned their backs on him with pity and contempt, saying, if they were going to bother to mention him at all, "Oh, that idiot!" There were some who even said, "That villain." And he concluded, from the fact that they could say it with impunity, that high-school study came entirely to an end with the final examination. So he enjoyed his allotted time with his students to the full, clutching it and squeezing out of it all the satisfaction that was denied him afterwards—squeezing it until the blood came.

Professor Artur Kupfer, known to his students as God Almighty Kupfer, had come to see, by dint of clear thinking, that when a command to "sit down" no longer carried such weight, the divine and absolute power of his reign came to an end. He was a god of limited staying power. But where he clung on, he clung like a bur.

II

Entry of the Gladiators. Strike the Gong.

THERE WAS NO FIXED TIMETABLE yet for the next day, so the students had plenty of scope for guesswork. And yet it was also a school day like any other, since one thing was certain; Kupfer was their class teacher.

Almost all of them had quickly adjusted to the idea. Thick exercise books with pages of graph paper and black covers, drawing instruments and a triangle already lay in the desks of the particularly hard-working. It never hurts to be well prepared. And if a test can't be avoided, it's best to do it with a smile and not morosely and reluctantly, which after all will do you no good. Exercise books have to be bought, so better do it today than tomorrow.

Kurt brought neither exercise books nor any other teaching aids with him. Going halfway to meet a teacher without express orders struck him as an unnecessary and indeed reprehensible show of over-eagerness. He even hated speaking up from his desk when someone else was being tested up in front by the blackboard and was stuck for an answer. And why be so keen to do Kupfer's bidding that you'd bring exercise books to school without being sure whether he was going to turn up at all? All these pitiful precautions "just in case"! He hoped that the industry of those keen to curry favour would be for nothing. Yet he knew that they wouldn't draw any conclusions from that; they would meekly turn up with their exercise books again the next day.

However, industry was rewarded. Soon after the bell rang Kupfer did come into the classroom. As he made entries in the register, Severin, unnoticed, put the seating plan on his desk.

He had worked on it carefully, with red and black India ink, marking the position of the teacher's desk, the door, the stove, the windows. Now he was clearly waiting for appreciation, but pretended to be surprised when it came.

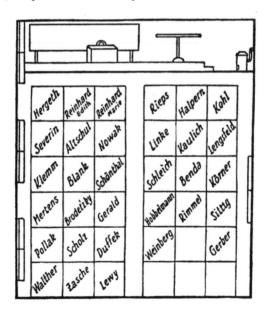

"Who was it did this? Ah. So you are… Severin. Very good. You don't have the proportions of the windows quite right, and the distance between the steps up to my desk is rather greater."

Kupfer smiled ("I am putting on a show of eccentricity!") and benevolently called, "Quiet!" when a couple of those who had appointed themselves to laugh at the professors' jokes showed their understanding and appreciation of his by muted giggles.

"Come over here and explain it to me!" said Kupfer, and drew his notebook towards him, still smiling. But now it was a different smile, contented, replete with the horrified astonishment of the students. Would you believe it? Testing someone in the very first lesson! And moreover, the very student who had rendered him a service! It was enough to shake the tried and tested foundations of sycophancy!

Confusion was aired in suppressed murmurs, some students shifted where they sat and looked at one another in dismay. Only Lewy and Lengsfeld smiled in a wise and superior way. They knew about this kind of thing. Rimmel turned to look at Kurt Gerber, wanting to know what position to adopt. But Kurt had been prepared for anything, and merely shrugged his shoulders.

Kupfer noticed the restlessness. He changed tack. "What is going on?" he asked sharply. "Do you by any chance think I'm going to waste a lesson just because this happens to be the second day back at school? Quiet there! Gerber!"

"Sir, I—"

"That will do. I don't want to know. If you like you can come up to the front of the class instead of Severin."

Kurt restrained himself. Damn. He hadn't taken this into consideration. He was not a diligent student, the Professor could mark his answers "Unsatisfactory" at any time—and only now, when Kupfer made insinuating remarks, did Kurt see that he was in danger.

"Very well, then!" With composure, Kupfer turned to Severin. "There's nothing we can do about the angle of the steps now. That will be for the next lesson. Now we'll have descriptive geometry, then mathematics from nine to ten. Good." He imparted this information casually, well aware of its terrifying effect. As if it were perfectly natural for him to take two lessons in succession. "Now, Severin, think of the stove in relation to the window again. As what geometrical figure can it be regarded? Use a little of the imagination that I trust you have! Well?"

Severin squirmed with embarrassment in the face of so much confidence. He was one of those inconspicuous students who generally refrained even from trying hard at school for fear of attracting attention. The inconspicuous passed their written examinations by dint of some skilful sleight of hand, with luck just scraped through the oral tests, and one day were declared worthy of their *Matura* certificates. They would use some favourable situation at the beginning of the year to make a good impression, and if they succeeded that was all they wanted.

Severin had been trying just that in providing the seating plan—and now there he stood staring at the stove, thinking strenuously and making faces, as if he had to find the most cogent of all answers for the most difficult of all questions.

Kupfer, who was quick to pick up a suspect scent, asked, "What were your marks last year?"

"Good in both semesters."

That surprised Kupfer. He didn't know exactly where he was. Was Severin in fact an able student, just confused at the moment? Did he, after all, know so much that in these circumstances it would be disgraceful to let him fail over such a childish question? Well, he'd soon find out. For the time being Kupfer passed it over.

"The stove most resembles a cylinder." (Kupfer pronounced the word with pompous precision, as he did all words borrowed from languages other than German.) "Is that right?"

Severin nodded, relieved.

"Good, then let's go on. Imagine the stove standing in that corner by the window. Let us suppose the sunlight falls in at an angle of sixty degrees. We want to work out what shadow the surface area of the cylinder, that is to say the stove, will cast on the plane surface, that is to say the surface of the desk."

Severin was lucky enough to know how to begin this exercise—which was not surprising for a student of his stamp. When he started to hesitate, Kupfer intervened, added new complications and finished by solving the problem himself. Severin watched attentively, nodding from time to time to show that he understood, and repeated a few key words under his breath. This was the normal way of "making progress with the syllabus", in which the student played the part of dogsbody. The initial danger of a storm, in the shape of a test carrying recorded marks, seemed to have blown over.

"There." Kupfer put the chalk down and gazed affectionately at the board. "Was that so difficult, Severin? So now you see. Thank you, sit down."

Severin was on his way, mightily relieved.

"One moment!" Kupfer picked up the class register. "You were marked Good last year. Hmm," and with a grin, he entered something in the book. "Today I'm afraid it was Unsatisfactory, at best."

Another surprise and another point scored. Once again it struck home. Severin bowed, scarlet in the face, and went back to his desk. The class sat there, rigid.

Kupfer, unmoved, went on.

"As you see, everyday objects provide the best examples. We just have to keep our eyes open and not allow ourselves to be put off. Don't you agree? For instance, there was I in June 1916, lying beside the River Isonzo…"

"Going to laugh again today, Scheri?" enquired Rimmel, half turning.

"You'd all like that, wouldn't you?" Kurt muttered through his teeth. "Laugh yourself!"

Rimmel grinned, but no sound was audible.

"Hello, Zasche!" Kurt called in break to the rather simple student who ran errands for the others. Was he, he asked, on his way down to the stationer's to buy exercise books?

Zasche nodded, and opened his hand to show a number of banknotes. Kurt added a contribution.

"Get me two as well, will you? The same as for the others."

A little hanger-on, faced with a task that seems to him onerous, thinks it can be mastered only by stepping outside his own nature, and puffs himself up to unhealthy proportions, putting a strain on his lungs. Instead of reducing the task to its proper dimensions he screws himself up to what he supposes them to be, and then suddenly shrinks again, like a rubber band stretched tight and then abruptly snapping back. A melancholy sight—but at first no one thinks about him. Without considering what will happen, the gentle suddenly become rough, weaklings mimic strength, the naturally kindly arm themselves with severity and belligerence.

"Well-Then", as the stout German teacher Franz Mattusch was nicknamed, had never yet entered a student's name in the register by way of reproof, or summoned him before a staff meeting, or actually given him a mark that meant he failed. However, he had his black days when he was possessed by an inconsiderate excess of ill will. Anyone intruding on his preserves then seemed to be inviting total annihilation. These lapses remained within the boundaries of his own subconscious. Not even the class teacher learnt what had happened in the German lesson. For Mattusch was far too lazy to spin out affairs at length, even in his mind, and he was therefore regarded as a good sort. And so he probably was, although whether at heart or only on the surface no one really knew; but that made no difference to the fact that ultimately he presented no danger.

As if he were on the track of some misdeed, he came barging into the classroom with a lot of noise at ten, banged his briefcase down on the teacher's lectern, and looked around the surprised students with brows thunderously drawn together. Then he let fly, and his remarks—he was a fast talker anyway—were wheezed out so asthmatically today that you could hardly understand what he was saying.

"Outside the door I heard one of you saying: 'Good, here comes Mattusch.' I know who it was, of course."

(He paused, and every student present thought that he was meant. In fact, Mattusch had just wanted an excuse.) "Well then, you needn't think you can lead such an easy life with me, right?" ("Well then" and "Right?" were Mattusch's favourite expressions, and he used them all the time, snapping them out crisply.) "Well then, you needn't imagine I'll let everyone who's lazy off so lightly, right? And no trying to argue with me, right? I'm the one who knows best, I always know best. Well then. This is your last school year, and you gentlemen will have to put in a bit of work, right? I'll make sure you do. Well then, it's not so good if 'here comes Mattusch', right? Kindly remember that. Sit down!"

And during the lesson Professor Mattusch paced restlessly up and down between the rows of desks, pouncing on every offence against discipline, and never forgetting to conclude the lectures he then read the students with: "Well then, stop and think what you're about. Your *Matura* exam is imminent, right?"

Professor Prochaska, who had taught the class history and geography for the last three years, was not his usual self today either, and the consistency with which he kept up his new attitude throughout the lesson made the students fear it might be a permanent innovation.

"Young ladies, young gentlemen," he began quietly, yet oddly abruptly, and after the long break his strong Bohemian accent was particularly noticeable. "I'll ask you not to make life difficult for me in this last year of yours. I'm an old man, I'm soon to retire. You're the last class I'll be preparing for the *Matura*—so show that you're grown-up now! But you must also, if you please, kindly keep quiet."

The class fell silent. Quiet for Prochaska. What was this? A strangely weighty sensation hung in the air, pressing down on the thirty-two students in their final year like the hushed sanctity of a cathedral. The students, who in their different ways had reached different stages in their work, suddenly all felt equally bad, as if it were their fault that they were Professor Prochaska's last class for the *Matura*. They also resented it. It limited their options; and what they had heard about the *Matura* so often recently, shaking it off easily again, now suddenly made sense. So the life upon which they were about to enter was really there, it stood before them, to be lived to the end, a furrow to be ploughed, grey, alarming. A mechanical mode of existence, its engine already switched off, began embarking on its final oscillations.

"I'm an old man, soon to retire…" Why is he telling us that? Is it our fault? We don't want to know, we don't want to escort anyone to his grave! So one door is closing behind us at the end of this year—fair enough. But behind him? He's all part of it. We want to leave him behind, too. However, not until the end of the year! We don't want to know, at the very beginning, that it's a last year in two senses. We don't want to think of a life that promises none of us anything but a long wait to say goodbye… why is old Professor Prochaska saying goodbye to us today? We all like him because he's kind, kind like anyone who's used up all the bad in him. Professor Anton Prochaska had used up the bad in him pretty quickly, for his reserves of it had not been large. He had become a likeable character much earlier than most other people. As far as anyone could remember, no student had ever said a word against him—and now were no students to know him again? Are we, the class wondered, to be the last to know and like him?

We'll like him, anyway. And it would be good to tell him so. Why doesn't anyone say anything?

"Professor Prochaska, sir!"

Kurt Gerber has risen to his feet. He'd felt that everyone was waiting for it.

"Professor Prochaska, sir, I promise you in the name of the whole class that your last year at this school will be the best ever!"

The rest of the class rises. They stand there in emotional silence. Prochaska cleans the inside of his glasses without taking them off.

"We'll observe a minute's silence in memory of the dear departed!" he says, with the smile that accompanies all his jokes. This time, however, no one laughs. It was almost the truth.

"Now, do sit down, please!" Professor Prochaska's voice sounded the same as usual again. "I'm particularly glad to hear our friend Gerber say that. I've always thought he was the right sort, even if he's sometimes been known to get rather rowdy playing a game of taroc. Or, come to think of it, was marriage the card game in question? Well, never mind. I'm sure we'll get on well, young people. I'm not worried about that. Of course, you'll have to work a little harder just before the *Matura* exam. And we don't want you two having headaches too often, Lewy and Weinberg, do we?"

Lewy said "No", and Hobbelmann said the same on behalf of Weinberg. Prochaska was so short-sighted that he hadn't even noticed Weinberg's absence. (Weinberg never came back after the holidays until the third day of school. It was his speciality, and he was not a little proud of it.)

"That's all right, then. And once again, young people, behave like the young ladies and gentlemen you are. No coming in late after the bell has rung and slamming doors. You know the close attention everyone pays to the eighth class when you're in your last year. So don't do anything silly. I hope to get you all through the exam, but you mustn't make it too difficult for me, young people, you must help me. It will mean a bit of effort, but, after all, you take the *Matura* only once in your life. At least, I don't want any of you having to retake it. Right, there we are."

The students looked at each other. They knew what Professor Prochaska's remarks meant. He would be telling everyone the individual questions in geography and history, the subjects they would be required to discuss in the exam, ahead of time. They had always heard rumours that he did that. However, the older students taking the final exam never said anything definite. So there was always anxiety: would it really happen? Now Prochaska had almost entirely dispelled that anxiety. He was a good sort. And to have him this year, too! What luck they had to be the last eighth-year class he would see through the exam…

The last lesson was given by Professor Filip, a young teacher with private means who was regarded by the other professors and the students alike as out of the common run. Everyone knew that he taught for sheer love of teaching, and there was probably some connection with his favourite subject of individual psychology. He taught introductory courses on methods of advanced study, logic and chemistry, and was not regarded as a great authority on those subjects. But he had wide general knowledge, which he readily imparted. So his lessons—in which art, politics, medicine and all sorts of other matters were discussed, rather than the ostensible subject—were the most stimulating of all. Filip also liked to depart from ordinary high-school conventions, disregarded any seating plan or other formalities, talking informally to the students, calling the girls by their forenames, and he was in mortal difficulty when there was an inspection. He would then call someone up to the teacher's lectern—someone who had shown evidence of ability in the few opportunities provided by Filip's lessons—and give him his head to say what he liked. Such students got the top mark of Very Good in his reports, most of the rest of them got Good and a few, who he knew for certain wouldn't mind one way or the other, were given a mere Satisfactory. This lax concept of education did not, of course, gain him any respect—for that it would have been necessary for him to be a teacher of one of the main subjects on the curriculum—but it did mean that the students confided in him and treated him (with just a touch of condescension) as a friend. That went so far that students in the lower classes, whose pranks Filip was unable to deal with, were beaten up by the eighth year on their own initiative out of an honourable sense of indignation. The eighth year liked Filip a lot. Unfortunately he was of no real importance.

And even Filip adjusted, in this first lesson he gave them, to the significance with which the coming *Matura* endowed them. It didn't seem like that at first. He arrived late, said not "Sit down" but, as usual and with a civil little bow, "Good day to you"—but then he began trying to force something out; he ran his eyes over the class, and he finally brought himself to make the following speech:

"Do please—I've no objection—do by all means sit any-where you like. We're going to have a weekly lesson in the chemistry lab, and another in the classroom here. I'd like just to ask you to keep to the same seating plan in both rooms. There has to be a little discipline and order in your eighth year, I'm afraid I can't help you there. You won't be taking the *Matura* in my subjects, but you'll need a good grade for a pass and the opinion of the examiners in general. So if I were you I'd bear that in mind. I certainly have no intention of making life difficult for anyone, but I can't allow things to go on this year just as they did last year, or I'll have to take drastic action."

"Cries of *hear, hear* on the right!" commented the occupants of the rows of desks from Lengsfeld to Gerber in the *Sprechgesang* choral style that they liked to use with Filip.

"Never mind the childish jokes!" (His tone of voice expressed a less than happy mood.) "It's your own doing if I treat you as though you'd already passed the exam. So can you please keep quiet?"

"We—will—keep—quiet!" replied the *Sprechgesang* chorus. And then at last, for a change, they did keep quiet.

Filip pulled the chair out from the teacher's tall lectern. "It's rather hot in here. I'll take off my jacket, if the ladies don't mind?" He hung his jacket over the back of the chair, and smiled at the two front rows. The students there returned his smile. "Hello, where's Lisa Berwald?"

"She left," said Sittig. "I'd have expected you to know that."

"I don't take such a close interest in the matter as you do, Herr Sittig. A pity, all the same. She was really charming."

Filip only just managed not to hear the "Shut up!" that came from the desk at the back.

Kurt had not had time since yesterday morning to think about Lisa, had kept putting it off, and now he was annoyed to be caught out in this omission. Something else to lay at the door of bloody Kupfer, whom he couldn't get out of his head. And now there Lisa was in his mind's eye all of a sudden, in surroundings from which Kurt still couldn't detach her.

The rest of them had no difficulty. "She left," was all Sittig had said, yet he was one of the students who had been particularly keen on Lisa. Now, Kurt supposed, he would just look for another girlfriend, and that would be that. In the same way as Filip says, "A pity," hangs his jacket over the back of the chair, and compares Lotte Hergeth's legs with Anny Kohl's slim hips.

And Lisa will never know how lightly everyone takes her departure, he thinks. She will never have a chance to notice that Kurt is the only one who misses her. Even if anyone tells her, she won't understand.

Knowing how pointless his intentions were, Kurt took his maths exercise book out of his desk and tore out a page.

No. What was happening wasn't something to put down on paper. It would have been hard enough to talk about it. And for that Lisa would have had to believe him, really believe him as they walked arm in arm, with smiling eyes, along a narrow, shady woodland path somewhere, or sat in the corner of a twilit terrace… then he could have tried to make her understand it, and not just that but everything else, everything—why did Lisa never talk to him like that? Months ago, that one unhoped-for hour in the park out-side the building where she lived, that first, inexplicably long, ardent kiss, followed by more and more, as if the kisses were startled out of them… but they had never been alone together after that, never again… In break at school, of course, there were exciting moments in passing, brief glances, quiet words. There was also his fear that it had all been mere chance, a passing episode, a tribute to a mild night—Lisa smiled when he wanted, but it was the same smile that she had for everyone who came into the room. Only Kurt took it differently. As the confession of something to come, something wonderful, as an apology for the fact that it hadn't happened yet, a promise that it soon would. If that "soon" always turned out to be "some other time", it wasn't his fault! What reason would Lisa have had to provoke him? And what reason would he have had to insist?

Now that Lisa had left the school, now that the whole unspoken shame of his love's possible dismissal as "only schoolchildren's love" was gone—now much would change. Was Lisa waiting for him at least to make the first move, to push at what might be an unlocked door? Lisa never began anything herself. He would have to remind her of her promise. Again and again. Until sometime it bore fruit.

Dear one,

As you see, I don't mind showing that I understand your superiority over us these last two days by writing to you on a page from my maths exercise book. It's twelve-thirty, and Filip, whose opening remarks to us were very light-hearted, is getting on my nerves now with his travel stories. So I'm writing you; I'd rather do it now than when I get home, where I'm not so sure of being undisturbed.

Are you interested in what goes on at school? In a kind of maternal way—so how are the little ones doing? Well, just fine, because guess what, God Almighty in person has descended into their midst and will be teaching them maths and descriptive geometry under the name of Artur Kupfer. So now Kupfer's got his claws into me. I had a little fencing match with him yesterday in the very first lesson, a kind of preliminary skirmish, it gives me some idea of what's coming. Then good old Prochaska was in here again, he really is going to retire after this year and is getting all tearful in his Bohemian accent. Well-Then is also still around; all the airs he put on about the *Matura* would have made the ends of his moustache twirl if he had one—but luckily he doesn't. We don't know the rest of the staff teaching us yet, but we expect them to be first-class, Niesset, Borchert and other big names. Think yourself well out of it!

Many thanks for the card from Bologna. I'd have been even happier to get one by inland post saying you were back. But of course the lady's not supposed to write first. Lisa, when are you finally going to stop tormenting me with all this waiting? I want so little from you. Is it still too much? You can answer that question with yes if you like, but you must answer it. Will you do that, Lisa? At once? Please do!

Here comes the school servant with the provisional time-table. Filip reads out the names of the teachers. Borchert for French—ugh! Hussak for physics, great! Niesset for Latin, again ugh! Seelig for logic, three cheers! Riedl for natural history, doesn't deserve even 'ugh!' Well, it could have been worse. But I don't want to bore you.

I'd have liked to tell you more: how dismal it is to have Lengsfeld sitting at your desk now, how terribly dismal! Did you think of that at all? And now it occurs to me that I haven't even asked why you left school. I hope to hear it from your own lips.

And not just that. I'd like to hear so much else from you, Lisa. Will you tell me?

Yours.

No signature. That was their way. As it happened, they only occasionally wrote to each other, or rather Kurt wrote Lisa three or four letters, and then Lisa scribbled a skimpy answer on a note, some kind of apology, something to fix their next meeting (which was then called off), and after that a few affectionate words hastily put down all anyhow, no salutation, no signature, just the bare bones of a letter.

Kurt's letters were always several times longer. He felt it necessary to write everything down, he always had far too much to say, and as he never had a chance to say it he wrote it all down indiscriminately, without stopping to think that his words would be out of date by the time Lisa saw them. Words of love age even as they are spoken. Before you have really finished saying them, before the person to whom they are spoken can catch them in their youth, just as you meant them, they have lost their first bloom. And words of love on paper age even faster. Events catch up with them, fade them, leave them meaningless to the recipient's eye. They have been on the way too long, nothing is left of the secret of their origin, only the obvious nature of their aim stands there four-square in its dusty nakedness—and yet they are bashful and amazed, and don't know what to do with themselves. You put those words down somewhere, anywhere that happens to be empty, and sometimes that can be the place that's right for them, but if so it's by pure chance… it isn't easy to deal with written words. And even with spoken words, only a willing, affectionate mind knows what to do with them, a mind that also pays attention to the pauses between them, and fits itself into them as if into a trough between warm waves on a wide, wide sea, letting the air stream over them, breathing them happily in, looking up at the sky and only the sky…

Afterwards, Kurt felt annoyed about that letter. It seemed to him particularly badly written and superficial—and yet he had written it out of a sense of great need. Lisa won't notice any of that, he thought in hopeless desperation. Because I always worry about how she may be feeling in advance. She might happen to be in a cheerful mood, and because she doesn't much like "difficult" letters anyway, she wouldn't have liked one that said any more. Oh, great—I love in the subjunctive mood of the future perfect tense. I ought to let Niesset know. Translate for us, Gerber, please! *Ex abrupto!* Does a man like Niesset ever write love letters? Not letters like that, anyway. I'm the only one who writes letters like that. And I think well of myself for doing it—what a fool I am.

At the end of the lesson, Filip was surrounded and involved in a debate about the *Matura*. Other groups of students were also discussing the day's events.

"This is getting serious, my children!" Blank nodded, looking melancholy. "If even good old Filip is talking like that…"

"He only wanted to show off," said Mertens.

"You don't say so! They all want to show off, of course they do—but there's something in it this time. This is when the crunch comes."

"I wish I had the whole wretched thing behind me," muttered Schleich, sounding depressed.

No one said anything. Kaulich tried for a change of mood.

"Look, we can feel sure Prochaska will tell us the questions. At least that's something."

"And how about Kupfer? And Niesset? And Borchert? Don't they mean anything? That old paralytic Prochaska wouldn't have dared to fail anyone, anyway."

"Calling the only decent one among them names now, are we? We're too hard on him."

"The confession of a sensitive soul!"

Körner, at whom this sally was directed, took offence and walked off. The others were strolling towards the exit as well. Just as Filip passed them, Gerald was saying gloomily, "The hell with this whole school!" Once again, Filip appeared not to have heard. Maybe he shared that opinion himself. What he had said about the marginal importance of his subject for the *Matura* had sounded very forced. But Mattusch had been genuinely bawling them out, and Prochaska had been genuinely sad, and finally, Filip had genuinely thought that he had to say something…

The eighth-year students were tacitly allowed to light cigarettes outside the school building, although strictly speaking they, too, were forbidden to smoke "in the vicinity of the school".

"What do we really make of Niesset?" asked Klemm. "Is he worse than Borchert or not?

"They're both about as bad as each other. A dead heat, coming in just behind God Almighty Kupfer." Lengsfeld said that with such a wry expression that several of the students began to laugh.

"It's not funny," objected Mertens. "Just imagine if we'd had Birdie for maths as well." By Birdie he meant Professor

Hussak, who had acquired this nickname because he called the students "my birdies". "Wouldn't it have been terrific? Birdie instead of God Almighty Kupfer!"

"For Heaven's sake, can't any of you stop your teeth chattering?" Kurt was impatient on his own behalf, too; it was worrying to find the others confirming his fear of Kupfer. "We do have God Almighty Kupfer, and there's nothing to be done about it. But if you're going to be scared shitless before he even lifts a finger, you'll be falling at his feet like ripe plums later. Why are you all so frightened of him?"

"Not everyone's as good at maths as you, my dear Gerber!"

"And thank goodness not everyone's such a fool as you, my dear Schönthal! We none of us know so much that we're immune to failing. Not even you!"

"Oh, really? I don't know about that."

"Well, I do. What's more, there's no point in arguing about what we know or don't know. We'd do better to think how we can disarm God Almighty Kupfer!"

"I don't know what use that would be!" Brodetzky was considered one of the best of the year at maths, and was not in the least afraid. It would have been extremely awkward for him to get involved in any mass protest that could do him no good. "God Almighty Kupfer is only a teacher like any other. It's normal for someone who knows a subject to pass and someone who doesn't know it to fail. Never mind God Almighty Kupfer—"

"Which isn't as hard as all that!" said Pollak, finishing his sentence. He felt as sure of himself in maths as Brodetzky, and had no plans to rebel.

Slowly, the groups of students dispersed, and in the end only Kurt and Lewy were left.

Kurt looked at the thin figure with the strangely old face for a long time. He had sympathetic feelings for Lewy—now, in particular—as the most dismal proof of Kupfer's machinations. Because of them, Lewy had been forced to repeat a year twice, and had therefore been at the school for two years more than the rest of them. Kurt would have liked to show his friendship in some way—but Lewy dismissed any sympathy with cold contempt. He seemed indifferent to his own fate at this school. He didn't bother much about the other teachers, either. But he had a fanatical hatred of Kupfer, and would even have been ready to sacrifice his twenty-first year of life to it.

"Well, what do you think?" asked Kurt.

Lewy shrugged his shoulders. He spoke monotonously, his tone suggesting a lack of interest, his lips twisted ironically, and he was probably well aware that most people put that down to arrogance on his part. "God Almighty Kupfer has outwitted people better than that lot. But he'll pass them all."

"Yes, I'm afraid he will. That's sad."

Lewy snapped his fingers. "If you ask me, Lisa leaving is even sadder. Such a nice, firm body!" A lascivious look came over his face.

What was all this? Intentional or chance? Kurt was afraid of giving himself away, and hardly knew what to reply.

Lewy didn't seem to notice his embarrassment.

"It's too stupid. The only one of the girls who might have been good for something."

Kurt bit his lip. He did not like such conversations in the least. And he could do nothing about it, or Lewy would be dropping some remark tomorrow and the whole class would happily seize on it.

However, Lewy's ideas had a logic of their own. "And by the way," he said, "there's a new dancer appearing at the Cockatoo Club tonight. A friend of mine knows her from her last engagement. Like to come with us?"

"No, thanks. I'm expecting my parents back from their summer holiday this evening."

"Well, maybe next time."

"Maybe. And please—no meaningful hints at school tomorrow!"

"Meaningful hints? What kind of hints?"

"Oh, nothing. See you tomorrow."

They said goodbye, and Kurt went into the stationer's shop near the school. "Rudolf Lazar. School Supplies," said the sign. The owner, an ever-friendly man with a goatee beard and a way of cracking jokes containing sly double entendres that he stepped up according to the age of his customer, said good day. "And what may I have the honour of selling you, Herr Gerber?"

Kurt asked for a number of exercise books, refills for the pen he used in his compasses, and an eraser.

"A rubber, yes, to be sure, guaranteed unbreakable," the stationer assured him, disappearing into the premises behind the shop.

Kurt took the letter to Lisa out of his pocket. "Lewy sends regards," he wrote on the back.

"Anything else?" The stationer had come back with what he had asked for.

"Yes, an envelope, please."

"A nice cold envelope, just coming."

Kurt addressed the letter there and then. As he was writing "Frl." the stationer said, "I'd think a little less about the

Fräuleins today if I were you, Herr Gerber. The study of Fräuleins isn't on the curriculum for the *Matura*."

Really, this was too much. Had no one anything better to do than think about the *Matura*?

"That's my business, Herr Lazar!"

"Oh, I wouldn't dream of interfering in your business, which you're quite right, is none of mine, although—"

Kurt cut him short abruptly, but he couldn't avert a mollifying, "Well, well, well! I didn't know it was so serious, I'm sure the young lady will be pleased. Such a handsome young gentleman…"

At this point Kurt gave up. He was unable to think of an answer, so he paid and walked home slowly, his head bent. When the letter began to feel moist in his hand, he hastily put it into the nearest postbox.

Kurt does nothing to break the awkward silence that fell between him and his parents once they had arrived home and greeted each other. At supper it is not so noticeable, but then it becomes oppressive and intolerable. A sense of stagnation builds up in the air. His mother opens her mouth to say something several times, but can't begin. Kurt himself is not even searching for a remark. And as for his father, he just wants to rest after the stress of the journey home, and before the day-long business meetings that always put such a strain on him, since he holds a leading position in his firm. His father has other anxieties. It costs him an effort to tear his mind away from them and, finally, ask his son what has been going on at school.

Nothing, says Kurt, without looking up.

Did he really, his father enquired, mean nothing?

Really nothing. What, Kurt asks, does his father think could have happened on only the second day back at school?

That was exactly what he had asked, his father insists.

And that was exactly the answer he had given, replies Kurt angrily.

"Kurt!" His father brings his hand down on the table, making the glasses clink.

"Leave him alone, Albert! You mustn't get worked up like that." His mother anxiously reaches for the hand of the man she has loved dearly for twenty years, and for whom she has feared all those twenty years at the slightest provocation, because of his weak heart. Then, with a touch of reproof in her eyes, she turns to Kurt, who is staring morosely ahead of him.

"Who is your class teacher this year?"

"Well, at least that's a question I can answer. Kupfer."

Kurt says that in an indifferent tone, and goes on studying the pattern of the tablecloth. But when there is no reply for some time, he looks at his father after all. He is sitting with his head bent forward, his eyes half closed behind his gold-rimmed glasses, his breath coming irregularly, as it always does when he is badly upset. Now small beads of sweat slowly form in the deep folds on his forehead. And just as Kurt, horrified by this unexpected reaction, is about to say something mollifying, his father draws a deep, vibrating breath and speaks firmly, as if winding up a long discussion.

"Then you'll just have to leave the school." And after a pause, as if that were already decided, he gives his son a choice: he can either go to another school or have private coaching in business skills, and then take up a position in his own office. That will certainly mean jettisoning any idea of the doctoral degree he hoped to achieve after studying law or philosophy at university, but, says his father, it seems to him probably the best solution.

Kurt smiles. He feels that his father is making an over-hasty decision, simply to get away quickly from the reason for it. He isn't used to such unthinking haste in such a clever man. His head must be in a state of confusion. Kurt tries to calm him down. "But Father, none of this is worth making a fuss about."

He has struck the wrong note. "Not worth making a fuss about? What *is* worth making a fuss about if not my own child? When may I get upset if not now, when your future life is at stake? And I am not handing over your future life to that…"

His father doesn't complete that sentence. Sharp resentment at the remarks made by Kupfer during the summer holidays, which he had half forgotten, the fury of a father against someone meaning ill to his child—all that is raging in his mind, unable to find expression. Kurt is strangely shaken. Is the school really so important?

"I'm sorry, Father! But I think you're making too much of something that after all—don't misunderstand me—doesn't matter all that much. My future life—what does that mean? You surely don't think that a cretin like Kupfer can really have any influence on my future or my life? In ten months' time he can go to hell! And until then—" Kurt makes a dismissive gesture, wondering how best to prove the unimportance of those ten months.

"You're mistaken, Kurt!" Now his father's voice sounds warm and calm; once again he is a clear-headed man, with a wide-ranging grasp of business, putting his analytical mind to a given situation as if it were a proposal from a partner in a contract. "You're mistaken!" he repeats, with emphasis, and Kurt has no idea just where he is wrong. "That's not the way things are. I'm very glad that you are not afraid of Kupfer—"

"Maybe he's not so bad after all," interrupts Kurt, not sounding as if he really believes it.

But his father is not to be contradicted. With the painful force of conviction, he demolishes the foundations of any point made by Kurt, showing that his rashly inflated expectations were bound to shrink in the face of facts, like the limp remains of a child's balloon. Without making accusations—for after all, there was nothing for it now—he shows his son how foolishly he has acted in his seven previous years of high school; as a result, it's not to be taken for granted that his recent good progress will continue, and if it does it will be a godsend. He weighs up Kurt's goodwill against Kupfer's vengeful sentiments, forcefully marshals all the arguments for and against Kurt's options, and comes to the conclusion—less and less ably interrupted by Kurt himself—that it would be a useless waste of energy to embark on a battle when its outcome is already decided by Kupfer's entering into it.

"I'm sorry this has gone on so long, but let's get it all out in the open now. You'd be in difficulty over the *Matura* even without Kupfer. At least I am not letting him have the satisfaction of hunting you down."

Hunting him down. Now Kurt sees only an enemy stalking him, and one whom he is not to oppose. Why not? Was Kupfer really so powerful? A fresh surge of energy makes him double his resistance.

"I'm not running away from a man like Kupfer!"

"Please, let's have no heroic posturing. You won't be running away from Kupfer, but from the self-inflicted consequences of your behaviour so far."

"All right—then I'll change all that. This is my last school year anyway."

"That's the very reason why changing will do you no good now."

"That's ridiculous. You talk as if there's nothing I can do about whether I pass or fail."

"That is my point exactly."

"How can you say so? I've never really put my mind seriously to studying before. If I make a great effort now, surely it will work!"

"I doubt it. I even doubt whether you *will* make a great effort."

"Suppose I promise you I will?"

"You can keep your promise at a different school. There's still time to make the move."

"I don't see why it wouldn't be possible if I stay where I am."

"I have just shown you why not."

"You've assumed that events are certain when there is no reason why they should happen at all."

"They'll happen."

"Why? I'll make sure they don't."

"You can't make up, in a single year, for what you neglected in the last seven."

And so it went on, a ding-dong battle of Yes and No. Often there was little difference between them; often they found themselves on the same side of the argument. For Kurt,

argument in favour of staying at the same school was for
something to which, fundamentally, he was indifferent—but
it became significant only because he was giving his word
to work hard, and he was not having his word doubted.
And in fact his father's secret intention—almost irrelevant
of the occasion for it—was to strengthen Kurt's belief in
himself, stimulating the vanity without which achievement
is impossible.

Kurt's mother's eyes went alternately from one to other of
the two men, lighting up with affection when they lit upon
the taut face of the younger, widening in anxiety when a
vein swelled in agitation on the elder's forehead. After quite
a short time she had no idea what it was all about, but
only felt it must be something very bad to get her son, with
his easy, youthful confidence, and his experienced father,
with all his concern for him, into such a hostile argument,
opposing each other but united in opposition to something
of which she knew only fleeting external details, gleaned
from Kurt's very rare stories of school, but also from the
changes in her own household that had taken place in the
school holidays. There had been only a single experience
of her own. She had once, tormented by anxiety, gone
to the school to ask about the result of an examination
that Kurt was taking that day; it would decide whether
he went up into the next year or had to stay down. The
professor she met had spoken to her in a condescending,
unfriendly way, informing her that it was none of her
business, that she and "that fine young gentleman" her
son—how cutting that sounded!—would find out all in
good time, and then he had walked away without another
word, leaving her feeling somehow ashamed. Since then

she had had uncharitable thoughts about the school, and avoided going near it again.

Kurt's father could not withstand his son's insistence in the long run. Although he was composed now, when he looked at the facts he could see many flaws in Kurt's eager torrent of words, but he was tired of exploiting them. He was to some extent reassured, but he still had doubts. More than fifty years of life had pulled the net of his experience too tight for Kurt to be able to undo the knot; he could only break it with wild impetuosity. His father stopped opposing him.

"I'll just point out," he said as Kurt's mother tried persuading them that it was time to go to bed, "that the responsibility is yours now. I've warned you, I can do no more. If you won't listen to the dictates of reason you'll have to see how you can manage for yourself. It's not impossible, to be sure, but it would be easier without Kupfer. He'll persecute you, he'll keep making digs at you, he'll—ah, well, I don't want to discourage you entirely. Go to bed."

A surge of paternal warmth had suddenly come over him. He turned away.

Bewildered, Kurt went to his room. He felt, dimly, that there was more at stake here than a *Matura* certificate, and it scared him.

He lay down on his bed, depressed. His fluttering thoughts would not be shooed away—his father had left them hovering over him in too dense a flock for that. Only a few days ago Kurt would still have laughed heartily at any prediction that he wouldn't pass the *Matura*, would have asked the prophet who made it whether he was crazy. But no one had said any such thing to him, even his enemies among the other students would have shrunk from saying so. Kurt Gerber, not pass the exam?

Now that it had been spoken aloud, however, its effect was doubly strong. And the prophet had not been struck by lightning for such malevolent remarks, but had produced evidence, solid, sturdy evidence. No, it was not impossible after all… Kurt Gerber, fail the *Matura*?

Kurt's spirits had sunk to well below average, to the point of vacillation. He began thinking ahead from this point.

Ten months—was that really a long time or not? It made no difference. He had to get through them. Yes; he could make a great effort without losing face. Of course he could. It would be a fine thing if he couldn't! I'll pay attention in lessons, he thought, keep cool and pay attention; if I'm asked questions I'll answer them—no more than necessary to show that I can deal with the subject. I'll ask someone really good at maths to help me with my homework, and I'll be really down to earth about it—amazing what Scheri can do, who'd have thought it… yes, let's amaze them, I'll tell them my opinion and God Almighty Kupfer will get to hear about it too. Professor Kupfer—why should I call him Professor? If at least he had a doctorate, but he isn't even Dr Kupfer, the great ox. Herr Kupfer, you needn't think you've got the better of me, my father is a sick man, and if I haven't given you a chance to vent your wrath on me it was a sacrifice I had to make for his sake, you were lucky, Herr Kupfer, ha, ha, ha, there he goes talking about good-for-nothings, and it turns out he has not the slightest thing to find fault with, not the slightest. I ask you, what a joke! I can't wait for the moment when God Almighty Kupfer tests me for the first time… there, you see, Gerber, it's fine, you just have to want to do it… I think I'll even enjoy it, but not the way he expects; he thinks I'll knuckle under and put up with his remarks in silence, and he'll look at me in surprise, oh yes, he'll feel some respect too, and before the next lesson Scholz will come and ask me, Hey, Scheri, how did you construct that cross section with the plane, come on, tell us—well, yes, the prop of the pyramid stands with its main foundation on the second plane of projection, then we can do it by shifting the parallel, oh, thanks—listen, Pollak, this is how Scheri thinks we should do it… interesting, wouldn't you say? Very interesting, in fact, all kinds of extremely interesting things are going on—guess what, you can be a good student without crawling to anyone, or swotting, I'm trying to think of a case, a single case where *that* worked! No, my dear Weinberg, I wasn't swotting when I spoke up voluntarily—well, I had to speak up, he expected it… but between ourselves, Weinberg, just between you and me: of course I'm swotting, but I can't help it, I have to pass the *Matura*, I have to, I have to… oh, my dear good father, if only I could get you to understand how very unimportant all this is, how childish, how infinitely childish, but it must be done, right? You're a different person with a pass in the *Matura* behind you, oh, and what have you studied, Herr Gerber—ah, unanimous pass marks in every subject, well, delighted to hear it, the post is yours, but I don't want that kind of post ever, ever, and let's hope you get the news you want, ah, excellent again, three children and a wife, and what did you make for dinner today, my dear, liver dumplings, was it? And then I'll tuck my napkin into my neck instead of spreading it over my lap, and it will all be forgotten, no one will ask me if I ever failed the *Matura*, but first I must pass the *Matura*, oh this is terrible, terrible!…

Kurt tossed and turned in bed, tormented by his thoughts. It was all so narrow-minded, so undignified. Then he had to smile. What had all this to do with him? Young Gerber—top marks. From eighth in the class up to first. And after that, what?

For a moment emptiness lingers in Kurt's head. Then he sees a large, radiant image before him: Lisa. And next moment Lewy appears beside her…

That stupid business at midday today. Why did it upset him so much? Kurt could have listened with indifference to a conversation showing that the girl he loved was sleeping around. To him she wasn't, to him that part of her didn't exist, say what you liked. But he wouldn't have anyone turning directly to him and saying, Hey, yesterday I saw you with her outside the theatre! Because no one else would ever understand what had gone on between them outside the theatre, because people might believe they were discussing the weather—that was all right, whereas at that moment she had just given him an extraordinary glance. That glance was his property, it belonged to the image he had made of her for himself. And Kurt demanded respect for that image. He didn't mind what other people thought. That was why he insisted that they should be indifferent to his image of her, that they must not try to reveal it, they were to leave him alone with the girl whom he loved just as *he* saw her, they were to stop short of what was accessible only to him, what he had shared with her. No one must desecrate that by intruding on it without permission, no one else must make free with his preserves.

Lewy—as he now knew—had had no right to inform him that Lisa's body was nice and firm. Lewy, and all the rest of the class, had no right at all to say things about Lisa to him. Twenty-six male students in the eighth year. One of them knew what Lisa was really like, so the other twenty-five had to keep their mouths shut in front of him. Because all they could say would have been as nothing compared to what *he* could say. However, he could never get them to see that. And if someone were to ask, tomorrow, "Who's she sleeping with these days?" and Kurt told him to shut up, then they would all be mocking his "righteous anger" in protecting "the honour of his lady love".

Did they really know he loved her? It hadn't seemed so, when he was talking to Lewy. But Lewy was one of the few who didn't habitually think much about these matters. The others certainly do think something, thought Kurt, and they certainly have the wrong end of the stick. Luckily! Because if a rumour were to get around the eighth year that one of the young men loved one of the girls, really loved her—oh, unimaginable! They never have anything in their heads but one idea, always the same idea.

You'd never understand that the mere pressure of a hand can be a miracle, he told them in his mind.

And I'm still there with you. Thank God, she isn't there with you any more. But I am. At school. There I am in front of God Almighty Kupfer, like all of you. Or no, it's worse. Few of you have to fear him as much as I do. None of you, in fact. It's me he's going to torment, me he's going to persecute...

A white palfrey has to wear a yoke for a while... and then it will be free... free as the wind... a noble white palfrey... leaping through the night... a thousand and one nights... and there's the princess... Lisa, Lisa, Lisa...

III

Three Encounters

S UCH A BRIEF, insignificant period of time, those seven
years. No one bothered about them, but what happened
now became doubly important.

So you set about it with double diligence. If you knew
the answer to a question you didn't simply call it out from
your desk—you volunteered to speak, you did so in serious,
measured terms, you sat down again, thinking of the *Matura*,
and you firmly believed that when the moment came the
professor now questioning you would remember the answer
you had just given. And that the professor took note of matters fraught with significance, was sparing with praise and
blame alike, with encouragement and admonition, and if
now and then he said, perhaps, "Yes, good, sit down, you'll
be all right!" or, "Hmm… that was no great shakes, was
it? How will you manage when it comes to the *Matura*?"
his comments sounded fateful, final; if that was how things
stood, enormous efforts must be made to change it.

The days flowed by like lead, hesitating indecisively in
the face of their purpose, coming closer and closer to the
great day. That day couldn't yet be seen in its entirety, but
it rang like a bell at every sound in the classroom, haunted

the teacher's lectern, loomed grey and shadowy behind the blackboard—and yet in reality it was still very far away. It would have been better not to think of it at all. There was no need to worry yet. But the fear of omitting to do something, the sombre anxiety of the idea that the great day could suddenly come upon you, taking you by surprise, forced you to stay drowsily on guard. You didn't really know what you were afraid of. But afraid you were. You fulfilled your daily quota of fear.

It was hopeless for summer to resist; it gave way to autumn. One day the first coats were hanging on hooks in the cloak-room, a sad and stunted sight. Soon it was raining. The windows stayed closed during break, smokers stopped going out into the alley and shut themselves into the toilets, in groups. And when they were first caught at it, when there was an entry in the register under the heading "Other Remarks" for the first time—then there was no longer any doubt: the school year had firmly taken the students in its grip.

After that they slunk to school, and suddenly they stood there like lethargic buffaloes with their horns lowered; the first written tests in class. German, soon after that Latin and French. It became very difficult to copy from someone else. The professors paid closer attention than ever. And other students who always used to be ready to help seemed to have to force themselves to do it now, making their unwillingness obvious. In break, several eager beavers got together, talked with muted excitement, and made no secret of the fact that they were disinclined to pass on what they knew. With expressions of self-satisfaction, they saw the brief, anxious glances cast at them by those in need of help, and stout, self-confident Scholz, whose fat face was embedded in a triple chin and whose neck was almost non-existent, Scholz whose nickname was Hippo, was the first to refuse his aid outright. During a Latin test, Mertens asked him for a word. He got no answer. Scholz ignored him, didn't even turn round. Martens asked a second and then a third time, raising his voice, until Professor Niesset warned him, and thereafter kept a sharp eye on him. Others did the same in their own ways. When Severin asked him a question, Altmann, for instance, gave him the information he wanted in such a loud voice that the whole class could hear it, and so, of course, could Niesset; Nowak, on the other hand, mumbled an answer so indistinctly that it was impossible to make out what he was saying, and then turned away in pretended regret. Schleich and Pollak acted as if they were too busy with their own work to have time for anyone else, and Schönthal even let out a curse through his prominent teeth. "For God's sake! You should have done more preparation!"

Some of the students openly declared war. It was a struggle for existence, they said in self-defence when a few genuinely helpful students—Kaulich, Benda, Weinberg—showed their disapproval. "*Tunica proprior palliost!*" quoted Klemm. Among the general murmuring, Hippo's unctuous voice was heard: "Say it in German so that Mertens can understand."

Kurt Gerber kept quiet. So far, in the rather isolated position intentionally allotted to him in the classroom, he had not had much chance to help anyone, and almost had to offer his support. Even then the offer wasn't always accepted. The others were afraid of having to reciprocate, and because Kurt needed help in maths, where everyone wanted to do as well for himself as possible, they were very reserved. Kurt didn't want to force himself on anyone. He knew who his friends were; there were not so many of them, but they were true friends. Weinberg, Kaulich, Gerald, Hobbelmann, maybe Benda too, strong, calm Benda, would have done anything for him. That was enough. He didn't want all and sundry helping him, oh no! He didn't want everyone to be able to say: Kurt Gerber is grateful to me for helping him. They all had a right to receive help, only a very few the right to help others.

The year before, Lisa Berwald had offered to let him copy an answer in the maths test from her. (He had been sitting behind her; Professor Rothbart was not a stickler for the same order of seating every time.) Kurt had shaken his head, saying, "Thanks, but no," as if she had offered him a sweet. Then an odd thing had happened: Lisa, quietly angry, had simply pushed it his way on a piece of paper, saying in a forceful whisper, "You don't want to come a cropper, do you, idiot?"

Later Kurt had decided to see that incident as the beginning of his love. That was when what was different about Lisa first dawned on him in a clear light. None of the other girls in the class would have been able to salvage a touch of femininity from that silly little scene...

Now he had had no news of Lisa for weeks. She had not answered his letter; he had heard that she was abroad. Kurt refrained from trying to find out for certain. He was satisfied. He didn't believe the rumours of Lisa's engagement to a rich manufacturer. Even when they grew more numerous, even when some people claimed to know the man's name, others his age, even though they were all agreed in saying it was no more than they'd expected. After all, said Kaulich, Lisa was definitely nubile. Which couldn't be said of all her girlfriends in the class, added Weinberg, in a tone of unsparing clarity. Six girls contemptuously turned down the corners of their mouths, hoping to show that they, untouched by any rumours as they were, were better off.

And one day, in ten o'clock break, there was Lisa, suddenly standing in their classroom. Young, beautiful, light-hearted, wearing a trench coat and a pale beret from which a lock of her brown hair emerged, she stood there, composed, as if she just happened to have arrived late by chance; yes, here I am, what's so surprising about that? Oh, because I was away so long? There must have been a mistake, that's not so, look, I'm here now!

Kaulich, the first to see her, shouted, "Lisa!" and started running towards her with a broad smile on his face. He would probably have flung his arms round her, but he didn't get as far as that. Lisa was surrounded by the girls already. They knew how to behave; with surprising ease they took the situation as if it were routine. They could hardly contain their delight at seeing her again. They made Lisa go forward to the front of the classroom, sat her down on a bench; Well, what are you doing these days, that's a pretty coat, how brown you are—their chatter swelled louder and louder, the circle around her grew denser, and Lisa, enjoying all the fuss, although she ought to feel well able to deal with being the centre of attention, had to keep her bright smile ready on her lips and renew it whenever she offered her hand to anyone. And she offered it to everyone. To stout little Hobbelmann who came up, panting and pushing, just as affectionately as to simple-minded Zasche, who stared at her as if she were a funfair attraction.

The whole class was gathered around Lisa.

Kurt was the only one who stayed sitting in his place. He didn't like such crowd scenes, and since he could hardly have welcomed Lisa as he would have wished anyway, he waited.

A few people moved away from the group. Nowak passed him.

"Lisa's here, Scheri."

"So?"

"Why don't you go and say hello? That's the thing to do when a former classmate turns up."

"I can wait."

Kurt looked at the front of the room. Now he could see Lisa clearly. Then she turned her head to him and waved, with a happy light in her lovely, lovely face, and said nothing but waited for him to come over. A warm current ran from his head into all his limbs—mine, she's mine! My love! But then all the glances that he thought were turned his way dispelled his joy. And as, with some hesitation, he walked over to her, he was annoyed to see Lisa behaving like this.

"At last, Scheri! How are you?"

I don't want her calling me Scheri, for God's sake. I'm not just a classmate of hers.

"Thanks, Berwald, I'm fine. How about you?"

Lisa presses his hand. Presses it down. She doesn't want him to kiss her.

"Why so formal, Herr Gerber?" asks Ditta Reinhard with a sharp smile.

"I can talk dirty if you'd rather, Fräulein Reinhard."

"Oh, Scheri!" Lisa gave him a little tap. "Can't you control your tongue a bit better?"

"In front of a lady!" adds Lotte Hergeth caustically.

"You want to show some respect to a distinguished visitor!" snaps Else Rieps. Green-eyed jealousy couldn't be kept permanently down.

"Oh, please, don't all laugh at me!" What superiority Lisa's words convey, ordinary as they are; what else could she have said? And now she's talking to the others again.

Kurt waits. Why doesn't she take me aside? After she waved to me… One moment, I have to speak to Kurt Gerber, I know you'll excuse me. And she can speak to me, too. Saying what? Well, whatever she has to speak to me about.

Maybe she'll say that in a minute.

But no. She doesn't.

"I have to catch up with some physics," says Kurt suddenly, going back to his desk. He will intercept Lisa before she leaves and discuss the most urgent point with her. On the way to the physics lab, where the corridor is dimly lit.

The bell rings. The class sets out with exercise books, textbooks and drawing instruments. Lisa is at the centre of the students, and Kurt, walking on one side of the procession, is looking for a way to detach her from it, since it seems she can't detach herself… or doesn't want to?

The physics lab is on the next floor up. The corridor bends twice, getting darker all the time.

There's no holding them now. One after another, they press eagerly forward, all of them making it look as accidental as possible. Kurt sees that Lisa is soon hemmed in by the whole horde. He is overcome by fury. No longer because now he won't be able to speak to her. No, it's his old hatred for their undignified, brazenly lecherous advances to her, they're all driven on. They want to be there, gain access to the delicious Lisa, be excitingly close to her. Trumping each other with familiarities that are nothing but a confession of their dismal inability to do anything about it. And it's done with a certain indifference at that: well, we might as well go along with the others, all in the spirit of the thing. Now Sittig's hand brushes her breast, as if by chance. Now Körner is putting his arm around her shoulders. Then they both retreat, they've done their part, others come up… Kurt's fury knows no bounds. It's jealousy, yes, jealousy a thousand times over, but he's not ashamed of it now, he knows how superior he is to these wretched youths, pressing close to Lisa like randy farm labourers around a milkmaid. And it makes him indignant to think they're making Lisa no better than a milkmaid with their clumsy little advances; there's nothing to be done about those because they're disguised as harmless friendship, and no one is supposed to notice them on pain of appearing ridiculous.

Cowards! Rip her dress off, someone, why don't you? Push her into a corner. Throw yourselves on her! At least then you'll have done something. Your behaviour is no less than disgustingly slimy.

The class begins to fill the physics lab. Lisa is still outside with the girls.

Suddenly Anny Kohl has an idea.

"I tell you what, Lisa, come in and stay with us for the lesson! I'm sure Birdie wouldn't mind."

This proposal meets with great approval. Lisa doesn't hesitate for long, she goes in with them.

Professor Hussak is surrounded. "Guess who we've brought with us!" He's glad of the distraction, and readily allows Lisa to stay for the lesson. "But you must keep quiet and pay attention, Student Lisbeth Berwald!" he says.

After twenty minutes full of experiments, Lisa gets restless and asks Hussak for permission to go. Some of the students stand up to wish her goodbye; Lisa nods gravely and says, "Sit down, please!" and then goes quickly out of the door. The class laughs.

Kurt sees and hears this, unable to grasp it, cheated of his new hope. In desperation (he *must* speak to Lisa, nothing else matters) he puts up his hand. There's no going back now.

"Professor Hussak, sir!"

"Yes?"

"Please can I leave the room? I'm not feeling well."

"I see, birdie." Hussak makes a face; he doesn't mean ill, why would he, but some of students nudge each other and chuckle. Kurt turns pale. This is the end! He veers off course, believing in his own excuse now.

"Yes, sir. You don't think I'm a liar, do you?"

That was stupid. But Hussak is far too sensible to exploit the situation with silly jokes. He looks up briefly in surprise, his smile gives way to what is almost concern (of course you don't feel well, anyone can see that) and lets Kurt go with a magnanimous wave of his hand. Kurt leaves the physics lab slowly, feverish with shame and triumph.

There is still chuckling behind him—now he can't hear it, the door is closed. He breaks into a run—they can chuckle all they like now—two steps, and Hussak into the bargain—three steps, Lisa was acting so strangely—what's happened?—faster, faster, Lisa is waiting for me—four steps… Kurt stumbles, falls, catches himself up, forward, no time to waste, if only the gate is open, yes, thank God it is, with one bound he is outside, almost knocking a fat woman down, Lisa isn't in sight, he runs on along the road, a car brakes, tyres screeching, and turns abruptly aside, the driver calls something angry after him, but Kurt has left it all far behind, he has seen Lisa turning the corner… and gasping for air, knees weak, smudged with dirt, hesitant, there he stands before her like—well, like a schoolboy. He wishes he hadn't done it, he feels limp suddenly, almost uninterested. What was all that in aid of? Well, here is Lisa staring at him. Now what?

"Why, Kurt! What does this mean?"

"Mean? That I—that you…" Kurt doesn't say those words except in his head; he alone hears them, and they sound to him ridiculous. He can't say that.

"I came after you."

"Yes, so I see. And you got dirty too." She brushes him down and strokes his hair, which is wet with sweat, back from his forehead. Simply like that, without making much fuss about it. That's her way. Not bothering with why, she goes straight to the fact that it happened. There is something curiously self-assured about her attitude.

"Well, come on, Kurt. We can't stand here like this."

Of course not. Come on. Where to? That's of no importance. Anywhere.

Kurt walks beside her. As she doesn't ask any questions, as she doesn't find it odd that a student is walking in the street during a lesson because of her, it suddenly doesn't strike him as important to talk to her about it. Or about what happened at school. That's over now. Over and done with.

"Did you get my letter, Lisa?"

"Yes, of course. Don't be cross because I haven't answered it yet."

"I'm not cross. You probably didn't have the time."

"No, I really didn't. You know—" And the letter, which was so important, is already dismissed, she is already talking about her recent return and a hundred other little things, as if there were nothing else to discuss…

"That's very interesting—but wouldn't you rather tell me when we have more time?" He stops. Lisa remembers.

"Oh yes, you have to go back to school. Am I holding you up? I wouldn't want to make things awkward for you, Kurt."

How good that sounds, how affectionate, how full of love. Now Kurt is perfectly happy again and relaxed.

"Don't worry, Lisa." He raises his hand and strokes the air around her head—touches her, and takes fright. "When will you have time for me?"

"Well—that's a very difficult—"

"It will be all right, just think when."

"Wait a minute, this is Wednesday."

"And tomorrow will be Thursday."

"Amazing! Then the day after tomorrow will probably be Friday?"

"If nothing happens to prevent it."

Lisa laughs. She has wonderful teeth, and her bright peal of laughter, so merry, is nothing but that, happy laughter that will suit any occasion. Kurt adores that laugh. It is not for him in particular.

"I don't have much time, Lisa. When, then?"

"I probably can't make it this week. But you can always call me at work. I'm working in an arts and crafts studio."

"Oh. I didn't know that." Kurt is surprised; Lisa has a career, she is out in the world. He feels a little ashamed of himself.

"Yes, the Dremon Studio. You'll find it in the phone book. It would be best to call me about the middle of the day. But you must say you're Dr Berwald, that's my brother, you see. My boss doesn't like me to have phone calls. Do it just this once, all the same, because I honestly don't know when I can be free. And I would like to see you."

"Would you really, Lisa?"

"Of course. Why ask such a silly question?"

"I'll call on Monday, then. Is that all right?"

"Fine, Monday. Certainly. I'll keep it in mind." She gives him her hand. He pushes her glove back and kisses the lightly tanned skin, a hot, long kiss, and Lisa doesn't mind. Suddenly she gently strokes his hair. She doesn't do that often. Kurt trembles. His chest feels constricted, he turns and walks quickly away…

The streets are not busy at this hour of the morning. Not that this is the first time Kurt has seen them in the morning. He has often been out of the school building during lessons, has often played truant, he knows the tingling delights of forbidden mornings when you are a school student.

But now he was here for a reason that had nothing to do with school. He was one of those going down the street on his own lawful business. The pavement, the noise belonged to him like the rest of the passers-by.

He took out a cigarette and asked one of them for a light. The man obligingly knocked the ash off the end of his own cigarette, fitted its glowing tip neatly into the cigarette reached out to him, turned it around this way and that, and replied to Kurt's "Thanks" with a civil, "You're welcome", even lifting his hat slightly, and Kurt felt very remiss in having no hat on his own head. But what did that matter, by comparison with the delightful freedom of his gait, making him a rightful part of the general public around him. Good day to you, my dear fellow! You're in a hurry. So am I. We have urgent business to see to. You have to go to the bank to withdraw a sum of money, I have a little meeting with one Professor Hussak. What, you haven't heard of him? Oh, he's a great physicist, a scholar. He's expecting me, I have to discuss certain matters with him, confidential matters, man to man. I wouldn't like to keep him waiting, he's a nice fellow, did me a favour recently, rendered me a great service in an affair close to my heart. Yes, that's right, there's a woman in the case. Do I love her? Oh God, yes, I do feel what they call love, don't they? Well, we're past the age when—

"Gerber! Can't you be civil enough to give me the time of day?"

A figure bars his way, standing right in front of him, an unfamiliar male odour rises to his nostrils, but he knows that voice. Horror paralyses him, he raises his head, stares stupidly into a face that, for a second, is twisted with malice, and next moment is merely stern, stern as iron, and cold.

Kurt is bewildered. He is still standing motionless; he stands there for a good minute. Kupfer narrows his lips.

"Well? What are you doing out and about in the street at this time of day? To the best of my knowledge, there are lessons in progress at school."

Now Kurt understands the position he is in. He makes a plan at lightning speed. Only imperturbable impudence can save him. It must be audible even in his voice. A note of self-confidence.

"Professor Kupfer, sir, I—"

"Would you kindly stop smoking when you speak to me?" Kupfer interrupted him tartly.

Dear God, the cigarette! Kurt drops it to the ground and treads it out, his mind elsewhere. He has been thrown off balance.

"S-sorry," he stammers. "I entirely forgot—"

Kupfer is master of the situation. "I see. So you're also still smoking?" He nods, satisfied. "You can expect repercussions after this, Gerber. And now you'd better get back to school. The rest will follow in due course."

Kurt flares up. He hastily tries to make good his mistake.

"Please listen to me, Professor Kupfer, I fell on the stairs, my knee is bleeding, don't you understand? Professor Hussak sent me to see the doctor—"

But Kupfer isn't listening to him. He has already walked away, paying no attention to Kurt's stammered explanation. Kurt is left standing there, his head bent, watching Kupfer go, his left trouser leg turned up. He just stands there, looking totally ridiculous, until at last (when someone jostles him roughly, saying, "Adjust your sock suspender somewhere else, can't you?"), at last he begins staggering away. He can't even guess what the consequences of this encounter will be. He drags himself wearily on, his eyes cast down, a conman unmasked. His leg really is beginning to hurt now.

The clock on the wall on the first floor said a quarter to twelve. There wasn't much point in going back to the physics lesson now.

95

Kurt limped to the washbasins in the toilets; his injury looked nasty, with clotted blood on his shin.

The pain did him good, however. He closed his eyes. For you, Lisa. I'd suffer even more for you, Lisa. And you don't even know it.

The bell rang. Kurt tied his handkerchief round the injured place on his leg. Then he went into the physics lab to collect his things.

The lesson was just over. The students were noisily making their way to the door.

Hussak was standing behind the tall desk. Kurt wanted to avoid him, but the teacher had already seen him, and beckoned him into the lab. Kurt followed; there was nothing to fear here.

Hussak was hanging the black lab coat he wore for lessons on a hook, putting on his ordinary jacket, and seemed to be looking for something. Then he locked the door, pointed to a chair, and sat down astride the lab bench himself.

Under the profound, long look from his blue eyes that Hussak gave him, the last remnants of Kurt's belief in his own cause melted away. He was ready to agree with whatever Hussak said.

They went on looking at each other, until first Hussak and then Kurt smiled. But Hussak immediately looked grave again.

"I'm afraid this is no laughing matter, my friend," he said with concern. "I only wish it were."

"Has something happened?" asked Kurt with ready sympathy, as if it were for him to lift a burden of anxiety from the physics master's shoulders.

"What would have happened? At the most an inspection by the Headmaster. There's been no disaster either. No, no. The way you ran away from my lesson today is not so bad."

Kurt said nothing. He was full of vague forebodings.

"Naturally, I would rather have been able to test you today. You know, of course, that we have a staff meeting next week, to discuss marks for the next set of reports—"

"No, I didn't know that."

"Well, we do, and that leaves another three lessons, no more. Then you can be sure that Zeisig will carry out an inspection. What the verdict on your own progress will be I don't know. But that's not so important either." Hussak's brief gesture dismissed all minor fears. "There's something else that *is* more important. I've been meaning to say this to you for some time, and today I have a clear reason to do so. You mustn't be so thoughtless, my dear Gerber, not so thoughtless. Or you may come a cropper over the *Matura*."

Kurt looked at him enquiringly.

"No, no, you have nothing to fear from me. And I don't mind at all if you stay away for once. Only," and here Hussak's tone of voice changed, "and I say this purely in passing: only not for such a childish reason!"

Kurt went red, actually blushed with embarrassment. In front of this man, he felt very much a schoolboy, or rather, he felt that Hussak was very much a teacher. And almost a friend to whom, now, he can say, "It isn't childish, sir. Please believe me, it isn't childish."

"Oh—then you must forgive me; I wasn't to know that." The subtlety of this remark makes Kurt doubt that it is meant seriously. "But that's not the point of our conversation. I wanted to tell you that you had better pay more attention to what you do, Gerber. There are those who don't wish you well."

"I'm aware of that, sir."

"Then why don't you act accordingly? Why are you always laying yourself open to attack from certain quarters?"

Kurt has no answer to that. He looks at the floor. Hussak is working himself up.

"That little pretence today doesn't matter. And I can understand it. But for that very reason it shows me, yet again, how careless you are. If things go on like this, Gerber, I don't see how it can end well. Stop and think: this is your final year! The fact that your colleagues are already laughing at you—"

"I couldn't care less."

"And I've no objection to your saying so. But do you think it will stop at that? Everything gets around. In the staffroom, we hear about everything, and you know yourself that anything can be exploited to your disadvantage."

"Yes—but why—"

"Why? Why? Take your maths master, for instance, might it not enter his head to do a little spying? Please don't take this amiss, but think—suppose he had seen you out in the street just now? Think of the consequences—"

Kurt, who has been slowly straightening up, raises his pale face to the startled face of Hussak: "Sir, he—he *did* see me."

"What?" Hussak jumps up, clasps his hands behind his back and paces hastily back and forth. Suddenly he stops short, close to Kurt, puts both hands on his shoulders and shakes him.

"Gerber, you idiot! My poor, poor Gerber!"

And then he goes on pacing about the room, stopping now and then to fidget nervously with the pieces of apparatus, then stamps his foot, turns round, and says, calmly, "This isn't a promising situation—and if I may give you my advice, I think you'd do well to change this school for another one as soon as possible."

Kurt wearily waves this away. "That's what my father said." And quietly but very firmly, he adds, "It's out of the question."

At that moment the bell rings for the next lesson. It goes on for a long time. When it stops, the two of them are looking at each other almost like a pair of lovers lost to the world after their first embrace.

"You'd better go back to your classroom," says Hussak, his tone matter-of-fact.

Kurt goes up to him.

"Thank you, Professor Hussak, sir!" He holds out his hand.

"There's nothing to thank me for. Understand?"

Kurt understands. He bows briefly and turns to leave.

"Nothing at all!" Professor Hussak's voice follows him. It sounds like a voice from the grave.

IV

Meditations on x

S TAY AT HOME!
That was Kurt's first thought when the throbbing pain all down his leg woke him next morning. Stay away from school. For a few days. How stupid Kupfer would look! Although he didn't like the thought of skipping Hussak's lessons. However, it would all turn out all right in the end. At worst some of his marks would be left an open question. Including for maths and descriptive geometry. Kupfer hadn't really tested him yet. There were to be written tests on Saturday and Monday. If he missed those—and it seemed very likely that he would—then they'd have to grant him a supplementary test; after all, he'd been away sick.

His over-anxious mother wanted to call the doctor at once. Kurt protested; he was afraid his injury wasn't so bad that he couldn't be sent to school. However, when the glands in his groin swelled, and his temperature rose to thirty-nine degrees, Dr Kron was summoned.

Dr Kron, a jovial elderly gentleman with a grey Vandyke beard and pince-nez, a medic who talked about operations the way other people speak of coffee parties and who loved to strike a note of earthy humour, had been the Gerbers'

family doctor for years. He addressed Kurt like someone he'd
known all his life, and after a cursory examination of the leg
waxed indignant. Why hadn't they sent for him before? It
was blood poisoning, and how, might he enquire, had that
idiot Kurt come by it?

"I was clumsy and fell on the stairs at school, doctor."

He'd fallen, had he? Running after the little girls again
in too much of a hurry, the doctor supposed. Lord knows
what gets into these snotty-nosed lads!

Kurt scented an allusion to Lisa behind all this, forgetting
that good Dr Kron didn't even know of her existence, and
though he usually liked the doctor he snapped at him, "I
don't go running after little girls!"

"Not now, you don't, Herr Gerber. Or not for the time
being, anyway. That'll be all the running you do for a while."
Then Dr Kron gave his orders, and threatened to splint the
leg if Kurt didn't keep it still. He'd call again tomorrow,
he said.

The next day Kurt woke up feeling strong and full of
well-being. Forgetting that there was anything the matter
with him, he tried drawing his legs up. It hurt so much that
he fell back on the pillows with a muffled cry.

Later in the day, Weinberg came to see him. He was greatly
surprised to find Kurt actually in bed.

"Very clever of you." he said appreciatively. "Even God
Almighty Kupfer couldn't send the caretaker to check up on
you just like that." Kurt put the covers back and pointed to
his knee. Weinberg looked bewildered: fancy someone not
coming to school because he was sick!

"My word! If I'd known, I'd have come yesterday. We all
thought you were bunking off today to spend time with Lisa."

Kurt said nothing, thinking of Monday. Maths versus Lisa… In the end he thought it best to see this as a classic conflict between duty and inclination, which amused him. He laughed out loud. Weinberg looked at him, baffled.

"So that's what you all thought? What put such an idea into your heads?"

"Excuse me, but you needn't think we're stupid! All that with Hussak made it clear enough."

"I see. And now the *Matura* candidates have nothing else to talk about."

"Of course not. You know how they seize on news like that."

"Are they making a big fuss about it?"

"Well, quite a fuss—I mean, no, it's not really so bad." At this point Weinberg notices what way the conversation is going. He would like to spare his friend annoyance.

"What are they talking about, then?"

"Nothing of any importance. I don't think it need bother you."

"It certainly doesn't bother me." Kurt tries to act unconcerned, but the opportunity is too tempting. Furthermore, he has something else in mind, a revolutionary idea. "I'd like to hear what they're saying, though."

"Oh, go on, you're being childish."

"Call it what you like. But tell me what they're talking about, all the same. I'm interested."

Weinberg's jaws are working as if he were chewing the cud; it is distinctly visible, and he always does it when he's at a loss. Suddenly he says briefly, firmly. "No. What good would it do you, you cretin?" Then he stands up, sits down again, takes out his comb and gets busy with it on his rather unruly hair.

Kurt sits up. "Fritz!"

"Yes?"

"You mustn't think I'm asking out of silly curiosity. Listen, will you? I'm in love with Lisa."

Weinberg gasps. This is too much for him. What, his friend, his good, clever friend in love with that silly, affected doll, throwing himself away on her? That's incredible! And Weinberg bursts out:

"Oh yes? Well, if you really must know, you're a figure of fun to the whole class. I wouldn't have told you, but you make me. I always thought you'd realize that for yourself, or you already had realized and were secretly laughing at it. But you're out of your mind. In love with her! Say it again."

Kurt lies on his back again, looks up at the ceiling and says slowly, smiling, "I—am—in—love with her."

In his agitation, Weinberg doesn't notice how far away and happy that sounded. If he had, he would probably have stopped at that point instead of going on with his diatribe: They were all heartily amused, he says, specially the girls, because Lisa took no notice of Kurt, and left the lab early yesterday just so that she wouldn't have to talk to him; that was clear enough, you fool, but you go running after her like a dachshund; the class fell about laughing, they all think it's such a joke, and she thinks so most of all; of course, girls like that, you want to put them over the edge of the bed and make love to them, but that's all, people don't fall *in love* with them, least of all you, you're showing your inadequacy to everyone… and so on in the same tone, but it goes right past Kurt, whose mind is elsewhere.

"Kurt, are you listening to me?"

"Of course. Carry on."

"I've finished. You say something now."

And Kurt says something. Quiet things, in a quiet voice. Still looking up at the ceiling, and after a few words forgetting that there is anyone in the room listening to him. But he isn't talking to Weinberg, he is talking to Lisa… Weinberg's feelings and thoughts, good as well as bad, are always perfectly obvious. You only had to look at him when he was angry—and you felt you could sue him for impugning your honour. He is one of those people (a breed rapidly dying out in a climate that does not suit it) who resemble modern book advertisements, where the book stands on a rotating plinth in the shop window, showing the public page after page… Now, for example, when Kurt had finished, Fritz Weinberg hung his head like a scolded child. Then his thoughts took a couple of sudden leaps and landed suddenly on a simple reflection. "Why are you telling me all this?" he asked, and there was a touch of longing in his voice.

"Not for my own sake, Fritz. I want you to do Lisa justice."

"Well, I'll do my best," was all that Weinberg said. And then he abruptly began talking about school. Not much has happened, he said, since the day before yesterday. Mattusch gave back the German tests written in school and read Kurt's aloud as the best, then there was another of Filip's chaotic lessons, and then, yes, then today God Almighty Kupfer announced the names of those who hadn't done enough to be assessed yet, and Kurt's name was listed for both his subjects. Would it be absolutely impossible, Weinberg wondered, for him to get to school to take the maths test tomorrow?

"I'm not well," said Kurt reluctantly. He had not considered this possibility, nor indeed had he been thinking of school at all, and now he found himself abruptly faced with it. He could have borne having these stupid things said to him, but to be asked to take them seriously, to make objections, take up a position one way or the other—oh, it was too much! And now, at that! Couldn't Weinberg come and say all this another day?

Hardly possible, when time was too short for that. And if Kurt could possibly do it, said Weinberg, he ought to try. God Almighty Kupfer could easily make a rope to hang him out of a few questions unanswered in a school test, might also assume that his sickness was malingering; and even the best-case scenario, the idea that he could be tested later, either orally or in writing, was bad enough. It would be relatively easier tomorrow or Monday.

"And you might make God Almighty Kupfer look more kindly on you if you come limping to school to please him and—"

"I don't care about that!" Kurt interrupted in annoyance. But looking at him, Weinberg could see that he was feeling small and embarrassed. This was all very uncomfortable. Kurt was gnawing his lower lip. Anyone could see that he was really unwell at any time, he said sharply, even God Almighty Kupfer would have to see that no one could go to school with a knee oozing pus, could he? And when Weinberg said nothing, Kurt worked himself into more and more of a state of artificial indignation. What an idea! He had no intention of endangering his health and maybe his straight limbs for the sake of a silly school test, it would be different if he had to improve on several downright Unsatisfactory marks; however, you couldn't be graded, *couldn't*, on the strength of a few questions asked orally as you sat at your desk, so he had no reason at all to go to school next day.

"That's what you think," said Weinberg, unperturbed. "Let's hope you're right." He looked at the time, and got to his feet. "I'm off to get some sleep. Riedl will be testing us in geology. Good night." And Kurt was left alone, with his thoughts in turmoil.

Now they whirr restlessly around in his head, mocking all his efforts to chase them away, they startle him out of his light sleep in the middle of the night, they torment him so that he cannot bear to stay in bed any longer; in his helpless bafflement, he gets out of bed—stands up—walks about—what's this stuff surrounding his leg?

Slowly, he remembers. But how is it possible that he's reached this point? He leans gingerly against the wall, raises his foot, tries to bend his knee—it works. Without any special pain. The bandage doesn't bother him, it has come loose, his knee is bare: red and blue and yellow, with swellings and inflamed skin and pus. It is not a pretty sight, but he can walk on that leg.

And now—is he to be glad that he is better and can walk again? Because that means… yes, it means he can take the maths test at school tomorrow. He has felt that at once, and he knows there's no escaping it now.

All the same, he begins to try persuading himself otherwise, looks for reasons why of course he won't do it, and finds them, reminds himself of Weinberg and his "That's what you think"—sheer madness! He hasn't even been able to prepare for it, hasn't revised the work they have done since the semester began, would be making straight for that Unsatisfactory if he went to school tomorrow. But come to think of it, Weinberg sits beside him, Weinberg is good at cheating, he'll be able to get hold of something of Benda's,

106

one of his solutions to a problem, one of Weinberg's; that will be enough, he may be able to solve one for himself, after all, he understood a lot of what they'd been studying about progressions and differentiations. In a few hours he has almost come to the conclusion that he's not so totally dependent on his neighbours after all; if Mertens and Linke and Severin and Blank can solve these problems then so can he… What you're saying is lazy, very lazy, my dear Gerber, because if that were so you would have nothing to fear from a supplementary test on your own later. You don't know anything. You don't know the first damn thing about it.

"Not the first damn thing!" says Kurt out loud, and the strong language makes him feel calm and peaceful for a brief moment. But then it all comes back to him, nagging him, won't leave him alone; he tries to recite a few formulae from memory, the integral of x to the power of n times dx equals x to the power of n plus 1, x—whew!—n plus one, say the n plus one very fast, remember that, so that anyone can tell it all belongs together, otherwise it might be thought that you meant x to the power of n minus plus one, which would be a bad mistake—so what's the formula? He repeats it as fast as he can… now then, Geeeerber! That's what God Almighty Kupfer always did. He went up and down between the rows of desks, and after every word there was an endlessly long pause, he dragged out the final syllables; if he was at the back of the class he looked at the front, as if to choose his victim there, and then suddenly called the name of someone sitting in an entirely different place, or tapped the student beside whom he was standing on the shoulder with his forefinger; and the student, thus taken by surprise, naturally stammered and couldn't answer, even if he had just memorized the formula fluently. During the pauses between Kupfer's words—sadistic pauses, the students called them—some of the good mathematicians, those with nothing to fear, sometimes amused themselves by timing the length of those pauses with a stopwatch; the record to date was sixteen seconds, and it had gone like this: work out... (eight seconds)—in your head... (twelve seconds)—whaaat... and that pause lasted for sixteen seconds, and then Gerald had fallen for it, that was God Almighty Kupfer's way... What *was* the formula? Kurt writes with his finger on the white bedspread:

$$\int x^n \, \mathrm{d}\, x = \frac{x^{n+1}}{n+1}, \text{ for } n \neq -1$$

if n is larger or smaller than minus one, and how does the second formula go?

$$\int (a + b\, x)^n \, \mathrm{d}\, x =$$

But he can get no further; he traces the equals sign a couple of times with his finger, as if on the board at school, and finally, in a bad temper, turns the bedspread over. He wants to get it all out of his head.

But a decision has to be made; and he has to think again after all, and he can't get to the end of his thinking, realizes that his thoughts are going round in circles once more. In addition, at last he feels very tired. Just before sleep over-comes him, he decides: if he wakes up in the morning early enough to get to school and take the test in comfortable time, yes, and if his leg isn't hurting, not a bit—then he will take that as a divine judgement and he will go to school…

Only when Kurt saw the school building did it all come back to his mind, sombre and terrible: waking up at nine-thirty, his mother's anxious questions, his answer, always the same, like a formula: quick, quick, I have to get to school or I'll fail… and now he was really standing there, heart thudding, trembling in sudden fear: what he intended to do—and would do, for he was going through with it, wouldn't turn back—suddenly seemed to him so incredible that he couldn't believe it was true. No, no, it can't happen, it's impossible, the test is postponed, Kupfer is unwell…

But there lay the big blue exercise books, gaping at the air with a single rectangular eye.

The little note-cards had already been made out. Kurt recognized Ditta Reinhardt's steeply sloping handwriting (so Severin had retired from the job of secretary) and read the words long familiar to him over a period of seven years, with only the Latin numerals for classes changed: High School XVI, 1st Semester, Class VIII, Name: Gerber, Kurt; Contents: mathematical tests—it was so cold and indifferent. Kurt opened his exercise book at random and found the poor-quality sheet of bright red blotting paper between the pristine pages of blue graph paper, one after another, open wide and ready. Suddenly hope came to his aid: as he is so self-sacrificingly doing his duty, he thinks, dragging himself to school while he isn't well (the leg is hurting again), Kupfer will show clemency, will close an eye if Kurt tries copying from someone, will mark his work leniently, may even let him off the geometry test…

Kurt has arrived in the middle of break; he is greeted by only a few, and fleetingly by those few, the eighth-year students are short of time, feverish restlessness fills the whole room. Some students are pacing nervously up and down, replying impatiently if anyone addresses them, others are scribbling figures and letters on thin strips of paper in tiny, tiny writing; most of them are whispering formulae to themselves with their eyes closed, in tones of urgency, each on his or her own, and yet all bound together. The formulae are like magic spells, like prayers—and now Kurt knows what the scene reminds him of, something he recently read that occurs to him: it was about a pogrom in a synagogue, and there the congregation sit in fear, in terrible anxiety, waiting for the Cossack hetman to come in with dreadful news. Kurt can imagine them all bursting out weeping and wailing—but no, that probably won't happen, after all they have "prepared" for the test, learnt their lessons, some are so sure of themselves that they even chat to one another—those are the experts, they inconsiderately talk out loud. Kurt listens: "And I know for a fact that we'll all be getting differ-ent problems," claims Klemm. "God Almighty Kupfer will bring along thirty-two papers with four different questions on each." That doesn't bother Klemm's friends. "Let him!" says Pollak dismissively, and Schönthal says quickly, cuttingly, showing his teeth, "Well, if anyone has the nerve to try copying—" Then he feels Kurt's eyes on him, ducks his head and makes a sign to the others. They look surreptitiously and with malice at Kurt, darkly afraid of that alien gaze; it makes them uncomfortable to see anyone who has the time and inclination to look like that now, they feel that such a glance comes from a place where all the mathematics tests in the world disappear into ridiculous insignificance—and that won't do, it is bold, it is even impudent, arrogant, particularly from someone who would surely give much to be able to talk lightly in their own carefree manner…

The bell rings. They all fall silent for a moment, look up, startled, and then plunge headlong into their work again, as if under the lash. Now the stragglers arrive; some have been smoking, Kaulich is among them, then Benda comes in, quiet and thoughtful, taking long strides, and Weinberg as well. He expresses no surprise at seeing Kurt there, just smiles. "It will be all right."

"But I haven't done any preparation," says Kurt, pointing to the students still revising hard around him; even now he has not been able to get anything into his head—then the door is opened, stands open briefly—there's a breathless silence—careful—and in comes Kupfer.

The class stands in tense silence, like the silence it preserved in the first lesson of term. What now?

Kupfer sets about taking the register. Else Rieps, who always hands him the pen, shifts impatiently from foot to foot. Kupfer says, almost under his breath: "I take it the same as yesterday are absent? That'll be Lewy, Nowak, Kohl, Gerber." He writes quickly, in a businesslike manner. Else hasn't noticed Kurt's presence, she nods…

"I'm here, Professor Kupfer, sir!"

Kupfer looks up. And what a look. It slowly makes its way towards Kurt. Impossible to describe the mixture of avid amazement, wily triumph and malicious expectation in it. "Well, well," says Kupfer slowly, striking out the name Gerber in the register again. "So you thought better of it in time."

"Yes." Kurt has no idea where this is leading.

Kupfer nods. "There would have been unfortunate consequences for you if you had persisted with your fraudulent claim to be sick, thus missing the test."

"It wasn't fraudulent, and I'm here, Professor Kupfer, sir."

"You don't say so!" remarks Kupfer sarcastically. "I seem to remember that you were out and about in town in perfect health during lessons on Wednesday. And you were away sick on Thursday? And today you're well again? Strange."

Only now does Kurt see the trap. Kupfer is baiting him with malice aforethought: maybe he will yet be led to commit a punishable offence. He swallows all the retorts already on the tip of his tongue and says calmly, "I'll bring a doctor's certificate to school."

Kupfer makes a dismissive gesture: "Yes, we know about that sort of thing."

Some of the class are beginning to shuffle their feet impatiently. They are afraid of a long argument and, stimulating as that might be some other time, today every minute counts. Kurt says nothing.

"Well?" Kupfer tilts his head to one side and drums his fingers on his desk. At that, Kurt slumps forward, his throat swelling; something appalling is about to happen—but Weinberg has already grasped Kurt's clenched fist under the desk, and he holds it firmly. His jaws are working, but otherwise his face shows nothing.

Making a superhuman effort, Kurt regains control of himself.

"I have nothing else to say, Professor Kupfer, sir."

But Kupfer trumps him with his closing point. "You astonish me. Please sit down."

Kurt drops back into his seat, shaking, his fists opening and closing. Weinberg claps him on the thigh and says—Weinberg always knows the right thing to say, he can turn a situation right round with a few words—says quietly, as he concentrates intently on writing "1st Maths Test" and the date in his exercise book, "The hell with Kupfer!"

Kupfer writes an Arabic numeral 1 on the board with a flourish. First question. So much for the prophecy that he was going to bring thirty-two different questions in order to prevent any copying. God Almighty Kupfer needs no such precautionary measures. That would look like weakness. Like fear of someone cheating. Kupfer and fear? No one cheats in Kupfer's test. Not God Almighty Kupfer's.

There are already several white letters on the blackboard. Mysterious signs, like those Chinese magic flowers that unfold in water. Does anyone know what they'll turn into? Does anyone know the particular meaning of that letter x? x can mean so much! x is not just a letter of the alphabet or even a mathematical sign. x takes many forms. For instance, x can have a small number 1 under it, and then it is the co-ordinate of a point of intersection with the axis in the general equation of the circle. But x can also be arithmetical, for instance as a factor in an endless geometric series of the first order. For while the geometric series is pure arithmetic, the arithmetical method is pure geometry. And x is everywhere. There is no fraction line on which x will not thrive.

x, in general, is a modest little thing. If you treat it properly, it will let you bend and twist it as you like, and then, out of the thousands of fruits it can bear, just the right one will fall into the lap of its careful handler. All ways pass through x. Without x there is no life. And if it wasn't there from the start it is sure to come along later, forcing itself through a tiny crack in the calculation, crossing its spidery legs in peaceful enjoyment of its existence and waiting—often waiting only to be dismissed again, to be "eliminated". And often waiting for something that is equal to it. There are factors whose whole purpose is to be equal to x. For love of them, you often have to fetch x back from infinity. It hasn't been around all this time, there didn't seem to be any necessity for its presence, but suddenly it comes along, with a little equals sign hitched to it, the team of horses pulling a carriage, and wants to be treated accordingly. That's x for you. By what right? Why? To what end, for what purpose? Who gave it this rank? And why x in particular? And how is it established that x equals this and that? There's something not quite right. There's a gap somewhere. x starts out like an amusing toy, lending itself to all kinds of tricks, and then suddenly turns bitter and incomprehensible. $x = $. Equals what? Some quiet agreement? There are some people who don't get asked. They were ignored when the agreement was being concluded. Suppose they now refuse to consent to it?

Only they can't. Because x is stronger. Its extremities grow and bend, wind around the body and throat of the agreement, until they have acknowledged the existence of x and manipulate it as it demands.

And suppose they still won't agree? Or they want to, but they can't? Suppose they toil, sweating with torment and misery, in the iron embrace of the great unknown, and can come to no conclusion? Suppose they suddenly run out of breath?

Then… well, then they can always go and shoot a bullet into their temples out of a small black object resembling a trapeze with a half-ellipse attached to it, or they can drink some kind of fast-acting fluid from a cylindrical vessel, or they can put a noose round their necks and attach the other end to a rectangular window frame, or they can throw themselves on two iron rails tracing exemplary parallel lines and allow several massive wheels with a circumference of $2r\pi$ to pass over them—death itself is an explicitly variable quantity, and even x is not so merciless as to prescribe one particular solution in this case…

All four questions were up on the board now, and intent expectation gave way to busy activity. All the students were keen to show that they were able to begin on the questions at once without pondering them for a long time. It was not a good idea to be visibly thinking. Kupfer might notice, and draw conclusions that were either wrong or, even worse, right. So activity was called for.

Kurt immersed himself in the exercises, wanting at least to try making something of them on his own. He soon gave up. Not one of the questions came from those areas of the subject where he was reasonably knowledgeable. No probability calculus, no differential quotients, no series. All integrals, by the look of it. And he had no idea, as he realized after briefly looking at the exercises, of the way to deal with them.

He let his eyes wander round the room. They were all working, except for Zasche, who was chewing the end of his pen with a vacant expression. Even Mertens and Severin and Hobbelmann were writing busily, drawing lines, scribbling on the wood of their desks. What were they doing? Where did all this briskness come from? It was alarming.

Weinberg was also writing. Kurt squinted at his exercise book in the row in front of him—he couldn't see anything. A pang of fear that his friend might let him down overcame him. He craned his neck—

"Gerber! If I see that once again I shall confiscate your exercise book. Move to the corner!"

No, God Almighty Kupfer knows no mercy. He isn't interested in the fact that Kurt's mere presence here is an achievement in itself.

Meanwhile Weinberg is placidly writing on, as if none of it was anything to do with him.

"Zasche! You move to the corner too! You can drop these ridiculous attempts to dupe me. I notice everything. And now I don't want to be disturbed any more."

Kupfer leans back in his chair, takes a newspaper out of his briefcase, and immerses himself in reading it.

After a few minutes some of the students begin moving, surreptitiously at first and then, as Kupfer does not seem to notice them, more and more openly. Kurt watches what each of them is doing anxiously; so far as he is concerned, much may depend on their success.

Suddenly Kupfer raises his head—all the students freeze where they are at that moment—and looks enquiringly round the class. Has he seen anything?

No. Nothing. He simply says, "Quiet there!" and goes on reading. (Another teacher might have stationed himself by the window at this point. Checking up on them with mirrors? God Almighty Kupfer can do without such simple tricks.)

Again, some time passes before work is in full swing again. But it is mainly the mathematical experts who are getting in touch with each other, full of chivalrous civility. There is unpleasant derision in the caution with which Scholz and Brodetzky begin conversing, probably about the more elegant calculation of an instance of volume, and beside them Mertens is shifting back and forth in growing fear—his early activity was just bluff, he hasn't answered a single question yet—and as Scholz ignores him he is trying to pick up something from their quiet conversation. He does not succeed; the few words he hears lead him to no kind of conclusion, and he is pale with useless effort.

Kurt sees that there are only twenty minutes left. He clears his throat.

Weinberg nods three times and goes on writing. All Kurt's senses are on edge—help ought to be coming now—then Weinberg leans to one side, just for a moment, straightens up again—and halfway between them a small note is lying on the bench.

Slowly, Kurt puts out his arm.

As he does so, he keeps looking at Kupfer so that he can spot the slightest danger.

But Kupfer is holding the newspaper, opened right out, in front of his face. Another few seconds, and Kurt will be safe.

His arm, moving little by little, comes ever closer to the note.

Mustn't hurry, a hasty movement can ruin everything, his ruler could fall to the floor, or something else happen.

Another second. Kupfer is still reading…

Kurt has the note in his hand. Done it! And as slowly as he retrieved it, he brings it close to him. Everything is all right. He will pass the *Matura*.

The note lies in front of him. He carefully unfolds it, holding the refractory sides of the paper down with his spread thumb and forefinger. There are two of the problems on it, all complete and solved, he has only to write them down in his exercise book –

"Ah, my dear Gerber. May I ask you to stay in exactly your present position?"

Without haste, Kupfer puts down the newspaper, gets to his feet and comes very slowly towards Kurt, eyes fixed on him.

Kurt sits there motionless, as if hypnotized, the note with the answers that will save him lying on the bench with the two fully completed exercises on it, needing only to be written out, he is still holding the note between his thumb and forefinger— and makes a pitiful attempt to push the blotting paper over it with his other hand, but of course Kupfer notices. "Don't move!" he shouts, and without quickening his pace he comes closer, and now he is there ordering, "Hold up your hands!"

Kurt obeys, still as if he were in a dream. Kupfer takes the note between two fingers, holds it up and says, in a tone of friendly reproof, "To think you consider me so stupid! I told you that I see everything."

Then he shakes his head as if in astonishment, tears the note into many little pieces, and lets them flutter to the floor right in front of Kurt's face.

None of the eighth-year students turn to watch this. (To show sympathy would make you guilty too.) Heads bowed, they have only listened, and now they are busily writing again, unmoved. And when Kupfer warns them to hurry—"Mind you finish the test, the bell will be going in ten minutes' time!"—they make sounds of alarm to confirm that his information has had the intended effect.

Kurt sits there, apathetically tracing meaningless figures in his exercise book. He can do no more. It's over.

When Hobbelmann pushes a note towards him, he revives slightly, feels a last weary hope—but then his fountain pen won't work, and the bell goes before he can refill it. Kupfer in person collects the exercise books without waiting a second; he doesn't look to see if anyone is finishing writing a solution, just takes the exercise books, as coldly from those who hand them to him with satisfaction as from those who sit in pale horror, unable to take in the fact that matters have reached this point. Then, without a word, he leaves the classroom.

Is it by accident or design that he has left the newspaper lying on his desk? Hobbelmann suddenly pushes his way through the circle of sympathetic students around Kurt, waving the newspaper in the air.

"What a bastard!" he cries breathlessly. "What a bastard!"

They knew that anyway, say the eighth-year students.

"Here—there—look at that! What a cunning bastard!"

Three small, circular holes have been cut across the middle fold of the newspaper with scissors…

Weinberg went home with Kurt. They did not talk. His friend was feeling guilty, reproaching himself for not having sent the note sooner. He had wanted to make quite sure it was safe—and then it ended like that.

But it wasn't all over yet.

"This is only October," he said outside the gate of Kurt's building. And when Kurt did not reply, "We've hardly started yet."

V.

The Palfrey Stumbles

T HAT WAS TRUE. It was October, and work for the school year was only just beginning.

But then came November, and it was still only just beginning.

And that was the terrible part of it, impeding your breathing, constricting your throat, casting hopelessness over everything: this eternal beginning. Always accumulating more and more days behind you and saying: it's not all over yet. Now the real part is beginning. Always pretending that this time, yet again, you were only making a trial attempt, it wouldn't be real until next time—and then it would be real in earnest. Accepting everything happening at the moment with the excuse that it could safely be forgotten in the light of the more significant future. There was still so much time before the important reports came halfway through the school year! And then there would be another staff meeting about the marks. And then there would be the final report at the end of the year. Only then the *Matura*. And by that time!...

So what did it matter that a week later Kurt (whose knee was almost entirely healed after that first setback, but who was not able to go out yet) found in the post one of the notorious "blue letters", an official communication to "parents or responsible guardians", for which no postage had to be paid, informing them that the school student concerned had not done well in this or that subject during the period for which marks were now allotted? Was it so terrible if such a letter came into the house?

Dear Herr and Frau Gerber,

In the staff meeting allotting marks held on 29 October this year, Kurt Gerber, student in Class VIII at High School XVI, is reprimanded for extremely Unsatisfactory work in *mathematics*, Unsatisfactory work in *descriptive geometry*, and is *warned* to show more industry after inadequate results in *Latin* and *Natural History*. Moreover, the said Gerber, Kurt, is *reprimanded* for late attendance at the test and receives a *stern rebuke* for various activities contrary to the school rules. Accordingly, we are sure that you will…

Kurt was shocked. He had not expected it to be as bad as this. The two warnings in particular were entirely unexpected. He remembered a few poor marks given by Niesset and Riedl, but surely they couldn't have had such a dire effect. Or was it because he hadn't been at school for the last few days before the marking period ended? So that they couldn't test him any more? In which case that precious pair had exploited their rights on paper, clinging to Kupfer's coat-tails, and struck a blow at a helpless student, that was it. Well, you weren't examined in Natural History for the *Matura*. And Kurt felt confident about his knowledge of Latin. We'll be having a word about that, Carrot-Top. (Niesset had red hair.)

But the reprimands from Kupfer... the maths result might be fair enough. The other was scandalous. And then that reprimand for late attendance! That was the end! They were looking on the worst side of everything! Late for the test, instead of praising him for turning up at all. Imagine hanging on, for days, to such an artificially constructed account of the facts! As if Kupfer's double triumph in the test hadn't been enough for him! But no. Kupfer let nothing escape him. A major success did not confuse his mind. No sooner had he struck a devastating blow than he turned with equal determination to the next. "Reprimanded for late attendance at the test!" It was as if a man condemned to death were given an additional sentence of twenty years' loss of his honour.

Kurt came to the conclusion that this report on his marks was the most outrageously underhand trick ever to be played on an innocently absent student.

Of course, his parents would never understand that, they would probably think the teachers were right. "Educational method", people called it.

And what was that worth? More agitation on his part, more annoyance—all to no effect. He could spare his sick father anything so useless. There was good morality behind his little fraud.

After a few trial attempts, Kurt felt sufficiently sure of himself to sign "Albert Gerber" on the dotted line left for "Signature of student's father (or responsible guardian)".

Weinberg had not visited him during these last days, perhaps for one reason out of a lingering sense of guilt. So it was not until Kurt was back at school that he learnt what had happened about Lisa.

Monday, when Kurt had been going to phone her at work, was when he had been at his worst; his temperature rose to nearly forty degrees, and the next day he couldn't bring himself to call her. After all, she had expected him to phone on Monday, and it wasn't good for her to get calls at work… He finally sent the parlourmaid to school with a note for Weinberg, asking him to make his apologies to Lisa. It might work in his favour, he speculated.

Now he drew his friend aside. What had happened with Lisa, had he done as Kurt asked?

Yes, of course he'd done it. Or rather he meant to do it, he was going to give her Kurt's apologies, but—

But?

This time Weinberg was much more thoughtful, apparently glad of something, beating about the bush, but not in the same way as before.

"Well, with the best will in the world, I couldn't," he said. "Couldn't deliver your apologies, I mean."

"Oh. Why not?"

"You see, it was like this: Lisa got in first."

"I don't know what you're talking about."

"You will in a minute. So I phoned on Tuesday: Dr Berwald speaking, may I speak to my sister? Thank you. Hello, Lisa…"

"For God's sake, get a move on."

Weinberg did not get a move on, but finally it all came out. Lisa hadn't given him a chance to say his piece; she thought it was Kurt on the phone, and apologized profusely for not being there yesterday, but she hadn't had any time, no time at all, and so on. "Yours, Lisa. That was all," concluded Weinberg, not expecting Kurt to ask, "Did you say who you were?"

"Yes. She didn't even seem very embarrassed about it."

"Why should she?"

"Why should she?" Weinberg mimicked him, unable to understand that Kurt was not furious with Lisa for such behaviour. "Why should she? Because it can't have been too nice for her to have a third person know about her lie."

"What lie? She didn't have time, full stop."

Weinberg was stunned to find his own healthy suspicion come up against such credulity. He made one last attempt. "I suppose you wouldn't like to tell me why she didn't call you first?"

"Of course." Kurt was in command of the situation again. "For one thing, she doesn't know my phone number—"

"It's in the telephone book!"

"—and for another she guesses that it would be awkward for me to get phone calls like that at home. It might lead to unfortunate developments, now of all times when my parents are keeping a sharp eye on me because of school."

"She's as considerate as that?"

"Yes, she *is* as considerate as that."

"A wonderful girl!"

"A wonderful girl."

Weinberg turned away angrily. But after a while he came back, and said in a more conciliatory tone, "She said she hoped you'd be better soon."

Along with his parents' written explanation of why he had been off school sick, Kurt placed the signed letter of reprimand on the lectern. Kupfer didn't notice the forgery. That at least had worked.

Moreover, Kupfer was able to observe, with satisfaction, that young Gerber was paying particularly close attention in this lesson. So when the bell had gone, and the class was standing to attention, he began his address to them by saying—with a regretful expression, and without leading up to it in any way—that he was very sorry...

"I am very sorry to have to inform you, Gerber, that the account you gave has turned out to be inaccurate."

Kurt stood there, turning pale. He didn't know what Kupfer was talking about. It was some time since he, Kurt, had been in school. Surely anything he'd done was long forgotten.

Oh no. Almighty God Kupfer never forgot anything.

"I have found out that Professor Hussak did not give you permission to go and see the doctor, but that you left his lesson on the pretext of having a headache."

Only now did Kurt remember. So that's what he meant, he thought, he keeps track of all my failings. I wish he'd get to the end of this.

"You not only left the school building without permission and deceptively, you not only smoked in the vicinity of the school, which is also forbidden, but above all—" and here Kupfer was no longer pretending to be sorry, he raised his voice, he was thundering from on high—"above all you lied in the most shameless way to two members of staff. If Professor Hussak lets you persuade him that you have a headache, that's his business. I am not interested in that, any more than I am interested to know what the connection

125

was between your sudden indisposition and the presence of the former student Berwald here."

What I ought to do, thought Kurt, is go up to him and slap his face. But he was too tired for that, and preferred counting the grooves in the wood of his desk.

"Only objective facts matter to me, and they weigh heavy enough. I was obliged to call a staff meeting to decide on the appropriate disciplinary measures to be taken against you. The meeting decided on four hours' detention. Let that be a lesson to you, and in future let the thought of it rule your conduct. You know what the consequences of a second detention would be, particularly for a student in such a precarious position as yours has been since the last time marks were given. You are to inform your parents of the detention, and have the fact that you have done so confirmed by your father's signature. You will be told the day and hour of your detention later. Sit down."

And in an icy silence, Kupfer left the classroom.

After some time, it turned out that, for once, the whole class was united in feeling the amount of malice brought to bear had been unusual. The eighth-year students crowded round Kurt with expressions and cries of impotent regret, of the baffled sympathy with which one looks, for instance, at a horse that has fallen in the street.

The palfrey had been broken in. It lay there with its flanks trembling. It felt dirt on its white coat, muddy droppings soiling it, a sensation even worse than the lash of the whip laying the palfrey low on the ground.

Then the dirt suddenly seemed pleasantly soft, forcing the palfrey to stretch out and wallow in it, feeling apathetic and indifferent to its own fate.

"When were you thinking of phoning the emergency services?" asked Kurt, forcing a thin smile to his lips.

The students around him grinned, not sure what he meant. But when his glance moved slowly from one to another, many of them turned away. It was more than they could take.

At that moment there was hardly one of them who would not have been ready to mount an attack on their maths teacher Artur Kupfer at a nod from Kurt Gerber. At that moment something of significance might have happened. But it didn't.

All that did happen was that Kurt Gerber got to his feet and said, imitating the voice and gestures of Well-Then, their German teacher, "Well then, Kaulich, give me a cigarette, would you? As you may notice, that's what they call Romantic irony, right?"

But the irony did him less and less good. His talent for mockery began to fail him. Incidents that only recently might have amused him became major problems. The whims and fads of the teachers—each had his speciality, for instance Riedl had recently taken to testing students only where they sat at their desks, spending half an hour calling names, asking the student addressed a question and then saying, still in the same tone of voice, "Sit down," so that you never knew whether the answer had been right; Borchert would suddenly demand repetition of something learnt long ago; Niesset held written tests unannounced—all that used to make Kurt smile, as the comic intoxication with power of the bourgeois let loose; but now it seemed to him intentional tyranny, aimed principally at his own downfall.

At this time Kupfer's first formal examination up in front of the class was hurrying towards him (so far tests had been done at the students' desks), and Kurt thought it perfectly normal that he could not answer the question he was asked, and was marked Unsatisfactory. It was an unemotional affair, with nothing to show that this was really the first battle in the open field, in which two people who hated one another fervently clashed for the first time—it was an ordinary exam, and those who were no good at the subject would not be up to passing it.

School was closing in more and more on Kurt's mind. Here and there enemy patrols were already making their way into his last sanctuaries. It sometimes happened that he closed a book in the middle of reading it, left the theatre in the middle of an act, because he had suddenly remembered an exam tomorrow. Fear had a hold over him, sheer fear of inevitable events. It so entirely paralysed him that whether or not he might escape those events was something he left to chance. Doing anything by dint of his own powers seemed impossible. If he did try, however, with his brain reeling, he soon felt such disgust that he gave up. Not knowing whether it was the disgust or his fear that shook him, he took refuge in a book again. And closed it again in the middle of reading. There was a void in him that he had so far thought was entirely physical, a feature of an empty stomach. But now his mind was losing its appetite.

The void was worse when he thought of Lisa. By this time his self-confidence was badly undermined. Sometimes it seemed absurd for him to approach Lisa, who was living in very different circumstances, offering her what he thought of as love at all. He had assumed rights that were not his from

128

the mere fact that they had been at school together. Lisa, a woman like any other—or no, not like any other, a thousand times better than any other—Lisa could be worshipped from afar, that was all. And any time he spent with her, however short, was like an unexpected mercy for which he had to spend a long, hard time waiting. It was not just chance that she had left the school. Lisa had nothing at all to do with school and the trouble brewing for him there. She must be kept apart from it for ever.

Weinberg would have to be kept out of it, too. He hadn't come up to Kurt's standards. He had thought Lisa was lying. Even if she had been, he wouldn't have Weinberg thinking so.

Kurt had nothing to cheer him up. The achievement of fooling Kupfer twice running (for the signature he faked on the confirmation of his detentions had also escaped notice) was not a triumph. What harm had it done Kupfer? None, none at all. Well, if Kupfer had noticed the fake, had recognized it for what it was and phoned his father, and his father had said in surprise, "I don't understand, Professor Kupfer. That looks like my signature!" it would certainly have been awkward. But as things stood?

Nor did Kurt take much satisfaction in the fact that since his treacherous "warning", Niesset had been avoiding him, that he no longer asked young Gerber questions, even when he was the only one volunteering to answer them, and if Kurt did simply call out an answer he fingered his tie nervously, and that was all. Clearly that red-headed crocodile had taken fright once his malice was activated. But Niesset was denying him the satisfaction of actual capitulation, and preferred to wait in ambush. By ignoring Kurt's attentive participation in Latin lessons, he positively forced him to turn his attention to something else. And Kurt felt almost ashamed of the eager interest he had been showing, and immersed himself bitterly in the opposite, ostentatiously reading large books in class, doing homework, without even trying to keep these activities secret for the look of the thing. But nothing happened. Niesset, whose conscience pricked him, feared that young Gerber, if given another warning, might return his attention to the lessons and make his mark by giving the teacher some unfortunate reason to remember him.

Only once, when Kurt ceremoniously unfolded an English newspaper of gigantic dimensions on his desk, could Niesset not refrain. Eyes narrowed, he squinted at Kurt and made a throaty sound rather like a snore: "Mnnn, Gerber!" Kurt glanced up and, looking amiable but surprised, acted as if some stranger had addressed him. "Yes, that's my name, Kurt Gerber! But how do you come to know it?"

Now it did look as if something exciting might happen. Niesset's red face twisted into a grimace, he swallowed, now he *must* do something to assert his authority—but as most of the class had failed to notice what was going on, and went on talking undisturbed, he controlled himself and just managed to avoid a scene in which the ticklish subject of that warning might have come up. It came in quite convenient for him that at that moment Pollak's full bass voice was heard singing, at considerable volume, "Figaro, Fiiigaro, Fiiiigarooo!" Niesset could probably have done without what happened next; some of the students laughed and clapped, calling, "Da capo!" Soon the whole class joined in, and it took Niesset a long time to quell the noise. When he had, Kurt rustled his newspaper loudly. Niesset jumped, and lowered his head over his textbook.

At break the students congratulated Pollak warmly on his musical performance, and Kurt himself received appreciative comments from the few who had noticed his little clash with Niesset. Something like a relaxed atmosphere had spread in the class, and even Kurt was slightly affected by it. When he came back to school after his time off sick, it had struck him that the eighth-year students were no longer concentrating so purposefully and with such unnatural stiffness. That might have been the result of the staff meeting to allot marks, or the realization that there was no need to wear themselves out so long before the end of the year—for instance, following the subject in Niesset's lessons was impracticable, and taking down Prochaska's remarks word for word impossible (his opening address to them at the beginning of the year was long forgotten); sooner or later there must be a setback, and if so, sooner would be better. Some even ventured to copy from each other again in a Latin test and helped one another with vocabulary in French. There was a good spirit at large among the eighth-year students. It fumbled successfully at the chilly armour with which they had surrounded themselves, cutting them off from each other. In many lessons light air seemed to waft through the classroom, fanning their faces and their hearts, and they recognized it and greeted it with melancholy joy: it was a breath of that carefree air they had breathed long ago when life was not so serious, when they were still children with short trousers and bare knees, when they looked up to the eighth year with awe, and couldn't imagine ever being in the eighth class themselves. It seemed like the height of achievement. And now here they were,

Now we're the eighth year ourselves, they thought, but the students in the classes below us are cheeky and disrespectful, defying us behind our backs out of pure childish stupidity. We weren't like that in the fourth year, were we?

Only in Kupfer's lessons could no such atmosphere be felt. The students had other things to do then than wax elegiac. You had to answer him back with his own methods, and there was no liberation from the iron tension that reigned.

But finally relief did come. And from someone of whom it would never have been expected, a student who had never said a syllable too many in seven years, who was obviously bored to tears by the whole business, who never spoke up in class, and only let it be seen, in exams, that he knew much more than it was necessary to show here, indeed that he was almost amazed to find himself giving the best answers to all these questions, petty and stupid and unimportant as they were, and he couldn't get over that amazement. He was incontestably a good student, his reports said nothing but Very Good year after year, and as he shone not only in any one subject but in all of them alike he did not seem to be brilliant, didn't want to; he was that unique phenomenon, a good student who could not be blamed for showing off, or cramming to excess, or indeed for anything at all, who had firm opinions and yet was successful, who in all probability was a genius; and his name was Josef Benda.

This Josef Benda gets to his feet, not very enthusiastically, when Kupfer, in a bad temper, addresses him sharply.

"Benda! In the ten o'clock break yesterday, that is to say *after* the ten o'clock break yesterday, you were seen in the corridor when lessons had already begun again."

Benda wrinkles his brow. He seems to consider Kupfer's remark an unwelcome irrelevance. Or it may be that he has to stop and think what ten o'clock break and lessons are. He replies slowly, with some surprise, "Yes."

"Don't you know that you have to be in the classroom when the bell has gone?"

"I'd left the room." By this Benda means something that the irritated Kupfer fails to understand.

"I know that, for God's sake! That's why I'm calling on you to explain yourself."

Benda says nothing.

"What had you left the room to do?"

Benda is visibly surprised now. What are all these questions about? Then he says, with a smile intended to be bashful, but it comes over as avuncular, "Well, what one usually does when one has to leave the room."

The two of them are talking at cross-purposes, which Kupfer takes for intentional provocation on his student's part. He lowers his voice menacingly.

"Don't you try playing games with me, or you'll find it's the worse for you! I ask you for the second and last time: where were you?"

Now Benda sees the misunderstanding. His face clears. He grins slightly. Anyone coming in by chance would take him for a total idiot (which makes the probability that Benda is a genius a near certainty). He replies, benevolently, "I was in the water closet."

Whether because of the deep voice in which he says this, or the thorough way he utters the words "water closet", making them unintentionally funny—why doesn't he say WC, or loo, or toilet, and why does he speak with such exaggerated care, slow, clear and correct: water closet? At any rate, suppressed laughter begins breaking out in the classroom, like water from a leaky barrel.

"Quiet!" screeches Kupfer, and the startled class falls silent. Then he cuttingly echoes Benda's words. "Oh, so you were in the water closet. Couldn't you have done that earlier?"

Kupfer is throwing caution to the winds, running headlong into a field where his powers are, after all, to some extent limited. But he will not admit to himself that he can hardly be in command of his students' need to obey the call of nature. As long as they are in the school building, they ought to!

Benda himself seems to notice that this is not going too well. That he has various options. Couldn't he have done "that" earlier? What a stupid question! Of course not, or he *would* have done it earlier. He says, very firmly, "No."

"Oh yes, you could!" snaps Kupfer. "You could have done it earlier. Indeed, you *ought* to have done it earlier. Ought, I say. That's what break is for."

Now Benda is getting into his stride. Nothing in his tone of voice seems to change, but sharp ears can pick up a distinct undertone that shows he is enjoying himself.

"Professor Kupfer, sir, I can't take a pee to order!"

The self-appointed official laughers in the class make themselves heard. Their giggles are intended to suggest that no one gets anywhere with an oddity like Benda. But the barrel is beginning to gurgle and leak in other places as well.

Kupfer misses his last chance to withdraw in good order. He snarls at the class, threatening them all with detention, and then turns back to Benda. His eyes are flashing.

"Listen to me, Benda, don't you go too far!" Here his voice cracks. He stamps his foot. "Let me point out that you have no business in the corridor after the bell has gone, and that your actions are punishable."

Benda stands his ground.

"But if I need to take a pee, Professor Kupfer, sir…"

The girls have had their handkerchiefs stuffed into their mouths for some time. Distorted red faces with eyes and veins standing out are to be seen at all the desks. It can't go on much longer.

Kupfer gasps for air, and shouts at such volume that he makes the class jump, "Then you just have to hold it in until the next break!"

The hoops round the suspiciously gurgling barrel are beginning to crack, and when Benda says, with an insistence that removes the last doubt of his purpose, "Oh, but that's very unhealthy, sir. The astronomer Johannes Kepler is said to have died of urine retention"—when Benda says these words there is no holding them now. The barrel bursts, a great roar of laughter surges out, the class is in fits of merriment, many of the students gasping for breath and hooting out loud, the girls at the front screeching with mirth and falling into each other's arms. Hobbelmann has put his arms over his belly, rocking up and down in his seat like a bouncing ball, Kaulich has taken off his glasses to wipe the tears from his eyes, Gerald is bent double, arms outspread, writhing with laughter; the roars swell again and again, feeding on themselves; any student who looks at another is set laughing all over again, there is no end in sight, no moderation, thirty-two eighth-year students are beside themselves with glee. No, only thirty-one. There stands Benda, calm as ever, scratching the back of his head as if wondering: good heavens, what have I started? He thus represents such a contrast to Kupfer that it sets them all off again. Kupfer was frozen rigid at first, but then life comes back into him, his mouth moves, he is probably shouting, his face is red and bloated, he shakes his fists, sends the big wooden triangle crashing down on the floor, scribbles something in the register, paces back and forth—the sight is irresistibly comic, the class laughs even more, more and more—then an idea occurs to him. He contorts himself once more, opens his mouth wide, and then he sits down at his tall desk, braces his hands on the edge of it, and calms down.

The class too becomes calm, uncannily calm. Kupfer could leave this calm to take effect, but he is still too agitated for that. All the colour has now drained out of his face, his chest is rising and falling heavily, his breath is not yet regular, and only when the small black notebook is on the desk in front of him is total silence restored.

He begins at the end of the alphabet.

"Zasche. Come out to the front of the class. What do you know about the shadow boundary of angular radiant bodies?"

"The shadow boundary—the shadow…"

"Thank you, sit down, Unsatisfactory. Walter. The curves of the trigonometric functions. Well? Thank you, sit down, Unsatisfactory."

And so it goes on all through the alphabet. Kupfer calls names, asks questions, and marks all the students Unsatisfactory. Without any further comment at all. It is all he says when he gets to Benda too. Benda is the second in alphabetical order. Before him—or rather this time after him—there is only Altschul. What now?

Now Benda is called to the front of the class for the second time, and is marked Unsatisfactory again.

Is he going to go back all the way through the alphabet?

No. He calls Benda to the front of the class once more. And as soon as he is sitting down again—Kupfer takes meticulous care that Benda is sitting properly with his exercise book open—he is called back to the front of the class.

The fifth time, Benda stays on his feet beside his desk.

"I said sit down."

"But as, anyway, I'm—"

"I didn't ask you a question. Sit down."

Benda sits down.

"Benda!"

Benda gets to his feet.

"Well?"

Benda stands there in silence.

"Come to the front of the class."

"No."

"Are you aware that this is disobedience?"

"Yes."

"Will you kindly come to the front of the class?"

Unexpectedly, Benda does go to the front of the class without a word, and stands there without a word, not even making any attempt to answer, as he had before. Kupfer's hopes are dashed. He stops the questioning and begins to teach in a low voice. And any remnants of triumph that he might still be feeling come to nothing. Towards the end of the lesson Benda speaks up.

"Benda?"

"May I say something?"

On the lookout, for the last time, for a clear offence, Kupfer says yes.

"It's not part of the lesson," Benda assures him.

"Go on!" snaps Kupfer impatiently.

And Benda says, slowly and seriously, "I made a mistake just now, Professor Kupfer, sir. It wasn't Johannes Kepler who died of urine retention, it was Tycho Brahe."

No one laughed this time. But they all felt that, on the devastated face of Kupfer as he turned away, inextinguishable grief over something that had never been known before was imprinted...

The general opinion was that nothing could happen to Benda, it was, all of it, too unimportant. Only the five Unsatisfactory marks gave some cause for concern.

But not to Benda, who thought that Kupfer would let the whole thing rest at that. He probably also said so to make the Unsatisfactory marks of the others, which after all they owed to him, seem harmless.

It didn't work with one of them: Egon Schönthal.

Schönthal—known to those who walked reasonably upright as "the toad", and who was always annoyed by being asked if he'd crawled out of his mother's body just like that—was the perfect example of a lad who would crawl to anyone without thought. The question of to be or not to be never bothered him, only the question of to be good or even better; he would go to any brutal or humiliating lengths when they were to his own advantage. If Kupfer's unapproachable attitude after today's pitched battle had not been so alarmingly icy, Schönthal would undoubtedly have been ready to kiss the dust of Kupfer's shoes and swear by all the saints that he, out of all of them, had never once laughed. Schönthal could do more than that, he had more than once wormed his way out of a noose prepared to hang him. He did not shrink from being the only one to make true solidarity impossible, the only one to plead pathetically to be let off a detention imposed on the whole class; he denounced others both openly and in secret, lied with incredible subtlety to get himself out of a tight place—damp and toadlike, he crawled over all obstacles until he reached the peak he meant to climb. And indeed, he was the only one apart from Benda who never got a worse mark than Very Good. But what seemed an inevitable necessity in Benda, one that he simply accepted as just about permissible, was in Schönthal the exhausting pinnacle of achievement, a blessed certainty that no one could do better.

So the toad went about looking sullen, making pained faces and showing the gums of his prominent teeth, thinking of the shame represented by a mere Good in the column of Very Goods. He was furious, but did not quite like to adopt an anti-Benda stance. His only consolation was that the splendour of Benda's own series of Very Goods had also suffered. At last he said venomously, "Yes, very amusing, all well and good, but who's going to get me my Very Good back?"

The students looked at him in amazement.

"Very well, don't gawp in that silly way—what I mean is, how did I come to lose my Very Good?"

Some shook their heads, embarrassed by his attitude, never as inappropriate as now. Finally Lengsfeld, who had twice been obliged to stay down a year, broke the silence in his high voice.

"Listen, will you? If everyone, and I mean *everyone*, were to worry over whether this incident could harm them, then you're the last to have any reason for it."

Schönthal ducked his head. "No one asked your opinion, but I'll tell you something all the same: if it's all the same to everyone, and I mean *everyone*, how they're marked, then it isn't all the same to me."

Lengsfeld, not a very pugnacious character, withdraws. As Benda also leaves the group, Schönthal looks challengingly from one to another. He thinks he has won.

And indeed, his last argument does have some effect. Scholz, Pollak and Brodetzky nod thoughtfully. Hmm, he has a point. How do we deal with this? You toil away for eight years, and then maybe you whistle your advantage down the wind for some childish nonsense like this. It's not such an open and shut case as it seemed.

"It's not all the same to any of us how we're marked!" Kurt's voice is sharp and menacing, there's a lot he wants to get off his chest. This scene has been the nastiest for quite some time. But Schönthal doesn't let him go on. He casts Kurt a poisonous glance and says, venomously:

"Thanks. I'm grateful to you for that information. But you just listen to me. For you—" (his forefinger stabs the air from below) "for you in particular, of course, it makes no difference, because you're going to fail anyway."

For a moment Kurt does not take in the real meaning of Schönthal's words; he only senses their vicious hostility, and he says nothing, repelled.

Then something shoots past Kurt. A body. It is Weinberg, who has got up on the bench behind him and now jumps down. He makes straight for Schönthal and punches him

140

hard in the face. Schönthal staggers slightly, his glasses fall off, he stares wide-eyed, with a stupid expression, and covers his face with his hands. A drop of blood seeps through his fingers, and then another. He takes out a handkerchief and runs out of the classroom. Without a word, the others watch him go. Weinberg brushes something that isn't there off his hands, turns abruptly and goes back to his place.

"What an achievement," says Brodetzky, scornfully. Murmurs of disapproval swell. It is quite clear now that the mood of the class, or part of it anyway, has come down in Schönthal's favour. But the bell and the entrance of Professor Borchert rule out any further debate.

Borchert is a small, dithering man, distinctly fond of himself and the importance of what he says. If anything goes against the grain with him, the little eyes behind his pince-nez begin to blink nervously, then he draws himself up to his full height, and his comments always begin with the words, "In *my* lesson..." For the rest, he is not unpleasant out of a passion for being unpleasant, like his colleague Kupfer, only a man of erratic changeability, which can sometimes make him seem a little irresponsible. He may admit to being unfair and makes up for it, or he may suddenly fail you in a test for reasons you don't know. Kindness, insight, an often surprising understanding of his students' concerns—and petty vengefulness, fits of anger worthy of Nero, and pedantic inaccessibility change place in him at breakneck speed, creating confusion and anxiety. At heart he means no ill, but he is dangerous.

Today, as usual, he has forgotten to check the register. As the class has been fully present for a long time (you don't miss days lightly in the eighth year!), he notices the absence of Schönthal at once.

"*Monsieur Schönthal, est-ce qu'il est absent depuis la première leçon?*"

"*Non!*" reply several students. "*Il est présent!*"

"*Alors, où est-il?*"

Borchert gets no answer to that. The class, feeling awkward, does not reply. Borchert begins to suspect that Schönthal is missing "his lesson" on purpose, and is about to enter his name in the register. The eighth-year students don't know how to correct this misapprehension.

Borchert has opened the register. He stops in surprise, then reads quietly, but so that everyone can hear him: "Benda disrupted the lesson in the most outrageous manner by refusing to obey my orders and giving impudent answers when reproved. He thereby caused an equally reprehensible breach of discipline in the class as a whole… *Monsieur Benda? Je suis profondément étonné! Qu'avez-vous fait?*"

Benda stands up but does not reply, from which Borchert concludes that the case is nothing to do with him. He, too, however, has noticed a regrettable change in the conduct of the eighth-year students recently, and he is much surprised that Benda, of all people—in any case, he is about to enter Schönthal in the register.

But at that moment Schönthal comes through the door, his handkerchief still over his mouth. During the subsequent interrogation, matters are revealed that, once again, leave Borchert *profondément étonné*. He delivers a lecture of some length, making various allusions, and Kurt, whose nerves are on edge after what has happened, relates them all to himself, becomes restless and wishes all this would come to an end. Borchert reproves him several times, but leaves it at that. At last he interrupts himself: Zasche is playing with his pen-holder instead of listening.

"Zasche! *J'observe que vous n'êtes pas très intéressé!*"

Zasche, who has not understood a word of it, looks at him in alarm and nods, to be on the safe side.

Borchert likes to exercise his not very inventive wit on the half-idiot youth. Since Zasche replies *Oui* or *Non* at random to Borchert's questions, a delicious idea comes to the teacher. "*Vous êtes fou, n'est-ce pas?*" he enquires in a friendly, encouraging tone of voice.

And Zasche, concluding from that tone that his consent is expected, says accurately, "Oui."

Borchert titters, and the self-appointed official laughers of the class join in, full of appreciation for the hilarious joke. Zasche stands there helpless, bright red in the face. It is a repellent spectacle, and Kurt's indignation turns to it at once and uncontrollably.

"Congratulations, sir," he says. "But why not make such jokes about me instead?"

The class falls expectantly silent. A verbal duel, Borchert against Kurt—this could be amusing. Borchert apparently in good humour, Gerber, they all know, fully charged with caustic explosive. The eighth year sit up straight. Körner imitates a fanfare, and Schleich says, audibly, "In the Great Hall of Toledo". All the conditions for a dispute are present.

Nothing comes of it. Borchert blinks vigorously, then nods regretfully: "In *my* lesson, Gerber, you should refrain from such arrogant conduct. *You* of all people need to do so. You ought to have an eye on your predicament. *Alors, la dernière leçon…*"

And he has simply swept Kurt aside.

This is too much for Kurt. Schönthal's words still ring in his ears—you're going to fail anyway, you're going to fail anyway—and now this humiliation, this unmistakable hint at his position. Kurt feels weak at the knees.

He is going steadily downhill, failing several tests, and, moreover, when he is sent back to his desk with an Unsatisfactory again, he sees a malicious grin flit over Schönthal's face. He tries to spur himself on to work hard—I'll show that idiot! But such an ambition soon seems to him so degrading that for a while he does not answer questions put to him even when he could. Herr Schönthal was not to think he had the slightest wish to convince him; no, maybe I don't know anything about gneiss, granite and mica schist, and I'm not interested in them, I know other things, things of which *he* has no idea, and I don't want to know the stuff that he prides himself on, I'd be ashamed to know it, I won't say a word...

One day Professor Seelig takes him aside after the lesson and speaks to him urgently, warning him to try a little harder, not make it so difficult for the few teachers who are still on his side to speak up for him. Kurt tries morosely dismissing this, but Seelig looks at him so sadly out of his deep, dark eyes that Kurt pipes down. And above all, Seelig goes on, he must try to sort out that business of Kupfer and his detention, he must, and Kurt promises to do so almost tearfully, like a child trying to be good. Oh, sometimes he would be so glad to have everything all right again, everything in order, it hurts him so much to be hated and have to hate in return, what's it all for, why is Schönthal glad to think of me failing, why is Kupfer so unpleasant to me, so deeply unpleasant, why, what's got into him, perhaps he is a very unhappy man and could be kind and soft-hearted if he had someone to love him… And Kurt told himself to stop falling apart like this, shored himself up with good intentions, went over to Kupfer and began speaking in a gentle, amiable voice—but Kupfer hurled the sharp dagger of arrogant implacability at him, and Kurt guessed at the existence of a huge and horrible Never; we cannot run against it headlong, or it will fall like a gigantic wall and force us to the ground, and if we get too close it will crush us…

It hadn't come to that yet.

The palfrey had tried to get to its feet. But it stumbled and collapsed at the knees again. Its strength was wasted. The whip rose without haste after every lash, fell again without haste, rose again, regularly, up—down, up—down, twenty-four hours, a full day, and here came the next lash, the palfrey already felt nothing more, and its eyes were slowly losing the glint of fear and the gleam of hope alike—until one day the whiplash remained in the air and did not come down.

The Christmas holidays were here.

VI

A Young Man Called Kurt Gerber

T HERE WERE TIMES when Lisa Berwald, shaken by sudden ideas of the aimlessness and pointlessness of her existence, did not know what to do about Kurt Gerber and his devotion to her. When that happened she mentally clothed her naked perplexity in a wrap that billowed out around her; she hoped it would be seen as plain lack of interest, so that she could resist any attempt to make her go on strenuous forced marches of emotion. It seemed to her entirely pointless to scale peaks when in the course of nature every ascent must be followed by a descent. Why go to the trouble of such feats of mountaineering? Very well, you'd reached the top. And then what? See the beautiful view inevitably disappear again, go back down to the grey plain and live there even more discontented than before? Was she to take the trouble of loving vows on herself just for the sake of a promise which was always going to be impossible to keep? Why should she set out to exert herself, plant hopes, tend and raise them?

Lisa Berwald saw no need to exert her heart and brain, her thinking and her feeling any more than the moment required. And so, not having used up her energies in making unusual demands on herself, she always got the maximum achievement at the minimum expense. Down-to-earth people would call that a "practical disposition". And they would not be wrong. To have a practical disposition means not doing anything useless. However, because all that is beautiful has been proved to be entirely useless, the practically disposed do not usually lead beautiful lives, and Lisa Berwald did not. That is true of those who do have a practical disposition, but to say so of Lisa would be to do her wrong, because she lacked their calculating egotism. Lisa Berwald had no idea at all about her own nature. What she did, she did instinctively, and because her instincts were good she always did what was most advantageous. But she didn't think about it, was not calculating, and so did not get any further use out of her instinctive reactions. She was never in command of a situation, only faced with it. She was indifferent to the facts of it, and so they dwindled in importance until, as she ignored them, they were finally entirely lost from view. There was something strangely generous, even noble, in her thoughtlessness.

So when people told Kurt Gerber that Lisa was stupid, he smiled secretly at such a comical conviction. At the most he would concede that she was not, maybe, highly intelligent, but no one was asking that of her, and all the same—

That "all the same" covered several contingencies. From time to time, Lisa had fits of enthusiasm. Then she would devour, in motley confusion, the most difficult reading matter she could find, she learned languages, went to the opera, surprised acquaintances with her unspoilt judgement—and the fit would suddenly wear off again. Not a jot of all the culture she had swallowed wholesale remained, she was an empty vessel once more, sitting without a word for hours on end and looking sadly into space.

The sadness might arise from the fact that Lisa, having been intellectually overstrained, was thinking of something just the opposite, and if she did not consciously identify it she felt what it was: she had never been in love. She hadn't even had the usual teenage crush on anyone; when at the age of thirteen she let someone kiss her for the first time it was no picture postcard of an Adonis for whom she yearned, but a chance-come neighbour in the summer holidays, a bank clerk with thinning hair who took advantage of Lisa's being left alone in the apartment that evening. At the time she had felt flattered because he was, after all, grown up, and once back in the city she cherished fantastic expectations, contemptuously rejected the burgeoning wishes of her male fellow students at school, and was greatly disappointed when no one else came along. The boys she met at dancing class, with their smooth words and the dirty jokes they told in private, bored her, but as she, the prettiest of the girls, did not want to be the only one without a boyfriend, she would let first one and then another kiss her, and at the age of fifteen she knew everything that a kiss had to offer. And then came a dismal, trying time full of dry sobs, sombre nights and burning days, when she simply did not know what to do about the urges of her young body, and went about in a daze. It was then, too, that she took to putting up with the knowing way her fellow students pestered her—until one day, when Lisa was between seventeen and eighteen, Otto Engelhart came along. She hardly knew where from, she didn't love him, didn't even like him when he was introduced to her and she bowed awkwardly. What happened next was also unimportant to her: how they came to be sitting in a car side by side after going to the theatre on a rainy autumn evening, kissing wildly, and then she was lying naked in a strange bed, and woke up naked in a strange bed, and she still wasn't in love with Otto Engelhart. It could just as well have been anyone else, she thought. But it hadn't been. And he was followed by this one and that one (she was the one who made her choice now, and she did it like a queen in full knowledge of all her powers), and then even Otto Engelhart said nothing and kept away—but she felt it was no coincidence when he came back one day, his angular face pale, his throat rough with emotion, and there lay Otto Engelhart at Lisa's feet and Lisa didn't like to see it, so as he would not get up she lay down on the floor beside him. After that they stayed together. Lisa Berwald was "walking out" with Otto Engelhart. It almost amused her that rumours about her began going the rounds at just this time. Now that she was being faithful to one boyfriend, people began looking at her askance, calling her flighty and flirtatious. At school only the energetic support of the more liberal professors kept these slurs from having further consequences. Then one day her parents were wringing their hands—people she didn't know had thought it their duty to open their eyes, was it really true, had their daughter sunk so low? Lisa saw all the uselessness of a frank discussion, and neither wanted one nor felt that she would be any good at it, so she soothed them, assuring them that it was just silly talk, good heavens, the things people would say… and like it or not, her parents had to be content with that.

However, people did not stop whispering about her, and that became a real nuisance. Particularly when Otto

Engelhart himself began complaining. Defiantly, she now allowed others to "succeed" with her, as they put it. Nor did she object when Otto Engelhart had similar success with other girls. She knew that he could not break free of her any more than she could break free of him, that whatever happened they would always find their way back to each other with the inevitability of a boomerang, however far it is flung.

Their reconciliation after such interludes (if reconciliation is the word for it) was without scenes or bitterness, and it was also without any emotion that, lying in Otto Engelhart's arms, Lisa said one day that, now she was nineteen years old, she would soon be getting married.

However, there was painful surprise in his voice when he asked, "Who to?"

She didn't know, said Lisa indifferently, examining her fingernails. Probably some paunchy businessman supplied by her parents or a helpful friend of theirs.

Well, said Otto, he was sure that would be a good thing for her. They couldn't have gone on in the same way as before anyway.

To which Lisa unexpectedly asked, "Why not?"

And Otto Engelhart, eyes wide with surprise, repeated, "Yes, well, why not?"

Then there was a long silence, while they were both thinking the same thing, and both thinking it with the same hopeless fury.

But it was no good. Lisa left school, where she had been for too long because at home they couldn't think of anything else to do with her. On her summer holiday in Italy she was introduced to a manufacturer considerably her senior, who could boast of owning a car and an unnaturally high voice for a man; these went with an easy-going nature. His surname, very inappropriately, was Brumm, denoting a low growl like a bear's, and he was what is known as a good catch. He knew nothing or little about her earlier history, or else he knew it all and didn't mind, because Lisa was very beautiful and very young and was nice to him. He would certainly have married her, if only to possess her, and she seemed happy enough with that; but when they went home to the city, Lisa suddenly took fright at her unimaginable future, and one day she was back with Otto Engelhart. At home she explained, briefly, that she had thought it over and she really couldn't go about with a surname like Brumm for the rest of her days, and she rather liked to think that she would now be considered an excitable and hysterical young woman.

That had been in September. Since she didn't want to be entirely a burden on her parents, who were not pleased with her anyway, and also to find a substitute for school, she took a job in an arts and crafts studio, where she embroidered cushions, made decorative tea cosies topped by china dolls' heads, was highly valued by her boss and was even popular with the rest of the staff, because she was pleasant to them, obliging and not ambitious. At the beginning of November the young and very rich son of an estate owner started idolizing her, heaped luxuries on her, and quarrelled with his family on her account. She enjoyed this for a few weeks, and then suddenly dropped him. In the Christmas holidays she was going to visit a winter-sports resort not far away, with Otto Engelhart and some of his lively assortment of friends.

A pleasant weariness had overcome her. Surveying her existence, she saw the possibility of living for several endlessly long years just as she liked. For the time being that was enough to put her in the right frame to think, with a kind of agreeable emotion, of Kurt Gerber and his wild, ambitious love, which in its purity put something of a strain on her. In such a mood, her intention of denying him the fulfilment of his dream, but in the most painless and gentle way possible, grew and flourished; she would do it with many kind words, even with many passionate kisses. For she was firmly determined that Kurt Gerber must not entertain such ideas. There had been a brief period when she would have yielded to him, because she liked him, and at the time she didn't mind much about her current boyfriend, the fourth or fifth. But Kurt had failed to take his chance at the time. When she realized that he had refrained from doing so intentionally she had been very cross at first, and the next moment more moved than ever before. Then she took fright at the wide range of turbulent, uncontrolled feelings he showed he had for her. She could not understand how anyone could take a kiss so seriously, and because she herself had such very different feelings she thought Kurt Gerber's love was childish (although she respected the fact, particularly striking in the surroundings of school, that he was so adult in other ways). A maternal feeling for him had developed from this attitude, although it had nothing to do with the concepts of "friendship" or "platonic love" misused by schoolgirls. It was a strange way of reciprocating his feelings that made his devotion seem inappropriate. As she knew that her views were free of any false cowardice, she thought she could satisfy Kurt in the way she planned. Indeed, there was a certain esteem for him in it. She did not want to have slept with Kurt "too", did not want to see him as just one of several. He had no idea of this. The fact that he knew he had had predecessors inflamed him; he would show her that, for his part, he did not want to sleep with her "too". And so they both, but from different causes, shrank from a relationship that was like many others, and loved at cross-purposes without knowing it.

Lisa, undoubtedly far less clear about all this in her mind than Kurt, ultimately found his persistence uncomfortable: why can't he accept that I don't want to be loved like that? He could be in clover if he'd only stay within the limits I set! She was annoyed. And when a girlfriend asked what sort of relationship she had with that Kurt Gerber, people were saying he was a nice young man, and where looks were concerned could well be in the running, Lisa would reply with more irritation that she really felt: yes, very true, but after all, she couldn't do as everyone wanted! She had really said that out of embarrassment; it sounded as if she genuinely disliked him, and really she didn't, on the contrary—but that was what she had said. And she liked the phrase, it put down roots and grew, becoming a firmly established intention which was not going to change. Sometimes she felt quite sorry she had come to that conclusion, sometimes, when she was with Kurt and he said nothing, and she looked at him—then her attitude softened, she felt that the young man beside her was different, you couldn't just shake him off like anyone else, and then she suddenly stroked his hair or kissed him gently on the cheek. Yes, that might sometimes happen, not very often, but it didn't change anything. Lisa Berwald had made up her mind not to give herself to a young man called Kurt Gerber.

Puffing listlessly, the train is making its way through the twilit snowy landscape. Sometimes it stops with a screech, lets out a loud and particularly bad-tempered gasp, limps a little farther and then comes to a halt; the masses of snow in front of the engine are too large, and must be shovelled off the line. Only when that has been done does it move shakily away again. No point in this, creak the wheels, no point in this. It has to stop again.

A ski-resort train. The local council of the village that at this time of year proudly calls itself a "winter spa", a "skiing paradise" and so forth runs these trains several times a day on its own (very lucrative) account. They often take the more ambitious skiers several miles away to the finest pistes. They spare them the trouble of the upward climb, in fact; only the upward journey, because almost every downward course takes the skiers well below the village, and at the end of the trip they have to climb up again, unless they come to a halt earlier. With the trains on hand, however, you can ski all the way down; the "boozed-up old tub", as it is known, of the train is down at the bottom and will take tired skiers back from the plain up to the place where the village clings to a slope halfway up the mountain range.

This is the last train, and because it has been snowing all day it finds progress difficult in the evening, as twilight falls by almost visible stages over these regions with their clear air—a gauze curtain, and then another, another—until you see nothing any more. Now three have come down, and as it is still snowing, earth and sky are the same milky grey colour.

The powder snow was too tempting, and most of the holidaymakers have stayed on their skis until the last train arrives. So it is full to bursting, passengers are so crowded in the carriages that some even have to stand on the outside boards, which is not very comfortable. They try to keep their limbs warm by moving all the time and shake themselves now and then, sending the snow flying off them in dusty clouds. Then they look longingly at the insides of the carriages, but there are still no empty seats, everyone who could get inside is glad of it. Across the roofs of the compartments, from luggage net to luggage net, countless skis are stacked as if they were dead hares, their ski bindings dangling like entrails. Water drips persistently from many of them—they belong to the beginners, damn them, who have forgotten yet again to scrape encrusted snow out of the grooves; sometimes it's almost raining, and then those who have to stand get their chance to congratulate those sitting inside, who are getting a shower in the comfort of their armchairs. But then they have to stamp their feet again where they stand, to keep off the cold.

Good old Willi Wagenschmid is a splendid fellow. There isn't a torn binding that he can't repair at once, no young plantation of trees through which he can't guide you, no inn where he can't get the best possible deal however much the innkeeper may curse his persistence. And God knows what useless Sunday skiers would be occupying those two rows of seats now if Willi Wagenschmid hadn't found the only open window in the whole train. While hand-to-hand fighting was going on at the doors, he climbed through that window, staked a claim to all eight seats, and defended them against all comers until the others arrived.

It turns out that Paul Weismann has a whole bottle of cognac with him. He hadn't been going to bring it out on

the way up to the resort, but now Gretl Blitz and Hilde
Fischer have secretly opened his rucksack and are holding
the bottle up in triumph. It's to be emptied, they say, to the
good health of Willi Wagenschmid, their rescuer.

There is enthusiastic assent to this proposal, and Boby
Urban even suggests that Paul himself shouldn't get any
of it, to punish the grasping bastard for his meanness. But
then Lisa intervenes. Lisa—she is looking radiant, and
her pleasure in knowing it infects the others—won't have
any disagreements, even as a joke, she wants unclouded
good humour; and because she puts all her charming
kindness into her efforts to achieve it (not that they are
recognized as efforts) she always succeeds in creating
that happy, light-hearted, weightless, relaxing and relaxed
atmosphere of merriment that has no beginning and no
end, is simply there. She goes from one to another of her
companions like a fairy-tale princess, embracing each in
turn and whispering in every ear, "Did you ever imagine
anything in the world could be as nice as this?" It's a
merriment that is only really true and genuine when you
catch yourself feeling it, when you stare abstractedly at
the ground and think, "Why, oh why can't it always be
like this?"

Kurt thinks so too when it is his turn to drink, and he
takes a large gulp from the bottle, closes his eyes and lets
the cognac spread pleasant warmth all through him, feeling
very, very happy. He would like to fall down in front of Lisa
in consuming love and gratitude, because it was she who
invited him to join the party, and because she is so good to
him here, almost too good, what has he done to deserve it?
Now Lisa is smiling at him. "Do you like it?" she asks, and

Kurt says, "Yes!" He says it quietly, bashfully, like a child reproved for being naughty: "There, now do you see that you were wrong?"

In fact all of them are very friendly; some have even taken him to their hearts. He is particularly flattered by the affability of Paul Weismann, the painter, and Boby Urban, the composer. But even Otto Engelhart, of whom Kurt has been slightly afraid, turns out a nice fellow. Not the smooth society sort, but you can rely on him not to spoil anyone's fun; it's only in minor matters that he is curiously obstinate. He has been very affable to Kurt, with a hearty handshake when they met: "Ah, so here you are!" Apparently Lisa has told him something about Kurt, who only wishes he knew what! The others also make out that they have heard a lot about him already, and Kurt takes a childlike pleasure in the ease with which they are soon acting as if he had always belonged to their group.

So now they are sitting in that boozed-up old tub of a train, seeming even more in accord than before under the influence of the cognac (and that is saying something, since they always get on well together; there's never any quarrelling among the young people, who all seem to know and understand one another very well).

Willi Wagenschmid and Boby Urban are smoking short-stemmed pipes with their legs stretched out; they look a gruff couple in their blue Norwegian ski suits, green wind jackets and huge boots, and because the train is rolling and listing like a ship in a storm at sea, they strike up a few sea songs, amusing the whole compartment.

It is getting darker all the time outside, the gauzy curtain between the window and the air grows denser, the telegraph poles behind the train race past like shadows in a hurry. But you can still see the separate wires.

Boby Urban stands up and looks for the electric light switch on the wall. The occupants of the carriage, crammed close together as they are, move aside without much goodwill. At last he has made his way through, presses the switch, presses it again—hello? What does this mean?

One of the bystanders speaks up: he could have told him at once. However, the passengers in standing room only feel quiet satisfaction when the nobs from the comfortable seats have to push their way through and then turn back, disappointed.

"I suppose the power's off," says Boby, not very imaginatively.

He supposes right. It's been tried several times, he is told. Absolutely hopeless.

Boby goes back to his own seat and delivers his report. Would Willi like to try his luck?…

Willi would not. He's tired out, almost asleep.

Soon protests are heard from other parts of the carriage. Put the light on! Where's the switch? What, not working? Rotten luck.

And still two hours' train journey before they arrive at their destination, and no sign of any guard aboard! (He would have tried in vain to push his way through the overcrowded train anyway.)

By now the whole carriage knows about this mishap, and the passengers are accepting it as best they can. Someone opens a window and leans out. There are no lights anywhere along the train. The sparks from the engine up in front are visible as little red-gold points.

And suddenly it is as if an abrupt realization has come over all the passengers, sitting and standing alike: they're in a train in the middle of the dark night, full of people. Men and women alike.

The conversation is quieter now. Those who are couples move closer to each other. It will soon be pitch dark. And they all know what is bound to happen. They fold their hands in their laps and put their heads together. They wait. Like a flock of lambs silently but willingly letting themselves be driven to their watering place.

Some have already fallen silent, others are still talking in whispers. Here and there a match furtively flares up, is held carefully in the hollow of a hand and soon goes out again. No one wants to disturb anyone else. They are considerate.

The compartment is full of a quiet humming sound. Sometimes a brief laugh rises like a fish jumping up from the dark surface of a lake, and dives down again into the desultory chatter; its regularity is curiously exciting.

Night has fallen.

Kurt strains his eyes, trying to exchange glances with Lisa. She is sitting diagonally opposite him, and he does not regret that arrangement. He wonders what he would do sitting beside Lisa. Probably nothing. The feeling that he ought to be doing something would make him uncomfortable. Anything he did would probably be wrong.

And yet…

Hilde Fischer and Paul Weismann are sitting on his left, closely entwined, moving only now and then. Paul would probably rather be getting some sleep, but Hilde is so much in love with him that she will miss no chance.

Boby Urban and Gretl Blitz are different, not to mention Lisa and Otto Engelhart. Boby is asleep on Kurt's right, his head propped in his hands. Opposite, Gretl Blitz and Willi Wagenschmid are asleep too, leaning against each other. Then there is Lisa, the only one still fully awake. And Otto Engelhart is dozing in the corner by the window with his arms folded.

Deep night reigns.

It worries few of them that it has fallen on them as they sit in a train. Night is night. The question is not: should we kiss now? It is: why should we *not* kiss now? The answer was given long ago. We are young. Who knows how often those of us who want to be with each other will get another chance to meet in the dark? Who knows whether you, my neighbour in the next room, will be going away again tomorrow? Whether you, found on the piste with a broken ski, don't have someone waiting who will take you away from me, or whether you and you are simply compliant out of boredom, or you and you will stay away from me for a long time, for ever? Who knows?

No one knows, and no one is watching. It is cold and dark, and we are young.

Deep, deep night.

Kurt moves his foot, which comes up against something. A wooden strut? A heating pipe?

Then—a warm shock passes through him—then there is a response to its pressure. At first he dares not believe it. Then he presses more firmly, and the response is firmer too.

After a few minutes he has Lisa's leg firmly clasped between his, and through the layers of thermal padding and flannel Kurt feels the sinews of her strong thigh sometimes twitching briefly, as if the leg had a heart beating in it.

Happiness surges through him. And, because a stroke of luck seldom comes on its own, the train shudders to a halt—so abruptly that they all wake with a start, and Kurt thinks disaster is imminent.

Meanwhile, once calm is restored, Paul Weismann sleepily expresses a wish to lie down for a bit; he probably had too much cognac, he says, and now he has a headache.

Then someone will have to stand up, says Boby in some concern, and he stretches in his seat with obvious comfort. Otto Engelhart has snuggled down under his windcheater again, and Willi Wagenschmid, who made sure they all had seats, can hardly be asked to move. So Kurt gets to his feet and says, with pretended reluctance: well, he supposes it's up to him, as the youngest, to pay for the sins of certain habitual drunks.

They all go along with his suggestion. And while, in the beam of a flashlight, Kurt despairingly watches a new seating arrangement being made, Lisa suddenly stands up and says, in a tone that will brook no contradiction, "I tell you what, children, you can make yourselves even more comfortable. I'm not at all tired, and I don't mind standing until we get back—it can't be long now." So saying, she steps out between the two rows of seats and takes Kurt's arm. "Anyway, it would be rude to make poor Kurt stand on his own."

No one notices how firmly she presses his arm, and no one is surprised to find that once again it is Lisa who is fully in charge of a situation.

"Well done, girl of my heart," mutters Boby, using Paul's head, now in his lap, as a cushion. "Don't forget to pay me a little fee when you take over this brothel on wheels!" And as he cuts any response short by grunting with satisfaction he stretches out in comfort, and obviously takes no further interest in the universe.

So now the opposite row of seats is occupied by Otto Engelhart, the two girls and Willi Wagenschmid, who switches off his flashlight now that everything is settled. It is pitch dark again, the train moves off once more, puffing, and soon all six are asleep.

Some of the passengers who were standing before are hunched on the floor now. So there is some room in the corner by the connecting door between carriages. Enough room for two people to be able to move slightly in it. Over there. Very cautiously. And keeping their voices down.

"Are you all right, Lisa?"

"Oh yes." She feels for his cheek, strokes it a couple of times.

"Aren't you cold?"

"A bit."

"I'll warm you up, Lisa." He is close to her, his voice shakes, he breathes the words out.

Her arm lies lightly around his neck. And suddenly she puts her other arm round him too and holds him close, very, very close, and her firm body rears up to his, and now he has found her mouth and his teeth are digging into it, he grinds them, he sucks her lips, they are intertwined in a hot, untiring searching and finding and searching, as their tongues caress like two beasts of prey in an amorous game...

Whispered, meaningless words, hotly stammered out in incredibly blessed ecstasy. What happiness to be able to

disregard the pitiful inability of words to express their feelings, what happiness to be able to give themselves up to
uninhibited enjoyment again and again, what tearful, smiling, explosive happiness!

He strokes her profuse, waving hair, firmly, urgently, as if it
might fly away from him. Her soft hand caresses the parting
of his own hair, much more calmly.
   "Lisa—why—why can't it always be like this?"
   "It can!"
   "Then why—Lisa—why wasn't it like this before?"
   "Don't talk, not now."
   What an excess of happiness—alone with each other!
Both with our own burden of happiness. It gives to us, it
takes nothing away. The ultimate torment of unfulfilment:
will you be my companion for life? Until we reach the same
end—and I don't know myself where that will be.

"Listen—when you stood up, just now—was that on purpose?"
   "Silly you!"

No train is thudding along, no engine is puffing towards us.
Fiery swarms of glow-worms fly past our intoxicated eyes.
They fly away behind us, into the dark.
   How unearthly, how strange that we can see them at the
same time, one and all together.
   You shouldn't have done it, Lisa, you shouldn't have kissed
my hand. Do you want me to burst into tears?

I haven't really wept in front of you yet. I was far too sparing with my tears. Forgive me!

No, not like that… I want to kiss your eyes, your forehead, your hair. Like this.

Perhaps you'll weep again in my arms. That would be good…

The time races past, a captivating, carefree time.

Willi Wagenschmid keeps finding new routes on the tourist map, many a slope suddenly opens out ahead of the downhill skiers in virginal expectation; the tracks of the narrow skis cut through its smooth and dazzling skin like weals, so that afterwards you feel almost sorry to have destroyed its untouched beauty. Before, of course, all you feel is joy swelling in your breast, as if you had discovered a new part of the world and were now, rejoicing, taking possession of it. And when only the ends of the skis, turned upwards, emerge from the snow, gliding ahead of the skier's body as if at the pressing of a magical button, and fine, white clouds of snow rise like dust around his feet, the strong pressure submits to the will of that body, and when you hear nothing but a quiet crunching, and you feel nothing but the clear, free air and see nothing but the glittering sky, then—yes, what then? Then the powers of the brain fail in the face of this unparalleled experience.

Lisa has adopted a curious attitude towards Kurt; she singles him out, but in such an easy, unselfconscious way that with the best will in the world no one can sense anything behind it. Deep down, maybe Kurt expected a secrecy born of mutual understanding, a surreptitious pressure of their hands, something they could have been caught out doing, and he is just a little disappointed that nothing of the kind happens. Then he puts it down to Lisa's great cleverness. It's all right. Was he expecting her to draw him aside and say, with a soulful whisper, "Oh, you... do you still think about that?"

Yet somehow or other, surely she could show him that *she* was still thinking about it?

Sometimes it seems as if, once again, she doesn't remember anything. On the morning when their party gathers downstairs in the breakfast room, Kurt feels as if he is being introduced to Lisa all over again.

Good morning. Haven't we met somewhere before?...

Kurt sees Lisa's hands moving as they handle various objects. Did those hands hold him close? Kurt sees Lisa smile at others. Sees it without envy. After all, he never kissed those lips. Kurt sees Lisa's brown hair blowing in the wind. Surely it's impossible that he ever stroked that hair and his lips caressed it.

What would happen now if he went over to her and did that very thing? Unimaginable. They'd all think him crazy. Lisa would probably even say so. With a surprised smile, a little forbearing, as you might speak to an invalid. For instance: "Oh—have you by any chance lost your wits?"

No. Or rather, yes. It seemed to me that I had—I only wanted to make sure that—but it must be a mistake. Maybe a case of confusion.

"Why are you talking to yourself like that, Kurt? Yes, I mean you!" Now Lisa really has spoken up. How odd. That tone of voice—

"Me? Talking to myself?" Kurt gives her a bewildered smile. "Now that would really surprise me. I mean, I've disliked myself for quite some time, so I'm not on speaking terms with myself."

Laughter. How they all laugh. How Lisa laughs. To think how little she guesses of the difficulty that went into that joke.

"Skis all well waxed? Bindings all right?" asks Willi Wagenschmid. "I don't want anyone's ski binding coming off halfway down the slope—I don't fancy running after a ski with a life of its own."

"Oh, shut up about it, do!" mutters Hilde Fischer, who recently had that very accident.

And then they are off again for another day on the slopes, followed by another cheerful evening and then another cheerful day again, and one misty afternoon they go to the bar, which is on the basement floor of the biggest hotel in the resort, and is always full of Sunday skiers and other undesirables.

The eight of them sit at a round table requisitioned for the party by—who else?—Willi Wagenschmid, and make critical comments on the dancing couples, their faces strained, moving through the low-ceilinged, smoke-filled room to the music of an ailing piano.

"Hey, young beau, give us a dance!" cries Boby, clapping Kurt on the shoulder. "Off you go! The pretty girls are waiting!"

Kurt is not particularly happy to comply, and indeed is at something of a loss—but gentle, blonde Hilde Fischer, always ready to help, frees him from his difficulty with tender understanding, stands up and says, "Come on!"

Kurt is very grateful to her, but he doesn't venture to talk to her about Lisa.

"What were you gawping at while you danced?" Boby asks him when they return to the table. "You look like a dolphin washed up on shore!"

"I haven't either," says Paul dreamily.

"You haven't either what?"

"Oh, I thought someone just said he'd never seen a dolphin dancing."

"Here's to your demise in the near future!"

"Cheers!"

But it is no use, Kurt has to dance again, with Lisa this time. He takes fright, starts by asking, "Would you like to dance, Lisa?" And Lisa—does she understand him?—nods her head at the crowd and says, "The dance floor is so full," but then Otto Engelhart, who doesn't usually say much and just laughs along with the others, intervenes, "You're not going to turn him down, are you, Lisa?" and Lisa says, "Of course not!" and off they go.

It is the first time they have danced together, as he realizes only now. Kurt is a very good dancer, holds her lightly, begins to lead her steps—and immediately stumbles over her foot.

"Sorry."

"Don't mention it."

Lisa does not dance well. Kurt notices that, and now he feels released from his fears. He also knows *what* he feared: he feared that Lisa would dance very well, too well. He wouldn't have liked it at all if she had let her body follow every movement he made, shamelessly, demandingly, with a challenging look.

167

But she doesn't. Lisa follows his steps only hesitantly, although she is obviously trying. Kurt can tell that her awkward resistance isn't intentional, that she can't help it.

Lisa is wearing a casual, sleeveless outfit. Her body shows much more clearly than it did in her ski suit. If he has to hold her a little more firmly as they turn in the dance, he distinctly feels her backbone.

And her whole body, like her dance steps, is hard. Her body—her movements—all so strange, so unexpected—you could call her attitude defiant, or no, imperious—no, neither of those words is right: demure! Her body feels austere and demure.

Once again, Kurt feels the blazing heat of love stream through him.

"Lisa—"

"Yes? Do I dance very badly?"

"No, far from it. You dance splendidly."

No response.

"Tell me, Lisa—"

"What?" She says that so lightly, so brightly. There's no replying to it with words of passion.

"Five days ago, Lisa—didn't you say: it can always be like this?"

"What do you mean?" As if she really didn't know.

"Why are you acting like this, Lisa? You know very well what I mean."

"Yes, of course I do."

"Well then—"

Again no response. The pianist embarks on the recapitulation of the tune for the third and last time. Kurt grits his teeth.

"Have you forgotten?"

"No, Kurt. Why do you ask?"

"Lisa—how can you talk like that? Don't send me crazy—why haven't I been able to kiss you again since then? Why do you do this—do you think I can stand it a day longer—Lisa, darling, tell me when! Oh, say something!"

Kurt has brought these words out hastily, almost imploringly. Now he looks anywhere in the room at random to keep the others at the table from noticing. Yet he would so much like to look at Lisa's face.

"Yes, but why do you come out with such things just now?" asks Lisa.

"Such things?"

Crash, bang—the pianist concludes the piece with a low bass chord. Over. They go back to the table.

Paul Weismann taps Lisa's arm with his finger.

"Elisabeth—if dolphins do dance, I'll bet they dance like you."

Lisa laughs.

Who'd have thought laughter could hurt so much? Kurt feels despair overcome him, tries to subdue it—but in vain. The bar, the music, the people become intolerable to him. That includes the company at their own table. Suddenly Boby Urban's jokes strike him as tasteless and always the same, Paul Weismann isn't so different, Hilde Fischer's dreamy glances make him nervous, Gretl Blitz is boring. He dares not even think about Lisa. Indeed, when he goes on thinking along these lines the entire company repels him. It shouldn't be like this.

Abruptly, Kurt gets to his feet.

"You'll forgive me, I hope? The air in here is too stuffy for me. See you all at dinner."

169

And before anyone can say anything, he is outside.

The evening air is cool and mild around him. Groups walk slowly over the sparsely lit market place.

Locals, Kurt realizes as he passes them. They are talking and laughing out loud. It annoys him that he can't understand every word of their dialect. What's amusing them so much?

A sleigh passes very close to him. "Gee up!" calls the driver. The mere sound of the human voice offends him.

The hooves of the horses have a hollow sound as they clatter by, in alternating rhythm, on the hard, yellowish-grey frozen snow. Their little bells jingle.

Kurt is disturbed. The cold, threatening regularity of the high mountain peaks all around makes him feel uneasy.

Ridiculous, those mountains. They'll never reach the sky.

The moon, faded and weary, hangs in the black sky, bleakly revealed.

A wintry evening idyll…

Back in his tastelessly furnished and not very hospitable room at the inn, Kurt flings himself down on the divan, smokes and stares into space.

Now and then he hears a log crackle on the fire. Scraps of conversation come up from the street, along with laughter and the sound of sleighs.

All as it should be. Unalterable. Yet he could be joining in the laughter. The sound of the sleighs could still appeal to his ear…

Kurt is lying in bed, already undressed, still staring into space, when the door opens and Paul, who shares the room with him, comes in.

Why wasn't Kurt at dinner, he asks.

He probably fell asleep and missed it, replies Kurt without any particular surprise.

Paul sighs slightly, and without another word begins to get undressed.

Next moment, Kurt feels, something is going to happen, he will either burst into tears or laugh out loud. Anyway, some kind of loud noise must break this unendurable silence.

There—laughter, words, footsteps. A knock on the door. And Lisa's voice.

"Why didn't you come down for dinner, Kurt? Aren't you feeling well?"

Lisa's voice, warming and caressing his heart. Now he realizes that he wouldn't have laughed, he would have wept.

"Thank you," he said with difficulty, "but I'm fine."

He is afraid to look at her. When he does all the same, he sees Otto Engelhart standing behind her, and is glad that his eye can choose where to rest.

"Sleep well," says Lisa, in no way embarrassed, "and see you in the morning. Good night, Paul."

Kurt wants to say something civil, along the lines of "Very kind of you to ask after me," but he doesn't. If one of the servants had fallen ill, Lisa would probably have knocked on his door to find out how he was. She is naturally friendly.

She has already left the room. With Otto Engelhart. And for the first time Kurt feels resentment. Now they're going to sleep together. Or maybe not. That would be even worse.

"Do you love her very much?" Paul suddenly asks from the bed beside his.

Kurt is not at all surprised. He has been sure for a long time that all of them know he is in love with Lisa. And as they are reasonable people it doesn't bother him. Paul's question is not really ill timed.

"Do you think it's surprising or—I don't know how to put it—improper, inappropriate for me to love her?"

Paul does not answer that.

"Don't feel embarrassed. I've already heard worse of her." Kurt smiles. The mere possibility that someone might speak slightingly of Lisa brings him round to her side again.

"You won't hear anything bad from me. In principle I don't do any woman the favour of speaking ill of her. Note that, Herr Gerber. Great Thoughts of Paul Weismann, number 407."

This is something that fascinates him about Paul: he had no consideration for either others or himself. His cynicism is part of him, like a sword in a sheath. However credibly and fervently he speaks, you can't shake off the fear that at the end of his cleverly constructed, irrefutable remarks he might say, "There, now you see that I'm right. But if you like I can instantly prove the opposite." (Sometimes he really does say that, and is as good as his word, which is terrible.) Kurt waits until Paul speaks up again.

"Lisa dabbles in the sewage more enchantingly than almost any other girl I know. When a man is young and silly—and you can take that as you like—he can even love her too. It doesn't matter. It will pass off."

"A very original saying."

"Hush. If I get original you won't understand me at all. Anyone who wants to be understood must steer clear of originality. Great Thoughts of Paul Weismann, number 408. The very fact that so many people dislike the Porta Pia makes

172

it almost certain that it's the greatest thing Michelangelo ever created. And no one but Michelangelo knows why—well, what I meant to say was: one can love Lisa. But not the way you do. You don't love her the right way."

"What do you mean by that?"

"Nothing."

"Well, you certainly succeeded there."

Paul grins. Kurt's readiness to rise to the bait obviously pleases and stimulates him. But he means well.

"You're the youngest, put the light out. I don't like looking at your rosy boyish face."

Now it is dark in the room. Slanting moonlight falls only into one corner.

"I mean," says Paul, and Kurt can tell from his voice that his eyes are closed, "you're not doing her any favour by being in love."

"I don't understand you."

"And no one would expect you to, but you will in a minute. Listen—" (Paul turns abruptly to face Kurt) "I strongly suspect that you haven't slept with her yet."

Kurt does not reply. He knows that Paul didn't mean to cast aspersions on his virility or anything like that. It is something quite different. Something unknown until now, to Kurt anyway, that is shaking the foundations of his ideas.

Paul's voice makes its way through the darkness again.

"I'm not asking you out of curiosity or prurience, or any personal interest, so I ask you straight out, in the plainest words there are for it: have you had Lisa Berwald yet?"

Kurt is startled. Something unguessed at begins to dawn on him. What Paul says has something magnetically enticing

about it, if he could grasp it, suggests intoxicating triumph…
"the kneeling queens await the victor in the tent"… isn't that
in a poem by Heine? "To Youth"? And—this surprises Kurt
most—he sees nothing bad or wrong in it.

"I'll point out that in any case I must answer your question
with No. Take that however you like."

"So you haven't had her yet," says Paul, calmly and firmly.

And at that moment Kurt knows that he himself can't go
to wherever Paul gets his calm superiority. Not yet. Maybe
he will later, if necessary. But not now.

He takes a deep breath. The attack has been repelled.
Happiness has overcome.

A sense of satisfaction takes him over so powerfully that
he doesn't hear what Paul says next.

"That's a great mistake. You won't get anywhere that way.
It's all very well that you aim higher with her than most do,
and no one could begrudge her that. Something could be
made of Lisa. But you can reshape only what you possess.
You can't plough a field before it's your own. Incidentally,
how long have you been in love with her?"

Kurt does hear that question.

"Almost a year, Mr Investigating Magistrate, if you must
know."

"Then there's no going back for you anyway."

"Going back where?" asks Kurt, baffled. Nor does he
understand why Paul turns on his other side, with a reluctant
growl, and wishes him good night.

Kurt hasn't finished yet. He feels, in a way, drunk with
victory, he thinks he has achieved the same success as he
did with Weinberg, success that he now remembers with
a smile.

"Paul!"

"Oh, let me get some sleep."

"I only want to ask you something else. I suppose you think Lisa is the kind of girl you have to sleep with at once?"

"It all depends who's doing it. And not necessarily at once, but soon. You'll never get Lisa."

"Are you so sure of that?" asks Kurt, amused.

"Yes. But anyway it doesn't matter now."

And when Kurt says nothing more for some time, Paul Weismann suddenly turns to him, places one hand on his head, and says with a warmth of which Kurt would never have thought him capable, and which therefore moves him very much, "You're going to get a great surprise, my dear fellow. A great surprise."

The next morning, when the white-clad waitress comes over to their breakfast table with a huge tray and says "Eight of you, right?" Otto Engelhart says, "No, only seven, one of the ladies is having breakfast in her room today." Then, turning to the concerned questioners, he says, "It's nothing much, Lisa pulled a muscle; her ankle is slightly swollen and she thought she'd stay in bed today. Nothing to worry about."

Hilde Fischer stands up and says firmly that she won't be going with them today either.

She'd be doing Lisa no favours by staying behind, objects Otto Engelhart. Lisa wouldn't like that at all, and had asked him to make sure none of the others spoilt their day on her account. If she needed anyone, he'd stay here with her.

Hilde sees the point of that, if reluctantly, the others also say they're happy with the arrangement, and they set off.

No doubt about it, something is missing. There is a slight but perceptible sense of depression. But, as soon as the downhill run begins, that is overcome. Only Kurt, when they are about level with the little resort, feels a strong wish to unstrap his skis and go back to the hotel. He thinks of running into a tree to give himself an excuse.

"Watch what you're doing, for God's sake!" he hears Boby's voice close behind him. But his right leg is already high in the air, he tries in vain to straighten it, the weight is too great, his body tips backwards as he slides on, uncontrolled, he somersaults, rolls a few metres sideways… and then he is head down in the snow. It is like having a cold sponge pressed over his mouth; he has lost all sense of exactly where his limbs are.

At last he gets to his feet (on his own, because helping a fallen skier up is the kind of thing that Sunday skiers do), and looks around, dazed. Far below him, at the bottom of the slope where the woods begin, Willi Wagenschmid is also coming to a halt by abruptly swerving to one side, shouting something up; the others are standing some way off, behind and to his left one ski is sticking out of the snow, its point dug in, and to his right Boby, who has fallen too, is angrily brushing snow off himself.

The language of skiers, which is basically no more eccentric than other kinds of human language, calls a fall like that "bringing down a star".

Kurt has brought down a star, then, and a large star at that. For the rest, his limbs—he doesn't know whether to be glad or ashamed—are all intact.

With a good deal of difficulty, he straps his ski on again, and skis on downhill in wide, exploratory hairpin bends. As he does so, he gradually remembers how the fall came to happen, and now he really doesn't know what he ought to do.

At the bottom of the slope, Willi receives him with some forthright remarks. "I'd very much like to send you straight home. This is disgraceful. A little pimple like that—" And, shaking his head, he points to the slope, falling steeply away; by no means just a pimple, it is a hill of considerable size.

Kurt stands there sheepishly, unable to say anything much.

"Don't shout at the poor man like that!" says Hilde Fischer, the peacemaker. "Maybe he's hurt himself."

"What?" growls Willi, but he is concerned. "Have you hurt yourself?"

Here's my chance, thinks Kurt. Careful, now.

"Hurt myself? No. At least, I can't feel anything wrong yet."

Willi looks at him and says, kindly enough, "I don't want to offend you, but you'd do better to go back to the resort now rather than later. I'd think you can see that for yourself."

Kurt puts on a great show of remorse while Willi shows him the way on the map. Being able to get away so unobtrusively puts him in a curiously undecided mood, he could think about things like chance and providence now—but the others are already wishing him a good journey back, and parting from him, so he must set out himself, and watch the way he is going…

His real feelings then erupt, and remain almost inexplicable. Kurt has never been able to explain to himself why he suddenly turned and followed the group with feverish haste. He was almost weeping with joy when he saw them ahead of him.

And he would probably also have wept—but not for joy—if he had ever learnt that at the same time Lisa Berwald was standing naked in front of the full-length mirror on the wall of her heated room, stroking her hips with trembling fingers, and that the first thoughts to pass through her mind led for the first and the last time to the body of Kurt Gerber...

Then Lisa Berwald fell asleep, and when she woke she told herself she was being irresponsible and careless. Her determination was firmer, her love for Kurt Gerber gentler and, in her opinion, purer than ever.

But Kurt Gerber never knew any of this. Even if he had had an opportunity of doing so, unexpected circumstances stood in the way.

"Lisa says would you visit her," says Otto Engelhart after dinner that evening.

Kurt is slightly startled and a little pleased, and anyway rises without haste and asks, "How is she?"

"She's fine. She'll be fit again tomorrow."

On the stairs, Kurt thinks how different it would have been if she had sent her message through the waiter. It occurs to him that there is something insultingly unconcerned about the free and easy way Lisa summons him to come and see her.

Lisa is lying in bed, her head on a pile of pillows like a fine fruit lying on its own in a handsome dish, so that you can all the better see how delicious it is. She is wearing white silk pyjamas, and the quilt on the bed is white too. A picture of tender, cool purity, driving away all thoughts of the body under the quilt.

"So here's the great man! Has to be asked to come and see a lady! You'd never have thought of visiting me of your own accord!"

Although she says that jokingly, and puts her hand out to Kurt, he takes it as a serious and well-deserved reproach; no, it wasn't right of him, his secret diplomacy is now revealed to the light of day. He says, awkwardly:

"You must forgive me—I came a terrible cropper on the way down today, what they call bringing down a star, and I'm still feeling the effects a bit."

"Dear me!" cried Lisa, horrified.

"It's nothing, really. How's your poor ankle?"

"There." Lisa brings her foot out from under the quilt.

Intentionally, or just unconcerned again? He leans over and examines the ankle carefully, like a doctor. Lisa flexes her instep; her leg is now a single perfect line… Kurt's lips move over the slender ankle.

"Oh, you!" She laughs, and her foot withdraws under the quilt.

And because she is still laughing, and because her mouth is so red and her teeth so white…

But then she closes her lips and turns her head firmly aside, so that Kurt immediately stops short, abashed.

"No, don't!" she says pleadingly. "Someone might come in." It reassures him slightly that she said "someone", not "Otto".

Kurt sits on the edge of the bed, saying nothing.

Suddenly he feels Lisa's hand gently caressing his. He looks up. "I'm no good, Lisa."

She presses his hand more firmly. "That's not true."

"But it's not my own doing. It's this dreadful, inborn urge: I mean the two of us, young and alone in a room—do you understand me? I'm afraid of being laughed at."

And suddenly he moves quickly forward, looks intently at her face and asks in an anxious whisper, "Don't you sometimes laugh at me, Lisa?"

Lisa lies there quietly. Then she moves a little way back, very gently, and looks frankly into his face, "Why do you think I'd do that?"

"You don't, Lisa? And you never will laugh at me, never?"

"Oh, go on with you—how silly you are!"

And that is all. They begin chatting lightly…

Nothing looks as incredible as true innocence. So perhaps we should avoid detecting it now—it is ten o'clock already—however cheerful and superficial their conversation is.

"It's time I went."

Kurt takes one of her hands, then the other, and puts his hot face between the cool backs of her hands. Then he turns so that his cheeks lie between the soft flesh of her hands as if in a comfortable pillow, and she keeps her hands firmly pressed to his mouth.

And then it is that Lisa says the greatest words of her life, softly, hesitating, like a child putting the ungainly words of a foreign language together in a brief sentence for the first time, a sentence brimming with understanding, revealing unknown depths—she says:

"I love you very much, too."

It is past midnight when Kurt returns to the inn from his walk through the silent streets of the little resort.

His room is on the first floor. He slowly climbs the creaking wooden staircase, turns into the dimly lit corridor—when Otto Engelhart suddenly materializes in a doorway, leaning against the doorpost, looking past him but looking at him as well. It is a little unsettling. Kurt stops.

"You went to see Lisa?" asks Otto Engelhart, but still not looking him in the face.

"Yes," says Kurt frankly. "You asked me to go yourself."

The other man nods slowly, as if thinking hard. Then he turns his face to Kurt, swings around abruptly, goes through the doorway and lets the door latch behind him.

Kurt watches, shaking his head, and is about to go on, but something he saw in Otto's face holds him back. He is in a good, calm mood; maybe he can do something about this dark figure, who seems so hard that he might hurt himself on his own sharp edges.

Curiously, Kurt opens the door.

Otto Engelhart is lying across the bed on his stomach, turned away from him, his head and arms hanging limp over the other side of the bed. All at once a long shiver runs through his body.

Shaken himself, Kurt stands there. Is the unemotional Otto actually weeping?

He goes carefully up to the bed, leans over the man lying there, and gently touches his shoulder.

Otto Engelhart sits up, staring at him as if he were a ghost. "What do you want?"

Kurt sits down on the bed beside him. "Otto—"

Until now he has avoided addressing Otto by his first name, and he is bewildered to find himself doing it now. Uncertainly, hastily, he begins to speak. "Don't be childish,

181

what's got into your head? It would hurt me if you were upset because I went to see Lisa. I mean, you know me, you know who I am." That was ridiculous; he goes on faster, yes, he admits that he is not indifferent to Lisa, he has never made any secret of it, on the contrary, he will say so to anyone, and for that very reason—Kurt doesn't know quite what to say to get Otto responding—"You really don't have to be jealous on account of me, Otto!"

Embarrassed, he gets to his feet and walks up and down the room a couple of times. Then he stops in front of Otto, who is still staring at the floor.

"Jealous?" says Otto Engelhart with a strange smile, taking a deep breath. "I wish to God there was something to be jealous about."

Kurt is looking at him in surprise.

"That's right, no need to wonder. But it's not my fault. Jealous? She doesn't love anyone. No one. Not me. Not you. No one. I give her all I have. Someone will come along and give her more. But she doesn't take it. Jealous…"

He has spoken these words jerkily, they are simple but still not clear. Kurt has some inkling of what is upsetting him, and would like to comfort him—then Otto laughs hoarsely and says, "Please go now."

And as Kurt gives him his hand, warmth comes into his eyes and his voice.

"I respect you. Not for what you may think. Cleverness? Talent? None of that matters. But you may be a real human being. And that's something. A young man called Kurt Gerber. That's something."

Otto Engelhart falls silent, and Kurt stands there with his hand held out, forgetting to withdraw it, for all this leaves him confused, his mind in turmoil. He tries to tell himself that Otto's words are nothing but truisms—but he feels something like awe for the man who uttered them so harshly and with such certainty, as if they had never been expressed before.

Kurt lets his hand drop to his side. Otto does not notice; he nods as if to add something more, then suddenly pulls himself together. "Good night," he says, and guides Kurt to the doorway.

What Otto Engelhart said about Lisa matters more to Kurt than anything. He won't believe it. He knows Lisa better. Maybe if Otto had spoken to him like that four hours earlier—but now, after that "I love you very much, too…" She said "too", and yet he hadn't said a word about loving her; she didn't mean it as an answer, no, she understood that what Kurt feels for her is love, understood it and welcomed it and confirmed it—oh, he knows that Lisa is not as she appears, and he is glad that Otto didn't let him say more, he might have made him, poor Otto, very unhappy, Otto who has slept with Lisa so often but doesn't possess her, possesses nothing of her… Think how much richer I am, and so far I've only kissed her…

Paul is still awake, reading in bed. He grunts vaguely as Kurt comes in, and then asks what kept him out so late.

Kurt sits down opposite and looks straight at him. "I'm very happy."

Paul looks straight back and says, in the same tone of voice, "You're very foolish."

"Comes to the same thing!" laughs Kurt, who was expecting to hear something of that kind. If Paul only knew…

183

When the room is dark, Kurt cheerfully says, "Didn't you make the bold yet daring claim yesterday, Paul, that I would never have Lisa Berwald, though I love her?"

"I did."

"I believe I can assure you that you're wrong."

"I'm not wrong."

"Want to bet?"

"No, because it's perfectly possible that one of these days you may sleep with a girl who's identical with the aforesaid Lisa Berwald. Good night."

If Kurt had not felt so mindlessly happy, these last words would have given him something to think about. But he did feel mindlessly happy, and fell asleep looking forward to the morning, when for the first time he would wake up entirely for Lisa.

However, even before he had tasted the indescribable joy of that awakening to the full, the chambermaid brought him a letter that made him catch the next train home.

VII

Kurt Gerber, Number 7

O N THE WAY, Kurt kept reading the few lines that his
father had written to him:

My dear Kurt,

I happened by chance to be talking to one of your
teachers. On the grounds of this conversation, I consider
it urgently necessary for you to take the next train home,
where I will tell you everything else. I hope that even
though your holidays have been broken off early, you have
enjoyed them, and with warm greetings I am

Your father.

As he was to hear everything else soon, it was unnecessary
for him to worry about it now. Kurt wanted nothing to do
with school for as long as possible, was reluctant to accept
the imminence of next term as you might delay putting on a
heavy coat, although the warmth of autumn is indisputably
over. His reluctance was ferocious, but the prospects were
hopeless. Kurt forced himself into the focal point of the
slanting and now fading rays of warmth that had filled the
last few days. Lisa had finally confessed her love for him, her

emotion seemed to him now almost modest and humble; Paul Weismann spoke to him as no one ever had before, and the certainty with which he assumed that Kurt would understand him was good; while Otto Engelhart—hadn't he seemed like the younger of them when he bared his soul to Kurt, telling him all his emotions?

All this was so delightful and different and promising, Kurt relived it all so vividly, that he didn't notice the arrival of the train at its terminus until he found himself alone in the compartment.

And then, in view of the unfriendly apartment buildings lining the dirty streets, that other world was suddenly gone in the city air, now doubly unpleasant to him. Kurt paid the taxi driver with the resigned lordliness of a baron fallen on hard times. And when his father summoned him to his study, he sat down in apathetic expectation, just as he remembered feeling about his exams in the last few months of school: interest, if any, lay in when the inevitable humiliation would come, and what form it would take.

This time it came promptly and with shattering force. Professor Mattusch—he was the teacher to whom his father had talked—took a very pessimistic view of Kurt's situation at school; it was his opinion that only getting extra coaching from a private tutor as soon as possible could help him, and then only if from now on Kurt applied himself diligently to making up for all the time he had wasted. "I am sure that Mattusch means you well," concluded his father, "and he will certainly have good reasons for giving me this information privately. It turns out that your good resolutions when I wanted you to go to a different school were nothing but meaningless lies." Then his voice softened. "But I'm not going to read you the Riot Act now, I know that these things give you no pleasure. However, there's nothing else for it. Here is the address of Professor Ruprecht, whom you will go to see at ten tomorrow morning. He has said he is ready to start work with you at once, and revise all subjects with you in the days remaining before school begins again."

His father fell silent. Like a judge regretting a sentence that he has passed, but believing it is all for the best.

"It may all turn out well yet. If you would only make an effort! You know that I shall happily show my appreciation of that. On the day after you pass the *Matura*, you can board the train for Paris."

"Yes," said Kurt. Then he rose to his feet and went out of the room, dejected.

The next day he wrote the following letter:

My dear, kind father,

I don't know what else to do. I don't want to upset you by a confrontation in person, so I am choosing this way of telling you that all attempts to find me in the course of today will be useless. I am not going to see Professor Ruprecht, and—just to prevent all unnecessary anxiety on your part—I am not about to throw myself into the river either, or go to my death in any other way. Of course that would fit rather well into what has happened so far, and might not be without desirable effects, but I don't intend to take my views of the school to extremes. I think I would be doing it too much honour to give up a life that, thank God, has nothing in common with it. My hope of that real life—and nothing else—will help me to bring the next few months to a happy conclusion without a private tutor, in spite of all those like Kupfer, and pass the *Matura*. It's not all lost yet, and the stupid farce of this high-school study can hardly reach the point where I'm really declared unfit to pass the *Matura*. Please remember what our Headmaster said when he answered your fears, that time when I delivered my talk to the last Students' Academy, by protesting, "Oh, please! You can't mean that seriously! Who would be judged mature enough to pass the *Matura* if not your son?"

If you cannot approve of my decision to do without private coaching, then please make sure the door is locked when I come home at eleven this evening. I shall then try to show my maturity even without a duly stamped certificate.

In any case, I ask you not to see this step either as a hasty boyish prank or the product of my imagination, for which you have so often reproved me. It is the result of long thought. And if I am giving you such pain that you cannot parade me to our family and friends, that I deserve to be struck out of the family as your son who turned out badly—if all that is to be so then I want to be struck out of the family *entirely*. I would like to spare you and myself failure in an atmosphere where a failed school examination is regarded as a mortal shame.

Kurt

At eleven in the evening Kurt put his key in the lock with a steady hand; the door was not locked, and opened—but the chain was over it, leaving only a small gap through which the front hall was visible. There were lights on.

Then he heard footsteps, and the sound of the chain being taken off. His father stood there in a long, black dressing gown. He let Kurt past him, closed the door behind him, and went into the living room without a word. Kurt felt that his letter had not had the intended effect. And he also felt something else: anything you stage with elaborate ceremony falls flat when it is put into performance. He felt that nothing is quite as bad as it seems—but thus, in a way, twice as bad too.

There was a note on his bedside table:

I am glad to hear that you are firmly resolved, I believe in your good intentions, and I hope you are right to be so optimistic. But one thing I will tell you: if you think that life has nothing in common with school, you are mistaken.

Things were looking up. Kurt couldn't explain it to himself, but they were definitely looking up.

Borchert was the first to say so openly. "You appear to have seen reason, Gerber! And about time, too."

Next was Hussak: "There, you see, birdie? You could have done that all along. Very good, sit down." And as if guessing Kurt's opinion of such praise, he added, "Carry on like this for another five months, and then—!" That sounded comforting.

Kurt also successfully passed a test set by Riedl; Mattusch, Prochaska and Seelig had always been happy with his work, and it seemed as if Kupfer had entirely forgotten that there was a student called Gerber in the back row. Did he guess, or did he know, that now Kurt really wanted the teachers to notice him? That he was always well prepared? Maybe Kupfer really did have informers who told him everything, maybe he had learnt that those excellent students Altschul and Nowak had taken Gerber, a candidate for failure, under their wing, and were doing their preparation for class work and tests, which was well known to be conscientious, together with him.

It had not been easy for Kurt to decide, uninvited, to go and see Altschul at his home. However, one day when by chance he overheard him fixing a time with Nowak: "Right, then, come over to my place earlier today, Nowak, around three, and we'll go through the history and geography together"—then Kurt made up his mind to carry out his plan. Just after three in the afternoon he rang Altschul's bell, ignored the surprise that he encountered, and when he couldn't take any more of the two students' anxious diversionary tactics he said directly:

"Look, I don't want to take up any more of your time— please would you tell me, straight out, will you let me sit in on your studies? What worries me most is God Almighty Kupfer. You're both much better than me at his subjects, probably better than most of the others." (Here Kurt paused for a moment, and however ashamed he felt of his present pathetic course of action, he found that he could still despise his two flattered fellow students, who took themselves for mathematical geniuses, as they modestly demurred.) "I'm convinced that you could keep me above water if you agree. I know what bothers you, and I have to say you're not entirely wrong. But I promise you I wouldn't disturb the work we did together by cracking jokes or making demagogic speeches or anything. You know about my position at school—so you must be aware that I mean what I say seriously, and you know why I'm saying it to you."

At this Altschul waved his hand with a grand gesture at a chair: "Do sit down. Cigarette? Here. We're just beginning on the geometry homework for tomorrow. An inclined prism, its base ABCD being a parallelogram lying in the second plane of projection, has a lateral edge…"

Kurt Gerber had now been studying with the two model students for two weeks, day after day.

And when Kupfer began the important semester exams, when one day he put the small, black notebook down in front of him and slowly leafed through it, when a deathly hush had come over the classroom and many of the students held their breath and ducked down behind the back of the student in front, afraid that Kupfer's glance might fall on their names at that moment, when their paralysing expectation went on for ever, not ending yet, not yet, oh, let him go ahead and give me Unsatisfactory, I don't mind anything, just so long as I can get this chunk of rock off my chest—when they were trembling as they had in a hundred lessons before, Kurt Gerber raised his hand suddenly, heard his name at the same moment, and went up to the lectern in the firm knowledge that he would be up to today's test.

Kupfer recorded his correct answers with barely perceptible surprise. He ended Kurt's test by calling the next student up to the board, without any comment at all. The next student was Mertens. He got Unsatisfactory, and was not alone in that, which considerably enhanced the value of Kurt's achievement.

After the lesson he went, as usual these days, up to the front of the class to have a word with Altschul and Nowak. They congratulated him effusively, Schönthal asked, with some sarcasm, where all this knowledge of his had come

191

from, and Scholz murmured appreciatively, "No one could have worked out the axial affinity better." But Kurt wasn't listening; he was trying to pin down a memory that was raising its bony finger to admonish him, what was it… a night a long time ago, some dreadful night he had already seen and heard this, all of it… when had Scholz clapped him on the shoulder like that?… and then he remembered that it was the night at the beginning of the school year when he had argued with his father about staying at the school… and then he had fallen asleep full of ideas of the future that were oppressing him at the time… and now it had turned out like that…

Pale, with hunched shoulders, Kurt returned to the back row. Weren't they all staring at him, all those who had been marked Unsatisfactory today, Mertens, Lengsfeld, Lewy, Zasche, with sad looks and painfully twisted mouths? Weren't they saying, quietly and slowly and penetratingly, "Traitor"?

Weinberg made as if to shake his hand again.

"Kurt, what's the matter with you? Aren't you glad to have come up to scratch this time? Kurt!"

Kurt jumped, and stammered in confusion, "Yes—yes, you're right—very glad, yes."

"You're also crazy!" said Weinberg. "Come on, let's go and have a smoke in the toilets."

But, in spite of everything, Kurt Gerber sometimes realized, with horror, that a sense of comfortable satisfaction came over him when he gave the right answer, when a difficult question was asked, and the teacher enquired, looking round the class, "Well, who knows that? Benda—Schönthal—Brodetzky—Scholz—Gerber—no one? Ah, Gerber?" How horrible it was to be named in the same breath as those students, how much more horrible to be glad of it! Was there no way out of his dilemma?

He tried to find one in the classroom, and didn't. Instead, he found out that the low-achieving students, his former comrades in his battles and victories and defeats, were distancing themselves from him. It was almost a social shift. The proletarians of the class who got low marks and had so far been his faithful friends, while he himself was perhaps the only one to have found an impeccable compromise, let him know with bitter clarity that they thought he should be ashamed of his sudden change of direction. So be it. His uneasiness after his successful test by Kupfer had not deceived him. He *was* a traitor.

It did not occur either to them, who were now shunning him, or to Kurt himself, who felt that their present dislike of him was justified, that any single one of them (with the possible exception of Lewy) would have turned traitor in the same way if they had only been able to.

Mixing with the bright students was no good either. He would have liked to numb his feelings by getting on friendly terms with them—but they were cool to him; perhaps they didn't really trust him, thinking he wanted to join their select circle only to profit from them, or perhaps they thought he didn't really know enough, his reputation was too new and not yet established. He was out of place in both sets of students. And sometimes Kurt felt dismally abandoned, almost shunned like a leper.

For that reason, an event that affected the others only fleetingly shook him deeply. One day Benda was absent, and as he had never been away sick everyone noticed at once. When he did not turn up the next day either, some were already passing on rumours about a bad attack of flu; and the day after that, Professor Seelig told the eighth-year students in the first lesson that their fellow student Josef Benda had suddenly died yesterday. "Such an excellent fellow!" he murmured, as the class rose to their feet. Then he asked who had been particularly close to him.

And no one spoke up. Although they liked Benda, he had not been close to any of the eighth year, his death left no gaping void in anyone. Including Kurt. He had thought highly of Benda, he mourned him as a human being of obvious value. But that wasn't what troubled him most. He was suddenly made to think: if I die tomorrow—who here will stand up and say they were close to me? Who's particularly close to me now when I'm among them, we all suffer the same fate, we have for seven years, and I feel it more fervently than they guess? What am I to them except another alphabetical entry in the register? Gerber, Kurt, Number 7. There was no room for more. The staff wanted to reign over a body of students. The arabic numbers 1 to 32 give a roman numeral VIII. Benda, Josef, Number 2. Josef Benda, strong and calm, with eyes always looking inward—no one really knew him, no one was "particularly close to him".

It surprised everyone to see Kurt Gerber going around looking so upset today. Why? If he and Benda had been real friends, then he could have spoken up, surely? But that wasn't it. Perhaps Schönthal had been right in suspecting that Kurt Gerber was sad because Benda had promised to explain two questions for the next maths test at school, and all that had now fallen through. It didn't sound good, no one would have thought it of Kurt Gerber—but well, school was serious these days...

An icy, unfeeling chill all around… it couldn't go on like this.

Even as he made a plan involving Lisa, he was aware of commonplace morality souring quiet heroism and self-sacrifice, affecting good intentions and their happy conclusion. There was something rotten about it all.

"Lisa," he wrote, "I have to be with you, at once."

You should only put the essentials in a letter.

But days passed before her answer came, and days before he saw her—days, so much time, so little time—who knows that, we tumble helplessly back and forth, as if in a dream about flies—and then we emerge somewhere and nothing is as we expected—or else it is exactly as we expected, who knows?

They were standing outside the coffee house to which he had accompanied her, not quite knowing what else to say. Once again Lisa was acting if this were her first date with him, everything went its familiar way, she was expected by some relations, she said as soon as they met, she must be there in half an hour's time, and then it had gone on as before, meaningless chatter, not a word of any memories, not a word asking why Kurt had appealed to her and why now.

Total disappointment is so powerfully convincing that any hopes previously nurtured seem deranged. Astonishment—how could it have turned out like this?—is not quite the same. It is more like: how could I have believed that it would turn out any outer way?

"There we are."

"Yes. I see. Of course."

"Well, then…" She puts her hand out to him.

"It's snowing," says Kurt, crazily.

"Goodbye!" She's still there.

"Goodbye—but when, Lisa?"

"Yes, when. Wait a minute… We'll all be at Paul Weismann's studio next Sunday. Will you join us?"

"Yes, of course, but—"

"Right, then you'll have to phone him, will you? We'll see each other up in his studio, then. Goodbye, Kurt."

And then her hand has gone, and so has she, and Kurt is still standing there open-mouthed.

It is snowing.

Better this way. What kind of "help" did he really imagine she was to bring him? Not the way she's suddenly beginning to take an interest in the school again. Asking him question after question about it. That was all he needed. How did your last maths exam turn out? What mark did you get for your French test? Terrible.

No, Lisa can't help him like that. How pathetic! His love would suddenly be just a schoolboy infatuation again.

Kurt stamps his feet. Only now does he notice how cold he is.

It is still snowing.

But once you have come to terms with the cold, the snow is a gift, falling gently and consolingly as if to show that cold can be more than just cold.

Kurt has come to terms with the cold. And it's good that snow is falling.

The snowflake falling on his lips is like a cool, fleeting kiss. A goodbye kiss.

He looks up at the falling snow, and his glance takes in the black sky and reappears on the clouded glass panes of the café windows, and glides down to the ground with a large, white snowflake like a many-pointed star.

Goodbye, Lisa.

Is there no hope for him, no hope?

Yes, there is one hope. He just has to make do with what he has. If he tries hard it will be all right.

His father. He is so happy when Kurt tells him about a success at school. It's enough to make anyone weep.

"There, you see, Kurt. I knew you wouldn't put me to shame. Keep up the good work, do your old father that pleasure."

Yes, my dear father, I will. Although I don't know that a scrap of paper with an official stamp on it means happiness. We carefully hang it on the wall, and never really need it again, and I have the impression that you don't entirely believe it means happiness either—but I can see it would be bad for you if your only son failed his *Matura*. No, my dear father, that won't happen. And in a few days' time we'll get our half-year reports, and there won't be a single Unsatisfactory on mine this time.

It is only of his father that Kurt is thinking when he goes up to the lectern and is handed the stiff, bluish paper with the familiar text, showing a pre-printed column of subjects on the left, and another column for the marks on the right, always filled in, in regular handwriting, by the class teacher… oh no, this is a silly joke… what curious words emerge when you put a few random letters together side by side… un-sa-tis-fac-tory… Unsatisfactory… mathematics, Unsatisfactory… descriptive geometry, Unsatisfactory…

funny, what on earth does it mean… probably nothing, nothing at all… the letters just don't belong together… they dance around… or no, there they stand up straight again and side by side: Unsatisfactory…

"Is there anything you want, Gerber? No? Then go back to your place."

Yes. Sorry. Is there anything I want? I'm going already. No.

The others take the piece of paper from his hand, read it and give it back to him in silence. Why should they say anything, when he himself is perfectly calm and composed?

Calm and composed. That's right. Not in the least upset or regretful. This piece of paper has no effect. It leaves him indifferent. Exactly.

And Kurt listens to Kupfer's comments with an expression of civil interest on his face.

The marks have turned out really very much as might have been expected, says Kupfer in an offhand manner, no better and no worse than suited the students' proven achievements. It was, he added, certainly unfortunate that seven students must be regarded as having an overall negative result, but although this half-year report, as the last before the *Matura*, does have special significance, its verdict is not yet final.

Kurt sizes up the students sitting there from the way they look. Who are the seven? But all of them are looking gloomy. The gravity of the moment demands it.

To be sure, Kupfer goes on in a rather firmer voice, to be sure those judged Unsatisfactory in the first half of the year will have great difficulties ahead of them. They had better recollect in good time that they are now in their eighth year, are they not? At that point you should devote the whole year to going full steam ahead. It would be ridiculous to assume that one or two better marks in tests just before the reports were delivered could retrieve the situation. (He means me, thought Kurt, no one else, he means me.) That, says Kupfer, would be too comfortable. He had, of course, seen through these tactics on the part of certain gentlemen. (Here Kurt has to smile: a nice name for me. I am "certain gentlemen".) It ought by now to be obvious that no one could deceive Professor Kupfer! (But no one tried to, Professor Kupfer, sir! I've learnt my lesson, sir! Four or five hours a day with those model students Altschul and Nowak, then a few more hours at home alone and in break, and I was always well prepared, sir!) As he had said, there was no final decision yet, that wouldn't come until after the final exam. The humble could be raised up; those on high could be laid low.

Ha, ha, ha, chuckle the self-appointed laughers.

"Well, you know what you have to do. Work! Or else!…"

He would have liked to hold out the prospect of slavery rather than work, and to add a chilly threat to that "Or else!…" But the way he suddenly breaks off and strides out of the classroom is very effective in itself.

The slaves, herded together there, wait in meek torment for their lord and master, who knows no mercy, to remove himself.

Some of the favoured, perhaps chosen to be overseers, are rubbing their hands. Others, condemned to damnation already, stagger away from their desks and are surprised to find that they can still walk anywhere they like.

You might expect them to crowd together, united by the same fears. But no; they avoid one another. No one wants to stand on the same bottom step as the others, each wants to be the one student to be spared that shame.

"The most vicious thing of all was what he did to Scheri," says Hobbelmann, who has an Unsatisfactory himself, but only in French.

"I wouldn't say so myself!" Schönthal has the nerve to say that out loud. He is seething with anger because his column of Very Goods has actually been disfigured by a mere Good in mathematics. It would have been so delightful—Benda being dead—for Schönthal to be the only one marked Very Good in all subjects. Damn Kupfer!

The identity of those predicted to fail gradually emerges. And while other students surround them, while gloomy and useless assumptions cast their shadow, in another corner Pollak is engaged in fierce argument with Brodetzky, hissing furiously in his face that he doesn't deserve his Very Good, and owes it only to the patronage he has had, while Scholz stands listening and nodding his large hippopotamus head—well, yes, very annoying, it has to be admitted…

Kurt's mother herself opens the door to him, putting a finger to her lips. Then she takes Kurt into his room and sits down opposite him. Only now does Kurt see that her eyes are red with weeping.

Father must have died, he thinks, and the room seems to sway around him. Now nothing matters. Nothing.

He waits to hear it.

But his mother raises her head and asks, carefully controlling her voice, what his report is like.

As if that mattered now! Is she trying to spare him?

"Why have you been crying, Mother?"

"Me—"

But then she bursts into torrents of tears again, and from her broken, stammered remarks Kurt gathers that—that his father is not dead. He has only had a very severe heart attack, with his stertorous breath coming short; little veins burst with the strain of it and he spat blood, but now he has had an injection and Dr Kron is with him.

His father is alive. So it isn't true that nothing matters now. Far from it.

How low I've sunk—down to animal level! I rejoiced—I actually rejoiced to think that now none of it would matter. Oh, God in heaven, thank you!

Kurt has a solemn vision of himself in a long black robe, a figure of priestly stature, arms outspread, saying in a loud voice, "In the face of death, may the school be thrice accursed! All evil comes from the school!" The priest raises and lowers his arms three times. Then he has gone. (Not for ever. He did appear to Kurt once more, but that was much later, and everything was different.)

Kurt looks up and sees that his mother is still in tears. He goes over to her and caresses her, a little clumsily. "It will be all right."

Slowly, his mother calms down and dries her tears. "But you haven't told me about your report yet!"

"So I haven't!" With forced laughter, Kurt considers what to say. "Well, this will make you laugh: I have two marks of Unsatisfactory from Kupfer." And he takes out the paper and acts as if he really expected his mother to laugh with him.

His mother has collapsed into sobs again. "Dear God!" she whispers with trembling lips. "And his first question was: where's the boy with his report? What's to be done now, what's to be done now?…"

Kurt paces up and down the room as if a thousand devils were after him. He doesn't know what to say. His breath sounds like a croak.

In the hall outside, a man's voice is heard asking for the lady of the house.

Kurt's mother wipes her face a couple of times, hastily straightens her clothes and goes out. Kurt follows, since she leaves the door open.

Well, says Dr Kron, at least the worst is over, the patient has had another injection and now he is asleep. If anything happens they must phone him at once, whatever the time of day.

With a faint whimper, his mother disappears.

"Kurt," says the doctor, his voice husky, "make sure your father has peace and quiet over the next few days. Absolute peace and quiet. No excitement, nothing at all to agitate him. I can say this to you, I know: his heart wouldn't stand up to another attack like that. Do you understand me? Well then, I'll be off—or is there anything else you want to ask?"

"Yes—doctor, you say nothing to agitate him—only the reports were given out at school today, and—"

"And what?"

"The reports—at school—"

"Yes, yes, what about it?"

"And I'm going to have to tell him that—well, in short, I have two marks of Unsatisfactory, and that's sure to agitate him."

Agitate him? Why? Dr Kron asks, perplexed. Two marks of Unsatisfactory, yes, but that's nothing to worry about, least of all when a man has just had a close encounter with the Grim Reaper.

202

"But my father thinks if I get marks like that, I'm going to fail the *Matura*!"

"Oh, come along! Fail the *Matura*! That's a good joke! Ho, ho!" Dr Kron claps him benevolently on the shoulder. "Don't you worry, Kurt, I'll soon talk your father out of any such notions. You'll have to tell him, of course—but you just leave it to me to see that he doesn't make a great drama out of such a little thing!"

With this, Dr Kron shakes hands with Kurt and nods to him, amusement in his eyes wrinkling up the little folds of skin around them. He seems to find the idea really entertaining.

"Fail the *Matura*!" he repeats at the door, with an air of comic concern. "Whoever heard anything like it?"

Kurt could have embraced him. At long last, someone with a healthy outlook.

He goes back into his room.

There's the chair where his mother sat in tears. There is the report. Mathematics: Unsatisfactory. Descriptive geometry: Unsatisfactory. There is his desk with exercise books and textbooks and the other musty old study aids lying on it, there is his diary up on the wall, with the note "Afternoon, Kupfer" written in for days ahead in the Afternoon columns. That is all it takes to make his healthy outlook fall sick again.

And in another room his father's breath is still gasping after the struggle with death that he so narrowly survived.

Where's the boy with his report?

VIII

The Hard Path to Failure

Too many doubtful glances were turned on Kurt these days. And he lost what had so far enabled him to defy all dangers: his spirit of contradiction. He was not resigned, he still took an interest in his fate, and that was the worst of it; he would agree with everyone who came along and put his oar in, giving advice or an opinion, with hope or with concern, with condescension or pomposity—he would let anyone convince him for the moment. Indifference still amounts to something like an opinion of your own, although of the most makeshift nature. Kurt didn't even have that.

Someone might come along expressing horror: "For Heaven's sake, what's all this I hear about your poor showing at school—you're not actually going to fail the *Matura*, are you?" Another might come along and tell him, "Don't lose heart, it will be all right!" Yet another might come out with downright malicious mockery—"Fancy that, clever Kurt Gerber, prodigy that he was, can't even do as well as thousands of average students!" Another would express lofty consolation: "Think nothing of it, plenty of important people have failed exams in their time!" Yet another might say, "You'll do it!" and the next comer would say, "You'll never do it." And always whoever happened to be speaking to him seemed to make the only valid point. Kurt would listen and nod. "Yes, of course, that's how it is, you're right, how could I have thought?..." And five minutes later the next to speak to him would be right.

So he staggered through the day, zigzagging between many positive and many negative opinions, none of them his own. It could happen that he stood in front of a teacher testing him with lips compressed, giving no answers—and then, in fear and trembling, ask the same teacher at the end of the lesson not to give him an Unsatisfactory, he had had a headache that made him unable to say a single word.

But worst of all, he had to convince himself of his own lies. And it takes seven more lies to atone for one. Seven again and again. No one could take the burden of a single lie from his shoulders. They were all too busy with their own lies.

So he went on lying to himself, and lying to his father, who was gradually improving and was full of hope for a complete recovery. With some shameless thinking on the subject, Kurt managed to present the two marks of Unsatisfactory so that they almost looked like a guarantee of passing the *Matura*, and he did not sweat as he described a conversation with Kupfer... Believe it or not, Father, but he gave me those two marks of Unsatisfactory just for form's sake, because I was so weak in his subjects at the beginning of the year. His own words—forgive me—were: "I'd prefer, and I expect you would prefer it too, for you to do badly during the early part of the semester and then be authorized to take the *Matura*, rather than for me to hand you a mark of Satisfactory now, and thus maybe lull you into a sense of security, unreliable and light-minded as you are, Gerber..." Yes, he assured his father, that was what Kupfer had said, it was indeed surprising, but the main thing was that it almost meant a guarantee, and so it did.

His father said, "Hmm," and sounded a little suspicious, but as Kurt went on from lie to lie, putting together an ever stronger chain of evidence, he let his doubts drop and forced himself to believe in it. He was feeling tired himself.

But one day clouds seemed to hang low and heavy over the dining table at lunch, and when his mother left the room and his father immediately began, "Why have you been telling me lies?" Kurt knew what had happened. His father had made enquiries at school.

Out of pure helplessness, Kurt raised his eyebrows, pretending not to understand. "But what—"

"You failed in Kupfer's subjects."

Kurt clung to the crumbling remains of his lie. "You can't very well call it failing in the middle of the school year—and then, as I told you—"

"Yes. As you told me. And did you tell me that you had a detention and forged my signature?"

Kurt did not reply.

"You tell lies," said his father. "You forge signatures. You deceive me and others. You go behind my back. What am I to do with you?"

That last sentence was spoken in a loud, trembling voice, and it was a genuine question. His father sat there waiting for an answer. His clenched fist hammered up and down rapidly on the table top, his lips were narrowed and his breath came fast.

No agitation—his heart wouldn't stand up to another attack like that—fail the *Matura*—that's a good joke. Why does he take it so seriously? Why does he force himself to get agitated? He doesn't have to.

Kurt almost felt contempt, even hatred for his father. Only for a moment, but that was enough.

He leant against the wall, pale, with his head thrown back. His fingers sought support and didn't find it.

His father had risen to his feet as well. He was shaking, and his words shook too, as if his whole body was uttering them.

"You don't know what you're doing—there I stand in front of that nobody Kupfer like a prisoner in the dock—I dare not look into his eyes. So your fine son forges signatures, he's going from bad to worse. I have to put up with that, damn you—what's to become of you? I had to lie myself, say, Oh yes, I hadn't remembered at once, but that was my signature, I said. You—aren't you ashamed of yourself, deeply ashamed?…"

His father had come closer and closer, and Kurt retreated slowly to the door. No, he was not ashamed of himself, he felt nothing. His feelings were dulled, he heard the words and could not take in their meaning, saw his father's hand slowly rise in the air before him and then drop again without knowing what it meant, and then he was standing by the door, opening it, went unsteadily up to his room, stared at his books like a calf staring at the slaughterer's axe, was suddenly in his hat and coat, wandering along the cold streets, taking an interest in the most insignificant things—and then it all went abruptly through his brain, he recapitulated, he was living through the story of his life, which did not run: "In his family circle, Kurt Gerber would sometimes talk about his schooldays, and his experiences of the time." Although he didn't know why, it was more along the lines of: "And suddenly Kurt was standing outside the building where Lisa lived—but not right outside it, and he didn't want to go in, he didn't want anything… would it always be like this? Always? Why was it all happening? The days were waiting for him, tomorrow, and the day after, and every day they were waiting for him, waiting to intercept him and send him on, each to the next day, the days were playing catch with him, going round and round in circles, never-ending circles…"

Kurt gave up his private studies with Altschul and Nowak. Their differences of opinion began when he stopped paying attention to the other two and made jokes in reply to their corrections. Then he imitated the teachers, would suddenly make an eloquent speech attacking the shameful life of secondary education, embarked on boring mathematical debates, only to cut them suddenly short by observing that nothing mattered anyway—until one day Altschul rather brusquely faced him with the alternatives of working with them as he had at first, or not coming any more. This conclusion was not unwelcome to Kurt, who got to his feet with an air of offence, flung all the contempt at the two model students that it is possible to fling at model students, and slammed the door behind him without a goodbye. After that he felt curiously relieved, as if he had brought something to an end, and it was some time since he had managed to do that; it restored his own freedom and resolution again, and allowed him to see more than merely himself.

Hundreds of things happened in a single day, hour after hour, and you didn't know why, or what the outcome would be. If they represented the result of certain considerations, what were the links in the chain? What was achieved by marking Zasche Unsatisfactory? Zasche, who would plod through life impassive as a beast of burden, who needed a *Matura* certificate for some kind of professional post waiting ready for him, Zasche who never did anything to hurt anyone, and was no more superfluous in the world than thousands of others who were full of their own importance. What good would it do anyone for Mertens to stand in front of the blackboard white as chalk, while he was given time to think about something he had never understood? Where was it all going? Why were students who all sat here together in their first year, many long years ago, all on a par at the time—why were they now divided up, sorted out, identified more clearly than they wanted to be identified themselves? Very well, so admittedly one had more talent than another, one would use it better than another, was more successful, was marked Very Good, and the other was not. But Unsatisfactory? Not Satisfactory? Who deserves to be told, "You are not satisfactory"? Who had given the teaching staff, and every one of its members, the right to determine the course of the students' lives for decades to come? To make the inviolable decision, once and for all, that this one could reach for the future complacently, sure that nothing would go wrong for him, while that one collapsed and crouched, a shipwrecked sailor on a desert island, surrounded by a desolate sea, desperately looking out to see if a little white dot wouldn't appear on the inexorably regular horizon, a little white dot that might mean mercy or chance or delusion?

The professors looking askance behind their official-looking glasses have their argument ready: "Those who are not suitable for high school shouldn't be there." Fair enough. But who decides on suitability? Let's come to you, Professor So-and-so, sir. Who knows what your verdict would have been on this or that student if you, sir, forgive my mentioning it, had moved your bowels more easily on a certain day, or if your wife, sir, had not burnt the morning coffee? And even assuming that you came to your decision objectively and conscientiously—what would happen if the whole teaching staff were changed, and another set of professors were brought in to make the decisions? Is it quite impossible that Brodetzky might fail, and Hobbelmann pass with distinction? And further assuming that, even so, as providence will have it, Hobbelmann fails and Brodetzky passes with distinction—what does that prove? That Hobbelmann is unsuitable? That he never ought to have gone to high school at all?

Did you, Professor So-and-so, sir, ever ask anyone if you ought to become a teacher? If you were suitable? And would you then have submitted meekly to a negative decision that, like yours now, could have been the result of a mosquito bite?

Probably not. And no one can expect it. You have won the right on paper to be a professor in roughly the same way as you now cause others to win the right on paper to leave school with a *Matura* certificate. And those to whom you owe that right have won it in the same way, and those before them too, and so on, back and back… that's enough. There could be only one way out: for the embryo to say whether it ought to come into the world at all. Absurd, don't you agree? But if that possibility did exist—who, who, who would have the right to tell the embryo it wasn't suitable to be born?

And who has the right to tell a young man who is alive, and may already be able to point to some achievement of his own—stopping a runaway horse, refraining from crushing a flower—whose only wish is to live through a certain part of his life, on which he embarked when he had no will of his own, but was wax in the hands of those who sent him to school and those to whom he was sent; whose existence makes your own possible, gives it a point, because you would not be a professor without him; whose every breath earns him the right to draw the next, just like the rest of us, but who has many more breaths to draw ahead of him than you do—who has the right to tell such a young man, "You're not suitable!" because he has forgotten a formula, or a historical date, or the future perfect tense of a verb? Who has the right to cast the first stone, a stone falling into the smooth surface of his youth where the stone sinks deep, making ripples run out from his soul to the shores of torment and back to his soul again; circles that will be imprinted on him for ever, unless the great circle forms that reaches beyond the shore and into death—does every chance-come schoolteacher have that right?

We can't change world affairs, neither you, Professor So-and-so, sir, member of salaried class number such-and-such, nor I, Kurt Gerber, student number such-and-such in the register. But I can try to convince you of your nonentity, to get you to see that you have to leave the wretched blind alley into which you have sent so many people on their way through life, and do it as unobtrusively as possible. It's your fault that it is a blind alley, because when we met you we were willing to take a more pleasant path, and it was up to you to lead us, but you led us into the blind alley; we have now fled from it, averting our faces, into the wide road—and whether I get away unscathed or not, whether I fail or not, these are my last months at school. Oh yes, I'll soon make up for what I missed. But not in the way you expect.

Kurt openly began making new overtures of friendship to those who were predicted to fail.

Each of the six who had scored fail marks during the semester bore the burden of his fate in his own way. Zasche didn't seem to understand what was going on around him. Duffek, who was considered one of the worst of the grovellers and who addressed the teachers in the most circumlocutory of terms, redoubled his servility, scurried busily about Kupfer, helped him out of his coat, moved his chair to the best angle for him, even tried—perhaps unconsciously—to arouse liking by holding out his forefinger and middle finger in a painfully correct manner when he responded to the reading of the register, instead of just raising his hand like everyone else. Mertens had been felled by his fate as if a tree had fallen on him at the roadside; he didn't know what had hit him, and why did it have to be him anyway? He went on studying and paying attention in class, but when he put up his hand to answer a question, and was called on to do so, he was so scared even to give his name that he stumbled over his words and really did deserve a reproof. Severin wrapped himself in gloomy silence, but uttered mysterious hints about influential personages who would intervene against Kupfer on his behalf, and although no one believed his chatter they listened to it readily, with much wishful thinking. Lengsfeld, who had already had to stay down in the sixth-year class, began cursing vociferously when the conversation came round to Kupfer—sometimes it amounted to a fit of frenzied rage—and had to be comforted by assurances that surely Kupfer wouldn't keep him down again, such a thing had never happened before… and Lewy, sitting in the back row, knew for certain that if such a thing had never happened before, then it was definitely going to happen now. Whether Lengsfeld would be the victim was not sure—but he, Lewy, wouldn't have bet a penny on his own chances.

Kurt Gerber belonged with these students. The really dim ones. They were followed, at a certain distance, by Hobbelmann who had failed in French, and Sittig who had failed in Latin. Linke, who owed an Unsatisfactory in natural history (which was of no importance) to the hostility of Professor Riedl, hardly counted as one of them.

It could not have been said that on the evidence they felt strongly bound together; they were not a company of condemned students to which Kurt ruefully returned after a brief defection. But in their smiles to each other after failing a test, their caustic jokes about their own misfortunes, their helpless grumbling about the major and minor tortures inflicted on them—yes, they had something in common here, and it was natural for Kurt to associate himself with it.

In Lewy he found a curious companion. Lewy had mastered a particularly black kind of gallows humour, intended to deprive his tormentors of any pleasure in their successful work of destruction. He was convinced, with good reason, that there was nothing he could do of his own accord to change his destiny, and that enabled him to watch his own downfall like a sardonic spectator. The impudence of his comments on his own poor answers was uncanny. And as it made no difference whether he was going to fail in only two subjects or all of them, he did not distinguish between the professors. He enjoyed it when Borchert, whose declared favourite he had been, brought himself, with difficulty, to give him an Unsatisfactory; he even managed to goad Hussak and Seelig into treating him badly. In that achievement he stood alone.

Around this time Kupfer decided to slaughter his victims in pairs. Perhaps two students would be able to answer more quickly than one, he said, and anyway it would be faster, he wouldn't have to waste so much time on the useless students and could keep more of it for the good, interesting specimens. This identification of what was good and interesting in some students, when it meant cruelly questioning the value of their own existence in others, aroused some indignation. The construction of an angle of inclination, the calculation of a differential quotient, things that could bring a student down—Kupfer thought them good and interesting, and there were certainly some who agreed with him. The question that had a student like Lengsfeld sweating with fear offered one like Brodetzky a welcome chance to shine. Black magic with special effects laid on! The gentlemen coming up from the audience when the conjuror summoned them to check that there was no deception, had to know all his tricks, or the great magician would reach into his inside pocket and triumphantly produce an Unsatisfactory.

Lewy developed a different idea of the situation. In time it became a sport; he collected bad marks as an athlete collects winners' medals. One day the fancy took him to compare the way Kupfer tested them in pairs to tennis matches. When he and Gerber were called up together, he whispered to Kurt on the way to the board that Kupfer, the world champion, was about to contest the men's doubles, with Lewy and Gerber on the other side of the net. "I forgot to practise at home," he whispered, adding, when he reached the lectern, "so we'll give him a two-point lead. Thirty-love to Kupfer!

Ready?" And so it went on through the test; Kurt often had trouble in suppressing his laughter. If he gave the right answer, Lewy would whisper behind him, "Well played, Scheri! Nice ground stroke! Advantage striker!" Kupfer asked him something, and without stopping to think Lewy murmured, "Good drive, I'm outplayed!" Kupfer ignored a correct answer, and Lewy whispered, "The ball was in! We protest!" It usually ended with one of the two doubles partners retiring from the game after an unreturnable service from Kupfer, whereupon Kupfer would deliver a mighty smash to win game, set and match. Those in the know were particularly amused when Kupfer noticed the whispering and dismissed it with a scornful, "If you please, what did *you* want to tell someone?"

But unlike Lewy, who genuinely enjoyed this game, Kurt was sometimes overcome by discomfort. His father would appear in his mind's eye, the train to Paris, the maliciously grinning faces of Schönthal and Nowak and Altschul… Then he would pull himself together; he didn't want to do this, he was thinking hard about a question that Kupfer had asked, disregarding Lewy's giggles, he was thinking, thinking, he had found what he wanted—but Kupfer was already growling, "Thank you, sit down, someone else!" And perhaps he would have managed to save himself with a good answer today, if Lewy hadn't disturbed him, and then he hated Lewy and the arrogant smile on his wry mouth, he felt he could have murdered him, he hated him so much… then Mertens would be next to be tested, standing in front of the board, very pale, trembling and still stammering helplessly when "someone else" had already replaced him… and then the Headmaster would come in to inspect the class, and Mertens would be called out; only five minutes ago Kupfer had sent him back to his desk, the problem was still on the board, unfinished, and now Mertens was to complete it, the same exercise he had failed to complete five minutes earlier… and at that Kurt would turn his hatred on Professor Artur Kupfer alone.

So he became closer to Lewy, and that did not go unnoticed. In time it was obvious that when short-sighted Prochaska asked, "Who's missing at the back there?" the answer was nearly always, "Gerber and Lewy".

"Those young gentlemen shouldn't stay away!" said the old teacher, shaking his head in concern. "Mind you, I have no objection, and if my subject doesn't interest the young gentlemen let them stay away—but someone might see them outside the classroom, and then the damage will be done."

The two of them heard about this from the others. Lewy said, "Thanks for the information." Kurt said, "It might be just as well if at least now and then we—" But Lewy interrupted him. "You stay here if you like. I'll find someone else to play a game of billiards." In an indifferent tone with nothing caustic in it. And yet in the next history lesson the same two were absent again: Gerber and Lewy.

One day Professor Seelig took Kurt aside.

"Gerber—it's none of my business really—you can mix with anyone you like, but I don't think it's to your advantage to be so close to Lewy."

"He's cleverer than the others!" said Kurt defiantly.

"Yes, that'll be why this is his ninth year in the school."

"That doesn't mean anything. I could fail the *Matura* myself."

Professor Seelig looked hard at him. "If that's what you have in mind!" he said quietly. And as Kurt did not reply, he shrugged his shoulders and turned away. It was a clear defeat for Kurt.

There was another defeat, and again because of Lewy. He attracted Kupfer's attention during the maths lesson by suspicious movements under the desk. God Almighty stormed over, delighted to have irrefutable evidence of cheating—and had to withdraw abashed. Lewy had had nothing under the desk, nothing at all.

"Good fellow, Lewy!" Kurt murmured to Weinberg when the bell had rung, as it soon did.

Weinberg turned away with unmistakable displeasure.

Suspicion, annoyance and above all the lust for battle that he had damped down for so long irritated Kurt into asking outright whether Weinberg was deaf, or was there some other reason for his very odd behaviour recently.

Weinberg's answer was evasive.

He'd better come out with it, Kurt demanded.

Weinberg said he didn't think that would help.

"Oh," said Kurt indignantly, "so you've given me up for lost. Well, admittedly you don't like to mix with a candidate for failure."

"You're wrong," said Weinberg calmly. "I just don't admire Lewy's jokes as much as you do."

"Then you're an arse-licker like the rest of them!" Kurt's indignation was growing. He felt a hit had been scored on him. It was a fact that Lewy impressed him; he just didn't want to admit it. Now he was hearing it.

Weinberg shook his head. "You're crazy. Do you want to be on a par with Lewy?"

"On a par with Lewy—on a par!" Kurt mimicked him furiously. "Wonderful rhetoric, that! You ought to be a class teacher!"

Weinberg obviously had no intention of continuing this argument, and indeed did no such thing, but sat in silence through the next lesson. In secret, Kurt had hoped he might say more—but Weinberg was consistent. Kurt envied him that.

And he was not the only one he envied. In a way they were all superior to him. All of them sitting here had a sense of direction. Just one. Even the ultimate crawler went in something like a straight line, even if it led him to lick the professor's arse. He was a crawler, that was why.

And what about him, Kurt Gerber? What was he? Did he think he was above such things? There was hardly a student in the class who wouldn't have claimed the same for himself.

But he had to prove it, prove it!

I, Kurt Gerber, will prove it. They can give me as many Unsatisfactories as they like, and I'll just laugh. Ha, ha, ha.

Then Hippo will stand up and say: "I'm laughing too, or rather I would be laughing if—. But there you are, no one gives me an Unsatisfactory. Just my luck."

And anyway, are you really laughing, Kurt Gerber?

Don't you ever sit at home for hours and hours on end, studying, studying, studying?

Why?

Because you must, Kurt Gerber. Let's drop the pretence that it's not worthwhile. If you've been sitting around here for seven years, you want to end the eighth with a success. Obviously. And if you don't know enough to do that, then you must just learn it, and that's that.

Yes—but then you must study hard, really study hard. Are you studying hard?

No, you are not. Only too often you're too lazy, or you feel too indifferent, or you have some other empty reason to back out of it, and then you'll get Unsatisfactory, and you'll imagine you're a martyr to your own temperament. A dismal pretence.

Haven't you ever found yourself, having intentionally done no preparation, making efforts to pass a test all the same? You suddenly take fright in break, and you begin swotting it all up, and getting the students you despise to slip you answers during the test, don't you? And if none of that is enough, and the professor has told you to go and sit down—have you never regretted it, Kurt Gerber? Haven't you ever gone pleading to a professor, and haven't you felt flattered by the different tone of voice he adopted in such a private conversation?

Yes, you've done all that. And much more. You're a spineless poseur, Kurt Gerber.

Moral platitudes? The others don't do any better? Success is what carries weight. Have you succeeded, then?

No, you have not. And as you're not stupid, there must be some other reason.

They wish you ill. They have the souls of petty tradesmen, so they persecute you with hatred and disfavour. They are unjust. That's it.

There's something fine about being hated by everyone. Then at least you've succeeded in one way, in your own estimation.

But you haven't even done that, Kurt Gerber. Even, did I say? As though there could be any greater success!

You're always excusing one kind of failure by another, Kurt Gerber, and then vice versa again. You're playing a pitiful game. You lack backbone, composure, honesty. You despise school, do you? It's yourself you ought to be despising…

And Kurt did begin to doubt himself. He felt he was the most degenerate person in the world, worthless, useless, superfluous, unable to do anything for himself or anyone else.

Or for anyone else? Was that necessarily true? Maybe doing something for others might help him, too? That was supposed to be the incentive for rendering almost any kind of aid: afterwards you could say, "See how powerful I am! I can help people!" Altruism as deception, pleasing in the eyes of God. Even the most anonymous would-be benefactor turns his eyes to heaven: maybe someone up there has noticed… Yes, well, long ago Kurt had been able to devote himself to the interests of those who had suffered some kind of injustice. A mistaken admonishment, perhaps not really given with any bad feeling, an entry in the register for which the professor concerned could answer in any forum, a sharp word, an unfair mark: ah, then Kurt Gerber stood up and fought to the last, took blame on himself without another thought, and without another thought made someone else's cause his own. Because he did it *for the cause*.

But now he would fight for himself, now he wanted to show that *he* was right. If it was also for the cause, well, that was a nice extra, and he would pat himself on the back afterwards: hey, look, we're in this together.

As for the others, however, the reptiles who made all this possible in the first place, they wouldn't spot the difference, they wouldn't notice, appreciatively, that even if no one had asked Kurt Gerber to intervene in any way, he had done what he could…

If Borchert had not also been teaching German at this time, standing in for Mattusch, who was off sick, it would all probably have turned out differently. As things were, however, the timetable for that day had German from nine to ten, and French from eleven to twelve.

Borchert's vanity led him to all kinds of extravagant fancies, and the eighth-year students, whom he was teaching only as a substitute, did not go along with them as he wished. They didn't take him seriously when he taught this subject, they even mocked him slightly. Borchert had soon had enough of this, his highly strung nerves brought him to the verge of hysteria; and suddenly, before most of the class realized what was going on, an argument between the Professor and Schleich, not usually a pugnacious student, had degenerated into a shouting match. Borchert descended to vulgar abuse, Schleich rejected his remarks vigorously, threatening to complain to the Headmaster, and Borchert, now entirely out of control, responded with more abuse. Schleich tried getting past him and marching to the door. Borchert, whose twinkling eyes looked extremely comic in his scarlet face, barred his way. Whether Schleich had tried to push him away was not to be ascertained—but at any rate he suddenly got a resounding slap in the face. The class was baffled, and even more baffled when Schleich turned without a word and went back to his desk. Borchert, pale and trembling, laboriously went on until the end of the lesson, and concluded it when the bell began to ring.

The class was in turmoil. Some of the students were offering to go to the Headmaster with Schleich at once, but Schleich himself resisted the idea; he had changed his mind, he said, it would probably be better if he sent his father to do it. He could say no more, because all the others were giving their own advice at the top of their voices. Kurt tried to calm the tumult down a little, and since the eighth-year students—as he discovered to his surprise and pleasure—would still listen to him on such matters, he succeeded. But then the bell rang, and old Professor Prochaska entered the classroom.

One thing was certain: something had to happen in the next lesson. From time to time Kurt thought that all eyes were fixed on him, and it went through his mind, again and again, that they expected something of him. Yes, action of some kind was called for; the eighth year must show that they wanted something out of that damn rite of passage the imminent *Matura* besides just the duty to swot for it. Now or never!

How different this was. There was no sign now of the petty self-interest that he had expected to govern his conduct. Whether it had really gone away or only retreated far inside him he didn't know. Nor did he stop to think about it; it was all the same at this point. Full of an impetuous desire for action, he surveyed his troops.

Prochaska was standing at the front of the class, as usual, between the two front rows of desks, supporting himself on them and leaning slightly forward as he ploughed through the details of the new Bohemian constitution of 1627. The students in the front rows were busily writing it all down, in the middle rows they were just taking brief notes and at the back of the class no one was taking any notice of what the old man said—the seating order there also changed with every lesson, and with his poor eyesight Prochaska didn't notice a thing. Today, for instance, Altschul and Lewy were sitting side by side, their heads propped on their hands, and in a melancholy mood setting out the chessmen of a travelling chess set. In line with an unspoken agreement, they always played game openings that forced them to exchange pawns at once, so that the absence of two pawns each wouldn't impede the rest of the game. Rimmel and Sittig were solving crossword puzzles, Kaulich had his legs stretched out and was almost lounging at his desk; Mertens was reading a fat book which he had concealed, with excessive foresight, under his atlas, so that he had to lift the atlas whenever he wanted to turn a page, and a French textbook, a French dictionary and a book of exercises and lists of vocabulary lay on Severin's desk. He was obviously doing French homework ready for Borchert. Kurt remembered that he, too, had really meant to spend this lesson in the same way, that he should really be doing French exercises now—but wouldn't it be shameful, when a man had slapped your comrade's face so recently, to try impressing the same man with what you knew in the next lesson?

Kurt tore a page out of his geography exercise book:

"Anyone who likes the idea of responding to the injustice done to our friend Schleich by showing total passive resistance in Borchert's next lesson, please sign below."

And he signed his own name in large lettering under his appeal, folded the sheet of paper, wrote on the back, "Pass it on," and pushed it over to Lengsfeld, who was dropping off to sleep beside him (Weinberg sat in front of him). Lengsfeld perused it and did not seem enthusiastic.

"What's the point of that?"

"There isn't any!" Kurt snapped, handing him the pen. Lengsfeld shrugged and signed. Then he pinched Hobbelmann's buttock and, as he abruptly turned, held the sheet of paper out to him.

"I wonder if they'll dare," remarked Lengsfeld, turning to look at Kurt again.

"Just so long as you do."

"Count on me."

"…isn't that so, my young friend Gerber?" Prochaska had noticed the inattention in the classroom.

"Yes," said his young friend Gerber, agreeing to he didn't know what. Then he put his hand out to Lengsfeld.

"Give me your word."

Lengsfeld shook hands with deliberate man-of-the-world demeanour. He could be sure of Lengsfeld, then.

But what about the others? Kurt peered at the rows ahead. Severin was just passing the note on, and then went back to leafing through the dictionary. So he was doing the French exercise all the same, which was suspicious… The circular letter had now reached Körner, who turned to glance at Kurt. Kurt looked back at him as if by chance, without moving. Körner signed.

Kurt couldn't see exactly what went on after that. But before his appeal reached the front rows of desks the bell rang for break. Prochaska murmured his usual, "Until next time, then," and left the classroom. Kurt stayed sitting at his desk. He was feeling slightly uneasy, like the director of a play getting stage fright: would it go down well?

Then Schönthal was coming over to him. He slammed the piece of paper down on the desk like a playing card. "I ask you! What do you think this is going to achieve?"

Kurt did not reply. Without changing his position, he unfolded the paper. In all, there were eight signatures, not counting his own and Lengsfeld's. Hobbelmann, Lewy, Gerald, Weinberg, Kaulich and Körner had signed. (Körner had written his name very small and illegibly, to be on the safe side.)

Only eight ready to do battle, then? Still—a quarter of the class. No, not a quarter, just eight individuals. Where were the rest? Kurt had guessed that the girls wouldn't sign. However, he thought he could manage without them. But the twenty-five boys, one of whom had had his face slapped?

"Why didn't you sign, Schönthal?"

Schönthal bared his gums, which were an angry shade of red. "Because it's my opinion that it won't do Schleich or any of us any good to annoy a professor. The professors are stronger than us."

"As I've always said!" Körner's voice rose from the circle standing round Kurt.

Kurt ignored him. His glance travelled on.

"Klemm?"

"Why ask me? Ask the others."

"Schleich?"

"I'm personally affected! I can't sign."

"Nowak?"

"The note never reached me."

"Duffek?"

"I'll sign if everyone else does."

"Rimmel? Sittig? You? You?"

Silence surrounded him, sank over him, was soft like mud around him on all sides. And suddenly it occurred to him that French was the next lesson, and he hadn't done his homework. He felt like spitting at the whole bunch of them standing there smirking.

"It's all nonsense anyway!" said Körner, summing up the general opinion.

Kurt assumed an artificial air of calm. "Speak for yourself!" And seeing that Körner was about to reply, he added, "If it's all nonsense, then why did *you* sign?"

That was a mistake. With an argument like that, Kurt was pulling out the rug from under his own feet. Körner knew it, too.

"Don't you like it? Then I can cross my signature out again."

"Do that. If you don't feel for yourself—and that goes for all of you—" (Kurt had jumped up and brought his fist down on the desk) "—if you cowards don't feel for yourselves what's at stake, then—" Tired and discouraged, Kurt sat down again. He couldn't carry on.

"I don't know why you're all so worked up." That was Hippo, dissociating himself. "After all, it's Schleich's private business!"

"You're wrong there, Scholz." At least Weinberg was backing him. "If something happens to one of us that might just as well happen to anyone else, it's no one's private business any longer."

"The bell will go in a minute," said Mertens.

"Friends!" Kurt tried one last time. "Will you or will you not go along with me? I can do without your signatures. Your word will be enough!"

His appeal failed to take effect. There was only an indistinct murmur. This rabble don't even have enough courage to show cowardice, thought Kurt. He picked up the piece of paper. Meanwhile, when no one was looking, Körner had crossed out his signature. Kurt laughed.

"Anyone else want to withdraw his signature? I see. So I have Hobbelmann, Lewy, Gerald, Lengsfeld, Kaulich and Weinberg. Schleich, you have now," he said, turning to Schleich as if to introduce him to the class, "you have now had your face slapped again by all the others. By your fellow students, Schleich. You'd better say thank you."

The bell rang. No one said anything, except for Weinberg, who whispered as Borchert was coming into the room, "Bastards!"

Kurt grasped his hand. Weinberg shook hands heartily with him.

I ought to be feeling downcast, thought Kurt. But there's no time for sentimentalities. Now it's about something else. It's about me.

The petty feelings of his own that he had dismissed had only crawled into hiding, and now they came out again like snails.

Kurt read the signatures once more. He now had to write off not just Körner but Lengsfeld too; the appeal had gone to him first, and he had really just signed for the sake of a quiet life. As things stood now, he couldn't be counted on. What about the rest? Gerald was convinced that the campaign was just, and he could be considered reliable. And he had plump Hobbelmann on his side as well. He wouldn't venture to do anything in defiance of him (and now Kurt was in a mood to consider all resistance as directed against

227

him personally). Lewy had signed as a joke. Kaulich could afford to sign on a whim, he had nothing to fear. And he had no doubts of Weinberg. So if it was really only those six—but that was crazy.

A decision had to come soon, he thought. Borchert has now finished making his entry in the class register. Else Rieps goes back to her desk with the pen and Borchert opens the textbook—quiet, please, quiet.

His face thrust forward, Kurt stares at the Professor. Who will be called up to the front of the class? Borchert is leafing through his book. More slowly than usual, almost cautiously. Does he guess something? No. He lets his eyes wander over the class. Who will it be? Kurt would like to make his mark—but Borchert notices nothing. He is still looking around. Is he going to test anyone or not?

No! No, Borchert isn't about to test anyone. He perches on the lectern and says (Kurt jumps at the first sound he utters) casually and even in German, "Now, let's go on. We'll look at a poem by Victor Hugo, 'Les Djinns'. I'll read it to you myself first.

As he begins, Kurt relaxes, and the enquiring glance that Weinberg gives him seems to express his own thoughts: Borchert is going to let the grass grow over the whole incident, may even apologize to Schleich himself; it's perfectly possible, of course Borchert must feel he was in the wrong, and he'll be careful not to expose his authority to any other tests of how much we'll take, he's not going to test anyone, he won't call anyone up to the front –

"Kaulich!"

Kurt leans forward. What's this? So he'll venture to go on?

"Translate the first verse."

Kaulich slowly lumbers to his feet. Kurt's heart is in his mouth.

Kaulich stands there, awkwardly turning from page to page of the book as if he can't find his way around it. Perhaps he really did open it at the wrong page, perhaps he's just pretending.

"Sit down, and pay better attention next time!"

Borchert said that without any emotion, and now he is looking round the classroom again. Kurt might as well resign himself at once. It was chance that Kaulich was called on, chance again that he didn't answer, and now it will be the turn of one of the eager beavers to be summoned to the front.

"Weinberg!"

Kurt has to bite his lower lip in order to go on looking indifferent.

Weinberg has risen from his desk and is standing there holding the book, eyes looking ahead and not at the page.

"Translate the first verse!"

Weinberg says nothing, just stands there motionless.

"Don't you hear me? I want you to translate!"

That sounds angrier. But Weinberg grits his teeth. His jaw can be seen working again.

"Very well," says Borchert, pretending indifference. "Gerber, you translate, will you?"

Now Kurt is no longer surprised. As he stands up he wonders what would happen if he spoke now. For a fraction of a second he feels a scornful desire to do just that. Then, unmoved, he looks at the Professor's face.

Some time passes. They all look up from their desks. At last Borchert's slowly spoken words break the silence. "So that's how it is! Well, we'll soon see about this. You can sit down, Gerber!"

Kurt had never before felt such dislike of that "we", that royal plural expressing long-accepted arrogance. It's a crying shame: one person standing there saying "we", everyone else sitting below him, all saying "I". Borchert goes to the lectern desk, pulls out the drawer and opens the register.

"Someone give me a pen!"

Then something wholly unexpected happens: no one does as he says.

"A pen!"

In the front row, Else Rieps moves as if to stand up. It's not clear whether she is being held back or not—but anyway she stays sitting there.

Deep joy goes through Kurt. They're not so bad after all, they do have a sense of solidarity when the crunch comes. Borchert will have to reprimand the entire class in his report.

"I can wait," says Borchert calmly, folding his arms and leaning back. A dull, leaden silence reigns in the room.

Borchert's eyes are twinkling all the time. He could stand up himself, go over to someone's desk and pick up a pen or a pencil. Kurt imagines what it would be like (and now it seems to him not impossible), if the owner of the pen said, "Excuse me, Professor Borchert, sir, but that pen is my private property!" Would Borchert dare to confiscate it?

So the whole class will be reported for a breach of discipline. The silence preserved by Kaulich and Weinberg will suddenly look quite different—what amazing luck that Borchert didn't call on any of those who backed out!

It was nice of Else Rieps not to stand up. He wonders if she's in love with him? Why not? There's so much about Kurt to be loved.

Except that Lisa can't see it. Lisa—why does he have to think of her at this moment?

Because he's happy, that's why, very happy for the first time in a long while. Whenever he's happy he has to think of Lisa. If he walks through a park in the evening, and a white swan, neck held high, passes the weeping willows bending down over the pool, when everything is as soothing and full of relief as tears very quietly shed; or when he stands on a hill at night and sees the thousands of lights in the great city twinkling down below and the stars above; or when he sees anything else beautiful that makes his chest expand, filling it entirely—then he has to think of Lisa, every time, there's no help for it, and he misses her so much, he doesn't even long to kiss her, only to feel her breath on him, maybe share her silence, her peace and calm…

Peace and calm! Kurt comes back to his senses with a start. Where is he? In the classroom. And Borchert is still sitting on his desk with his arms folded. And no one moves. A car drives by down in the street. The noise it makes dies away within seconds. Then there is only silence again, almost tangible, like a heavy blanket against your face and then you hear a strange whistling sound.

The noise of someone clearing his throat breaks off abruptly. If the Headmaster were to come in now! But Kurt can't think that out to the end. The peace and quiet hums like a distant engine. He holds his breath. How much longer is this going on, for goodness' sake, they're only halfway through—there—what's that?

Borchert, without batting an eyelid, with an expressionless face as if nothing has happened, as if what he is doing is perfectly natural—Borchert puts his hand in his pocket, brings out a fountain pen and writes something in the register.

Several people are coughing now, desks are creaking, paper is rustling.

Then Klemm is summoned to the front of the class and translates the first verse of Victor Hugo's poem "Les Djinns".

Just as all imaginable misfortune falls on a defeated commander, just as the last of his loyal followers leave him, as he always has to fulfil new conditions, put up with new humiliations—everything now turned against Kurt Gerber.

His defeat in class, which sheer good luck had seemed to avert, was now out in the open. Most of the students were sorry for him, but there were some who could hardly hide their glee behind murmurs of regret.

Even more incredibly: at the end of the lesson Schleich went to see Borchert in the staffroom and apologized to him. Schleich apologized to Borchert. Borchert had called Schleich a cretin, a snotty-nosed youth, useless. In front of the whole class. Borchert had slapped Schleich's face. In front of thirty others. And Schleich apologized to Borchert— because, well, Professor Borchert would soon have a chance of doing something much worse to Schleich than slapping his face, wouldn't he? So it was probably better for the student Schleich to admit remorsefully that he was wrong, yes, Professor Borchert, sir, I was stupid, I know, Professor Borchert, sir, you're under great strain, and I ought not to have contradicted you, forgive me, Professor Borchert, sir, for getting my face slapped by you…

Borchert was gracious enough to forgive him. He also forgave young Kurt Gerber, who turned up in the staffroom shortly after Schleich, and he said he was prepared to let the matter rest there. For indeed, young Gerber had begged him fervently to do so. It was easy to see that he didn't find it easy to apologize. At first, that is. Later it was better, he knew how to convince himself of the terrible consequences there would be for him if his class teacher, Professor Kupfer, got to know about the incident, he was deeply sorry that he had let himself be carried away without considering such factors, that he... well, in a nutshell, it was Kurt Gerber who succeeded in persuading Borchert to withdraw his report of the whole class for indiscipline. In fact the other professors did read it, in spite of the two red lines crossing it out, and shook their heads—but the almost inevitable influence it would have had on the staff meeting soon to be held to allot the latest marks was averted, what could be salvaged from the wreck had been salvaged; indeed, at the end of his conversation with young Gerber, Professor Borchert had even found a few friendly and encouraging words to say...

That was Kurt Gerber's greatest failure.

IX

"Wednesday at Ten", a Trashy Novel

A FEW DAYS LATER the results of the last staff meeting to allot marks were announced. And the fact that Kurt Gerber had again scored Unsatisfactory in maths and descriptive geometry, that his situation now seemed utterly hopeless, that his father received the news in a silence where pain and anger, concern and anxiety seemed to mingle in wordless misery, and he now saw nothing for it but to ask his father, of his own accord, to engage a private tutor to coach him—all this was like the full stop at the end of a sentence. The machinery of torment worked of its own accord and with inescapable precision, hardly letting all the feelings that he had to cope with enter his mind, and he was greatly surprised when he rang Professor Ruprecht's bell and the tutor was not at home! Then, when he was told to come back in an hour's time, he felt that that, too, was right and proper, had been foreseen, shame coming in two instalments, redoubled…

"Hey there, young misery!"

Someone clapped him on the shoulder. Kurt jumped as if a revolver had been held in his face. Then he recognized Boby Urban.

"You certainly look down in the doldrums! What sends you marching past me with your head bent?"

The doldrums? Why was he going on about being becalmed at sea? "Hello," says Kurt, taking Boby's proffered hand.

"That's better!" laughs Boby Urban. "I thought your joy at seeing me again had stopped up your mouth."

Someone is laughing. Where does that laughter come from. He's still laughing. I suppose I'd better laugh too. Ha, ha. How was that?

"Know what I'm smiling over, my little lost lamb?"

No. No idea. What *are* you smiling over? Kurt shakes his head.

"I'm smiling all over my face!" chuckles Boby.

I know that one, thinks Kurt. And suddenly he realizes that he is glad to know the joke already. He doesn't know why, but he is glad—so he laughs too, a loud roar of laughter.

"I knew it!" nods Boby. "Good old Boby Urban"—he seems to be in high good humour, and practically belches the U of his surname—"he can always cheer the place up. Spray essence of Boby Urban around! It will get into the tiniest nooks and crannies."

And slowly, at first to his own astonishment, Kurt finds himself drawn into a conversation, question and answer and counter-question, easy and unforced; if he has nothing to say then he says nothing, and gives no offence.

Where was Kurt off to, asks Boby. Hadn't he said he was going up to see Paul Weismann recently? They'd all expected him, but he never turned up. What was the matter with him?

Kurt doesn't know what to reply—he genuinely doesn't know. What was the matter with him? Wait… wasn't that when I just missed the tram? No, that wasn't it… oh, now I know. I think I've tracked down the reason. Yes. But I can't tell him that…

Lisa had been really cross, adds Boby. And quite right, too. Fancy just not turning up when a lady invites you.

Hmm. To say that—no, I can't tell him it was because of Lisa. But for other reasons, too.

"You see, Boby, I don't really like entertainments of that kind. Sitting together in the evening—yes. But a studio party—it was a studio party, wasn't it?—you feel as if you absolutely have to—""

"Nonsense. We just call it a studio party so that it'll look like something familiar. We don't really set store by such things. Thank Heaven, we have other opportunities."

"Maybe *you* do."

"What do you mean?"

"Nothing." Kurt stops short, suddenly distressed. Then, just for something to say, he asks where Boby is going now.

Boby is on his way to meet Paul Weismann. The coffee house is quite close; why doesn't Kurt join them? Does he have time?

Not really.

Oh. Why not?

"Well, yes, it'll be all right," says Kurt. And he goes to the coffee house with Boby Urban…

Two hours later, when Kurt Gerber climbed the stairs to Professor Ruprecht's apartment, he thought he felt a little part of the cheerful mood, which he had had some difficulty in sharing at first, now ebbing away with every step. And once the door had been opened to him there was almost none of it left. Or only enough at least to be aware of the unfriendly reception that Professor Ruprecht gave him.

Professor Ruprecht, who taught mathematics and descriptive geometry at a different school, stood in the doorway in an open-necked shirt and red check jacket, and with his bushy facial hair and broad shoulders looked like a woodcutter. His remarks were inhospitable to match, and were spoken in a strong Sudeten German accent.

"Could have turned up earlier, eh? I've been waiting an hour. Waste of my time!"

Kurt went red, and stammered out a few apologies: the tram had been—

"All right, the tram, of course. Always the same excuse." Professor Ruprecht shook his head with a raucous laugh. Then he pointed to one of the basket chairs round the little table in the front hall. His voice became a little friendlier. "We can't use my study at the moment. Never mind. I can't give you a lesson today anyway, you should have turned up earlier. You need every lesson you can get. Right, sit down, then."

Kurt obeyed almost anxiously. What kind of a "sit down" was that?

"Well then," said Professor Ruprecht, lounging at his ease in another chair, "so you're in a bad way with mathematics. And descriptive geometry too. So I hear from my colleague Kupfer and your father. How did the marking go?"

A few minutes ago Kurt would have snapped back that he supposed he'd know if he had spoken to Kupfer. Now he said tonelessly, "Unsatisfactory in both."

"I see. I see. How is it going to be with your *Matura* in a few weeks' time? We'll have our work cut out for us. Why didn't you come to your senses sooner?"

Kurt did not reply.

Professor Ruprecht stroked his moustache, took a deep breath, and said:

"Well—we'll have to plunge in. We'll make a start very soon." He took out his notebook, opened it at the calendar and his timetable and laid it flat on the table. "The Easter holidays begin on Monday... I tell you what, take a bit of a rest then first, I could do with one myself. Today is Friday, so when shall we start?"

"Whenever you like."

"Right, then shall we say—shall we say... Wednesday? Will that suit you?"

"Of course, Professor Ruprecht, sir."

"Good. Wednesday at ten, then. You'd better make a note of that."

Without thinking, Kurt put his hand to his breast pocket, although he wasn't carrying a student diary with him these days.

"No notebook?" asked Professor Ruprecht impatiently. "Want me to lend you a piece of paper?"

"No, that's all right, thanks, I have something here," said Kurt. He had found a card in his left-hand pocket, but for the moment he couldn't remember how it came to be there. He took it out.

It was Paul Weismann's visiting card, with his address and telephone number. Kurt turned it over. He went pale.

On the back of the card he had written: Wednesday, ten o'clock.

Kurt stared at the letters. All the conflict of his life opened up like a chasm before him.

Wednesday, ten o'clock: that was when he was to phone the painter Paul Weismann to arrange to meet at his studio.

Wednesday, ten o'clock: that was when he was to go for a maths lesson with Professor Adolf Ruprecht.

Wednesday, ten o'clock; Wednesday, ten o'clock.

"Well, does it take so long to think about it?"

Kurt pulled himself together and added a few meaningless squiggles to the card.

"Right, agreed then!" said Professor Ruprecht.

If he says "Wednesday, ten o'clock" now, I shall strangle him, thought Kurt. But Professor Ruprecht said no more. He rose to his feet and opened the door. "Goodbye."

Slowly, treading heavily, Kurt made his way down the stairs.

All in order, he thought. I'm living out the novel of my life. I just wouldn't have expected it to be such a trashy story.

Wednesday, ten o'clock.

Kurt stepped out of the telephone kiosk near Professor Ruprecht's apartment and into the street. He hadn't been able to get connected at first, and when he did he had quite a long conversation with Paul Weismann. Now he wondered, as he was arriving late anyway, might it not be better to call Lisa at once? Paul had advised him to do that, indeed he almost made it a condition. Kurt should establish contact with Lisa again, and then the meeting could be arranged much more easily.

Kurt was glad to find that Paul took it so seriously. Lisa was angry with him. Did he mean enough to her for that?

He had walked on, deep in thought, and suddenly he was outside the building where Professor Ruprecht lived. He went upstairs.

A woman in a blue apron with her hair pinned up opened the door to him. She looked as if she might be the cook.

"Good morning," she said in friendly tones. "You've come to see my husband, haven't you? You must be Herr Gerber?"

Herr Gerber... Kurt said yes.

"Adolf!" called the woman out loud, looking in another direction. "Come out, will you? Herr Gerber is here for his coaching."

Soon Professor Ruprecht appeared. He growled a greeting to Kurt, took him into his study and turned to go again. "Sit down. I'll be back in a moment."

Kurt looked round the room.

So this is where I'll be sitting. On a chair. The chair stands at a rectangular table. There are three other chairs at the table, a sofa covered in red velour and an upright piano with a music stand.

How does there come to be a piano in the room? Who here plays the piano? Maybe Professor Ruprecht himself. No, nonsense; maths teachers don't play the piano.

Otherwise the room looks perfectly normal. Of course. How else would it look? Did I expect to find a tall teacher's lectern and a blackboard here?

Somehow I think I did. Or no; no, I didn't.

Just a room like any other.

Who lives here?

"Adolf!" It was the voice of the woman again outside the room. "Adolf, won't you have a quick bite to eat? A ham sandwich?" Then a door closed. What was all this about?

Well, all it meant—just a moment—was that someone here was called Adolf, and Adolf was eating a ham sandwich, so all it meant was that maths teachers are perfectly ordinary people.

No, no, no! For God's sake! That's impossible.

Teachers don't have any private life. No.

Kurt hastily opened his book of mathematical formulae, stopped listening to sounds outside the room and stared at the densely packed numbers and signs on the page.

Adolf? Professor Ruprecht!

Adolf Ruprecht, Professor of Mathematics and Descriptive Geometry at High School III, came in.

Kurt looked at him as if seeing him for the first time. He had difficulty in suppressing a smile. This man, he thought, has just been eating a ham sandwich.

The Professor sat down opposite him, took out his watch and placed it on the table.

"You can never arrive punctually, I see!" Then, unexpectedly, he grinned. "I thought as much—you slept in for a while."

So what? You slept in for a while. These things happen. And if a student does sleep in for a while and arrives late, what about it?

"Does a young man good to sleep in, am I right?"

Definitely. How many people are you going to bawl out today, my dear Professor? Do wipe the crumbs off your chin.

"Then let's make a start. Where are you weakest in the subject?"

Everywhere. And you have a bull neck too, you woodcutter.

"Well?" asked Professor Ruprecht impatiently.

"I—I think—in integral calculus."

"Ah. How's your knowledge of the formulae? Let me see."

Kurt pushed the book of formulae his way.

$$x^2 \cos x \, dx =$$

When the lesson was over (in the course of it Professor Ruprecht, shaking his head, had more than once expressed serious reservations), and Kurt went out into the front hall, the woman was there. She said, "Goodbye," and he still heard her voice when he was at the door. "Come along in, Adolf, do."

Maybe he's henpecked, thought Kurt as he went down the stairs, and maybe that's the only reason why so many students at High School III come to grief, racking their poor brains for a thousand reasons.

I wonder what it's like when Ruprecht hands out an Unsatisfactory? When Kupfer eats a ham sandwich?

It's all so ridiculous…

Kurt went into a telephone kiosk and called the Dremon Studio. His heart was thudding.

"Dremon Studio," said an expressionless, businesslike male voice.

"Yes—hello—Dr Berwald speaking—can I speak to my sister—" Kurt began.

"Who is this? I don't understand you."

"Dr Berwald. I'd like to speak to my sister—" Kurt tried again, his voice shaking, but once again he was interrupted.

"Who? Speak more clearly, please! Who is this?"

Then Kurt was overcome by a crazy fear that he had been recognized. He hung up and hurried out of the kiosk.

Out in the fresh air, it all seemed very comical. I'm not responsible for my actions, he thought. I'll go and see Dr Kron. There's something about the *Matura*—shut up, this is ridiculous. Why did I hang up? I ought to have insisted. Shall I call again? I was disturbing them. No, better not. Anyway, she wouldn't like me to.

All of a sudden a wild longing for Lisa took hold of him. An ardent longing such as he had never felt before. Lisa seemed to him all that could still give meaning to his life, something to support him, yet he knew that she would never understand that. But it was not hopelessness that surrounded him, nor the despair of unrequited love; it was the fear of being loved but not in the way he wanted, and the even greater fear that that was done intentionally.

Kurt decided to wait outside Lisa's workplace that evening.

The Dremon Studio was in one of those narrow alleys in the city centre that the press of traffic seems to leave alone. The more it races past them, the greater seems their silence. The little alley leads to a square with an old church in it. The rays of the setting sun were not strong enough to light up the cupola entirely, but cast a little glow on it. Milk-white curls of cloud stood in the pale-blue sky, getting whiter and whiter. A gust of mild wind raised a sheet of paper from the asphalt and blew it a little way farther. Then it settled on the ground, calm, satisfied.

Kurt noticed that it was spring weather, and was glad of it.

The church clock struck three times for a quarter to seven. Electric light was on in several shop windows. Shutters were being rolled down in front of others. Lisa must turn up soon.

People are already coming out of the shops and businesses and into the alley, going away singly or in couples, many of them arm in arm.

Why isn't Lisa here yet? Maybe she hasn't been to work at all? Maybe she isn't well?

Ah, there—no. But he must keep a good lookout now, because more and more people are coming into the alley.

And then no more at all come out. Where is Lisa?

It's getting quite dark now.

Kurt paces restlessly up and down, minutes pass by, a girl looks at him with flashing eyes, stops outside a shop window, then slowly walks on, turning twice more to look at him... She must think me an idiot, thinks Kurt, knowing very well that he is not going to speak to her... wondering whether to go up to the Dremon Studio, which is on the first floor, and its three large windows facing the street are still lit up...

He takes a couple of hesitant steps—then he has to wait for a car to pass—and as he is going on again Lisa comes out of the building.

She has not seen him, and goes down the alley towards the church. Kurt slowly follows her, enjoying the sight of her upright gait, and he is sure she, too, would rather he did not accost her outside her workplace.

She turns right. Kurt walks faster, full of happy hope, and trembling slightly.

Now he, too, has turned the corner and is three or four steps behind her.

"Lisa!" Kurt stops. But his throat is so strangely dry that his voice sounds low and rough. Lisa has not heard him; she quickens her pace a little.

The alley bends, becomes busier, he has to give way to passers-by. There is a car over there.

At last he is right behind her again.

And as he calls her name softly once more…

At the very moment when the word "Lisa!" passes his lips, a figure comes out of the gateway of a building, or through a porch, or maybe just along the side of the wall… the figure of a man who greets her—Kurt hears him, who kisses her hand—Kurt sees him, and next minute he has passed them, having quickly pressed his hat down over his forehead. He doesn't want Lisa recognizing him, that is his last clear thought, and then there is a rushing inside his head as if it were being hammered from all sides, he must get away fast, fast, didn't Lisa just call his name in surprise, isn't she looking at him as he walks away, shaking her head, fast, go on, get out of her sight, there, turn right—damn it, not a side street but a barred gateway set back from the street, and locked, now I can't go either forwards or backwards…

Groaning with shame and rage, Kurt hunches up his shoulders, makes himself small and presses himself into the niche, face turned away; he can hear footsteps and Lisa's voice, Lisa's voice—he can't make out what she is saying for all the uproar in his head, but she is talking to someone else, probably smiling; Kurt grits his teeth, and clenches his fists in his coat pockets.

At last he turned. There they went. He watched them go, and the strain ebbed, slowly relaxing him. His arms dropped to his sides.

There they went. He could still see them. Now they were stopping.

Then he put his hand in his pocket, it was almost cooler than the black metal thing it held; there was a brief bang, another, the man at Lisa's side flung his arms in the air, stood motionless for a moment and then collapsed. Kurt Gerber put the revolver back in his pocket, laughed scornfully and stepped out of the dark doorway.

Of course Kurt Gerber did not do any such thing, he just thought about it, for it had crossed his mind again that he was living in a trashy novel where a dramatic effect like that would have been in place. But once again, Kurt lacked the requisite solid foundations: he had no revolver on him.

So it was that Kurt, without having spoken to Lisa first, turned up at Paul Weismann's place on Easter Sunday, when the "studio party" had been arranged. Professor Ruprecht had given him today and the next day off—on Wednesday school began again—and so Kurt set off feeling less gloomy than he had feared.

Paul Weismann let him in. The room was dimly lit by bulbs fitted into niches in the walls. It was filling up already, with about a dozen people sitting on two low couches or in basket chairs in front of a long, narrow table fitted out as a bar along the wall.

Several of his friends from Christmas came over to shake hands with Kurt, now and then he was introduced to others whose names he did not take in, and then he saw Lisa sitting in a corner—Lisa—and she didn't look up when Kurt came in, but went on talking vivaciously to Gretl Blitz, who was the first to greet Kurt. Lisa didn't seem to notice his presence until he was holding out his hand to her.

"Good evening," she said. Her hand was cold and lifeless. Then, taking no further interest in him, she turned away as if to go on talking to Gretl Blitz, but by now Gretl had moved elsewhere.

Lisa glanced another way, looking bored, and fidgeted with her dress. Kurt stood in front of her feeling extremely embarrassed, and unsure what to say. Should he apologize at once? Maybe she was only putting on a show. Should he mention Wednesday? Perhaps she really hadn't seen him…

Lisa's arms lie along the arms of her wicker chair, as she looks at Kurt, twisting her lips. "Well?"

"What—how are you?" Kurt sits down beside her, pretending to be at his ease.

Lisa turns a look of pert surprise on him. "Why are you interested in that all of a sudden?"

"Because—I—Lisa, you must believe me when I say that—"

"Yes?"

Losing the thread, Kurt shifts his legs uneasily. His eyes wander over the room. The others are talking in loud voices, no one is taking any notice of the two of them; there's a door covered with wallpaper behind the bar, where does it lead, maybe he could ask Lisa—no, probably better not…

"You interrogate me as if I were a criminal!" Kurt tries to smile, but Lisa's expression is unmoved. That leaves him totally helpless and confused. He looks at her intently. All his torment is in his eyes.

Then, slowly, Lisa's mouth softens, her lips and her eyes begin to smile and she stands up.

"Come with me, you terrible fellow! You don't deserve to have people being nice to you, but I'll spare you a public lecture just this once."

She has gone behind the bar and is opening the little door.

Kurt follows her. He feels weak at the knees, and has to keep himself for shouting out loud with joy.

Beyond the door, Lisa switches on the light. It reveals a kind of lumber room full of easels and other artists' materials, and the one piece of furniture is a sofa. Lisa sits down on it and begins scolding him with mock seriousness for not getting in touch before, and being so childish and so obstinate, and her happy beauty carries him away until, unable to control himself and—

And then it is as he feared: Lisa's eyes stay open, looking vacantly up at the ceiling, her arms hang limp at her sides. Kurt holds back for a moment, and then his mouth is on hers.

She does not resist. But her lips are moist and cool. Kurt stops.

"Lisa?"

Lisa sits up. All of a sudden she is only a little girl. "Do we always have to kiss straight away?"

"Always? How often have I kissed you, then?"

"Well, and you'll kiss me often enough yet, Kurt, believe me. But not just now." Her voice is gentle and comforting. "It's not always right, don't you see?" She caresses his hair, and once again she is much, much older than him, superior, almost forgiving.

Kurt does not entirely understand, however hard he tries. If she loves me, and she told me she did (he feels now as if the last time they were together was at Christmas), then… He takes hold of her again, hesitantly. "Lisa—!"

She drops a light kiss on his forehead.

"Come on. We can't stay here too long." And unabashed, she precedes Kurt out of the door covered with wallpaper.

"Put out that fire, men!" cries Paul Weismann, whose eyes happen to fall on them. "Why did you switch on the light?"

Kurt walks into the room.

Otto Engelhart, with four others, is lounging on a sofa and lighting a cigarette with an air of indifference.

His indifference is acting, Kurt suddenly thinks, it's pretence, it can't be anything but pretence—he's playing at indifference the way Lisa is playing with me—why did she lead me into that room—why does she torment me—but she isn't tormenting me at all, not even that…

Boby Urban, when Kurt sits down beside him, spreads both arms wide and declaims, "O great Queen, what a wonderful thing is a sex life!"

"Idiot!" snaps Kurt.

The other man slowly turns to him and nods a couple of times. "My boy—"

Something in his voice makes Kurt pay attention. He feels as if it were concealing something on which all the others are agreed, but they are considerate enough to keep it secret from him…

And then the evening turned out as was to be expected. They were merry as they had been on the best days of the Christmas holidays, and Boby Urban played the piano, and a girl Kurt didn't know sang *chansons*, and then the room was darkened, and from the gramophone the soft song of a crooner filled the room, curiously moving in the darkness, and the girl whom Kurt didn't know showed a lot of interest in him, and the little door covered with wallpaper opened and closed again a couple of times, and once, as it did, the crooner was singing "I can't give you anything but love"; it couldn't be helped that he sang that, and Lisa commented on how sensuous the record was and wondered whose good idea it had been to put it on, and then Kurt was set free of the black fear that it was Lisa who was just going into the lumber room, and he loved Lisa very much and ignored the unknown girl beside him, ignored the interest she was showing in him, didn't want to notice when she touched him as if by chance, and had to in the end, and the hammering senses of his nineteen years, and the warm proximity of a willing female body made the darkness unendurable to him… and he loved Lisa so much… and thought, when the light came on again, that he was now at the end his courtship, and nothing could be denied him any more…

One of the group going along the street with Kurt at four in the morning, weary and heavy-footed, began praising the gramophone record.

"I can't give you anything but love," Lisa hummed.

Suddenly she interrupted herself.

"Terrible trash, really," she said.

With those words in his ears, Kurt said goodbye. Trash. A trashy novel. All trash.

And it was also trashy that the unknown girl squeezed his hand so hard when they parted, much harder than Lisa, with an air of promise. Trash.

However, Kurt was aroused again. Next time I'll go with her, he thought.

Lisa, why didn't you let me go with her? She wanted me, and I wanted her. Yes, I did want her. I'll go to see her tomorrow and sleep with her. You have no right to stop me.

But Kuno resisted all temptation, and next day was able to take his beloved blissfully in his arms… I'm a terrible moralist, I do it out of pure cowardice. What will happen tomorrow, Kurt wonders, what?

Next day is a Tuesday. And Kurt knows what will happen that day. Although the night is not cold, he shivers, and turns up his coat collar.

You didn't care about me, Lisa. You'd probably even have been glad if I'd done it. Well, you can still have that pleasure. Nothing simpler than…

Then a strong, vulgar perfume rises to his nostrils from right beside him. Glancing up, he looks into the face of a streetwalker, very close to him.

There is a smile around her mouth, as if someone had thrown it into her face and it had stuck there. "Well, laddie? Give us a cigarette, will you?"

Kurt jumps, and quickly walks on, impelled not by bourgeois fear of a social outcast, only by alarm. He is ashamed that he cannot even feel sorry for her; she looked old and unappetizing, and had gold teeth in her broad mouth. The idea of kissing that mouth makes him shiver.

There is another one, too. She is simply dressed (not got up like the other, who had a feather boa and a big hat), and now that she turns round he sees she is pretty.

Kurt comes closer, he soon reaches her. He slows down and stops.

The girl looks past him, not exactly past, but at something farther away—where has he seen that sad look before?

That's right, the trashy novel. Of course. I have to think up something like this, or the trashy novel wouldn't be complete.

"Come with me," says the girl quietly.

She still does not look at him when he asks, "Where to?"

She can't have heard this question so very often yet. It is some time before she replies with a smile meant to be enticing, "To where we'll be alone." Then she looks down at the ground again.

What has come over Kurt? He'd had no idea of sleeping with a streetwalker, it is absurd for him to do such a thing, and he won't do it, he will run away, now, will leave the girl right there, at once, next moment—but he is still there, and the girl is still looking at the ground.

"Come on!" says Kurt suddenly.

He walks very fast, and the girl beside him has to take many small steps. Noticing, Kurt slows his pace, and looks sideways at her—she keeps her head bent—oh, this is ridiculous—and yet there's something there, no similarity, not that—but something like melancholy that knows nothing about itself.

Oh well. All we need now is for her to tell me a sentimental story, how her father is an aristocrat fallen on hard times, that sort of stuff. This is a fine thing!

Kurt looks at her again. The girl bends her head yet lower, as if his glance were burning her body as it runs down it.

Terrible, thinks Kurt. Terrible, and it makes no difference whether she is really sad or not. Maybe she is really sad.

And maybe, up in the room they take in the *hôtel garni*, she would have cried if he had suddenly said no, cried not just for the loss of business but because some vague memory came to her—yes, she might have cried.

So Kurt put out the light and got into bed with her, and she pressed him close with her slender, childish arms, and sighed briefly only once.

She did not put on a great show of lasciviousness, and they said the bare minimum to each other. She addressed him by the formal "you" pronoun, and after a moment of surprise he stopped using the familiar *du* to her, as one usually would to a prostitute.

Now they lie in the tumbled sheets of the double bed, side by side, naked, drained of desire, strangers to each other; and when Kurt touches her arm, which is cold, he says, "Sorry!" without noticing how comic it really is to say a thing like that. Then they fall silent again.

Suddenly she props herself on her elbows, lets her glance rest on Kurt for a long time, and says softly, "I bet your best girl loves you very much!"

That was odd. She uses the *du* pronoun suddenly, and it feels warm and good, it reminds him of the time when he used to run after the pupils of the girls' school in the summer holidays, and felt very much the victor if one of those young girls let him use the familiar *du*... Only then does he take in her words and stop smiling. He looks up at the ceiling.

"You think so?"

The girl nods. "Yes."

After a little silence, she slips out of the bed and has soon finished her *toilette*. From the sofa, she watches Kurt getting dressed.

"You have such a handsome body!"

So that was what she meant! You're wrong, sad little girl. Lisa and I haven't reached that point yet.

Kurt knows, by hearsay, what he ought to pay her. All the same, he asks. At first the girl does not answer, but then, when Kurt presses her, she names a slightly higher sum, and gets it at once.

She holds the banknote, stands up and looks at him undecidedly. Suddenly she puts her arm around his neck, kisses him quickly on the mouth and asks, "Give me a little extra, will you? I have to pay for this room."

Kurt, sunk in his own misery again, suddenly sees himself facing someone with very different problems, and does as she asks.

Then they leave, the girl walking quietly behind him.

As they pass the porter's lodge, he hears a voice inside ask, "Well, Anni?"

The porter is sitting in his armchair, leaning forward, his peaked cap askew on his head, and he winks with unmistakable meaning. The girl, half turned to him, makes a face in Kurt's direction, which accompanied by a gesture says something like, "Fooled that one nicely!" putting her finger to her lips at the same time. When she realizes that Kurt has seen it all she breaks into raucous, shameless laughter, calls, "What are you looking at, then, dumbo?", slaps her thigh and disappears into the porter's lodge. Kurt hears the porter say, in simulated protest, "Now, now, Anni!"—and then he is out in the street, stumbling past shabby buildings already a dismal grey in the dawn light.

His trashy novel had gone straight to an important point. The rest of the story was going to be a penny-a-liner.

X

A Storm on Two Fronts

H ERE WE GO.
They were all thinking that, and many of them said
it out loud. There were about five weeks left now before the
written *Matura* examination, and soon after that the leaving
certificates would be handed out. There was something
mysterious about this in itself, heightening expectations and
apprehension; everyone had to take the written examinations, but admission to take the full *Matura*, awarded on the
grounds of the oral examinations, was granted only on the
basis of the leaving certificates.

The portentously busy activity in the classroom was obvious. To some extent there had been a foretaste of it at the
beginning of the school year. Students were visibly less willing to help each other now, and sometimes there was bad
feeling between them. Some of the professors made caustic
remarks; others, whose subjects were not examined in the
Matura, began gradually closing their lessons down—first of
all Professor Filip, who announced one day that chemistry
teaching for the present school year was over, and he planned
to fill the rest of his lessons with debates on themes chosen at
random. Unfortunately his lessons were particularly chaotic

because the fevered atmosphere generated in the lessons on other subjects was explosively discharged in them, with certain rows of desks competing to chant in chorus, as well as much shouting and bawling; and when Filip, in desperation, resorted to draconian measures (making entries in the register, holding tests in class, threatening detention and failure) they simply laughed at him. He wasn't taken seriously; everyone knew that he never made himself heard in staff meetings, it was unimaginable that anyone would be failed in any subject at his request, and the certainty that he would not in fact make any such request left him the laughing stock of the class. The eighth-year students exploited his harmlessness with diabolical subtlety, and it was pitiful to see him trying unsuccessfully to control the pack, once it was let off the leash, by shouting or pleading or appeals to their sense of "maturity". The class itself felt that its conduct was shameful, but good resolutions remained unobserved. Professor Filip, perhaps the only one of the teachers to bring energetic idealism to his post, was condemned to be a lightning conductor for the storm clouds that had built up into an unbearably sultry atmosphere in the lessons given by the professors whose subjects mattered more.

The same applied, but a little less riotously, to the deadly boring geology lessons of Professor Riedl. He showed fossilized plants under a microscope that he had brought with him, and the students had to go up to the teacher's lectern and look through it. At first they confined themselves to uttering loud cries in a show of enchantment and great interest; later Linke thought up the idea of keeping a record of the time each of them spent looking through the microscope. They actually drew up tables, and Pollak, who had looked through the lens without moving a muscle for two minutes seventeen seconds, earned loud applause. Riedl issued stern bans on such silly tricks, but with little success.

Prochaska's lessons were relatively calm. Throughout the class's schooldays he had dictated the material on which he would be testing them, and now he divided it into sections, providing them with titles and numbers; and he let it be understood that the section on which each of them would be tested for their final set of marks would also be what they needed to know for the oral part of the *Matura*. So if someone was called out and told, "Now, my young friend, we would like to hear something about the French Revolution!" or, "Tell us, if you please, what you know about mining in Central Europe!" only those two topics from his history and geography lessons were of any further interest to that particular student. It was on his knowledge of them that he would have to pass the *Matura*. Sometimes the old Professor would express anxiety—"You must go carefully, young people, I do beg you, steer clear of any scandal; this is my last year, you know!" But the students reassured him: nothing had gone wrong in thirty years, so why would it go wrong this time? They would take care, they said—and Prochaska, with a sly smile, would call up the next student.

In common to the languages taught by Borchert and Niesset was the fact that a student who had passed the written test for his final marks better in one would later be examined orally on the other. (If he had equally good marks for both, then preference in the oral exam was given to the classical language.) As both teachers had their favourites, the grotesque situation arose that in their cases it was a good thing to have a poorer mark for the written work in their better language. Borchert wanted Altschul to take the oral *Matura* in French—and so informed him that he could give him only Good as the final mark on his leaving certificate. Niesset planned to show off with Scholz's prowess in Latin in the oral *Matura*, and so advised him to make some mistakes in his final written exam. There were pitched battles between the two teachers for certain students, followed with interest by the others, for both Borchert and Niesset entirely forgot about the students who were weaker at languages and whose main concern was to do well enough to be allowed to take the oral *Matura*, and were glad to slip through by this means. If Borchert sometimes went for them ferociously, or Niesset warned them not to take anything for granted, they buried themselves even deeper in unobtrusive reserve and were soon forgotten again. They would reappear only when the *Matura* itself came—trusting that they could muddle through it somehow.

Hussak and Seelig also had something in common: they became less and less demanding and were content with only the most perfunctory achievements, knowing that the eighth-year students had more important matters on their minds now. It was also quiet in their lessons, and the respect they were both shown almost had a touch of awe about it. It was quite hard to believe that some teachers did not start out anxious to show their power for as long as possible, but quietly and modestly made the transition from their great importance to their even greater unimportance.

Not so Mattusch, who was close to bursting with self-importance. Red in the face, he would splutter out threats and curses if he caught anyone failing to pay attention, pointing again and again to the deciding influence of the

Matura in German in particular: "Well then, that's clear, clear, it all comes down to your German, isn't that right? Well then, we'll see who's just cramming and who knows his stuff, I mean in German, what else, right?" The safest way of proving that you knew your stuff was to take down his lessons in shorthand and learn them by heart. No surreptitious help was to be expected from Mattusch. But he wouldn't fail anyone, either.

And so the course of the last act of the drama was making inevitably for Kupfer. The rest of the professors, who were otherwise, each in his own way, perfectly capable, seemed to retreat respectfully before that master of his subject. There was general agreement that Kupfer was the be-all and end-all of this year's *Matura*. All might seem to be going well, satisfactory solutions found to everything—but the final decision lay with Kupfer, and a word from him could reverse the situation entirely. The others were only the stages, or steps, leading up to his throne—he, Kupfer, was God Almighty and the ultimate authority on whether a student passed or failed.

Kupfer was well up to the job of demonstrating his ever-increasing importance. It was as if an avalanche were slowly and with sinister calm rolling down on fettered victims. They couldn't get away, they could only look up, paralysed, they were alive, healthy, still alive—yet they knew that the avalanche would reach them sometime. It was coming closer, ever closer, without a sound.

Kupfer said not a word about what lay ahead. He conducted his lessons with a bored and indifferent air, in exactly the same way as at the beginning of the class's schooldays. If the fevered tension of the eighth-year students, which he emphatically overlooked, were to vent itself suddenly in a scream—Oh Lord! The *Matura* is in two weeks' time!—Kupfer would have raised his eyebrows in astonishment. So what about it? You've known for eight years that you'd be taking the *Matura* some day. And now that day has come. What did you expect?

And Kupfer went on teaching and testing and giving an Unsatisfactory here and there without adding any further comment; thank you, sit down, next… One student sat down, the next came up to the front of the class, puppets on strings being pulled by the puppet master to whom this was everyday business.

What was there yet for *him* to achieve? Nothing. He had determined on the path he would take at the start; now he had nothing to do but follow it to its predestined end. He looked down, with mild distaste, at the frantic, scrabbling efforts of that anthill, the class. Was one of them perhaps thinking of doing something about Kupfer's intentions for him, even planning to thwart them? How touching! What strange things we do find in this world! Why did that lad Zasche come to see me, asking me to suggest a private tutor to coach him? Why does that woman, Mertens's mother, pester me so tearfully? Why is Duffek dancing attendance on me? Why is Lengsfeld putting up his hand? Why all this? Strange… And as for *him*, as for Gerber! Why is he *not* putting up his hand? He did try it for a while, which was pleasing at the time—but now? Just sits there, paying only an average amount of attention, sometimes answering and sometimes not, a student like a hundred others, not at all diverting. I imagined it would be more exciting. More resistance, more struggling. But he's stopped defending himself. He dares to stop defending himself. What inordinate impertinence! Outrageous. He is perfectly calm! He isn't making a nuisance of himself!

"Gerber! Stop making a nuisance of yourself!"

Kurt tries to correct the mistake. "Professor Kupfer, sir, I wasn't—"

"Will you kindly be quiet at once? It is not for you to speak if you haven't been asked a question, understand?"

"But Professor Kupfer, sir, it's not true that I—"

"What's that? Not true? This is too much! Give me a pen!"

And Kupfer writes in the register, "Gerber makes a nuisance of himself by talking during lessons, and in spite of being warned about it answers back." Then he says, "There. Now you can sit down, Gerber." And turning to the board, "We will go on."

In grotesque American films, sometimes a storm picks up a whole house, carries it away and puts it down somewhere else. The people who live in the house, after a brief moment of surprise, get used to their new circumstances and go in and out of the house as if nothing had happened. It was the same here. For a moment, the students had done nothing but gawp, eyes and mouths open wide. When Kupfer was writing in the register, some had looked at each other, upset, but others, who had nothing of that kind to fear, simply shook their heads. Many of them glanced timidly round at Kurt Gerber, as if doubting whether he could still be alive—and then, as Kupfer said, "We will go on," they straightened up again and took a close interest in the shadows cast inside a hollow pyramid. They went on.

Kurt himself? His thoughts were in such confusion that he couldn't grasp just what was happening to him and how he felt about it; a terrible, painful void seemed to shrink and then expand his head, in and out it went, in and out—suddenly a signal flared brightly: Kupfer is going to test me now, next minute, while my mind's in this state! Kurt tried desperately to pull his ideas together, but they failed him. He realized, with horror, that he was unable to follow all that was being said in the classroom. The surface of the prism intersects the surface of the pyramid, yes, he could hear that and had a vague idea what it meant. But why does it intersect the shadow cast inside the pyramid? Why does it intersect—inside—intersect—intersect—well, why, for God's sake? What's it all about? Why? Suppose Kupfer asks him that? And he will, he certainly will, his eye has already fallen on him, he has made up his mind. Why? What is he going to say? Why? Help, help!

"Weinberg," Kurt whispers, "why does the surface of the prism—"

Weinberg gives Kurt a brief, baffled glance, doesn't understand what he is talking about. Up at the front by the board they have already gone on to something else, and Weinberg has to pay attention himself, can't offer any help, shakes his head, turns away—but to no avail.

"Weinberg, Weinberg, why, inside the pyramid?"

"Quiet, Gerber! And if you don't like it, you can complain after the lesson!"

Oh no, oh no, now Kupfer really will ask him, he really will, and at once, next moment, now, now…

But Kupfer doesn't ask him anything all through the lesson. Slowly, Kurt sees the danger disappearing; Kupfer's not so bad after all, Kupfer hasn't asked me anything, he doesn't want to give me another bad mark, nice of him,

God Almighty Kupfer is just, God Almighty Kupfer… And what was that he said? I can complain. Yes, of course I can. But I won't. Complaining just isn't done. No. Suppose, let's think this over, suppose I go and complain, who's going to believe me? Me, of all people! And if anyone does believe me—what use is that? The Headmaster will just shrug his shoulders: "Oh, come along—maybe you're not entirely wrong, but—I'm sure you can see this—I can't expose my colleague Professor Kupfer—and there must have been something in it, no one complains for no reason at all, right? What? The whole class witnessed it. You didn't really? Nonsense, everyone knows what to think of that—and then, well, we know you, don't we, Gerber? Very well, very well, I'll have a word with the Professor, perhaps—well, we'll see." That's what the Headmaster will say, no point in going to see him, he can't say anything else. Kurt knows that very well, he sees himself in the Headmaster's office, and Zeisig is sitting in his armchair listening to him civilly, and then he shakes his head, and then he says something, and then Kurt goes out, with a little bow… And maybe the Headmaster really will speak to Kupfer, and Kupfer will strike out his entry in the register, or maybe not, what's the difference… and then Kupfer will be after you again with all his methods of torture, Kupfer the villain, Kupfer the beast, Kupfer the bloodhound… what am I to do, what, what? Go to Kupfer and plead with him? But Kurt has done that unsuccessfully before, and besides—no, no meaningless beggar's pride. No. Go to Kupfer. Yes.

The bell rings. The eighth-year students stand to attention. And here comes Kupfer, looking straight ahead.

Kurt gets up from his desk and raises his hand. Now Kupfer is close to him. "Professor Kupfer, sir!"

"I have nothing to say to you!" rasps Kupfer, walking past, and then he has his hand on the door handle and is on his way out.

Kurt stands there motionless, he feels dizzy, he has to hold onto something—no, thank you, Gerald, I'm all right…

Kurt knocks on the door of the physics lab.

Didn't Hussak's "Come in!" sound unwelcoming? Is this hope going to be dashed as well?

Professor Hussak is tidying up the instruments in the lab with a couple of fourth-year students. He glances at Kurt, and gestures to the fourth-year boys. They disappear obediently.

"What is it, Gerber? Good heavens, look at you! Sit down, do!"

Kurt tells him what has happened. The Professor's face shows no emotion, although now and then he frowns.

"What am I to do, Professor Hussak, sir?"

At first Hussak does not reply; he is gritting his teeth.

"You can't do anything yourself. But send your father along, he may be able to get somewhere. He'd better go straight to the Headmaster."

"My father—I don't want him to know anything at all about this. He isn't well."

Hussak is taking long strides up and down the room.

"Professor Hussak, sir—couldn't you have a word with Kupfer?"

Hussak turns abruptly, then steps back, spreading out the palms of his hands as if to ward off the idea, and he shakes his head vigorously.

"I—have a word with Kupfer? No, no, my birdie—I want nothing to do with him!" And he makes a gesture of such aversion that Kurt gives up.

"Then I'm finished, sir," he says in an expressionless voice.

"Oh no, you are not!" Hussak stamps his foot. "And certainly not now! Wait until after the *Matura*, Gerber. Now—believe me, there would be no point in it at all. At the moment the decision is up to my colleague Kupfer and no one else. Wait, Gerber, and—".

But Hussak had nothing else to say, and could think of no way of hiding it but by quickly impelling Kurt towards the door.

Nothing achieved. "Wait until after the *Matura*!" The *Matura*... he couldn't even think as far ahead as that. The force of the immediate future was too great. What else might follow?

In the next break—Kurt had skipped the lesson, and heard by chance from Sittig, who was coming out of it, that Prochaska had asked to see "my young friend Gerber" to test him, but he had missed that too—in the next break Kupfer arrived. He slammed the door behind him, making the eighth-year students jump up from their seats.

"Gerber!"

"Here, sir."

"A staff meeting has just decided to punish your indiscipline with an immediate two-hour detention. It will begin at four this afternoon. You will be hearing the rest of what was decided later."

In the doorway, Kupfer turned.

"And you are to bring the letter about the detention, with your father's signature confirming that he has read it, by this afternoon."

Kurt was left reeling. There was not enough time left before the afternoon for him to make a plan. When afternoon came, and Kupfer asked for the confirmation, he resorted to the threadbare excuse that his father was away.

Kupfer did not reply to this, much to Kurt's surprise, and escorted him to the classroom where he was to spend those two hours. Nor was Kurt given, as he had feared, mathematical exercises to do, but could occupy himself as he liked. After two hours Kupfer dismissed him with the words, "And I want that confirmation tomorrow," adding, with emphasis, "signed by your father!"

There were a hundred reasons why it was unthinkable for him to forge his father's signature this time, but still less could he actually get his father to sign any confirmation. So Kurt saw nothing for it but to tell his mother the whole story. She listened to him in silence, trembling, all her anxious concern for her sick husband.

"If we can't find any way out of it," said Kurt, "I'm going to fail."

His mother said nothing.

A small gap, like the crack in a doorway when the door is ajar, opened up in Kurt's tottering mind, and for a moment he looked all the way to the end of the story.

"Yes," he murmured, nodding thoughtfully, "that's how it will be. That will be the reason. It's my second detention. That means that I'll get the *consilium abeundi*." (The formal term meant being "advised to leave" and led to actual expulsion.) "Before they throw me out. It's not difficult to make sure an expelled student fails the exam. No one bothers about him."

It occurred to him, suddenly, that this consideration in fact had nothing to do with the signature, that it would still be true anyway. He felt afraid. Had he really reached the end?

"You must go to see Kupfer!" he told his mother, looking at her as if to assess her suitability for this mission.

His mother remained silent. She slowly folded her hands, stared into space, and did not move even when the first tears fell into her lap. Then she sighed, like someone giving up the ghost on a bed of pain, and said quietly, looking away from him:

"Kurt—my dear Kurt, my poor child—you must pull through—you know you must—or else, oh, I don't want to say it out loud, it's unthinkable—dear God, dear kind God—". And then she burst into sobs, stood up and flung her arms round her son's neck. He felt warm moisture on his cheek and throat, and absent-mindedly patted her on her back, which was heaving up and down.

"Don't cry, mother, it's not guaranteed, it's not as bad as all that." He said this in a hard, dry voice; her tears did not go to his heart, as he could clearly tell, they simply irritated his nerves, and yet he felt so sorry for his mother, so sorry as she clung to him and caressed his cheeks.

"You will pass, won't you? Tell me, Kurt, you will pass the *Matura*—" And yet again her words were drowned in tears.

Kurt stood there with his thoughts in confusion, and suddenly he went ashen pale with shame; he didn't want to identify its source, yet it was a fact—with his mother's body so close to his, he couldn't help thinking of Lisa.

"There, lie down for a bit," he said softly, guiltily. "It's terrible the way that idiot gets you so worked up. Is it all really so tragic?"

"Tragic!" His mother's voice was tired and exhausted. "Suppose you have no father tomorrow—"

A dry rattle sounded in her throat. Kurt left the room.

No, there was no point in following his destiny back to its origins and lamenting over the course it had taken. Suppose it could have been changed? And what would have happened if...? Whereas now his fate threatened to roll on in a great torrent leading to something monstrous—*that* was what he had to face. Was there any remedy but flight from such a tide of misfortune?

What followed was crazy confusion. The waves broke wildly against each other—it was obvious now which way they were going—while a sea spray of malice and hatred rose high. Often it was hard to tell who wanted what as events came thick and fast, and only at the end was it possible to discern their outlines. Then peace, born of muted, heavy exhaustion, came down like mist, veiling what was yet to come.

As far as it was possible to disentangle the course of those events, it had begun when Kurt's mother knocked on the staffroom door during the break before Kupfer's lesson next morning; and when the nearest staff member asked what she wanted, she said she would like to speak to Professor Kupfer. Kupfer, who was sitting quite close, told his colleague to ask what her business with him was.

"It's about my son."

And who was he?

The student's name was Kurt Gerber, she said, and he was in the eighth year.

"Tell the lady," said Kupfer audibly, "that I'm not available to speak to her at the moment. I can be consulted from eleven to twelve the day after tomorrow."

Before this answer was conveyed to Kurt's mother, she went up to Kupfer, keeping her trembling under control with difficulty.

"Please would you make an exception, Professor Kupfer? This is a very urgent matter."

There was crushing arrogance in Kupfer's tone of voice. "I consider your behaviour very odd, Frau… er… Gerber. But let that pass—what do you want?"

He had stayed sitting where he was as he spoke, and made no move to ask her to sit down herself. She bit her lip until it was sore—but she clung with all her might to the thought that she must not harm her son by doing anything rash, least of all must she let her own person cause offence. So she put up with Kupfer's humiliation of her, and would probably have gone on standing there if two other professors had not brought up chairs at the same time.

Kurt's mother began speaking carefully, feeling her way. She knew, she said, she admitted that unfortunately her son—

Kupfer brusquely interrupted her. Could she kindly keep it short? He did not intend to waste his entire break, which was meant for his rest and refreshment.

The way Kurt's mother still managed to control herself was nothing short of heroic. She threw back her head and explained the situation to Kupfer, who sat there blowing smoke rings and looking bored.

"My husband is severely ill, Professor. He has an acute heart condition, and the doctor thinks any agitation would be extremely dangerous. My son will accept his punishment, I assure you. But please, would you dispense with my husband's signature just this once?"

Kupfer shrugged his shoulders.

"I'm sorry, but the rule is for confirmations of that kind to be signed by the father, if there is one." (Kurt's mother started in alarm.) "So even if I wanted to, I could not dispense with the signature."

Kupfer stood up, evidently about to end the conversation. Kurt's mother also rose. She had difficulty in staying upright.

"There may be a tragic outcome, Professor."

"I'm sorry, but I have to keep to the rules."

"I doubt whether your rules allow you to endanger the health and perhaps the life of another human being. You can't take the responsibility for that."

"You may leave what I can or cannot take the responsibility for to me. And if it is really as you say—then why have you not charged your son with *his* responsibility?"

"Professor Kupfer!—"

"That's enough. At least it will be a salutary lesson to him. I want the confirmation, signed by Gerber's father, tomorrow."

Kupfer turned on his heel and left the room.

Kurt's mother was almost fainting. One of the professors standing near (the last part of the conversation had been conducted in very loud voices) supported her.

"Dear lady, there is no reason for you to be so upset!" Others joined in too, reassuringly. "Our colleague Kupfer is sure to be ready to discuss it all, you mustn't take it so seriously!"

Kurt's mother hears none of it. All she sees, emerging again and again from visions of horror, is her husband breathing stertorously as he tosses and turns on his pillows.

In the taxi she is shaken by fits of silent, racking tears. And before, sinking into a chair at home, she has overcome them, Kurt's father comes in. Her weak attempts at concealment are fruitless; her husband insists on hearing the story, and has soon found out everything.

When he enters the staffroom, lessons have begun again. Some of the professors who are not teaching are there, including Seelig.

"Why, we were talking about your son, Herr Gerber. Your wife has just been here. What really happened?"

Kurt's father begins the story, briefly and in a composed voice. Now and then he has to wipe away the sweat breaking out in drops the size of pinheads on his forehead. When he comes to the nub of the matter, the detention, Seelig interrupts.

"Detention?" he asks in surprise. "What do you mean, detention?"

Why, on the decision taken at a staff meeting, Kurt had been given two hours' detention yesterday, didn't Professor Seelig know that?

Seelig shakes his head, raising his eyebrows. Then he turns and calls to the corner of the room where three other teachers are standing, "Borchert, do you know anything about a detention imposed on Gerber of the eighth year yesterday?"

Borchert does not. He comes closer.

"Interesting," murmurs Seelig. "Go on, please, Herr Gerber!"

When Kurt's father has finished, the two professors look at each other in surprise.

"A meeting of all the teaching staff has to be held before detentions can be imposed," says Borchert firmly. "There's something wrong. Either our colleague Kupfer imposed the detention without authority, or more likely it wasn't a real detention, your son was just asked to stay a little longer after school hours. But that doesn't mean he'd have to bring your signature to school. Well, we'll soon find out. Wait here, will you, Herr Gerber? Or would you rather sit in the next room? I'll tell our colleague Kupfer that you're here."

Only very confused accounts were heard of what went on in the next room. Some of the students said that in break the staffroom had been almost entirely empty, and loud, excited scraps of conversation had been heard in the room next to it, Kupfer's voice being heard particularly often. What it was all about the students did not know, because the professors present in the big staffroom kept shooing them away.

Kurt hardly listened to these stories; he spoke to hardly anyone these days, and so he had no idea of what was going on.

But when he went home at midday, Dr Kron was visiting again, and he did not leave. Next day, accompanied by Kurt's mother and Dr Kron, his father went to a large sanatorium in a nearby spa resort.

Kurt was not allowed in to see him; he couldn't make much of the few confused remarks his mother made, and only in later correspondence did he learn what had happened. On coming home, his father had called the doctor. Dr Kron had been able to prevent another heart attack just in time, and his father's health had suffered so much from his argument with Kupfer, along with the strong powders and injections prescribed for him and all the upsetting incidents of the last few days, that Dr Kron wanted him to go to the sanatorium for a long stay, away from all harmful influences. Otherwise, said the doctor, he feared the worst.

Kupfer had carried through his wish to impose a detention in an ad hoc meeting, without all the staff present, and the votes of Riedl, Niesset and Waringer were opposed by those of Mattusch and Filip. The decision to impose it was therefore not valid, and Kupfer did not mention the matter again. Nor was Kurt Gerber given the *consilium abeundi*.

It would have been sensible of him to take this as a hopeful sign that all was not yet lost, and even Kupfer's power had its limits. In fact, the affair of the detention was a defeat for Kupfer. But Kurt Gerber was unable to let his train of thought lead him to such a conclusion. He was impelled to keep on thinking, turning ideas this way and that, until he was defeated again and Kupfer was the victor.

When someone who has been lying seriously ill for a long time unexpectedly rises from his bed one day, and begins living a normal life again as the most natural thing in the world, the anxiety of those who wish him well has been so painful that they think this sudden cure is just a flash in the pan, a last flickering of the flame, and send the invalid back to bed willy-nilly to be treated with ointments and medicines. And then it can happen that he really does die. But it didn't have to turn out like that.

Nor did the affair of Lisa have to turn out as it did, although we must remember that Lisa may well have been going through a time when she felt that Kurt Gerber was a considerable weight on her mind. In any case, Kurt got an answer to his letter the very next day; it was a card sent by the pneumatic post system conveying items in canisters along underground tubes, and Lisa fixed an appointment for that very evening. He tried to feel glad, but dark forebodings stifled his attempts. What did it mean that Lisa answered at once? And in friendly terms, too? That was so far from her usual way that it seemed suspicious. (He did not dare to think that Lisa was acting of her own free will for reasons of insight and understanding, out of a sudden realization of what he was suffering and a wish to help him—in short, he did not dare to think it was because she loved him.) But perhaps she just happened to have this one evening free that week, and—oh, damn it, thought Kurt, crumpling up the card, I'll find out in a few hours' time. Do I *always* have to prepare for the worst?

So it could have turned out differently for Kurt—and perhaps the same may be said of Lisa. Kurt might have been over-anxious, seeing a last flicker of hope where only a temporary short circuit was planned, a final No where only a temporary one was intended—and perhaps none of that would have been of any importance if a blue light had not been reflected on the asphalt after entirely pointless rain… but fate is not to be changed by the use of the subjunctive.

So it was that, exactly at the appointed hour, Kurt and Lisa faced one another with expressionless faces, behind which strategy and calculation were constantly and secretly at work, with deception and cunning and in the hope that the other person wouldn't notice any of it…

The sudden shower in which Kurt was waiting had just turned to a slight drizzle as Lisa appeared. She turned up the collar of her trench coat and took Kurt's arm. "Come on."

How well she keeps in step with me, thought Kurt. How different it is from the last time a girl was tripping along beside me. How could I ever have seen any similarity? I must have been drunk! Comparing her to Lisa!

"You're looking very beautiful."

Kurt says that slowly and with emphasis, as if he had planned the words beforehand and would have uttered them anyway, even if Lisa hadn't been there. He would like her to keep quiet for a little while—but she is already putting her hand in its damp glove over his mouth.

"Oh, are you starting all that again? How often have I told you I don't want to hear it?"

Kurt breathes in and out deeply, with a challenging smile that shows all his teeth, and he repeats firmly, "Beautiful, beautiful, beautiful!" As he does so he squeezes her hand so hard that Lisa stops with a small cry and, thinking he may really have hurt her, Kurt looks so alarmed that Lisa utters a peal of glittering laughter, and everything is all right again.

They have stopped under the entrance to a cinema; no rain can get at them here, and the place can be seen only in the diffuse light of the advertising signs.

"Where are we going?" asks Lisa.

Kurt feels as if a wire brush were being held against his forehead: he has no plan at all! He didn't think of anything! He wanted to let things take their course—and they are indeed taking their course without a thought for him. This is where he has to be very strong and secure, master of the situation, *now*... But Lisa, for whom this is no problem, just a matter of the present moment—and she can always deal with those—says:

"Why don't we go into this cinema?"

Kurt goes dark red in the face. She oughtn't to have made the first suggestion; now she's ahead of him again and he has to follow her, *now, now*, his thoughts are racing back and forth, panic breaks out, and suddenly he hears himself say, "Lisa, there's no one else in our apartment—why don't you come home with me?"

He takes fright at his own words; it's like an electric shock going through him. He is sinking into a bottomless pit of fear that Lisa will turn round now and march away. But she stays put. "Look at the film they're showing! *A Story of Everyday Life*. Sounds amusing!"

Is that all she's going to say? Is she making out she didn't hear him? Did she *really* not hear him?

"Lisa—" he grasps at her avoidance of the question as a point of reference. "Lisa, you needn't be afraid I'll—". He stops.

"I know." Her tone of voice shows it, and is slightly derogatory. He wants to say: don't be so sure of that. The longing he has suppressed rebels in him. And he says harshly, disconnectedly, feeling his words sound wrong and wither away, "Lisa, just once—just one single time—one first time—can't you do me a favour? Don't you think I've earned it by now?"

"Oh, I'd love to go to the cinema—you know how little time I have these days!"

Her voice tugs with a thousand silvery chains at the cumbersome block of his resolution. He begins to waver. "Like a soldier with a maidservant," he says uncertainly.

"What are you thinking of this time?" asks Lisa, with comic severity.

"Lisa"—he speaks her name again and again, as if it had incantatory power in his mouth—"Lisa, don't be childish, I'm sure you get more chances to go to the cinema than to spend time with me. When I have you to myself at last, when we can be alone at last, surely we don't want to be with a crowd of other people!"

"But we can talk to each other in the cinema, too."

"Now you're getting your ideas all tangled up, Lisa! If we're going to talk it would really be better at home in my apartment."

"What bothers you about other people? We don't need to trouble ourselves with them."

"I suppose you're not interested to know whether I want to go to the cinema myself, are you?"

"Yes, of course I'm interested—why are you so grumpy?" Lisa pauses and presses herself lightly against him. "Kurt, if I ask you?"

"If you ask me, Lisa—if you ask me—then I'm lost. Please don't ask me!"

"This is terrible!" says Lisa, shaking her head. "We've been standing here for the last fifteen minutes, and I have to be home at nine-thirty. We could have been sitting in the foyer ages ago, talking more sensibly than here."

At that Kurt takes a deep breath, like a surgeon making up his mind to operate on a patient. In this case Kurt is both the patient and the surgeon. Every step that takes him closer to the ticket office is like the incision of a sharp instrument. And when he takes out his wallet he doesn't remember what has just passed. It is as if he met Lisa by chance and they went into the cinema on impulse.

The foyer is full of people waiting to be let into the next screening.

"Quick, Kurt, there are two seats still free over there."

Without a word, he sits down beside her in the deep armchair, and hears the muted music coming from the auditorium. Suddenly it breaks off, and a ripple of laughter at he doesn't know what comes through the closed doors. Kurt slumps in the chair with a soft groan.

"Aren't you feeling well?" asks Lisa. Until now she has been looking attentively at the photographs round the foyer.

"Oh, it's nothing."

"You're not cross, are you, silly?"

She strokes his hair and brings her face close to his. He sees her full, red lips in front of his eyes; their red is all he sees. And he feels some mysterious animal instinct rise in him, thinks of blood, takes fright, and lets his eyes move down, sees the creamy skin at the neck of her blouse, and the white strip of linen beneath it, sees the first curve of her breasts, guesses at more, and he begins to tremble and writhe in torment. His own hand shaking, he reaches for hers—but then she turns away with an air of comical regret.

"Oh no—you know, I almost wish we hadn't come in here."

And then she laughs.

Like a man in a hurry who sees the last train steaming away from him, he is seized by senseless rage, is almost bursting with it. He feels like jumping up and hitting out around him, shouting, with his eyes closed. He doesn't know why all these ideas come into his head just now; all he knows is that they are right feelings, they were bound to come to him, they might have come long ago, and now they are inevitably here, a pack of slavering hounds barking aloud as they break out of their enclosure. He glances briefly and sideways at Lisa, as if to see whether her filthy lies haven't started her body decomposing yet—it's a lie, all of what she has done to him is a lie, a shameful deception, he has been led up the garden path by a girl who laughs at him behind his back, not heavenly, silvery laughter, oh no, a screech of shrill, whorish merriment– there, there, now he knows, now he has found out the bold, liberating thing that will save him, and with his fists clenched and his teeth gritted he gets it out, and hopes it will singe her like a burning torch:

"You tart!"

Lisa Berwald didn't hear him. She had already got to her feet, surprised and perhaps slightly apprehensive, and just as the doors to the auditorium were opened she had walked on ahead.

Kurt dried the sweat from his forehead and followed her. He felt an endless sense of lightness, his anger had salutary side effects. He felt almost malicious glee at his own discomfiture, as looks of unconcealed interest followed them on the way to their seats in a box. Lisa really is extraordinarily beautiful, he thought objectively. No wonder if people envy him. Yes, take a look. You'd all like to be helping her off with her coat and sitting beside her, wouldn't you? Very understandable. Right, now you can turn round. And incidentally—in the box next to ours there is another very beautiful woman, her bare white arm lying casually over the low partition between us… suppose I made up to her when the lights go down? What would Lisa say to that? Probably nothing, she wouldn't even notice… or perhaps she is waiting for that herself… perhaps that was the only reason why she wanted to go to the cinema… how silly of me not to think of it before. Think how she pressed close to me outside… and if I were to ask you… no, you can wait for that, Lisa, I'm not falling for that kind of thing, not I…. I don't wait for darkness so that I can steal what I want to have in the light… I'm not going to touch you, no, no, no…

His warm glance moved over Lisa and stopped to rest on her face like a veil protecting it. Lisa was leaning back in her seat, her full hair waving softly round her cheek and the back of her head, her lips were slightly open, her eyes looked into a void below half-closed lids. At that moment her beauty was so relaxed as she concentrated on nothing at all that Kurt had to turn timidly away.

The music began softly. The lights in the auditorium went down, only a few red bulbs left on at the back. In the faint light they gave, Lisa's beauty seemed to him even more mysterious.

And to think that he, with a rough hand, had wanted to fall lecherously on this dream, this airy delicacy, this divine miracle!

Kurt Gerber was ashamed of himself. His shame was boundless, an awed sense of his own insignificance before so much grace, a barely grasped surge of gratitude. It had come to him at the last moment, the very last. He had very nearly—and then he would have felt miserable, vile and miserable. Slowly that realization rose in Kurt, constricted his throat and wouldn't move, however hard he swallowed, however low he bowed his head.

Carefully, he stood up. But the seat creaked slightly, and Lisa turned to him.

"What is it? Where are you going?"

"I have a bit of a headache, Lisa, that's all," he whispered back. "I'm just going out to the buffet to see if they have a headache powder."

Very, very gently, so that she is sure not to notice, he touches her shoulder and leaves. He goes out of the cinema, into the street, and feels like walking on and on for ever, never coming to the end, never having to stop. The rain is refreshing. Kurt holds his face up to it and breathes deeply, his mouth wide open.

Now Lisa is sitting in the cinema watching the screen, with no idea, none at all. How he envies her that. And at the same time deep, deep pity floods him, he doesn't know where it comes from or what its end will be. He knows only that he is the one person on God's earth to feel sorry for her like this—he knows that, and it makes him great and good. Poor, lovely Lisa.

Shouldn't she be permitted anything, shouldn't he accept whatever she did? Could anyone try disturbing the radiant aimlessness of what she does with dark, tormented intentions, with petty desires? Wasn't it a violation in itself that he had invited her home to his apartment, where he might have flung himself mindlessly on her? And wasn't the idea that she would probably have let him do as he wanted worse, more destructive than everything else?

Yes—but then why does he love her at all? What good is he doing her with his love?

He thinks of Paul Weismann, who had said exactly that to him at Christmas. And also: there's no going back for you now.

No, I can't. And I don't want to. But you are wrong all the same, Paul, and I'll tell you why. (Kurt thinks feverishly, feeling as if he and Paul were sharing the same room, and he puts his thoughts into the mode of expression usual between them.) I, my dear Paul, consider that the once exotic flower that now, thanks to the efforts of various scientists, grows and thrives by the roadside and is known as *coitus vulgaris*, ordinary sexual intercourse, is unimportant in the extreme. No, unimportant isn't quite right, I mean it's insignificant— that's better. It no longer lies at the heart of the matter. There's no objection to that, of course—on the contrary, we welcome with wild applause the fact that it is not of the essence any longer. If we had done so earlier, it would have been a cowardly lie. Sexual intercourse, as we call it, is not, it seems to me, what matters most. Love can flourish even without it, but doesn't have to divorce itself from physical matters. There has just been a little re-evaluation, perfectly logically, on the grounds of supply and demand. For instance, listening to the song of a bird together is less common and therefore more valuable than sleeping together. And as long as birdsong is not declared immoral in itself, as long as a kiss and the pressure of a hand (or even a glance and a smile) can be of more fundamental importance than the exchange of body fluids, which can be carried out elsewhere, I see no need to make love dependent on the granting or otherwise of that exchange. It isn't giving but refraining that's impor- tant in love. Great Thought number 409. With which I will conclude my reflections for today. Did you get the point?

No, you didn't. But that's not essential either. I don't love you, I love Lisa. It's Lisa I want to understand me. And she will understand me…

Kurt goes back into the cinema, feeling more victoriously cheerful than for a long time. He knows what he has to do. He has decided. Now, however, it seems that Lisa, too, has made her decision, and is planning to carry it out come what may. She has left only the preparations to her partner in the game, just as you wait in playing chess for the final checkmate until your adversary could dictate it in the next move. Lisa Berwald (white) is decidedly against a draw as the result of playing on. Kurt Gerber (black), after a wide-ranging endgame offensive, had to get himself into a hopeless position and surrender.

The last pause for reflection was cruelly long. Kurt tried to fathom it, but did not succeed. So he wondered if he had forgotten anything.

No. It had all been said. Everything that he had been carrying around for a year, everything that today, after struggle and need and confusion, had finally taken valid form—it had all been said.

And Lisa had listened to him, and hadn't yet replied. She walked beside him in silence, and was still silent when the rain came down harder again, and they found a little roadside shelter where they could stand. She said nothing, and avoided Kurt's anxious gaze.

Suddenly she laughed quickly and softly, turning full-face to him for a moment, looked away again at once, pointed to a nearby neon advertising sign and said, as if carrying on a conversation already begun, "Look, isn't that blue light pretty reflected on the asphalt?"

A first Kurt didn't know what she meant. Then he thought he must be deceived. Then he thought it a sign of her embarrassment. Then he suddenly smiled, because the whole thing seemed to him like a cartoon in a humorous magazine, and because it was in fact comic to think that Lisa might really have meant her words as an answer. Then it occurred to him that it was not really comic at all. And he remembered a porter saying, in mock indignation, "Now, now, Anni!" And he remembered much else.

And then nothing occurred to him any more, his brain seemed like a hurdy-gurdy gone wrong, churning out all its old tunes at the same time, enough to send you out of your mind, so he put both hands to his head. It would have been wrong to think he did it out of bewilderment and pain, or sudden understanding, or was moved in any other kind of way; no, he felt entirely unmoved, nor did he himself move; he stood there like a dead tree for some time. Then his arms began to sway like thin branches tired of life in the wind, he hesitated slightly, turned around; a surprised voice followed him, but he was far away by now, he was walking to the blue light that looked so pretty reflected on the asphalt, and he leant down to look at it, and slowly, slowly all became clear to him in that blue light. When someone tapped him on the shoulder and asked, "Have you lost something?" Kurt Gerber said, "No," and walked on.

XI

The Palfrey Collapses

Meanwhile, the end of the school year was coming closer and closer. It was barely two weeks until the written examinations; the majority of students had already finished their studies of subsidiary subjects, the first calculations of hours yet to be worked appeared, went from hand to hand, and were constantly adjusted by subtracting the number of hours worked at the end of the day, to the accompaniment of much cursing. Some particularly industrious students made sure of buyers for their textbooks in the present seventh-year class, the committee for the convivial farewell party was set up—it was the usual, traditional end-of-year turmoil, and everything would have been entirely traditional if one incident could have been overlooked, such an incredible incident that the eighth year began to doubt the natural order of things: Zasche, the near-idiot, suddenly came to life.

No one knew anything precise about the first signs of it, but when, after much dodging of the subject, one of the students first mentioned it, everyone else admitted to having noticed it too. Zasche began taking part in lessons. At first he confined himself to whispering answers to those sitting near him who were asked questions at their desks. To begin with no one listened to him, but when what he had said turned out to be right more and more often, his fellow students used his answers, if hesitantly at first. And soon Zasche was speaking up in class himself. Also hesitantly at first, and few really noticed; but then it became more and more noticeable, and finally he was holding forth so eloquently that it seemed as if the quiet fool had become a danger to the public at large. He flung his long arms far up in the air, moving them stiffly back and forth so that they looked like clock pendulums; and if he wasn't asked at first he would whine in a thin, pitiful voice, "Please, please, here! Please, sir, I know the answer!" His large eyes, which had hardly any eyebrows, burned with a strange fire, and his thin body was extended to its full length. There was something ghostly about these desperate efforts on the part of a student given up as a hopeless case, and it had an uncanny effect on students and teachers alike. Zasche was nicknamed "Spooky", and looking at him made you feel quite ill—in front of the whole school, at that. Students thought they would be glad to be rid of the place, if only because of Zasche.

Kupfer began paying attention to him, asked him questions a few times in a slightly incredulous voice, and had difficulty in hiding his surprise when the answers were right. And when a word of approval escaped him for once—"Good, Zasche, very good!"—Spooky gurgled happily, and a broad smile appeared on his face. Then he passed the first test with striking success, and the eighth year unanimously concluded that Zasche was a good student. When they were set a very difficult question for homework, one of the few who had worked it out turned half in amusement to him for information—and it turned out that Zasche's was the best solution of all. The eighth-year students tried in vain to find an adequate explanation of this miracle, and finally put it all down to the fantastic abilities of the private tutor coaching him. The other professors shook their heads too—and were very glad to think that now they would be able to let the supposed dunce of the class pass his exam with a clear conscience.

Around this time Kupfer began the tests on which the final marks would be awarded, as if he had suddenly realized that the *Matura* was imminent. And one day, at the end of the lesson, Zasche is called up to the board.

As the whole class has now become used to his mysterious qualities, no one is surprised that all goes smoothly. The others do not pay attention, but prepare hastily to be tested themselves.

However, it looks as if Kupfer is never going to be through with Zasche's test. He asks him more and more questions, and Zasche gives more and more answers, fidgeting jerkily, but his hands are perfectly steady with his compasses and triangle.

"He's working him to death today," whispers Kaulich to the students behind him. "Look sharp, Spooky!" Others are also whispering encouragement for their own enjoyment.

"Get a move on, Spooky!"

"Shake him off!"

"Quiet!" bellows Kupfer with unexpected violence. Then he turns back to Zasche, who looks as if it were nothing to do with him, and asks him another question, which is also promptly answered.

And suddenly the whole class knows what is going on in front of them: Zasche is being tested until, at last, he can be marked Unsatisfactory.

Kupfer's intentions are plain to see. Zasche is not to pass the test successfully. Zasche is to get the deciding mark of Unsatisfactory and fail. They all realize that. Except for Zasche. He stands up there answering every question. And then grinning.

Kupfer begins pacing up and down, asks for another construction, and another calculation, and another something else, leading to five more questions. He is in the grip of vibrant excitement, as if he were watching an interesting chemical experiment and waiting impatiently to see how the substances used in it develop.

The whole class is infected. A number of them are no longer working, just listening, some because they are so fascinated by the scene, others because they can't keep up.

Zasche has just finished a construction, draws the last line under it, and steps back from the board. He does not look at his work with pleasure and satisfaction, as you might expect, but turns his brown doggy eyes on Kupfer.

Kupfer ignores him, paces up and down with his head bent. Suddenly he stops and says:

"Well then. And now we will take—we will take—yes: the angle bisector LQ as the diagonal of a rectangle and inscribe it in the parabolic segment. If you please."

From somewhere comes a mutter of disapproval, running through the class, sending up little flares here and there, and disappearing again.

Kupfer does not hear it. He goes on:

"The rectangle is NLQR and is shifted to be parallel with the tangent T."

"That's it!" says Pollak, loud enough for most of the others to hear him. "Over and out. I can't go on!" In consternation, he pushes his exercise book away and leans back.

The little flames are flaring up again. "Outrageous!" someone murmurs. Others echo him. "What more does he want?"

"Poor Spooky!"

"It's scandalous!"

"Talk about dirty tricks!"

However, Kupfer notices none of this. Only Zasche exists for him. Zasche is not a student any more. Zasche is a matter of his prestige.

At last Zasche himself seems to understand. At a very slow pace that, in itself, could kill.

The expression on his face changes as if he were watching a process also changing. A race, for instance.

Then he stares foolishly at the board, which is covered all over with strong and faint and double and dotted lines, in three colours and with numbers and signs and circles and semicircles and many, many strange figures. The whole thing, if it ever had a point at all, is now completely pointless. That is how it must seem to Zasche himself.

"Angle bisector LQ... parallel to T with the index K," says Kupfer. "If you please."

Zasche looks at the board once more, steps quickly forward, places the triangle against it, turns to Kupfer, puts the triangle down again—a pitiful picture of total helplessness.

On top of everything, the bell rings at that moment.

It is not the class but Kupfer who breathes a sigh of relief. He will finish testing Zasche. And there can be no doubt how it will end. Unless divine inspiration strikes Zasche.

It doesn't. Zasche utters a muted groan, puts the triangle against the board again, draws a line that next moment can't be seen, then says, "The angle bisector LQ—" and stops short.

There is lively activity and noise in the corridor outside.

The class is restless, too, as the eighth-year students shift on their benches, scrape their feet, tap their desks and whisper.

"You are to construct a rectangle NLQR!" says Kupfer, very slowly.

Another student would probably have done something inappropriate at this moment, might perhaps have pointed out that the bell has gone, or tried a protest—"Professor Kupfer, sir!" But not Zasche. Zasche has nothing like that in mind, Zasche probably does not see Kupfer as a professor or indeed a normal human being, not as anything that can be addressed other than in mathematical formulae…

He makes a faint attempt to dig his compasses into the board somewhere, lets them drop again, and stares at the board.

"Well? Why are you standing there like an ox outside a new barn door?"

Kupfer has no idea how apt his comparison is. There really is something oxlike about Zasche's face, something animal in his alarmed distress. And the board really is a door. A barred door. Beyond it lies life, perhaps a happy mother, or love, or a position in the civil service, or something else. But Zasche will never get beyond it. The class is getting increasingly restless. Kupfer notices, but does nothing about it.

"Well? Can you do it or not?"

Zasche does not reply.

"Thank you. Unsatisfactory, sit down," says Kupfer. And although he has used his normal tone of voice, there is a note of infernal jubilation in it that would make the blood in your veins run cold.

Zasche stiffly raises his left arm, with which he is holding the triangle, then his right arm, with which he is holding the compasses, then lets both arms sink and stands there staring at Kupfer.

The class has put up with much from Kupfer. Now, however, it is indignant. Muted sounds of disapproval break out. Kupfer seems not to hear them, picks up his briefcase and goes quickly out.

For a moment the muttered disapproval breaks off.

And the sudden silence is broken by a long, penetrating scream, as if someone were trying and failing to vomit. "Aaaaaahh!—"

That wasn't Zasche, who is still standing at the front of the class, not moving.

The others swing round, not knowing what's up. They see Kurt Gerber, in the back row, slowly rising to his feet, hands half raised in the air, fingers spread, his eyes popping, his mouth twisted.

"Bloodhound!" he shouts. "Bloodhound!"

The eighth-year students stare at him rather anxiously, taken aback. Some of them, perhaps out of embarrassment, perhaps because it really is funny—begin to laugh.

"Ha, ha—what's the matter? Are you crazy?"

But the laughter soon dies down, and there is peace and quiet in the room again. Terrible peace and quiet.

Kurt climbs up on the bench in front of his desk. Saliva is running from one corner of his mouth.

"Someone hold onto him!" whispers a girl's voice from the front rows.

Kaulich leaves his desk and goes over to Kurt.

At that, Kurt jumps down, races past his baffled fellow student as he makes for the lectern, flings himself against the board, beats both fists on it.

"Bloodhound! Bloodhound!"

Zasche looks askance at him, utters some inarticulate sounds and hurries back to his own desk.

All is quiet again.

Someone outside the door flings it open, puts his head in, slams it shut again.

The noise in the corridor, after filling the classroom unimpeded for seconds, acts like a cold shower. The students' sense of oppression is almost tangibly washed away. And then Schönthal is on his feet, saying, "You ought to have done that during the lesson, Gerber!"

Kurt gives a start, closes his eyes and gropes his way to the door. He stands there, indecisively, and then leaves the classroom and locks himself into the toilets.

Someone outside knocks three times.

Kurt opens the door, and Kaulich enters the gloomy, evil-smelling place. He doesn't know quite what to say, so he elaborately lights a cigarette.

"You don't want to think too much of that," he begins.

Kurt nods, vaguely.

"Schönthal is a fool. I told him so."

"Did you?"

"Yes."

"Why?"

"Why!—"

Kaulich says nothing for a while. Then he drops his cigarette on the floor, looks at Kurt and still remains silent.

Suddenly Kurt begins talking, hastily, in confusion, muddling everything up. He has to talk, would probably have started talking even if no one else were there, but now he has someone to talk to, which is better. He talks about the test, about Zasche, about Kupfer, about himself, about the terrible time he was going through as that poor idiot out there was tested to death, about the torment filling him like the air in a fish's swim bladder until it all exploded in that pointless outburst. He feels so ashamed of it now that he doesn't want to go back to the classroom.

Kaulich listens without a word; it is impossible to tell whether he understands. In the end, he says, "But you'll have to go back to the classroom. God Almighty Kupfer will be on his own way back now."

He opens the door.

"I'll follow you in a minute," says Kurt.

Kaulich leaves, and Kurt looks out of the window. It offers a view down into the yards of a block of buildings. Construction work is in progress in one of them. Kurt looks at it.

A cart is just being loaded up with red bricks, and the horses are ready to be harnessed to it. Horses—the white palfrey—a trashy novel—the trashy novel of my life—who's editing it?—all over, all over.

One of the horses, a strong bay, is standing sideways on, almost at a right angle to the pole of the cart.

Right angle—

Now the horse is to be put between the traces. The carter comes up to it from behind and braces himself on the animal's flank. Kurt can't hear whether he calls a command to it.

The horse obeys the pressure only very slowly. The carter gets impatient and hits it with his fist. As the horse is still reluctant to move faster, he takes the whip from the horse collar, turns it round and hits the horse's flank with the handle.

That gets the horse into the position he wants quickly. The carter fixes the traces in place, then swings himself up on the box, and the cart starts off.

Kurt has watched this process enthralled, as if it were not an everyday occurrence. Why, he wonders, doesn't the horse defend itself? A single kick from its strong hoof would have felled the carter to the ground. But the horse retreated and let itself be harnessed up. Now it is pulling the cartload of bricks and the carter.

Why doesn't it defend itself? Why?

Kurt goes back to the classroom. Lengsfeld is standing by the teacher's lectern, trying to persuade the bystanders to come together in a joint action and do something in self-defence, to resist, not put up with such treatment any longer—it would be shameful, he says, if such a thing could happen again.

Only about half the class are listening to him. And as it is not clear what kind of resistance action he suggests, and as they know it won't be carried out anyway, they soon drift away, and Lengsfeld is left with an audience of only two or three.

The bell rings.

Kupfer comes in. He is in a jovial mood, makes a couple of poor jokes, and begins testing, turning mainly to the better students and testing with unusual benevolence, with the result that even young Gerber benefits; and young Gerber answers a little mechanically, but as the questions happen to relate to fields that he was going through with Professor Ruprecht only yesterday, he gives the right answers, and for the first time in a very long while he has two positive marks to his credit in mathematics and descriptive geometry… and he is delighted.

Delighted!

He knows, oh, he knows very well that he has achieved this success by walking over the corpse of Zasche. He has just been fulminating indignantly against the man whose offer of a good mark he is now accepting without a moment's hesitation. He is a deserter. He is climbing on the body of Zasche, like a hyena. "Yes, Gerber, good, you can sit down, next student!" And the hyena bows to the bloodhound—and is delighted.

Zasche sits in the back row, quietly shedding tears.

So he has skipped his lesson with Ruprecht, true. But you can't go on for ever without a little lounging around, smoking and singing. It has been going on for five hours.

Kurt decides to go to bed as soon as night falls. He sits by the open window, intending to wait for darkness as he looks up at the clouds, but the twittering of birds in the little garden outside becomes intolerable. He lowers the Venetian blind and gets into bed.

It is fairly dark in the room.

Kurt falls asleep while fearing that sleep may not come at such an early hour. His last clear thought is to wish he wouldn't wake up until after the *Matura*...

Abruptly waking from deep timelessness, Kurt sits up in bed, wide awake and feeling like a stranger to himself. His exhausted brain can make nothing of the darkness. Holding his hand in front of his face, he flaps it before his eyes. He can't see anything. Blind. I've gone blind. The thought flashes through his mind in unthinking confusion. God in heaven, not this. Light. I want to see something. A glimmer of twilight. As if to catch it unaware, Kurt abruptly swings his head round—nothing. All the night in the world is lying on him, enormous, sultry, impenetrable. He doesn't know which way round his bed is standing and where, doesn't know where the door and the window are. Madness seizes on him. He strikes out with clenched fists—and his second blow hits something hard. He is so glad that he ignores the pain. So that's where the wall is. Good, good wall. He can at least feel it. And he strokes the wallpaper, gratefully feeling its slightly embossed pattern. Then he pulls himself together: the wall is here, the bed is here. He is lying on his right side. Good. And the window is behind him. Slowly, eyes closed, he turns his head and opens his eyes, and—there! Thank God: light is filtering very tentatively through the cracks of the Venetian blind on the right, at the top. Kurt sinks back on his pillows, breathing a sigh of relief. Darkness is not so terrible now. Something is alive in it over there, and here—here a clock is ticking, or no, his watch—how late is it anyway? Kurt is aware of his right hand moving through the air, groping for—for the lamp, of course, the lamp on his bedside table, where else? To think that I forgot the lamp!

Is it still there? Soon I'll have bright light in the room, and everything will be all right.

But his hand reaches out too hastily, still trembling. With a mocking clatter, the lamp falls to the floor.

Now that he knows he isn't blind, that doesn't matter. He will go back to sleep again, he thinks, at once, quickly, before the thoughts come, those insidious thoughts eating away again.

But here they come. They refuse to be kept at bay for long. With great difficulty, Kurt has dismissed them from his mind, clatter, clatter, the shutters roll down over it, no one at home. That was how he managed to get over the blue light reflected on the road yesterday, by simply extinguishing it, that was how he woke in the morning today in clear, untroubled readiness for torment, and that was how, so far, he has managed not to think of all these things. His head is in two parts: in the front room he is awake and active, and everything is done in the front room. No one and nothing is allowed into the second room, it is locked, just as what has happened is over and done with. His heart and mind live in the mortal silence of that room, it is where Kurt Gerber lives, and now he feels he can't go on like this, he defends himself desperately against the thoughts pressing in on him, reaching out their thin hands to him like irritating petitioners, demanding, not to be turned away. The whole forecourt is full of them now, they are getting more and more insistent, Kurt wants to go away, to take flight from himself, so to speak, and give himself up to the devastation—but it is no good, they won't let him out, he must open himself up to them.

It is as if the thoughts find it hard to realize that they are being let in and out of the antechamber. Hesitantly at first, with some awkwardness, they take possession of him.

Kurt tosses and turns in bed, still defending himself; he doesn't want to think, he won't, no, he will not think, it doesn't help, and his brain needs peace and quiet to save itself for more important things... but what is more important? What? Kupfer? Lisa?

It was all there before. What are you looking at, idiot? All of it was sketched out in the plan for the trashy novel.

But why doesn't the trashy novel go on?

(So I'm thinking after all. Well, that's good too.)

Why does none of it hang together? I mean, if there were some connection between Lisa and Kupfer, if she were making a heroic sacrifice for me—but she has no such idea in mind. No. Wrong. Different. Kupfer has seduced Lisa, and I'm going to murder him. No, that's wrong too. Kupfer and Lisa—no, nothing. There is nothing between Kupfer and Lisa.

There is Kupfer, and there is Lisa.

Lisa is an entirely different failure on my part.

And if I get tested tomorrow, that again will be an entirely different failure. Self-contained. The end.

All of a sudden Kurt sits up in bed. A great idea has come to him: he will simply stay away from school tomorrow, there's no one at home to prevent him, not tomorrow, not the day after tomorrow, and if Kupfer sends the caretaker to find him—tell your Captain Kupfer he knows me. Slam the window shut. That will do. Excellent. That's what Kurt will do.

Then Kurt lies back again and knows he will do nothing of the kind, he will go to school tomorrow, and the day after tomorrow. And he also knows why. Every letter he gets from his mother is full of it. "Are you sure you're studying hard, my dear? Your father still isn't well—do I have to tell you what's at stake?"

No, no one has to tell me. So why do they do it all the same? Why do they torment me? Why? I'm really doing all I can. I passed two brilliant tests today, in both subjects. It was a scary kind of wedding, the bloodhound and the hyena getting married. They will give birth to a majority of pass marks.

In alarm, Kurt realizes that his thoughts are suddenly taking definite shape; he sees the bloodhound and hyena in animal form, and cannot tear himself away from the repellent picture of their embrace. Yet he is not dreaming, he is fully conscious, and no ghosts appear, no apparition of Kupfer brandishing a huge integral sign overhead; such things don't happen, it is all so void of mystery, so normal, so horribly transparent and logical until in the end… Kurt knows, Kurt is wide awake and well aware that none of this is so; but it *could* be so, he *could* be dreaming that he is condemned to death for high treason, a unanimous vote for the death sentence; and there is the gallows, a right angle $\ulcorner$; his escorts are moving towards it, all in black robes, waggling their heads back and forth, back and forth, their whole bodies waggle too; now they are surrounding him, and Kupfer asks if they have a last wish, and they'll stand in a semicircle under the gallows from which Kurt is already hanging, and point their arms and spit at him, and then they all fall flat on their backs—what has happened? Was he really dreaming? Kurt strains his eyes, peering into the darkness as if he could find something left there, something tangible.

There's nothing there. Only blackness.

But no, there is something: the hyena with the blood-hound. Get away, get away. Light! But the lamp is lying on the floor, broken.

Their terrible coupling lasts a long time, up—down—up—down. As if they were human beings.

And suddenly all the women who have ever been close to him are around him, lying in his bed, many naked bodies, and Lisa is somewhere among them, only a naked woman like the unknown woman at Paul's studio party and the prostitute and all the others… only half reluctantly he imagines crazy happenings before his eye; now at least there is confusion and mad oblivion, and again and again something strange reels among these images, torn scraps of formulae, spat out like blood; he can't bear it any more, he is too weak for this distress, he tosses back and forth, gasping in sombre torment, lies convulsed in the soft, soft pillows and buries his teeth in fabric wet with sweat, and feels his own body in a strange lustful state, knows why all this is happening, runs to oppose it, yet he wants Lisa, he is breathing stertorously, he wants Lisa… and she evades him again and again, and he chases her, an animal now, and then it's another woman, any woman… And then he is thinking coldly again, lying there limp and spent, and burning shame comes over him in the trembling aftermath, and a gentle, melancholy pleasure is part of it because it wasn't Lisa he'd been thinking of and that shakes him, all of it, shakes him thoroughly, until at last, at last he can sob, hot, beside himself…

It is not restlessness that has driven him to get up, get dressed and leave the house.

He simply had nothing more to do on that bed, churned up in the struggle. That's finished and over.

Only out of doors in the fresh air of the early summer night does he feel disgust at the sweetish smell in his room, and the soft pillows, and everything that happened there. He breathes in deeply.

It is half-past eleven. Kurt does not feel sleepy. Indeed, he feels free and healthy as he strolls through the streets, and a thousand faraway things that he hasn't thought of for a long time come into his mind.

It's so long since he has been in the company of other people!

And then he has an idea that, admittedly, is a little unusual, but easier to put into practice than the idea of a joint resistance action at school.

Last time it had been four in the morning before the company left Paul Weismann's studio. So it could be another four hours. It's worth a try. At worst there'll be no one at home. That would be no disaster either.

But he realizes, from his relief when the concierge of the building lets him in, if reluctantly, that for him it would have been; his fast breathing as he waits at the door tells him so, and his joy when it is opened.

There are even a few coats and hats hanging in the front hall. For once he's been in luck. About time, too.

But now he has to pull himself together, and make his late visit plausible to Paul Weismann, who stands there looking surprised.

However, Paul soon overcomes his surprise. Perhaps he is used to such things, perhaps he is one of those rare and precious people to whom appearances are of no importance—at any rate, he gives Kurt his hand without expressing any astonishment, and tells him at once that there's nothing left to eat, all he can offer is a drink or black coffee.

Oh, in that case, replies Kurt, joking, he has no business here and will leave again. So saying, he hangs his hat on a hook. But seriously, is Paul sure he isn't being a nuisance?

He could only be a nuisance, at the most, by asking such silly questions, Paul informs him.

They go in. The room is dimly lit, the gramophone in the corner is playing the record by the crooner that he heard before—yes, that's it—the first words of the refrain are heard. "I can't give you anything but love, baby—"

"But suppose she doesn't want his love?" says Kurt, and he suddenly feels close to tears again.

"That's the only thing I've plenty of, baby," the crooner sings on, wholly undeterred by the laughter of some of the company at Kurt's remark, and their loud greeting.

Kurt sits down on a divan. The unknown woman is here again. Lisa is not.

Lisa isn't here. And it was because of her that he came here. All because of her—

After a while the unknown woman sits down beside him. "Nice of you to honour us with your company again. How are you?"

Kurt was expecting something like that. And his voice is much less friendly than he meant it to be. "Why do you ask?" He wishes with all his heart that she would get up now, offended, and walk away. But she stays where she is. And Kurt knows that it is all decided.

The unknown woman is not even surprised.

"Because it interests me, my dear Kurt Gerber!" she says, pressing his hand.

He realizes that his hand is still in hers, and quickly pulls it away. He is suddenly angry with this unknown woman, who wants to give herself to him although he doesn't love her, who casts a light on the wretched nature of his self-deception by showing him his readiness to take her all the same.

"And why does it interest you?"

The room is almost dark, the crooner is singing, there is no one else on the divan.

"Because you are so young and stupid," says the unknown woman gently, caressing his arm. And as he says nothing, she puts her head close to his. "Little boy—"

"I am not a little boy."

"Stupid little boy!" The unknown woman's voice is vibrating close to his ear, mocking, lying in wait.

Then Kurt has sunk his teeth into her mouth, and she falls back, and—

"No—please—what are you thinking of?" she whispers sharply, firmly extricating herself.

Kurt lets his arms drop. This is too much. Yet another failure here! He grinds his teeth, desperate, and lies motionless on the divan for minutes on end.

Suddenly he feels a hand glide through his hair, first very gently, then harder and harder; finally she is pulling it as if to get him to stand up.

Kurt has followed the unknown woman through the door covered with wallpaper, feeling weak at the knees, and he has come back through that door, still weak at the knees.

But it was no longer his inflamed senses making him tremble; once again it was that limp, degenerate shame, that pitiful weakness, through and through, endless, with no consolation.

Except that now he can't sob. Except that now his thoughts are streaming back in a torrent, to where all is without end and without comfort, and suddenly the great river mouth of the torrent opens up ahead of him.

It seems to him as if he already knows what it feels like to have all eyes turned on him, gawping, as he feels them now.

Of course he does. And he knows exactly where, too.

There they sit, staring at him. Is he up in front of the class by the blackboard, unable to answer?

He tries to get his bearings and be back here. It doesn't work. Revulsion chokes him, aversion to everyone and everything.

He is already at the door.

"Please forgive me, I don't feel well. I'd better leave."

And he turns abruptly and leaves the room, followed by baffled silence.

Paul Weismann comes hurrying into the hall. "What's the matter with you? Was it something to do with Lizzie? Are you crazy? Come back in!"

"I have a headache," says Kurt wearily. "Goodbye."

The people in there can think what they like. Yes, it was something to do with Lizzie. Just as, back before this, it was something to do with Lisa. So the unknown woman's name is Lizzie. x equals Lizzie. I cross her out.

Kurt is back in the street.

No moon in the sky, only stars twinkling up there, fixed stars, never shaken from their courses.

Come up to the front, Gerber. We have here Orion, its five trace points with their co-ordinates x_1, y_1, x_2, y_2 and z.

We have here Orion. And it will always be there. Everything will always be there. I, Kurt Gerber, am of no importance at all.

But it's not about me.

By chance, now, at this moment, I am on the agenda. And for a tiny span of time to come. Then that will be over. Then we will have Orion again. And again and again.

We have here five trace points and their co-ordinates. Construct, if you please.

And they all gape at him, the way the guests up in the studio gaped now.

An arrogant company. And rather dim-witted at that. Was it something to do with Lizzie? Those are all the problems they have: Lizzie and the lumber room.

Did it occur to one of them, any single one, to ask me what I'm doing? What burdens I'm carrying about with me? What I drag around?

And suppose I'd told them? Told them the way it is, without any sense of shame? Suppose I'd come out with it of my own accord?

They'd shake their heads, baffled, and say: What are you so worked up about? We really thought you were over all this childish stuff. Do you think anyone's interested? We've all been through it. Been through it and forgotten it. We are alive and well. Don't shout like that.

Why am I worked up? Why? I have to get worked up because you don't. Because to you it's something childish. You've all been through it, yes. You've seen yourselves being murdered. And now you have forgotten it. You've forgotten yourselves, your dead bodies, and you smile. Do you know that your smile is the worst, vilest, most appalling smile there can be? It violates corpses, your own corpses. What was that? Oh, you're alive and well all the same? Alive? You? No, you stopped living long ago. What they have left of you, what their arrogance did not demand, that's alive. Alive? A gruesome kind of life. The final moments of a vivisected rabbit in a lab. And look, the experiment always works. They trample over your minds, they bend your backs, they subdue your wills, they duck and dive and deceive you and tear your hearts out of your bodies so that you won't notice—and you are alive. Alive and smiling. And wondering why someone is shouting in protest.

Good God, it's not me shouting! There are a thousand torture victims shouting out of me, with my voice. Please, Professor, may I shout? No, you may not. They've sent me all their cries, all of them. Black bats with huge fangs have flown into me. They are hacking at me, churning up my guts. So I have to scream and scream and scream—

Kurt opens his mouth wide, but nothing comes out of his throat and nothing gets into it, no air, his face swells, he falls on the paving of the road and feels something warm running, in a narrow trickle, down his forehead and over his lips, it doesn't hurt, he might have been able to stand up, but by now it is some time since he wanted to. He stays lying in the dark, empty alley, lying on the dirty paving in the soft horse droppings where he, the palfrey, lies.

XII

The Matura Examination

I T IS NEARLY one o'clock in the afternoon. There is the sound of muted movement in the corridor of the third floor. Time has been passing too slowly for the students in their last year, and one after another they have gone out. Now only Ditta Reinhard is left, the last of her group to be taking the exam.

The oral *Matura* had begun at State High School XVI.

Downstairs, on the blackboard, a stamped sheet of paper had been hanging for some days. It was signed by the eighth year's class teacher, the Headmaster of the school and the chairman of the examining board, Schools Inspector Marion. This sheet of paper informed twenty-eight of the students that they were admitted as candidates to take this final school examination. Of the thirty-two who had made up the class at the beginning of the year, then, four were now missing: as well as Benda they were Lewy, Mertens and Zasche. They had failed in Kupfer's subjects and were not admitted as candidates. Severin, on the other hand, whose situation had seemed very precarious, was admitted. Probably Kupfer was cancelling him out with something similar in another class; and then again, to be admitted

307

to the *Matura* as a candidate was not the same as passing it. However, it showed that Kupfer's power was no longer quite so almighty.

The sequence of exams was also given on the sheet of paper. The girls were given the first time slots of the day, irrespective of alphabetical order. It was not clear why, but as they always had the preference of the teachers no one said a word about it.

Today the first group were being examined. It consisted of Halpern, Hergeth, Kohl and Edith Reinhard.

The students had permission to attend the examinations, and they all made use of it. Even Lewy had turned up just before the examining began, when all was quiet, and had settled at his ease into one of the chairs set out for them, with the audible remark, "I want to see what I'm being spared!" Some of the professors wanted Lewy thrown out for that, but the chairman of the examining board dismissed the request, and the oral examinations began. The subjects, in order of testing, were: mathematics with descriptive geometry, Latin or French, German, geography and history. There was a long break before the German exam, and many of the students went home with their textbooks and exercise books for some final revision. It was the last chance.

Ditta Reinhard came out into the corridor, carefully closed the door behind her and put her tongue out at it. "Yah boo!" she said. She was quickly surrounded and effusively congratulated, for there could be no doubt that she had passed. She thanked the others with a happy smile, and said with fervent relief, "Thank goodness that's over and done with!" She was envied by all who still had to go in, all whose fate would not be discussed by the examiners until tomorrow, or the day after tomorrow, or even later, all who could not yet wait in suspense as the girls Halpern, Hergeth, Anny Kohl and Edith Reinhard were now waiting. Anny Kohl's eyes were red-rimmed with tears, for her performance in German had been very moderate, and now she was afraid she would miss out on the Distinction they all hoped for. The others comforted her, telling her not to look on the dark side, she was sure to get Distinction, as she'd see in fifteen minutes or so at the latest—but Anny Kohl was not reassured, she called Mattusch names, complaining that he had always looked down on her, and her parents would never forgive her if she came home without a Distinction. The conversation went round in circles, opinions of the value or otherwise of a Distinction were exchanged, and it turned out that suddenly none of them minded whether or not they got a Distinction, just so long as they passed and it was all over.

Kurt was leaning on the banister, a little way from the others. He knew what to think of the girls' attitude. He hated the whole thing. All this funereal pomp as the process of examination, long familiar to them, took place for the last time! The stiff self-importance with which the characters in the comedy were acting! It was enough to make you sick. Kurt shook himself.

The door of the examination room was opened, and Kupfer put his head out and called the four girls back into the room.

After a little while, Borchert was the first to come out into the corridor. "Halpern, Hergeth and Edith Reinhard pass with Distinction, Anny Kohl passes with voting unanimous. Well, that's the first four of you dealt with."

The first four could be seen through the open doorway, shaking hands with the chairman of the examining board and the professors, and thanking them; that was the custom. They came out again, the three who had a Distinction beaming happily, Anny Kohl in floods of tears.

So the first four were dealt with.

Kurt Gerber goes home. The air is warm, you can hear pigeons cooing on many of the rooftops.

So this is it. This is the end. This is all it was for.

Eight years. Have I been dreaming my life story, or is it true? Walther von der Vogelweide was born sometime between 1160 and 1170, they're not sure whether it was in Bolzano in the Tyrol or Brüx in Bohemia; he praised German morals and customs and German women as the best in the world, and he died in 1228.

Even Walther von der Vogelweide died.

We all have to die. Too bad.

He doesn't want his father to die. Not yet. His mother sounded so happy about the good effects of his, Kurt's, last letter. Really only the end of that letter had been important: "Oh, I almost forgot—I passed the written *Matura* and they've admitted me as a candidate for the oral part of the exam. And I suppose if they admit me they're probably going to let me pass."

Of course. There can't be any doubt about it. It has cost him a great deal of toil and sweat, unnecessary sweat, useless toil, superfluous torment, until that could be definite. Until he realized how ridiculous all his anxiety had been. It won't go that far, God Almighty Kupfer. You saw that too, just at the right time. It would have been such a joke: Kurt Gerber not admitted as a candidate for the *Matura*. What a laugh! Why, I may even be passed unanimously.

If you take a circle with a rectangle inscribed in it, with a tangent between each of its two consecutive sides, you get a new circle.

I can at least say as much as… as much as… well, for instance, Blank. Let's not presume too far. As much as Blank. Good.

Will Blank fail? No, he won't fail.

Why would Blank fail? Why would anyone fail?

But Lewy, Mertens and Zasche weren't admitted as candidates.

The bats hack and hack and hack.

The hyena bows to the bloodhound.

The palfrey lies in the mud.

Kupfer is an ox.

Is there a zoo in Paris? But I won't be going to the zoo anyway. No, Lisa, I won't be going there, I'll be going to the Folies Bergère, and after that I'll go and have supper, not on my own, and after that—yes, Lisa. I can do that.

I can do so much. I can prove that the normal layouts of plane figures are related by perspective affinity. The ordinates are the affinities, and the intersection of the planes of the polygon with the upper plane is the axis of affinity. Sit down.

Mertens's mother spent a quarter of an hour with Kupfer, crying. She ran after him to the door of the classroom, still crying. Then she took her son's hand and went away with him. Her son was crying as well.

The Zasches are poor, and the private tutor was expensive. Zasche wanted a post in the civil service. Now he'll never get one. The Zasches have no money left, said Klemm, who lives in the same building. Zasche has TB and needs mountain air. He'll never get that either.

The bats are churning, churning, churning up my guts.

My father is as ill as you, Zasche. And he has as much right as you to live, Zasche. But if I fail—oh, nonsense! I won't even think of it. My father must live. And I must pass the *Matura*. I'm not bothered about anything else. I must pass. I must.

Oh no, oh no, go away, bats.

It can be said of the geological structure of the Carpathians that the outer areas consist predominantly of impure sandstone or flysch. Good old Prochaska. You're the only one we can rely on!

The middle path. Yes. It's not so difficult, not so easy, not so important or unimportant as I sometimes think—after all, it's only the final examination after eight years of study at high school, isn't it? All in order. Keep calm, keep calm, keep calm.

Wednesday, when the group consisting of Brodetzky, Duffek, Gerald and Gerber was to be examined, had come.

Kurt had not attended the exams on Tuesday. Although Professor Ruprecht had advised him not to revise, he had spent the whole day on revision, and went to sleep very late. Now he woke feeling a little dazed, and looked around his room in the dawn twilight. The clock said a few minutes after six. So he could go back to sleep for another half an hour… Then his eye fell on the dark suit he had put out the evening before—the *Matura*! He jumped out of bed and stared at his suit as if it were a ghost. For a second his heart stopped beating, his throat was constricted, he couldn't believe that the time had come; that the idea of the "*Matura*", after taking on an almost legendary aura in eight long years, surrounded by all kinds of complex connections, was now actually taking shape, and would soon face him in the form of programmed events.

Then he reassured himself. Seen at close quarters, it wasn't so bad. Just something planned, he'd often been here before.

He dressed, without haste, and sat down for one last time with the exercise books that he had filled in his lessons with Professor Ruprecht. Many places had red lines through them; he read through those with particularly close attention. Professor Ruprecht had pointed them out with a fleeting twinkle in his eye, and said, "You may be asked about that. Take a good look at it." In fact Professor Ruprecht had sounded much more confident recently than could have been hoped when Kurt first began private coaching with him. When Kurt asked outright after the last lesson what to think of his prospects, Professor Ruprecht had replied, with much veiled meaning in his voice, "Hmm, one never knows for certain. But it ought to be good enough for you to scrape a pass. Well, best of luck, then."

Kurt tested himself on formulae, taking them at random, and was pleased to realize that he remembered almost all of them. He wasn't worried about Latin, he had learnt by heart what he needed to know on the two subjects set by Prochaska ("Geological Structure of the Carpathian Countries" and "The Age of Enlightened Despotism"), so he quickly skimmed a handbook of German literature and then stood up feeling reassured. It will be all right, he thought. It will be all right.

$$R = \frac{a}{2} \sqrt{2} = \rho \sqrt{2} \ldots$$

A sudden ringing sound startled him. What was that? A caller, now, at this time of day? A crazy thought crossed his mind—Kupfer was sending him the problems in advance—such things were not unknown. Why doesn't the maid go to open the door faster, he thought—faster, faster? There—the maid came in. Kurt saw, trembling, that she was carrying a folded piece of paper.

"A telegram for the young gentleman!" she said, putting the paper down on the desk and leaving the room.

Kurt sank into his chair, disappointed, furious with himself for his mistake. Reluctantly, he tore the flimsy form open.

"KURT DEAR BOY FATHER AND I THINKING OF YOU DAY AND NIGHT WE WISH YOU ALL GOOD LUCK SEND NEWS AT ONCE YOUR MOTHER." At the top was written: "Deliver before 7.30."

Kurt tried to feel pleased, or at least moved. To his shame, he realized that he felt nothing but morose. There they are sitting in the sanatorium, he thought, thinking of me and the stupid *Matura*. Believing they can do me some good with this telegram. I ought never to have written to tell them the date of the oral exam. Now my father will be on tenterhooks all day. Why did I? I'm an idiot. But that's what they wanted.

He crumpled up the telegram. Suddenly he stopped, smoothed it out again and put it in his pocket. All the love in those few words had struck him. "Your mother…" He imagined how it might have been. Maybe his father didn't know anything. His mother might have kept it secret from him to spare him agitation, might have slipped off to the post office unnoticed to send the telegram; she would have wanted a breath of fresh air, a change from the oppressive anxiety now approaching its end as she hesitantly faced it: "Send news at once…"

Yes, I'll send news at once. I'll come with it myself to enjoy your pleasure.

As Kurt went in, some of the professors were already sitting at the long green table in the examination room. He went straight to the place reserved for candidates in the corner beside the lectern. Brodetzky greeted him coolly, Duffek was memorizing formulae; only Gerald, who looked pale and as if he hadn't had enough sleep, smiled slightly and said, "And here is Scheri of the Eighth-Year Stables just coming up to the starting line."

"What do the odds look like?" asked Kurt.

"Not bad. Quite a solid field. Brodetzky has Distinction in the bag, Duffek is tipped for unanimous pass marks, and the two of us to get through with a majority of pass marks." (This was not entirely true; Gerald, too, was expected to get unanimous pass marks.)

They could make an advance guess, suggested Kurt. Prochaska, Hussak, Seelig and Filip were sure to be for them, Kupfer, Niesset, Riedl and Waringer were sure to be against. That left Borchert, Mattusch and Marion, the outside examiner. Marion had two votes, didn't he?

Yes, and thank God he's a linguist. He won't interfere with God Almighty Kupfer's marking in maths, but he might in Latin! Dangerous, that—cross-questioning! If he was in as bad a mood as yesterday…

Only now did Kurt remember that he hadn't been here yesterday. He asked about the results.

Gerald's eyes were wide with surprise. Didn't Kurt know yet? The first fatality!

Kurt felt weak at the knees. Who—who was it? All yesterday's candidates had been sure to pass!

Gerald too looked gloomily at the floor. "Poor Blank!" he murmured. "He was shattered afterwards, couldn't say a word."

So it was Blank, Blank of whom Kurt had been thinking recently. Blank, a safe candidate whose breadth of knowledge seemed to say something about him—Blank had failed.

"The other three got Distinctions," said Gerald.

Kurt spat. How was it possible that Blank had failed? "Who stabbed him in the back?" he asked.

"Three guesses."

"And the others? Didn't anyone—Blank was always— God Almighty Kupfer on his own isn't enough to—on his own he can't fail anyone, there must have been several of them—the others—"

Gerald made a weary gesture. "The others! They all had their own favourites yesterday and were working to get them their Distinctions. The only one they didn't care about was Blank, if you ask me. And then that idiot did something very silly. When it came to Prochaska's questions he rattled the answers off at top speed. It was bound to attract attention. He was slow everywhere else, and then in geography and history it suddenly went like clockwork. Prochaska is afraid he'll be found out, so he's angry too, and agrees to everything Kupfer says. And once there are four votes against you, the rest isn't difficult to guess."

No, thought Kurt, it certainly isn't difficult. There you are. Blank has failed.

Why did Blank fail? It was not at all what everyone had expected.

Well, for that very reason. That was the thrill of it, the divine sensation. If God Almighty wills it, then Blank fails.

But if God Almighty wills it, then Gerber, unlike Blank, can... Why not?

As if Gerald had guessed Kurt's line of thought, he said, "The outlook's not so bad for us, you know. Kupfer may be feeling satiated today. I don't think that on two consecutive days he—well, we'll soon see. Here he comes."

Kupfer had entered the room, wished all his colleagues good day and then turned his attention to his folder.

Kurt stared fixedly at him. He was painfully aware that he was looking for some good sign rather than expressing his own hatred and dislike. But not a muscle moved in Kupfer's face.

The other eighth-year students, who had been waiting around in the corridor until now, came in, waved and nodded to the candidates for examination, sat down and then stood up again; Marion, a thin, dry, stiff man in a frock coat of old-fashioned cut, came into the examination room in creaking shoes. The professors also rose for him.

At a slight inclination of his head everyone sat down again except for the four candidates, who remained on their feet. It was perfectly quiet in the room; by the third day the procedure had still lost very little of its alarming solemnity.

Kurt stood there looking pale, his heart thudding wildly. The *Matura*! Here it was, now, really and truly! A thousand thoughts flashed through his mind. Formulae, his parents, what would happen now, Ruprecht, Blank, Paris, more formulae, what do I look like, my father… hush, hush. But his headlong terror of what was to come didn't leave him. He felt like running away, far away, knowing nothing more about all this, it was all the same to him, just get away, quick—and then Kupfer's voice held him spellbound.

"Mr Chairman, may I introduce you to today's candidates?"

He had risen to his feet and was pointing to the four. They obeyed his gesture, walking in single file, and went up to the chairman of the examining board, who shook hands with them and nodded slightly as their names were given: Brodetzky—Duffek—Gerald—Gerber. Then they went back to their places.

"Brodetzky!" called Kupfer, and as Brodetzky hastily came up he handed him a sheet of paper. It contained the mathematical questions. You had to sit down with them in a place entirely separate from all the rest, known as "the electric chair", where you had a few minutes to study them.

Brodetzky had propped his head on one hand and was moving his lips quietly; anyone could see that he was preparing to answer. The room was still very quiet. Some of the professors exchanged remarks *sotto voce*.

Even before the time officially allowed to study the questions came to an end, Brodetzky stood up and signed to Kupfer that he was ready. Duffek took his place.

The oral examination began.

Kupfer took the sheet of paper from Brodetzky, who was already standing by the blackboard, and read out loud the first question as if it were entirely new to him:

"The radius of a sphere inscribed in a dodecahedron is fifty-seven centimetres." ($RGD = 57$ cm, wrote Brodetzky). "What does side a of the dodecahedron measure?"

Kupfer put the piece of paper down on the lectern, clasped his hands behind his back and began pacing up and down.

Brodetzky cleared his throat. Then he picked up the triangle, sketched the figure as described without a word, and only when he had done that did he begin speaking in a knowing tone of voice. He confidently described things of which Kurt knew so little that he soon gave up following.

Thank God, as it was Brodetzky's examination and not his he did not have to attend to it and keep up with it all.

All the same, it confused him that he had no idea what Brodetzky was talking about. Suppose… no, Brodetzky was a student destined for Distinction, so he'd have to solve particularly difficult problems. Kupfer was doing him justice.

Kurt nudged Gerald. "What's this all about?"

"Spherical trigonometry," Gerald whispered back. "Bloody difficult. I haven't the foggiest. Could turn out all right."

Kurt was about to ask something else when he sensed a glance directed at him. He turned round. Professor Seelig had a finger to his lips, telling him to keep quiet.

Kurt quickly nodded, and looked with interest at the board, where Brodetzky was just neatly underlining the solution of the first exercise. "$a = 40{,}675$ cm", read Kurt, without understanding it. Of course, I must keep quiet, he thought. How careless of me. If Marion had seen me, or

Kupfer—I don't want to start by making myself unpopular. Modest and unobtrusive, that's the best way.

It reassured him slightly that he knew one professor was on his side. For a brief while he felt a surge of hope and strength.

They disappeared at once when Duffek was called up to the board, and wrote out an exercise in progressive calculation. And Professor Ruprecht had specially indicated that as a field of interest! That would be it for today, then. What was going to happen to him?

Looking round, Kurt saw that he was on his own. Gerald was sitting in the electric chair, bent over his piece of paper, busily making notes.

It would soon be Kurt's turn.

Sweat stood out on his brow, and his hand was trembling so badly that when Kupfer handed him his paper, he twice failed to take hold of it.

Then he was sitting in the lonely electric chair, with the paper lying folded in front of him, just as he had received it. He dared not open it.

But, after all, he must—Gerald was now in the middle of his first question.

Kurt skimmed his own questions. It was almost uncanny that realizing he didn't understand them left him indifferent.

"No idea," he whispered to himself. "Not the faintest idea."

He scanned the paper again. Of course, this was bound to happen. Not a trace of progressions or of surfaces of the second order, the other field he had hoped for. A calculation of interest on a sum of money, and a construction exercise which looked as if you were meant to answer it algebraically. Useless to think about it now. He was lost.

Kurt looked at the board. Gerald had just faltered slightly, and Kupfer had to prompt him. Gerald was stammering, the examining board noticed, Marion made a remark, Kupfer responded: yes, quite right, the candidate ought to have mastered such a simple thing, hmm, hmm—the situation looked bad for Gerald now that he had begun to waver… but all of a sudden (you could almost see the idea that would rescue him dawn on his mind) he gritted his teeth, put his hand in front of his eyes and then recited a formula that Kupfer acknowledged with a lofty, "At last!" Gerald was safe, for now anyway, and he wrote out the answer to his second problem.

The examiners were overcome by tedium again. Some of the professors were whispering; Mattusch once even uttered a short bark of asthmatic laughter. Kurt cast him a glance of blazing fury. That self-satisfied bastard! Laughing. Laughing now, while there's a candidate sweating with effort—and Mattusch laughs. Well, that's nothing new in him. Like a professional layer-out of the dead who feels nothing at the sight of a corpse. It's just his business, he's used to it. And we're at the mercy of insensitive brutes like that.

Oh God, there's no point in thinking like this. I must pre-pare. Gerald will soon be finished, and I'll be sitting there… unable to help myself. And you… (Kurt glanced at the row of other eighth-year students listening)… you, my fellow students, sit there and you can't help me either. So close, so close, within touching distance—and there's nothing you can do for me, nothing at all, you'll have to watch me go to the slaughter, you're helpless, my friends, isn't that dreadful for you, aren't you shedding tears, friends, comrades, here I sit, look at me, why don't you look at me, my good friends, I love you all... They don't want to look at me, their hearts would break, they can't help me... Why are there tears in your eyes, Kaulich, your glasses are steaming up, Kaulich, look this way, do, Kaulich... Kaulich!

Feverishly, Kurt wills Kaulich to look at him. He passes his hand over his own eyes—a brief attack of derangement, he supposes—Kaulich wasn't shedding any tears—of course not—and he can help me, he can—

Silently, convulsively, Kurt moves his lips: "What is the tangential equation of the hyperbola?" he is trying to convey, and he repeats it three times: "Tan-gent-ial-equation-of-the-hyperbola!"

Kaulich indicates by signs that he doesn't understand, winks hard at Kurt, narrowing his eyes, cups his ear in his hand—it's no use. In addition, Niesset suddenly turns and sees what is going on, darts a venomous glance first at Kurt, then at Kaulich, and Kurt quickly looks down at his paper. "And now, finally..." he hears Kupfer saying, finally, finally, Gerald will be finished in a minute and I still have no idea, none at all...

A formula suddenly flutters into his mind and clings there, humming:

$$S_n = a_1 \cdot \frac{q^n - 1}{q - 1}$$

It is the formula summing up the geometric series. Armed with this formula alone, and knowing that it is useless to him, Kurt goes up to the lectern.

Kupfer looks at him, his lower lip drooping slightly in his otherwise expressionless face. And Kurt—what's come over him?—Kurt does not look down at the floor, Kurt looks at Kupfer standing there expectantly in the same way, lower lip drooping slightly. Suddenly he is perfectly calm; he feels so light-hearted, free, almost cheerful, he would like to indulge in some schoolboy prank, only what—ah, he knows what. Isn't it the candidate's right to answer the questions in whatever order he likes? Of course it is, yes. Obviously no one makes use of that right, who's going to make use of it when he's at the examiners' mercy—but it says so in the rules for the *Matura* examination, yes, and he also remembers that other silly sentence: "Any candidate who tries overtly or covertly cribbing—" ha, ha, of course cribbing is always covert, you're not going to show anyone what you're doing, are you? Those idiots don't even understand their own language, and they sit in judgement on our *Matura* exam—right, I'll tackle the second question first, here we go!

And Kurt lets Kupfer hold out his hand, goes up to the board with the paper and reads out the first question:

"Show the equations of the asymptotes of the hyperbola $4x-9y^2 = 36$, tracing them large and clear, and calculate their angle with the abscissal axis."

Kurt has written out that $4x-9y^2 = 36$ large and clear. There it is, $4x-9y^2 = 36$ on the blackboard. Large and clear.

$4x-9y^2 = 36$.

What does it mean? Who wrote that out?

What does what you have written out there mean, Kurt Gerber? What is x, what is y, what is the question, Kurt Gerber? Why are you staring at those signs that you wrote out yourself, Kurt Gerber?

That sense of freedom is gone, his mischievous wish for a prank is gone, all gone. What you wrote down says: $4x-9y^2 = 36$. Gone, all gone.

You're done for, Kurt Gerber. You wanted to do the second problem first, and you don't know how to do either the second *or* the first. There you stand, Kurt Gerber, helpless, broken, destroyed by your own lunacy.

And a professor is standing beside you, it's Kupfer, he stands there looking very surprised; now he says very calmly:

"If I remember it correctly, that is not how your first question runs. Give me your paper."

And you will give him the paper, too, Kurt Gerber. Oh yes, you will. Here.

Kupfer turns to the examiners, to Marion, annoyance in his eyes and at the same time amusement at such brazen conduct on the part of a candidate in danger. Marion makes a gesture that Kurt does not understand, but it looks to him like an exchange of the mutual confirmation of something discussed in advance. Maybe they think I'm crazy, thinks Kurt, they expected something like this so they won't hold it against me. Or maybe—I wish he'd say something!

"The first problem runs—?" says Kupfer, handing him the paper back.

Now everything in Kurt and around him seems unsteady. The people and objects in the room look to him blurred, and then clear again: Kupfer is staring into space with indifference, the other professors sit bending forward, here and there he sees a sarcastic smile. The class itself is frozen rigid.

Kurt turns his face to look at Kupfer. It is not his mouth speaking. A pair of lips which happens to be available to him by chance opens, and words come out:

"Professor Kupfer, sir, I have a right to answer the questions in any order I like. It says so in the examination rules."

Kurt began speaking quietly, his voice became steadily faster and louder and finally, although it is shaking, there is unconcealed defiance in it, a strange mixture of savagery and resignation.

He looks at the examination room again, seeking support, some recognition that, for once, a student is standing up for his rights—a weak student at that, and furthermore in such a situation—but there is no sign of approval. Seelig, Hussak and Filip are regretfully shaking their heads, Riedl lets out an indignant laugh, some of the class sitting at the back are tapping their foreheads.

Inspector Marion, confronted by something entirely unexpected, looks at Kupfer, and as Kupfer says nothing he himself says very casually, "Why, as a matter of interest, don't you want to work out the answer to the first question?"

It was put in such a way that you couldn't have given any answer, even if you knew one. But Kurt doesn't know one. He stares at his shoes.

"Please do not hold us up, then, and work out the answer to the first question!" says Marion, irritated. "The candidate before you has cost us a good deal of time already."

Kurt wipes the numbers off the board. The blackboard sponge has already dried up, is dusty, it leaves only a few damp streaks on the board, which is smeared with chalk—that will damage my prospects, too, thinks Kurt; and he reads out, in an expressionless voice: "A man pays a sum of 2,000 dollars at the beginning of every year for twelve years, so that from the 20th year on he can obtain a pension at the end of every year for a period of ten years. First calculate how large this pension will be, at 4% interest."

"It's a compound interest sum," says Kurt.

"Yes."

"A compound interest sum…"

Silence. An icy silence. It eats its way into Kurt, fills the void in him, brings him out in a cold sweat; he clearly feels the beads of sweat form on his forehead one by one, trickling over his cheeks, but he doesn't wipe them away; maybe they'll see me sweating with fear and take pity on me:

"Well? Work it out!"

Someone has cleared his throat, someone has closed a book. Time is hot on my heels. Quick!

Kurt begins writing on the board, slowly, carefully, to gain time. He wants time back, not pressing him on. Eight years—it doesn't all depend on a few minutes more or less, or so you might think. The board of examiners thinks otherwise.

"A little faster, perhaps!" says Marion sharply.

Yes. I've done it. There it is.

$$S_n = a_1 \cdot \frac{q^n - 1}{q - 1}$$

Kupfer looks up in surprise. "What does that mean?"

Oh, Kurt knows exactly what that means, it is the only thing he does know, and he's not going to toss out the information just like that. He wants them to know that he understands what he's talking about. He begins, in a strong voice: "The sum of a geometric series S_n, the sum of the first n-terms in the series—". Then he stops short.

Why am I telling them this stuff? What do I think I'm doing with the formula summing up the geometric series? I'm supposed to be calculating the amount of a pension—

"We don't want to hear about that," says Kupfer. "That doesn't belong in this paper. We are not interested in it."

Why aren't you interested in it? How can you say a thing like that, Professor Kupfer? You ought to be interested in it. Just look, S_n consists of the way you add up the terms, really interesting, $a_1 + a_1q + a_1q^2$ plus, and so on, and then a couple of dots, like this…

"Very well," says Kupfer suddenly, "you're right." He comes closer to the board. "So this is the formula for the sum of a geometric series, correct. And now, think hard, Gerber: how do you relate this formula to the calculation of compound interest?"

Kurt thinks he is dreaming. Is this possible? Is it true? Kupfer spoke without any hatred in his voice, benevolently, almost kindly, he wants to help me, and idiot that I am, I'm making it so difficult for him… I've not done you justice, Professor Kupfer, sir. I ask you, I humbly ask you to forgive me!…

"Please think: in what relation do they stand?" asks Kupfer in the same tone of voice.

Dear heaven, in what relation? Relation… nothing going on here relates to anything… Lisa… Kupfer… in what relation do you stand to Lisa Berwald… no, no. Quiet. Think.

Kurt looks at the board, his eyes narrowed, his fingers clutching the chalk so hard that it breaks—he can't think of anything.

"But Gerber!" says Kupfer, coming closer. "Think about it. The capital assets E are made up of the final values of

327

the individually paid contributions. And what are those contributions but—well, what?"

Jerkily, Kurt lowers his head, as if to make the answer come out. Kurt stands there with his mouth open; if he could only read something from Kupfer's lips, a little hint, then, he feels, it would all come back to him... what are they but... but... there, yes, he has found it:

"But the terms in a geometric progression," says Kupfer— yes, Kupfer says it just as Kurt was remembering it, and Kurt says it at almost the same time, slapping his brow angrily but with a smile: how could I forget something so simple, of course, the terms in a geometric progression, and then...

"Right," says Kupfer. "And now it's not so difficult."

Kurt feels he is in safe hands, he nods, shamefaced; no, now it's not so difficult, now—

"Now the final assets are the sum of those terms," says Kupfer again, with an encouraging nod. Kurt repeats it; it was just what he had been going to say, exactly that, you didn't really have to tell me, Professor Kupfer, I can manage by myself, it's so nice of you to help me out, but—

But Kupfer goes on helping him out, stands beside Kurt with a friendly smile, he has already written just what Kurt was about to write, chalk ready in his hand:

$$E = r \cdot \frac{q^n - 1}{q - 1}$$

And he continues in the same kindly tone, urging Kurt to think, it's not so difficult, he'll soon find the answer... and Kurt always does, and just as he is about to say so Kupfer has done it a fraction of a second ahead of him, and then he turns helpfully to Kurt, with that friendly smile; well, how does it go on—like this, right? Yes… but I was going to say so, Professor Kupfer, sir, why won't you let me speak? I know it all, sir, yes, that's it,

$$x = \frac{2000\,(1.04^{12} - 1) \cdot 1.04^{18}}{1.04^{10} - 1}$$

Why are you writing it out? I could do it too, why do you keep telling me to keep calm? I'm perfectly calm, I'm following the calculation—oh, help, where did that logarithm x come from, what am I supposed to do with it, now what?

"There. And now what?" asks Kupfer. Putting down the chalk, he steps back. "Now I think you could do a little of the work, Candidate Gerber. So far I've done it all. If you please!"

Only now does Kurt realize what has been going on. He turns as pale as death.

"Find the log," says Kupfer.

Kurt stands there dazed.

Inspector Marion disguises his own ignorance of the subject with the harmless question, "Don't you know how to work out logarithms?"

Kurt is at a loss. What—what logarithm is he supposed to find? There is a huge paddle wheel going round in his head, he stares helplessly at the board with all those strange figures on it, tries to say something, spurred on by sheer fear, stops, begins again.

"That will do," croaks Inspector Marion. "You can't expect any more! Thank you, Candidate Gerber." He makes a brief note on a piece of paper in front of him and then turns to Kupfer, who looks enquiringly at him:

"Shouldn't we move on to the second question?"

Marion hesitates for a moment. Then he says, "Ah, the second first question." He utters a hoarse laugh, moving his torso stiffly back and forth like a puppet on strings. Several of the professors oblige him by chuckling.

After a short pause Marion says grimly, "You really don't deserve any more of our time." More time passes before, with a dismissive gesture, he says, "But go on, please!"

Mechanically, Kurt writes: $4x - 9y^2 = 36$.

"The equations of the asymptotes have to be shown."

Kupfer does not speak up.

Bolder this time, Marion asks, "Don't you know anything about the equations of the asymptotes?"

Kurt hardly hears him, but looks past him at the class. Kaulich, Weinberg, Hobbelmann and others are frantically moving their lips, they are trying to tell him something. Kurt tries desperately to interpret the message; he leans forward, Kaulich crosses two fingers, Weinberg traces something in the air, they are all gesturing, putting their hands to their heads in horror—the answer must be something childishly simple, but Kurt can't think what it is, absolutely cannot, and they are gesticulating in more and more agitation...

Then Kurt sees Kupfer exchanging glances with Marion; he drops the chalk, he knows what is inevitably coming now—and it does.

"We have finished, Candidate Gerber!" says Kupfer.

And as Kurt staggers away from the lectern, feeling dazed, Marion says sarcastically, "And you wanted to answer that question first? Delicious!"

Brodetzky is already going up to begin the Latin exam. First he goes quickly over to the lectern, bends down, picks up the chalk that Kurt dropped. Then he sits beside Niesset at the head of the green table.

Kurt sits between Gerald and Duffek. No one is looking at him.

So that's what failing is like. Kurt imagined it differently, as something on a larger scale, out of the ordinary. But this was pitiful. The questions weren't difficult. He knew that himself. His eyes ran over the first question; yes, he had to work out the log of the factors of the numerator—only a little thing really—you have to be able to do it even if you don't need it at university (Kurt clenches his fists in sudden rage)—even if it's absurd to deprive someone of his *Matura* if he wants to study law or philosophy just because he couldn't work out a compound interest sum, and that was by pure chance, with Professor Ruprecht he'd always been able to do it... but there was no denying that two simple questions had been enough to bring about his downfall. Kupfer's behaviour was certainly another reason. On the other hand, he hadn't had to help him at all. The way he had done so, getting him first into full swing and then plunging to his doom—that was a little interlude, those two factors cancelled each other out. Kurt had definitely come to grief over those two questions, had definitely failed the whole *Matura*.

Failed? No, why? There were still three subjects to come! No, you didn't fail as easily as that. I didn't make it in maths, agreed, but there's still Latin, German and Prochaska's two subjects. Good heavens, I could have taken things more easily! I shouldn't have made all that effort, I should have saved my powers for the other subjects. Well—it may yet turn out all right.

Kurt calmed down. After all, anyone might have expected him to fail in maths. It was silly to have had any hopes of it. You don't have to do equally well in all four parts of the exam. If you did, you were unanimously awarded your pass, but who needed to be unanimously passed?

He wiped the sweat off his face. He was feeling very hot in his dark suit, his shirt was sticking to his body. Another silly thing is having to get yourself up in your Sunday best, he thought, just for an exam like any other.

Then Gerald was called up. Niesset came over to Kurt, opened a book and pointed, without a word, to the passage for translation, which was marked in red. Kurt skimmed it quickly. About thirty lines from Virgil's *Eclogues*, and they didn't seem to him difficult.

However, his performance was not quite up to what he had expected. His translation, so far as he thought he could judge, was indeed better than Duffek's and Gerald's, but some of the grammatical questions he was then asked gave him difficulty. Right at the end, when he was under crossfire from Marion and Niesset and didn't immediately recognize a very easy verbal form, coming up with one impossible future tense after another in his confusion; when Mattusch (yes, Mattusch, Kurt felt ashamed of himself) quietly told him the answer three times and finally gave up in exasperation because Kurt didn't understand him; when the bell rang for the long break period, and Kurt still hadn't decided between *aberem*, *abirem* and *abiturus sum*—right at the end Marion shook his head thoughtfully, saying slowly, "And *this* is supposed to be a candidate for the *Matura*!" With that Latin was over, and with it the first part of the examination.

Kurt went out into the corridor, and was surrounded by a group of his agitated friends all talking together.

"You idiot—what was that spectacle all about?—fool—can't answer the simplest questions and insists on changing the order of them—even a first-year student can't do that, but in the *Matura*—are you out of your mind?—it all comes from thinking so well of yourself—you always have to know best!—gets into difficulty, so he has to act impossibly to all the examiners—didn't you see what I was telling you?" (This was Rimmel, pulling him aside.) "You had only to take the equation of the hyperbola down to its normal form and then bring it out, child's play, don't you see that?"

Kurt stared in astonishment at his eager fellow student, who was now trying to tell him how to work something out. He was through with maths, after all, for ever. The whole maths exam, and its prelude, now seemed to him so far in the past that he wondered how the others all knew so much detail about it. Had it really been so important? Since then, after all, he had done pretty well in Latin, that made everything all right again—why didn't they say a word about the Latin?

Kurt waited. At last he asked them himself. "How was my Latin?"

The voices ebbed away, undecided opinions were hesitantly proffered; some of his fellow students shrugged their shoulders and walked away.

Kurt took fright. Did that mean—?

"You were all at sea at the end," said Klemm. "The translation was quite good."

Quite good, only quite good? Not very good? The conclusion, with that little mistake he had made, was not forgotten, and mattered? How could they say so with such certainty?

"Maybe you're just imagining that you shone in Latin?" said Schönthal venomously. "And anyway, it's obvious that Almighty God Kupfer let you talk on the way you did just to make sure you really would fail the *Matura*!"

Kurt swung round, and Schönthal retreated in alarm.

"There, there, there!" said Kaulich the peacemaker. "It was a very good average performance in Latin, and that's all you need if you're just after a majority of pass marks. You're sure to get that, Scheri, even if God Almighty Kupfer stands on his head. And a little while ago I picked something up, a conversation, Birdie was saying: and I'm not letting Gerber get failed because of Kupfer. Lengsfeld heard it too."

Lengsfeld confirmed Kaulich's remarks. Several other students made confident predictions. Anyway, the more difficult part of the oral *Matura* was over…

The bell rang again. The last time I ever hear it ring, thought Kurt suddenly, and he felt like rejoicing out loud. The happy idea of no longer having anything to do with school made itself forcibly felt, overwhelmed him. He went back to his place, humming quietly to himself.

The German oral exam was in two parts: first you had to offer your interpretation of a poem, and then a question about German literary history that had some connection with it was discussed.

When Mattusch put the book with the poem in it down in front of Kurt, he leant down a little and whispered quickly, "Well then, pull yourself together, show them what you can do in German at least, right?" With those words he was gone, leaving Kurt deeply confused yet again. Mattusch's good intentions were obvious, but sounded like a forlorn hope. What did that "at least" mean? Was his achievement so far as bad as that? Wasn't he fighting a battle that was already lost? Was everything decided? I'm not letting Gerber—but then that meant they must have discussed the prospect of his failing, didn't it?

"Gerber!" Mattusch was calling him up to be examined in German. And Kurt hadn't even looked at the poem yet.

"Well then, what have we here? A poem by Lenau, right? 'Autumn'. Well then."

Kurt was glad he could talk about Lenau; he loved his poetry and he already knew this poem. He would take care to read it with the reserved attitude that was right for it. Not in a warm, emotional voice—that was all wrong here. But then he read the last verse aloud:

> *And so my youth has passed away,*
> *Without the joys of springtide's gladness;*
> *The autumn winds blowing today*
> *Bring dreams of death and mortal sadness.*

And at that point he noticed, in alarm, that his voice was shaking slightly. Some sense of sublimity moved him in a way he had never felt so strongly before. It was not exactly unwelcome, just a little uncomfortable, something mighty and unapproachable—no, he could not have said what it roused in him. It was confusing. Kurt was used to knowing what his feelings were at once, and smiling at them if possible; he tried to do that now, telling himself it was an odd coincidence that he, of all the students, was to discuss a poem about youthful melancholy; maybe Mattusch had made a clever observation. But no, it was more likely chance, damn it, he thought; it's been like this since Wednesday at ten, from the streetwalker and Lisa and the crooner and *abeo abire* all the way to here, to another Wednesday and ten o'clock again—so stupid, the trashy novel is out to annoy me… But Kurt's thoughts took him no further, did not bring him to the heart of this unknown sensation before which all mockery died away… what could it be?…

"Well?" said Mattusch.

Kurt pulled himself together. No more trashy ideas.

But when he discussed the poem, hesitantly at first, trying to keep his way on the narrow path that left him the possibility of either choosing prosy, cliché-ridden language or being unable to make himself understood by the examiners—when he discussed the poem and came to the last verse that unknown sensation was back again. It flowed into him and would not let him go. Kurt tried to grasp it, to explore it—but it had too many facets. There was something about it like withered leaves, like floating away past a weary sun, something like apprehensiveness and peace, like growth and death. As if it would help him to escape the unknown sensation, for he felt timid in the face of it, he spoke forcefully about Lenau, his life and his madness, his death; he spoke cogently, ideas coming fast like ripples spreading out, and became so impassioned that Mattusch had to remind him to keep to the point. Kurt stopped. Where was he, then? Oh yes—taking the oral *Matura*, and there—brrr!—sat the professors around him. He looked at their faces. Seelig and Filip had propped their heads on their hands and were listening to him attentively. All the rest of them—Marion most intensively—were busy with something quite different, reading or writing or looking into space, Riedl had just yawned… Kurt sank back, feeling annihilated. An image appeared before him: he was standing in a large, high-ceilinged room, probably an official building of some kind, squeezed into a long line of people dressed almost the same, making their way towards a counter. Kurt did not really know why he was there. He was coming closer to the counter with every step he took. He could already hear the people in front of him putting forward their requests. He didn't understand what they said, only that it was always the same thing. Then he was standing in front of the official who stood at a little window behind the counter. But no sooner had he begun speaking than an opaque glass pane came down over the window, the people behind him were pushing, Kurt had to move on, and the little window opened again for the next comer. This happened several times. And the odd thing was that he knew he was speaking but he couldn't understand his own words.

Then the image suddenly disappeared, Kurt came to his senses, and was surprised to realize that he had really been talking all the time, mechanically churning out remarks on "lyric poetry in Austria at the time of the Young Germany literary movement". Doubtfully, incredulously, he passed his hand over his forehead. Was *this* real? Yes, it was! There were the professors, still sitting there.

He paused. Much surprised, and without understanding at once, he heard Mattusch's voice: "Good."

He was expecting another question, but Mattusch closed the book. The German examination was over.

"Finished?" asked Marion, peering up from the register at which he had been looking. "Thank you."

Kurt got up and went back to his place.

After this he couldn't get his thoughts straight. They assumed almost physical shape, they were stronger than him, they disappeared from him into mist. Sometimes he saw them emerge again very far away and go gliding past in ghostly form, they kept swirling around in pairs, he tried to follow them, but he didn't know the way; he groped around uncertainly, wandered off, got lost, then something that he had only recently been thinking jumped out at him again. Many thoughts came together, indistinct, intangible—yet always in such a way that they did not seem to him at all extraordinary or surprising, that he seemed to know all this from some time or other, that he felt his timidity as if it were a concern that he might find this or that was not the same as it had been at that mysterious last time, that—fully understanding the absurdity of it—he nonetheless always knew that nothing unexpected would really happen, nothing running counter to the outer course of events.

So he was not at all surprised when someone suddenly touched his shoulder, and next moment a white paper was lying on the table in front of him. It came from Prochaska, who would soon be examining him in geography and history, and thoughts of Prochaska and the examination in geography and history fitted neatly into the course of events—like everything yet to come; they went their way, were soon blurred and did not appear again until Prochaska called, "Gerber." Kurt had a feeling that he had been addressed several times before. He quickly got to his feet, picked up the folded paper and went to the map on the wall. Only now did he think about his questions. Yes, he knew what they were. And he began.

"It can be said of the geological structure of the Carpathian system that it—"

"Excuse me, young gentleman—er—Candidate—er, Candidate Gerber—er—"

What was the matter? Why was Prochaska interrupting him? Why was he shifting from foot to foot, hunching his head down between his shoulders and moving it back and forth? This is a nuisance. Kurt began again, with emphasis, setting him right: "It can be said of the geological structure—"

"That's not the question. Please look at the paper!" Prochaska had said that sharply and fast, as if taking a run up to a difficult obstacle, and then he immediately looked in another direction.

Kurt heard movement in the room, like the distant rushing of a waterfall, swelling louder and interrupted by an audible, evocative clearing of throats. He looked at Prochaska. But surely his question was "The geological structure of the Carpathian system"!

It was so quiet now that you could have heard a pin drop.

Prochaska said, "Look at the paper, please. You could really have done that before."

Kurt unfolded the paper and read: 1. Geography: Mining and the iron and steel industry in the succession states. 2. History: The causes and origins of the Thirty Years War.

There must be some mistake. He turned the paper over. No. It said: Kurt Gerber.

Suddenly he wasn't surprised any more. It was all in order. It would all go its way. He saw Blank turning a hurdy-gurdy—then he thought of Prochaska's first lesson that year—don't make life too difficult for me, young people, I'm an old man, I'll be retiring soon—something that Gerald had said to him (when?—he thought very long ago) ran past his ear—and then geography and history go like clockwork—he vaguely saw connections, they became clear for a moment, rage and hatred and indignation, and pity and understanding arose, airing themselves in one short, whistling breath... Then all was calm again, inside and outside.

"Then let's take the history question. If you please, the causes and origins of the Thirty Years War."

Kurt heard what the old man was saying, but it took some time for the words really to reach his conscious mind, put down root and bring more words out over his own lips. He began talking about what he dimly remembered, but what he said was so disjointed that Prochaska kept tearing it to shreds. Kurt nodded, spoke, nodded again; finally he brought some kind of train of thought together, and saw from a gesture by Prochaska that the examination was over. He went back to his place, and at first did not know why Gerald, the only one sitting there, stood up. Then he realized that the last who had been listening had also left the room. He followed them. The door closed behind him on the examiners and their discussion.

No one approached him.

Why not? You've nothing to fear from me.

Then someone does come up to him. Who is it? Weinberg.

"What a rotten thing for that old paralytic to do!" His cheekbones are working. "What a rotten thing to do!"

"But he's landed himself in trouble too," says Rimmel, who has joined them. "Now it will all come out. And we'll all be failed."

Someone says, "Mass failure. Like an epidemic." Some people laugh frostily.

Kurt hears this as if through a heavy curtain over a doorway. There is something he doesn't like about the laughter, but that, too, is all in the order of things.

The word "failure" has lodged somewhere in his brain, and now begins rumbling round it.

We'll all be failed.

The bats—no.

The screams? Not them either.

Only a sigh.

It was Kurt who sighed. Someone lays a large, heavy hand on the back of his neck, a deep voice speaks close to his ear. "Come on, Scheri!" It is Kaulich. Kaulich, who was crying. When? Yes. Why is everyone so quiet? Where's Blank? We'll wander the country together playing the hurdy-gurdy. Prochaska can collect the coins in his hat. Poor, blind old Prochaska.

Kaulich says, "Think nothing of it."

Of what?

"It's not so sure yet."

What isn't?

Everything will go its way. Say something, Kaulich, say something. This is probably all part of it. You're a good sort, Kaulich.

Kurt lets his head sink to Kaulich's shoulder. No one says anything.

Kurt looks along the frame of Kaulich's glasses. A tangent

on an ellipse. The tangent goes on, on and on. Now it comes to the logarithm cross. But no one spits. I've seen all this before. We'll get past it in a moment. Only a little more gneiss, granite and mica schist.

"His German was very good."

Here, clerk at the counter, I just want to tell you that I—but wait, please, why are you closing down? The opaque glass pane has come down over the window. It sinks lower and lower. Now I can't see anything any more.

"And his Latin wasn't bad."

"He'll pass on a majority of votes."

"I think so too."

"Of course, why not? Don't look so glum, Scheri! You're sure to pass."

Maybe, maybe. But now there are some people all in black standing in front of me, and they won't let me through. I wish they'd take their hands off my throat.

"Don't just stand there in that stupid way! Can't you see he isn't feeling well?"

Kurt feels his head being raised, far, endlessly far away.

He's dizzy. He leans against Kaulich again.

"Come on, Scheri, you'll soon feel better. Come on."

Kurt's legs are moving, he walks into a dark veil that becomes denser and thicker before his eyes. Then it suddenly breaks. Kurt feels something cold on his forehead: water. Kaulich has tied a wet cloth round his head. That feels good.

"Thanks," says Kurt.

Kaulich takes him under the armpit and leads him to an empty part of the corridor, where he props him against the wall near an open window.

Kurt meets the warm look in Kaulich's eyes and nods a couple of times, he doesn't know why.

"Believe me, Scheri," says Kaulich now. "I really wouldn't encourage you to be hopeful without good reasons, but what I heard from Birdie—you know, I'm sure you'll get through."

Kurt looks at him for a long time. Inside his head something is in great confusion, ideas and images all tumbling over one another, rushing, clattering—and then it is suddenly there, weighty, towering above everything.

"Do you really think so? Really?"

Anxiously, Kurt clings to Kaulich's arm as if the decision were his. Suddenly he sees it all with terrible clarity, as if he were still in the middle of it and yet he already knew how it would end. And then something comes crawling out, something he'd forgotten all this time, how could he possibly forget, for God's sake, no, no—but he already sees his father lying in bed, breathing heavily.

"Kaulich! Kaulich, have I passed?"

Kurt is paralysed by boundless horror; it streams over all the dams in his conscious mind. He hangs stiffly from Kaulich's arm, and Kaulich pats him on the shoulder and says, "Yes, yes, Scheri!"

Then, without a pause, he goes on. "Well, cheer up, all that's behind you now. I'm glad it's behind me, too. I tell you what, we can shit on it now. We really can. We discussed it before!" He swings Kurt round, speaking eagerly as if that could convince him that he has passed. "Think of it, Scheri. We'll go around at night, everyone has to take a laxative, and we'll leave a pile of shit outside their doors. Won't they just be surprised? Maybe we'll leave a card in it: Dear School—from your grateful *Matura* students. Ho, ho, ho.

That's what we think, and we'll let them know, and then we're free of it, Scheri, then—no need to think of it any more! We shit on you! Hohoho—ho—ho—ho—what—what's the matter with you?"

Kaulich's laughter dies away, he stares at Kurt's face, which is horribly distorted, grey as it rises above his collar, with flickering eyes and mouth wrenched open.

"What's the matter with you?" asks Kaulich again, flinching back.

What's the matter with me? And you can ask that again, you—no. You can't help it. You don't know about anything. Go away.

"Go away!"

Kaulich shakes his head, is about to say something else, then he turns quickly and disappears round the corner.

Kurt watches him go. He remembers that he asked him, "Have I passed?" He remembers that Kaulich said, "Why, yes."

Why, yes. Why, yes! So casual, so liberating, so wonderfully casual.

Kurt gradually relaxes, he feels limp. Relaxation becomes boundless, total exhaustion. The indefinable something comes close again, large, forgiving. He shudders slightly, raises his hand and nods.

"No need to think of it any more!"

His head sinks. Someone said that, someone still here and who is concerned more than ever. It isn't over yet, and they're already saying we mustn't think of it any more.

The bats are back again.

And the indefinable being.

Dreams of death and mortal sadness…

No, no! Not death! I want to go on living. And I want to go on hating! I keep thinking of that, always, always! Oh, rejoicing, tearful, lovely, lovely hatred! I love you, hatred…

Kurt leans against the wall, arms outstretched, with something in his throat. It isn't like retching, or a tugging sensation of the imminence of tears…

It is—how soft it makes him, how very soft—it is the indefinable being.

It wasn't that before. Only now has it got into his head. It is already coming his way again, tall, majestic.

Leave me my father, just for a moment. It's all so pointless. What is it for?

"If you think that life has nothing in common with school, then you are mistaken."

Was it his father who said that? Yes.

Is that it? The indefinable being—is it that? Was it that from the beginning?

I'll follow you, sublime one. Go your round.

The indefinable being is walking this way, very tall and white. It is a woman. It has—it has—Lisa's features. No. Not hers. The features of his love for Lisa. The features of all love.

Are you that—are you renunciation?

The woman is white, the pillows are white, his father is white lying on them.

If you think that life—

Kurt can't feel the floor beneath his feet any more, he is staggering, falling—then his hand catches the window sill and he hauls himself up on it, putting his head out of the window, drinking in the cool breath of a gust of wind.

A storm is gathering in the distance. It is too hot today.

Kurt looks down into the yard of the apartment block. There was once a horse there. Where is it now?

The indefinable being smiles and nods and disappears. And then the horse arrives. Not the same horse as before, and the vehicle it pulls is not the same. The carriage in which x drives about must look like this. And the figure getting down from the box is not the carter.

Hey! Who are you?

The figure comes closer. You can't see exactly what it looks like. It keeps changing.

I said, who are you?

The figure bows and smiles.

And here comes the indefinable being too. It points to the other figure with a graceful sweeping movement of its white hand and says: Mr Chairman of the examining board, will you allow me to introduce you to today's candidate for examination?

Well, what's his name?

The indefinable being says: Life.

What?

Yes, Life, eighth-year student.

Very well, Life. Come here.

What? You want me to go down there? I've no intention of doing any such thing. You want me to go down there—that's a good joke! You'll wreck my chances with all the examiners.

Come along, Life. Start writing on the board. First question.

What are you doing? Someone pays with all his love for twelve whole months, and then at the end of those twelve months—what? You must be crazy. This is inappropriate.

That does not interest us. The first question does not run like that.

Got it? Very well, the given facts are a professor and a student, isn't that right? The professor breaks the student's spirit. What comes next? No, wrong. However, the father—do not use such expressions here, we do not say, "The father is dying," we say, "The father is reduced to zero." Right. Do you know how it came to that? Look at the fraction line, Candidate Life. It is there because it is the sum of a geometric progression with n stages in it. The stages with the same coefficients stand out from the others. One after another. What we do not like is crossed out and replaced by other coefficients. If you please. Now, cross out all the coefficients with the index s and replace them with coefficients that have the index p. Why? Because the professor is superior to the student. $p>s$. And now I will tell you the basic factor to be used in your calculations: justice.

So?

Don't you know any more, Candidate Life? That will do. You really can't expect any more. You can sit down.

What? If I may say so, that's all the same to us. Well, let us try this question. The second first question. Good. What does that mean? Good, you are right. It would have been better to solve it in another way, but—just as you like. No one can be forced to love. Truth as a basic factor is unreliable. There, now you might do a little work yourself. So far I have done it all.

Well?

What's the matter with you? You don't know that either, Candidate Life?

You don't know anything about truth?

You don't know anything about justice?

You don't know anything about love?

You don't know anything about all that? Thank you, that's enough. We have finished, Candidate Life—

"Gerber! The discussion is over."

No, let that alone, Life. Pleading is no use. You're not worth any more of our time—

"What is it, Scheri? Come on! They're waiting inside!"

Who's disturbing me? A mean trick to play. What do you say about that, indefinable being?

The indefinable being is tall, and walks with majestic, inviting steps.

"Gerber!"

Yes, yes, just coming. Here I am. Why are they all standing here? Ah, Inspector Marion. My respects, dear colleague! I have just failed a student. What did you say? Life by name. Not fit for the *Matura*, no.

What do you want now, Life? No. There would be no point in that.

Why are they all so calm, staring at me.

Oh yes, I know now anyway. *Abeo, abire.* Yes. Hence *Abiturient* for someone taking his final exam. *Abiturus sum*: I go away.

Right through the middle. There is a table where the three of them are standing, there is a window above the table. Right in the middle.

Off I go through the middle.

Hush, hush! The indefinable being strides ahead.

I am coming myself, I shall enjoy your joy.

The priest spreads out his arms: Thrice accursed be—

"Gerber! For God's sake! What are you doing?"

The sun is so red, it is falling on me, all—

Newspaper Report

Another student suicide. During the *Matura* examination held yesterday at State High School XVI, one of the candidates, nineteen-year-old *Kurt Gerber*, committed suicide by throwing himself out of the classroom window on the third floor and falling to the street just before the results of the examination were announced. He died instantly of multiple injuries. It is particularly tragic that young Gerber, who undoubtedly went to his death for fear of failing, was declared by the examining board to have passed the examination.

PUSHKIN PRESS

Pushkin Press was founded in 1997. Having first rediscovered European classics of the twentieth century, Pushkin now publishes novels, essays, memoirs, children's books, and everything from timeless classics to the urgent and contemporary.

This book is part of the Pushkin Collection of paperbacks, designed to be as satisfying as possible to hold and to enjoy. It is typeset in Monotype Baskerville, based on the transitional English serif typeface designed in the mid-eighteenth century by John Baskerville. It was litho-printed on Munken Premium White Paper and notch-bound by the independently owned printer TJ International in Padstow, Cornwall. The cover, with French flaps, was printed on Conqueror Brilliant White Board. The paper and cover board are both acid-free and approved by the Forest Stewardship Council (FSC).

Pushkin Press publishes the best writing from around the world—great stories, beautifully produced, to be read and read again.